"Maquesta! You'd better get up!" Fritzen called. "You're needed on deck!"

Even before she was fully awake, Maq realized by the way the *Perechon* pitched and rolled that a storm had hit. Rain pelted the ship's portholes, and the wind keened like something alive. Glancing out, Maq saw it was still dark. They couldn't have reached the edge of the Maelstrom yet.

"Coming, Fritzen, com—" A high-pitched screaming and cackling cut through the shrieking of the wind. Alarmed, Maq yanked open her cabin door. She joined the half-ogre on the main deck in time to see a macabre scene illuminated by a flash of lightning. The eerie light revealed a red mist seeping up over the deck on all sides. The red cloud carried with it the almost unbearable sound of screeching and wailing. As Maq watched, the mist covered the deck and began swirling up the masts. When it reached her feet, a clammy chill crept up her spine.

Then, before her eyes, the mist took on solid form—dozens of solid forms—small red figures with horns, clawed hands, long sharp tails, and tiny pointed teeth.

From the Creators of the
DRAGONLANCE® Saga

WARRIORS

Knights of the Crown
Roland Green

Maquesta Kar-Thon
Jean Rabe
with Tina Daniell

Knights of the Sword
Roland Green
(available Winter 1995)

WARRIORS
Volume Two

Maquesta Kar-Thon

Jean Rabe
with Tina Daniell

DRAGONLANCE®
Warriors Series
Volume Two

MAQUESTA KAR-THON

Random House and its affiliate companies have worldwide distribution rights in the book trade for English language products of TSR, Inc.

Distributed to the book and hobby trade in the United Kingdom by TSR Ltd.

Distributed to the toy and hobby trade by regional distributors.

Cover art by Jeff Easley.

First Printing: July 1995
Printed in the United States of America.
Library of Congress Catalog Card Number: 94-68142

9 8 7 6 5 4 3 2 1

ISBN: 0-7869-0134-9

TSR, Inc.
201 Sheridan Springs Rd.
Lake Geneva, WI 53147
U.S.A.

TSR Ltd.
120 Church End, Cherry Hinton
Cambridge CB1 3LB
United Kingdom

Chapter 1

Preparations

"What do you think, Maquesta Kar-Thon?"

Lendle spoke deliberately, slightly formally, as gnomes are wont to do when talking to members of other races—even, as was the case in this instance, to someone he had known since she was a rambunctious child.

"What do you think?" he persisted, his black eyes wide and gleaming.

Maq knew by the jittery way Lendle was fingering the shiny cylinders and slender iron rods at the peddler's stall, coupled with—for him—his agonizingly slow speech, that whatever the objects were, the gnome wanted them with an almost desperate intensity.

Maq craned her neck to see if she could catch a glimpse of her father's ship from the rough row of stalls that passed for a marketplace in the bustling minotaur port of Lacynos.

"I don't *think* anything about those things—whatever they are. You know that, Lendle. If it doesn't have to do with masts and sails, I'm lost. Now come on. We've spent enough time here. We must get back to the ship. There's still much to be done to prepare for the race tomorrow." A hint of exasperation was creeping into Maquesta's voice.

But Lendle seemed not to have heard her. The gnome stood, almost transfixed, his stubby, deft fingers poking, probing, prodding, feeling every bit of the objects.

Maq sighed and decided to take another approach. "By all means, Lendle. These seem to be just what you need. I'm sure you can't do without them. In fact, I think you should buy them . . . if you think you can find the coppers to pay for them," she added under her breath. "After all these weeks without a decent job for the *Perechon*, I don't know how you have any coins left. I certainly don't."

"Yes. Yes, Maquesta Kar-Thon. I believe you are correct. These are just what I need." With that, Lendle reached into the sack he carried on his shoulder and pulled out a flat, rectangular leather box containing a number of small drawers and compartments. He pushed several colorful buttons on its top. Beaming, he explained to Maq that this invention of his had a drawer that would be opening any moment now—containing the exact amount of coppers the peddler quoted him. Instead, however, the box's bottom fell out, and the gnome's small cache of coins spilled onto the muddy roadway.

"Ohdearohdearohdear!" Lendle gushed, returning to his normal gnomish talking pace.

Maq stooped to help Lendle retrieve the coppers and watched as the suspicious stall owner, a stout human woman, examined each coin before handing over several rods and cylinders. Maq imagined the merchant didn't have much experience dealing with customers other than minotaurs. Members of foreign races were a rarity on the island of Mithas—unless they were slaves, in which case they weren't in a position to buy anything, or they were confined to lowly occupations, like peddlers. By the time she handed over the objects, Lendle had reassembled his mechanical wallet and stowed it away in his sack. In all the years Maq had known the gnome, he had never designed a device that performed as intended.

She steered him toward the dock where they had left the longboat they used to get from the *Perechon* to shore. The gnome was fairly skipping with excitement, moving so quickly through the crowd that Maq lengthened her stride a bit to keep up.

They made an interesting pair: the tall, lithe woman with ebony skin and curling hair the shade of midnight, and the diminutive, stocky, gnome with nut-brown skin and a mane the color of snow. As they made their way through the unpaved streets lined with massive, if unimaginative, stone buildings, few of the hulking minotaurs they passed gave them a second glance. In Maq's experience these bestial creatures had no interest in or use for other races—except as slave labor or sacrificial warriors in their gladiatorial entertainments.

Maq suppressed a shudder. She had no use for minotaurs either, and she was not especially fond of their city. Her attention, however, was caught by one of the city's natives striding toward her from the direction of the harbor. His curving horns shone as if they had been polished, and a gold hoop was affixed to the tip of one. The reddish color of the fur that covered his body was accentuated by the flowing red cape he wore thrown back over his massive shoulders. Straps of a leather harness crisscrossed his chest, holding a variety of knives and small axes with finely carved handles. The leather skirt that fit snugly around his slender haunches was studded with green and blue gems that winked in the sun. A sturdy chain trailed from his hand and ended in a thick collar around the neck of a creature Maq had never seen before. About the size of a dog, it looked like a giant rat, only with no fur or tail. It had six legs, and an upper jaw full of wide, deadly looking teeth protruded over its lower lip.

The thing scurried along behind the minotaur, who occasionally jerked the chain to speed its progress. Now and then the creature hissed menacingly when someone they were passing drew too close. This prompted an even harsher jerk on the chain by the minotaur. Maq could see that the iron collar had created a raw, oozing wound in the thing's almost colorless hide. Its close-set brown eyes stared with obvious malice at its master.

Maq's strides had slowed as she took in the pair. Lendle, oblivious to anything but his purchase, which he fingered even as they walked, was forging ahead of her. Maquesta reached out and grabbed him by the collar, gave him a quick shake to get his attention, and motioned with her head at the minotaur and his "pet." Lendle, looking for an instant as if he had been awakened from a dream, turned his attention where Maq indicated.

His eyes narrowed with momentary interest. "Osquip. Nasty creatures. Haven't ever seen one outside an underground ruin. In fact, can't say as I've ever seen one at all. Just pictures of 'em. Heard about them, though. They're supposed to be carnivorous, voracious eaters. I think. Hmmm. No, I could be thinking about otyughs. Now they are truly terrible things to behold. I never saw one of them either. But I had an uncle who came face-to-face with one when he was exploring an underground cavern. Much nastier than an osquip." The gnome's words started pouring out faster.

Just then, the osquip let out an angry hiss. Maq didn't know what had prompted it, but the creature leapt, snarling, at its master's throat. The heavy chain and collar limited its mobility, though. With surprising agility and speed, the minotaur stepped away from the attacking animal, pulled a short sword from his harness, and with a powerful lunge sliced off the creature's head. Blood spurted from its neck as the osquip gave a few feeble kicks with its legs and fell heavily to the ground.

"Take care of that," the minotaur ordered as he wiped his bloodied weapon on the osquip's hide. Satisfied the blade was clean, he sheathed it. Two mangy-looking human slaves who had been trailing behind their master moved up to the osquip's still-twitching body. One grabbed the creature's rear legs and started dragging, leaving a trail of blood behind. The other picked up the head and cradled it in his arms. They continued to follow their master down the muddy roadway that crossed the edge of Horned Bay. Maq stood watching and saw the slaves toss the body parts into the harbor—where the animal's remains joined the variety of other garbage that helped give Lacynos its distinctive aroma.

"Um. Well, that was pleasant. Minotaurs. In any event," Lendle continued babbling, "my uncle narrowly avoided the otyugh's tentacles—or arms I suppose, depending on your perspective. Though one of the tentacles had eyeballs on it. A half-dozen eyes, he said. So I suppose you couldn't call that one an arm. Well, I guess you could, since its eyes weren't on its head. So my uncle said, and he should know. Anyway, the beast had three or four legs and moved fast. But my uncle was able to outmaneuver the thing, and he found his way out of the cavern without having to kill the creature." Lendle smiled, finished with his tale.

Maquesta resumed her walk to the longboat. "Why have a pet if you're just going to treat it poorly and then kill it?" she muttered, shaking her head. "These minotaurs are the ones that are nasty and should be at the end of leashes. I'm glad we'll be leaving their company after we win the harbor race. I don't want to have to come back here for a while."

They walked along in silence, the incident having thrown Maq into a reflective mood. But when a salty breeze off the open sea managed to penetrate the dank atmosphere, hitting Maq in the face, her spirits improved. Stepping onto the wharf, with the twin masts of her father's ship, the *Perechon*, now in full view, she crossed the line into exuberance. Her gait picked up along with her disposition. She'd be at the *Perechon* shortly. She'd be home.

"Hurry up, Lendle. I'm sure Father is anxious for our return."

"I'm hurrying," the gnome replied, still inspecting his purchases.

Melas Kar-Thon's *Perechon*, with her patched sails and peeling paint, was not the prettiest ship on the Blood Sea—though her sleek lines and graceful bow kept her in the running—but the ship unquestionably was one of the fastest on Ansalon's waters. The *Perechon* was a two-masted pentare. Similar to a schooner, it was a warship that boasted sails for swift movement and oar ports that would help it maneuver in battle. It had a keel length of nearly one hundred twenty feet and had a ballista mounting on the bow. The weapon itself, a large crossbow that fired harpoons, bolts, spears, and any manner of other objects with a force harder than a man could muster, was being stored in the hold. Weapons were not allowed in the upcoming race. Despite its design, the *Perechon* had seen little fighting, being used most often as a cargo ship, and occasionally as a passenger vessel for individuals wishing to get somewhere quietly and quickly. Lately, the captain had been sailing the ship from port to port looking for work.

The *Perechon*'s railing was of fine mahogany, the posts carved to look like ornate columns, miniature versions of what might be found supporting temple roofs. The bowsprit, the spar extending from the bow of the ship, was made of hardened walnut. The main deck was stained oak that was forever being polished and swabbed, and the poop deck at the rear of the ship was made of white oak imported from an elven glade. Maquesta was nearly as proud of the ship as her father was.

Maq slipped the rope holding the *Perechon*'s longboat from the piling where it had been tied while they took care of their errands and pushed off, rowing strongly toward the ship. As they neared the *Perechon*, they glimpsed several crewmen polishing the rails. Others were hard at work repainting the trim. Maq suspected her father wanted the ship to look her best during the race. She grinned broadly—there would be time for her and Lendle to pitch in, too. She wanted everything to be perfect for her father, as this race was very important to him.

Melas's father had been a sailor and his father before him and his father before him. The Kar-Thons' blood was more seawater than anything else, the family liked to say. Melas knew his profession well. The modest dowry Maq's mother, Mi-al, had brought to their secret marriage—plus a lucky win at the gaming tables and proceeds from the sale of the Kar-Thon family's sloop—had given Melas the funds he needed to build his own ship. He knew what he wanted and what he needed to create: the most seaworthy and fleetest ship anyone had ever seen. He named it the *Perechon*, after a small seabird his wife loved to watch.

Mi-al was an elf, and Melas was confident a life at sea would keep her safe from those who hunted her kind. He hid her in voluminous hooded robes when she moved among the *Perechon*'s crew, and she ventured into ports with him only at night, when the shadows disguised her features. Only Lendle knew their secret—and shared Melas's sorrow. Mi-al had vanished fourteen years ago, shortly after Maquesta's fourth birthday, leaving Melas devastated and ending the possibility of a son to carry on the Kar-Thon sailing tradition. Still, Melas was determined to teach everything he knew about the science, art, and love of sailing to his only child. And so he had—after he had the child's ears trimmed. Maquesta, in all respects, looked wholly human, though she was well aware of her elven heritage. Melas wanted her to be safe, and Maq had no problem with the ruse. She wanted to stay alive, and she wanted to keep her father happy.

* * * * *

"You'll never guess who else is going to race tomorrow," Maq said to Averon, the *Perechon*'s first mate, as soon as she hauled herself over the side. She waved a partial list of names she had received in Lacynos when she registered the ship for the event. "The *Torado*," she sputtered, referring to another vessel that originated from Saifhum.

"Well that should make things interesting." Averon grinned, the mischief in his eyes more pronounced than usual.

"We'll have to fly our special colors to let everyone know that we're the ship from Saifhum to beat. I made the new flag myself. What do you think?" Averon motioned with his head toward the top of the *Pere-*

chon's nearest mast.

Maq suddenly realized that the rest of the crew had stopped what they were doing and were watching her and Averon with suppressed laughter. Her mouth dropped open as it always did when she realized one of Averon's practical jokes was upon them—and she was the intended victim. Maq's gut tightened. She looked skyward.

Flapping in the sea breeze at the very top of the mast, unmistakable in the rays of the late afternoon sun, hung Maquesta's bright yellow silk undervest—one of the few truly feminine pieces of clothing she owned, cherished because it was also one of the few items of her mother's that had survived years of seafaring. With a sharp exclamation, Maq leapt onto the rigging and skittered up the ropes to retrieve it, first shooting Averon a reproachful look.

How could he? Averon of all people!

Averon and Maq's father had been friends since childhood. They had been frequent rivals for the same women—until Melas met Mi-al when he was alone on a trading mission. Melas married her, ending the rivalry. Averon had been a frequent companion to the newlyweds, and often Melas wondered if Averon guessed that his wife was an elf. Averon had been with Melas on the sea voyage during which Mi-al disappeared, had comforted a four-year-old Maq when her father, for a period, had been too grief-stricken to remember he had a child. Averon, always impetuous and full of mischief, had been like a second father to her.

A sudden gust of wind caught at Maq, nearly tugging her from the rigging. She clamped her teeth together, grimaced, and shook off her foul mood. She couldn't afford to cry, couldn't spare a hand to wipe away tears, couldn't climb with her vision blurred. The sea winds had shifted, picking up power and causing the *Perechon* to rock. Maq needed all her senses, all her strength, and all her skill to continue climbing. Nor did she want any of the crew watching her to see that she was upset. Maq had grown up more or less as the *Perechon*'s mascot, indulged when crewmembers had time, affectionately regarded by all.

But as she'd left childhood, that changed. The sailors didn't know what to make of Maquesta as a young woman—sometimes she didn't know herself. They pulled back, not unfriendly, but watchful. And that wouldn't do. Not if Maquesta wanted to take over as captain of the *Perechon* someday. And she did. So she knew that any occasion could turn into a "test," as this surely had.

Glancing down, Maq realized none of the sailors could see the sad expression on her face. They clustered below her like toy figurines, laughing and pointing. The rough hemp of the rigging rope cut into her palms and drew blood, and the wind tugged harder at her body. But then she had the fluid silk of the undervest in her hand, and a smile crossed her lips. The garment was undamaged. Averon had carefully tied it to the mast rigging.

Climbing down as quickly as the gusting wind permitted, Maquesta jumped lightly to the deck. Her composure complete, she shot Averon a lethal look, then deliberately swept her glance over the faces of the surrounding sailors, daring any one of them to make a comment. Averon, for an instant, refused to meet her glance. Then, bending over in an exaggerated bow, he swept off an imaginary cap. "Well done, Maquesta Kar-Thon," he pronounced, raising his eyes, which were once again twinkling with mischief. "Well done indeed!"

Maq managed to resist Averon's charm for the space of at least three minutes. Just as she felt her lips start to twitch upward in the beginnings of a smile, Melas Kar-

Thon emerged onto the main deck from his cabin at the stern. Seeing a dozen or so crewmembers standing idly, observing Averon and Maquesta mentally sparring, he strode toward the pair and bellowed.

"What's this? In case you've forgotten, we have a race to prepare for. Averon—You dog! What mischief have you got up to that's keeping the crew from doing their jobs? Now back to work everybody —especially you two," Melas shouted, frowning at Averon and Maquesta.

Notwithstanding the harsh words, all of this was said with a good-natured gruffness typical of the *Perechon*'s amiable captain. Before all the words were out of his mouth, the sailors had jumped back to their tasks, an overall satisfaction with their captain and their duty indicated by the minimal grumbling.

"Now, you two. What am I going to do with you? You're supposed to be setting an example," Melas exclaimed with mock seriousness, attempting to throw his arms around Maq and Averon. Maq neatly eluded her father's grasp, but Averon was less agile. Melas got his arm around his friend's shoulder and quickly turned the embrace into a headlock. Not that it was too difficult.

The friends offered a study in contrasts: Melas stood more than six feet tall and had glistening black skin, darker even than Maquesta's. He was completely bald, making his large head, set on broad, powerful shoulders, even more striking. His muscular build had begun only in the last few years to reveal, with a thickening in the middle, his fondness for ale. Averon stood a good head shorter, and was slightly bowlegged. He had dirty blond hair that he wore long these days, hoping to cover the thinning spot at his crown. A thick handlebar mustache was his only neatly groomed aspect. His bronzed skin was weathered by the sun, sporting wrinkles here and there and making him look older than he actually was.

"What did you find out when you paid our entry fee, Maquesta? Anything that will help us tomorrow?" Melas asked, tightening his grip on Averon, then releasing him with a playful shove. The first mate stumbled for a couple steps, turned, and threw all his weight into a low tackle that sent the bigger man sprawling. In an instant the two were rolling around the deck, wrestling.

"Stop it!" Once again chagrinned at how quickly her father and Averon could revert to boyhood behavior, Maquesta put her hands on her hips and shouted more loudly, "Stop it at once! You both have to be in good shape tomorrow, or we won't have any chance to win. Now get up!" Honestly, sometimes she felt like their mother.

Her reminder brought the two to their feet, slightly winded. The coming race was important to both men, indeed to everyone aboard the *Perechon*. Solinari and Lunitari had cycled through the skies several times since the *Perechon* had seen her last well-paying customer. As usual, most of the crew had stayed with the ship. Melas, always content to "make do" from paying assignment to paying assignment—as long as he could sail while doing it—was not the most reliable paymaster. Sailors for hire on the Blood Sea knew that, but those who truly loved to sail loved to sail with him.

This recent dry spell had lasted long enough, though, that Averon had recently disappeared on one of his periodic departures "to seek my fortune," as he always proclaimed rather grandly. These jaunts were usually preceded by a scolding for Melas, whom Averon chided for not being ambitious enough. However, some time later, or sooner, he would track down the *Perechon*, bringing with him a bellyful of outrageous stories about his adventures and little else—with often not even two coppers to rub together. Then it was Melas's turn to offer some constructive criticism. Despite the ribbing back and forth, no serious disagreement had ever disrupted Melas and Averon's friendship. It ran too deep. And Maq always welcomed Averon's return, both on behalf of her father and herself. He was part of the only family she had ever known.

This last time, Averon had returned with news of the race in connection with the minotaur circus—no doubt the event was being held with the idea of minotaur crews inflicting humiliating defeat on nonminotaur entrants, all the while displaying their skill as sailors. Sort of a preparation exercise for the deadly-in-earnest circus contest. The purse was good-sized, Averon said, and it would carry the *Perechon* and her crew nicely for quite some time.

Now safely out of Melas's firm grasp, Averon took himself off to attend to preparations, voicing a mock-disgruntled rant about being underappreciated by the *Perechon*'s captain—and his daughter.

"What was that all about? Between you and Averon?" Melas asked Maq when they were alone. "And what is that you're holding? You looked ready to skin Averon when I came on deck."

Maquesta crumpled the silken vest into a ball, hiding it behind her back in her fist, somehow embarrassed to show the undergarment to her father.

"Averon . . ." she began, then hesitated and only shook her head. "Nothing. It was nothing." She knew, however justified her complaint about Averon's behavior might be, Melas would shrug it off. He always did.

Melas placed his arm lovingly around his daughter's shoulders and drew her toward him, planting a kiss on her forehead.

"Everybody's tense before a race. Whatever he did, I'm sure it was meant to give everyone a little fun. You have to understand, Maq," Melas said, giving her shoulders a gentle squeeze, "there aren't many friends as true as Averon. I'm sure he didn't mean any harm."

Maquesta hugged her father in return. "I know. And I'm fine." She pulled away from him and grinned. "But I am hungry; I'm going to track down Lendle and see what he's cooking up for supper. I hope it's not another version of dried eel stew."

Maq watched her father stride off to join a group of sailors checking the rigging on the mizzenmast, the smaller of the ship's masts, then she turned and headed forward toward the galley. "Sure, Averon wanted to give everyone a little fun—except for me!" she muttered to herself as she walked away.

As soon as she approached the galley's threshold, Maq knew that tonight's menu would, indeed, consist of dried eel stew, though it was mixed this time with some spices she couldn't identify. The tall pot simmering securely between brackets on the wood-fired stove emitted the fishy, oily aroma that unmistakably signaled the stew. Lendle, however, was nowhere in sight. Maq ducked her head as she moved over to take a closer look at what was cooking in the pot. The gnome had rigged up the galley so that virtually all his cooking implements—large spoons, soup ladles, double-pronged cooking forks, pots and pans—hung from a maze of movable belts suspended below the ceiling, with various leather pulls trailing down within his reach. Lendle insisted he knew precisely which thong to pull to set the belts in motion, bringing whatever utensil he needed to the stove or trestle table, with another tug releasing it from its latched hook into his waiting hands. In Maq's experience, however, this rarely occurred. More often than not the implement tumbled clanking to the floor—across the room from where Lendle was standing—or fell directly into whatever was being cooked. On several occasions, one tug from Lendle had sent all the paraphernalia loudly crashing down and bringing everyone running to see what had happened. And in one or two instances, a sharp cooking fork had slightly wounded an unwary visitor to the galley—but Maq suspected Lendle had contrived those "accidents" for crewmembers who had offended him or insulted his cooking. A fork hadn't fallen for quite some time.

She stood over the pot, considering whether to take a taste. The appearance of several slimy orbs that looked like peeled grapes but undoubtedly were not, and what Maq was certain was a tentacle roiling on the stew's surface, discouraged her. Instead she grabbed a piece of hardtack that lay on the trestle table next to a few wizened oranges and exited the galley.

Not quite ready to join in the race preparations after the undergarment episode, Maquesta made her way aft, back toward the raised poop cabin that contained separate quarters for her and her father. Lendle's quarters were just below theirs. The *Perechon*'s engineer-cook occupied a relatively spacious cabin, its size representing Melas's concession to Lendle's passion for tinkering and his relentless accumulation of *potentially* useful objects. Maq rapped loudly at the door, paused, then pushed it open and stuck her head in, knowing Lendle was sometimes too absorbed in his tinkering to hear a knock. As it always did, the cabin caused Maquesta to fight the feeling that she was trapped in an incredible, shrinking compartment. Every inch of wall space, most of the floor and ceiling, and any other flat surface was taken up by a vast assortment of miscellaneous objects, all labeled, boxed, and organized according to Lendle's private system.

Spools of twine and thin metal wire, loops of heavy hemp rope, and coils of chain links hung from hooks on the walls. Wooden boxes filled with everything from jagged-tooth gears to wooden slats to pulleys to bolts of cloth stood in neat rows on the floor. Nets filled with wicker baskets of varying sizes and more rope brushed Maq's head as she leaned into the cabin. The only exception to the organized clutter was Lendle's bed, which was bolted to the wall. It was a typical seagoing berth with high sides, foot, and head to keep him from rolling off during rough seas. Bolted to the floor was a small table with raised sides to prevent objects from falling off, illuminated by a hurricane lamp suspended over it from the ceiling.

Lendle typically stored his toolbox under the table, where it fit securely between four brackets he had pounded into the floor. But it wasn't there now, nor was the gnome. Inspired more by a vague curiosity than any burning, particular need to speak with Lendle, Maq closed the cabin door and headed toward the cargo hold. It had not in fact held much of anything in recent months. But Maq knew that Lendle sometimes made use of the space when he was diagraming one of his ideas for a particularly elaborate invention, or working on a project where he needed room to spread out.

* * * * *

"Fire!" Maq yelled the warning loudly, spun around, and began pulling herself up the cargo hold ladder before she was more than halfway down. Smoke was billowing wildly below her, and she hoped one of the crew would hear her and start bringing buckets of water.

"Fi—"

Maq felt one of her legs being jerked downward and away from the ladder rungs, causing her to lose her grip. As she fell, someone clamped a hand over her mouth, and also broke her fall. Her eyes adjusted to the flickering light released by the flames, and she blinked back tears brought on by the smoke.

"Lendle!" she scolded.

The gnome released her with a sharp admonition: "Quiet!" He stood over Maq, glaring at her.

"Lendle! What in the name of the Graystone of Gargath is going on? This time, you're going to destroy the ship!"

"The *Perechon* won't burn! I'm a good engineer!" Lendle seemed both hurt and excited. His words came very slowly so Maq could understand.

Maquesta peered at the source of the flames. They did seem to be contained in a brick enclosure, and the smoke was dissipating. A door in one side of the brick compartment stood open, with a pile of wood nearby. Nestled closely against the top of the bricks, which were built up around its sides, was a huge brass sphere, almost like a kettle, but closed at the top except for two pipes that connected to a large cylinder that angled upward, toward the trapdoor that led from the hold to the lower deck and the oar bay. In the dim light cast by the flames and a lantern near Lendle's feet, Maquesta couldn't actually see where the cylinder ended, or if anything was connected to it at the far end.

Closer to where she stood, Maq could see that the connection between the kettle and the cylinder wasn't complete. It sounded as if water were beginning to boil inside the sphere, and Maq noticed wisps of steam escaping on one side of the cylinder. She also noticed that Lendle was holding the pieces of pipe he had acquired in Lacynos.

"Steambenders," he said, indicating the pipe. "See this?" he added, waving a proud arm at his contraption. "This is for the times the wind dies and we're out at sea. This will help the *Perechon*!" Lendle nodded his head vigorously, agreeing with himself.

"We already have oars, ten pair of 'em, for when the wind dies down," Maq said, puzzled. Not that they were often put to work, she had to admit. The *Perechon* was well rigged and her crew skilled enough that the ship made good use of even the slightest breeze. There was that, plus the fact that none of the crew jumped at the opportunity for oar duty. It wasn't a point Melas pushed—one among many reasons for his popularity with his crew.

"It *will* help," Lendle repeated. "I will show you, Maquesta Kar-Thon. But not now. Soon. You must leave now. I have lots of work to do." Lendle started pushing Maq toward the ladder.

"All right, just be careful." Maq turned away reluctantly. "Wait a minute." She stopped with her foot on the first rung. "I came looking for you because I was hungry. We all are. When are we going to eat?"

"Maquesta Kar-Thon," Lendle said reproachfully, "I know my duties. I am not a wizard who can deftly conjure a meal at the last minute." Lendle wrinkled his rather large nose with disgust at the thought of magic. "Supper is already cooking. We will eat at the usual time. Now don't forget *your* duties. Go help your father prepare for the race. Be off!"

With that scolding, Lendle turned back to his contraption and Maq climbed up the ladder. She hated it when he talked to her as if she were still a little girl!

* * * * *

The *Perechon*'s crew ate on time that evening, and the dried eel stew was more palatable than usual. Those unattractive orbs tasted better than they looked. Lendle called them Blood Sea potatoes, an organism unknown to Maq. She decided not to inquire more deeply. Whatever they were, they helped fill her and the rest of the sailors, proving Lendle's inventiveness sometimes could produce good results.

Averon, however, missed the meal.

"Maybe he's off buying Maquesta some new articles of clothing. I understand the minotaurs on Mithas turn out some very fine and dainty garments that undoubtedly would look well on her," suggested Vartan, the helmsman, who originally hailed from Saifhum and was one of Maq's least favorites among the crew.

"Something in turquoise? I like turquoise," another quipped.

Several of the sailors snorted with repressed laughter at this. Vartan kept his tone light, but regarded Maq challengingly.

She fought down an impulse to blush. "Averon has more brains than to spend money on anything those ugly beasts could sew, and he uses his brains to think, not just as stuffing to give a nice shape to his pretty head."

Vartan, who was, in fact, good-looking and more than a little vain about it, flushed and turned his attention back to the stew as his mates hooted and laughed at Maq's response.

"Averon left to buy some good rum and a keg of ale, so we can start celebrating as soon as we cross the finish line tomorrow," Melas announced. "With the prize money we'll all get our pay—and our back pay. Let's keep our minds on that goal, not on anything else." Melas's eyes swept the galley, resting ever so slightly on Maq and Vartan.

With that, the captain bent his head over his bowl, and the others followed suit. Lendle, who had more fondness for ale than stew, downed a mug of the brew and started whistling as he spooned the last few servings of the meal into now-empty bowls.

Chapter 2

The Race

With her sails unfurled to speed her course, the Perechon greeted the early morning waves with eager grace, responding to every breath of wind under the firm guidance of Melas, who had taken the helm.

Maquesta, checking a line on the mizzenmast, marveled at the weather. They had been racing since dawn, and the sky had never held more than a few white puffs of clouds. The sea breezes had blown steadily and reasonably strongly. Without storms or lack of wind to worry about, Melas and his crew had been able to concentrate on their main challenge—the course. Maq grinned. It would be her turn at the wheel soon, and she couldn't wait to prove herself. She'd steered the ship hundreds of times, of course, but not in a race—at least not in one as important and potentially fruitful as this one.

The course would take them north and east, out of deep Horned Bay then around the island, past the Cracklin Coast with its strong currents and unfriendly bullsharks, and past the Blade, where the sea floor fell away to an immeasurable trench, creating unpredictable turbulence. The trench served, it was rumored, as a home for a colony of ghagglers—or sligs, as most sailors called them—large, distant cousins to goblins who breathed water as easily as air.

The *Perechon* had been increasing her lead when the lookout noticed one of the racing ships closest behind had fallen foul to something over a coral ridge. The *Waverunner*, a schooner from the Somber Coast, stood dead in the water.

"The crew's working with the sails, Cap'n!" the lookout called, a spyglass pressed against his right eye. "Looks as if they hit a bit of bad luck and the rigging's tangled. I don't see anything in the water that would've stopped them. No rocks or reefs, and not much turbulence today—no more than what we passed through. There's another ship farther back though. She looks under full sail, having no problems. But it doesn't look as though they can catch us!"

The *Perechon* would have to sail through where the treacherous Eye of the Bull narrowed between Mithas and Kothas, then around the rocky southwestern tip of the island, called by many sailors "Slim Chance." Then the course would take them back to Horned Bay—all before nightfall of the second day if they wanted to win the race—and they did.

The rules were wind power only, no oars, and every ship entering had to be at least a hundred feet from bow to stern, regardless of keel length. The *Perechon* had begun the course as one among a dozen. It didn't take long for their ranks to start thinning, though other ships were catching up during the late evening of the first day. But Vartan adjusted the rigging, and the *Perechon* pulled even farther ahead of her competitors.

Shortly after dawn Maquesta saw a merchant carrack, the *Saburnia*, and a slightly seedy privateer, the *Vasa*, driven off course into the northern Courrain Ocean by strong and unpredictable currents near the Cracklin Coast. Whether they would get back into the race, and what would happen to the other vessels that had dropped out of sight, Maq didn't know. The *Perechon* held her lead and began putting greater and greater distances between herself and the rest of the ships. She made good progress until midmorning, when the winds between a section of high banks that the *Perechon* was passing through dropped to almost nothing.

It was in that lull that two other ships, still benefitting from stronger winds, were able to draw near. Now, with the morning sun shining brightly and the wind about the *Perechon* picking up, Maq could see that there were no other contenders beyond the *Perechon* and those two—the *Torado* of Saifhum, captained by Limrod, who was well known to the crew of the *Perechon* as a worthy, though still inadequate, opponent; and a handsome ship that was a stranger to all of them, the *Katos*. A minotaur vessel, she had slipped into the Lacynos harbor in the last minutes before the race began, apparently already registered.

Maq watched her now with growing respect. She was just off the *Perechon*'s starboard stern, pursuing them with determination but, Maq was pleased to note, seemingly unable to close the final gap. Minotaur vessels were not particularly known for their speed. It would be a rare one indeed that could match the *Perechon*. The *Torado* sailed almost abreast of the *Katos*, but to the port side of the *Perechon*.

"Reef the topsails and everybody—mind your

posts!" As much as he hated the idea of slowing down and risking the *Perechon*'s lead, Melas knew it would be foolish to come round the southeastern edge of Mithas and attempt to pass through the Eye of the Bull at full sail. He felt confident that any time lost could be won back sailing up the west coast of the island.

The surface of the sea roiled as they approached, not in regular waves but an uneven to-and-fro that intensified at the point the ships needed to turn west, which was where the underwater ridge extending from the island dropped off into the Blade's trench.

"Keep your eye on the *Torado*," Melas told Maquesta, who had joined him for a moment on the bridge. "She'll make her move now, or I don't know Limrod."

He was right. Her sails bulging with the wind, the *Torado* began gaining on the *Perechon*. She also started to cut in closer to the coast of Mithas, whereas Melas was taking the *Perechon* around the outside edge of the turbulence, closer to Kothas. The *Torado*'s course would save the ship distance as well as take her away from the worst turbulence. But, Maq realized, the shallower coastal waters could prove dangerous for a ship as large as the *Torado*, especially because the rocky submarine ridge rose up at points very near the surface of the sea.

"Maquesta! Stop daydreaming and come give us a hand!"

The summons came from Averon, who with a few other sailors was struggling to tie down the mizzen topsail, a task made increasingly difficult by the freshening wind. The gusts, which often gathered force at this stretch of sea, contributed to the turbulence, as Melas had known it would. Embarrassed at her momentary inactivity, Maq glanced quickly at her father, but Melas's attention was now consumed with the handling of his ship. He hadn't noticed.

Maquesta scrambled up the rigging. By the time she

reached the section where Averon and the others were working on the topsail, they had succeeded in securing it to the yard. She swore at herself under her breath, but checked the rigging while she was up there. It made her look busy, at least.

"Don't be so downhearted, girl," Averon said with a wink as he began lowering himself down one side of the rigging. "If you're looking for work, there's plenty to go around. Come with me."

At least Averon didn't hold a grudge. Maq had started down the other side when they were both stopped midway by an ear-splitting crash and keening wrench, like that of a giant limb being split from a tree. For an instant, Maq thought the awful sound had come from the *Perechon*. Then, with the advantage of her elevated perch, she saw its origin.

The *Torado*, pressing forward through the shallow coastal waters, had run aground, snagged by the submerged ridge. The great ship had pitched to its leeward side, and Maq could see a jagged hole just above the waterline and almost directly under the bowsprit.

"Ha! That will teach Limrod," Melas called out from the helm. "He and his crew will be twiddling their thumbs on the shore or hiking overland to Lacynos when we sail into the harbor to claim our prize! We might even sail back to pick them up—after the race is over." Sailors on the deck of the *Perechon* hooted and whistled in appreciation of their captain's prediction.

With the *Torado* stuck a couple hundred yards off the *Perechon*'s starboard bow, Melas began gaining even more on his only remaining rival, the minotaur ship. As the *Torado* started listing, her crew began lowering a longboat over the side. The boat would have to make two trips to transport the more than twenty crewmembers to shore. Maq could imagine the sailors' mood. She almost felt sorry for them, but she quickly shook off the emotion, knowing a soft heart proved to be of little benefit on the open sea.

Having reached the bottom of the rigging, she was about to turn her attention elsewhere, to see where Averon had ventured to, when a strange turbulence in the water around the *Torado* caught her eye.

"Averon, what do you make of that?" she said, spying him over by the railing.

The first mate pulled a small, collapsing spyglass from his pocket and placed it to his eye. After a minute, he gave a low whistle. "Well, Limrod got more than he bargained for with his shortcut, that's for certain. Have a look." Averon handed the spyglass to Maq and called up to Melas to take his own out and point it at the *Torado*.

Maquesta could not, at first, divine what Averon meant. She could see Limrod still at the helm, gesturing at his crew. Then, scanning the ship, she noticed unusual seaweed formations clinging to the sides of the *Torado*. "Where did that seaweed . . ." Maquesta started to ask, then stopped, her attention riveted by what was happening on the *Torado*. "That seaweed's moving," she whispered.

Limrod was gesturing wildly now, his every movement communicating terror. His first mate, a handsome half-ogre, had a harpoon in hand and was spearing a piece of the seaweed that had oozed up over the railing. All the rest of the crew who were visible stood stock-still. The longboat dangled halfway between the deck and the water, swaying slightly.

The clumps of seaweed kept moving. Maq's stomach tightened; her knees felt weak. Even at this distance, she knew what the crew faced. Training the glass on a clump, she confirmed her suspicion. The seaweed was actually long, green hair attached to perhaps the most feared inhabitants of these waters: sea hags. Maq shivered, the appearance of the creatures filling her with fear. One of them turned to glance at the *Perechon*, and Maq saw its sickly yellow skin. Patches of green scales dotted the bony protrusions on its fingers, and its impossibly long fingernails looked like dirty claws. The thing's eyes were red pinpoints, the color of a sunset before a storm. For an instant it seemed as if the withered creature were staring back at Maq, but she realized the *Perechon* was too far away. The hags' ghastly appearance had the power to frighten intended victims into momentary weakness, allowing the creatures to move closer and cast a deadly paralyzing glance that rendered the victims helpless. Then they moved in for the kill. Sailors claimed the sea hags lived only to kill, and ate only a fraction of what they rended.

More hags crawled onto the deck from the far side of the *Torado*. There must be two dozen of them! Maq focused on one of the hags as it approached a sailor who had managed to fling one leg over the deck rail before being frozen in his tracks. Scrawny arms with hands that ended in nails like talons reached out from the curtain of seaweedlike hair and gripped the unwary man. Maq watched in disbelief as those seemingly decrepit arms snapped the sailor's neck with apparent ease, then ripped off the poor man's arm as though it were a leg of chicken and began chewing on it. The creature pushed the rest of the body into the water and began looking about the deck for another victim. The sea hags enacted similar attacks on every one of the *Torado*'s sailors. Only the captain and his first mate seemed to be putting up any kind of a fight.

"Can't we do something?" Maq heard herself say. "We've got to do something." But her words went unanswered.

She watched Limrod use his curved blade to gut one of the hags. A green-black mixture poured out of the creature's stomach and onto the deck. Still, the hag did not die. It glared at the captain and raised its filthy talons, raking them across his face. Maq was too far away to hear what was transpiring, but she saw Limrod's mouth open, and she imagined that he was screaming in pain. The captain was determined, however, and he brought his sword around once again, this time sending the blade deep between the hag's neck and shoulder. The hag thrashed about wildly and fell to the deck. Limrod, not stopping, stepped over the body and began battling another one. The *Torado*'s captain was strong, but he wasn't a young man, and even from this distance Maquesta could tell his sword swings were slowing with fatigue.

Maq chewed on her bottom lip and mentally urged him to move faster, to swing higher, to back up against the poop cabin for defense. She gasped in relief as the second creature he fought fell to the deck. But there were three more to take its place. The trio moved in slowly, perhaps relishing the moment, or perhaps being apprehensive of the big man who seemed immune to their paralyzing gaze. They started to circle him, and he danced around furtively. Choosing a target, he swung his sword and cleaved off the smallest hag's leg. The creature fell, writhing, and its two companions moved in, seemingly oblivious to their fellow's predicament.

One grabbed the captain's sword arm, digging its claws in, biting down hard with what Maq imagined were foul, sharp teeth, and making Limrod release his weapon. The other came at the captain from behind, raking its talons down his back. Maq looked away for an instant when she saw Limrod's skin and shirt shred like paper. When she glanced back, the captain was on his stomach, and the two hags were fighting over him. He wasn't dead, Maquesta could tell, for he was struggling to rise.

In that instant another sailor moved into her view, the Torado's first mate. The tall half-ogre kicked one of the hags off his captain, then drove a belaying pin between the shoulder blades of the other. He helped Limrod off the deck, then the two stood back-to-back, keeping an ever-increasing number of hags at bay. For a time, Maquesta believed they might actually be able to drive the hideous creatures away, but the hags were too numerous for the pair to handle. After three more hags were killed by the two, she watched with horror as the captain fell to his knees, at last succumbing to his horrid wounds. She scanned with the spyglass to see other parts of the *Torado*. A lump formed in her throat—the ship's deck was awash in blood. A red stream trickled lazily over the port side.

"If those creatures weren't reason enough to leave these waters, that blood is," Averon warned. "As soon as it hits the water, every bullshark and barracuda within miles will be headed here. Melas, can't we put on some speed?" Averon called out to the captain.

"Wait!" Maq grabbed Averon's arm. "Shouldn't we try to help? Can't we do something?" This time she got someone to listen to her, but little good it did.

"Do what, girl?" Averon impatiently shook off her hand. "Once we got within thirty feet of the *Torado*, those hags could use their powers to paralyze us—and all we'd be doin' is presentin' 'em with their dessert, served up nice as you please. No thank you, Maq."

Averon signaled for a few nearby crewmembers to help him unfurl the sails they had just fastened. As scared as they were, and as eager to leave the area, the crew hesitated, waiting to hear the order from Melas.

As Maq continued to stare at the gruesome sight of the *Torado*, the race suddenly seemed very unimportant to her. "But we can't ignore that crew. I see a few sailors still alive."

"All we can do now is help ourselves by getting away as quickly as we can, before the sea hags start looking for another target and before the bullsharks arrive. When a pack of those sharks gets together with their appetites whetted, they can batter a hole in a ship even the size of ours. Let's get going!"

This last Averon addressed as much to Melas as to Maq. Averon kept his gaze fixed on his friend and captain. Maquesta pulled her attention away from the *Torado* to look pleadingly at her father. Melas had not budged from the helm. He still held the wheel firmly. But she saw that his face had lost color beneath its burnished surface.

"Father . . ."

"No, Averon is right. There's nothing we can do," he said grimly. "Not unless we want to die with them. And I certainly don't. Besides, by the time we got there, Maq, there'd be no survivors to rescue." Casting a final glance at the *Torado*, he tightened his grip on the wheel. "Vartan! You and Hvel raise the mainmast topsail. Let's see just how fast we can thread this needle. We'll have to be quick, the *Katos* is moving up fast. We need to beat them through it!"

Melas was swinging the *Perechon* to the west, to position her to enter the Eye of the Bull, when Vartan, at the top of the mainmast, called to him. Maquesta saw the *Katos* gaining on the *Perechon*, not bothering to stop for the *Torado* either, nor even to slow to see what was transpiring.

"Captain—to the starboard, off our stern. What do you make of it?" Vartan's voice held an edge of fear. When Melas, Maq, Averon, and everyone else on deck looked where he had directed, they saw a cresting wave that appeared to be pursuing the *Perechon*. Beneath its white foam, the wave shimmered aqua in the morning light. It moved at an incredible speed, gaining on the *Perechon* instant by instant.

"What say you, Captain, should we man the oars?"

asked Hvel, who had been helping Vartan with the topsail. The crew paused in what they were doing, waiting for Melas's answer, and knowing that using the oars would violate the rules of the race. The crew of the *Katos* would see the oars extended and would win by default. The captain kept his attention fixed on the wave, using his spyglass to take a closer look.

"Vartan, take the helm! Averon, Maquesta—lower a rope ladder over the starboard side and stand by." Melas barked the commands almost angrily, then rushed down the steps from the aft deck as soon as Vartan reached the helm. Maq caught Averon's eye and she raised her eyebrows in an unspoken question. He shrugged his shoulders in reply. Averon obviously didn't know what was going on any more than she did. Maq watched the approaching wave apprehensively. A sea hag? It certainly wasn't a bullshark; the fish didn't move that fast.

"Look, the *Katos* is even with us!" one of the sailors called. "We can't afford to be stopping. We've got to move!"

Melas ignored the cry, and with impressive agility, he swung over the side of the deck and began climbing down the ladder.

"Father, what on Krynn are you doing? Be careful!" Realizing she still had Averon's spyglass, Maq pulled the instrument out and was about to use it when a high-pitched neighing checked her hand.

"Hippocampi!" Averon called. "A sea steed!"

Relieved but still curious, Maq leaned over the side, her mood now one of eager anticipation. All sailors knew the stories, or knew someone who knew someone else who had been aided by the benevolent marine steeds called hippocampi, but Maq had never seen one. She strained forward, staring at the wave, certain it was being generated by hippocampi bringing something to the ship.

Within a couple of minutes, Maquesta could make out three horselike creatures speeding toward the *Perechon*. Their equine heads, topped by manes of long, iridescent fins, rose gracefully out of the foam, appearing at first to be carried along by the wave. As they drew closer, Maq realized that it was the hippocampi themselves churning the water with their powerful front limbs. They were creating the crest.

The wave subsided as the hippocampi slowed their pace in their final approach to Melas, who now was at the bottom of the rope ladder, one arm linked through the rough hemp, the other swinging free. Maquesta could make out their features better with the water calm about them. One creature, closest to the ship, was aqua. Another was ivory, while the third was pale green, nearly the color of the sea. Their forelegs and torsos were horselike, covered in short hair. But their front hooves were webbed fins. Past the hippocampi's rib cages were long, thick fishtails. It was as if the gods had combined the best features of a horse and a fish to make the creatures. The tails, with their triangular-shaped dorsal fins, waved slowly back and forth in the water and kept the hippocampi's heads above the chop.

Two of the creatures hung back while the largest rose up through the water on its beating tail, trying to reach Melas. Its aqua-colored coat caught the sunlight and reflected back, so that the exposed pelt shimmered wildly. Three gills cut deeply into the skin on both sides where the creature's head joined its muscular neck, enabling it to breathe water as well as air. Up close, Maq could see that the mane was actually a flexible membrane that looked like a fin and that grew down the center of the hippocampus's neck.

The creature paused in front of Melas, fixing its intelligent eyes on the *Perechon*'s captain as it dipped its head down in greeting. Melas returned the gesture. Lifting its head to utter a gentle whinny, the hippocampus swung around to the side, presenting its flank to Melas. A tangle of wet clothes clung to the steed's back. Melas bent down and, with a powerful arm, scooped it up. Only then did Maquesta realize that inside the clothes was a person! Melas and the hippocampus bowed at each other again, then the hippocampus rejoined its companions and sped off. Melas shifted the person's weight to his shoulders and slowly climbed the ladder, a feat that would have been impossible for a smaller, weaker man.

"Call Lendle," Melas grunted as Maq and Averon helped him and his burden onto the deck. Maq's mouth fell open in surprise as her father laid the man on the deck. It was the *Torado*'s first mate, the handsome half-ogre she had watched battling the sea hags. His clothes were in tatters, and his bronze skin was crisscrossed by cuts from the hags' nails. In the center of his chest was a deep bite mark, where one of the hags had gouged him with its teeth. The half-ogre's hair was long and blond, braided from the nape of his neck to the middle of his back. But it was crusted with blood, and the leather thong that held it was frayed. A thin mustache was plastered by the seawater across his angular face, and a broad gash that still bled cut down through his right cheek and stopped at his jawbone. Maq mused that it would probably scar.

"His name's Fritzen Dorgaard," Melas announced. "He's sailed with Limrod for the past three years." Maq saw her father look about the deck, then point to a couple of muscular sailors. "Take Fritz down below to the crew's quarters and see what Lendle can do for him. I'm surprised the half-ogre would leave the ship. Of course, maybe he didn't. Maybe the steeds pulled him away. In any event, he must be the only survivor."

Melas and Maq looked down at Fritzen. His breathing was shallow, but his eyes were wide open and glassy. "Poor man," Melas said sadly. "He's probably seeing only what is playing out in his mind. If he makes it, I'll take him on. I've heard he's a good man, an acrobat who gave up the circus life for the sea."

The captain padded away from the half-ogre and strode toward the center of the *Perechon*. "As for the rest of us, let's get this ship moving! We've got a race to win, and time is a'wasting." After casting a last, concerned glance at the *Torado*'s first mate, Melas bounded up the steps to the aft deck, taking the helm from Vartan and shouting orders to the crew. Lendle, summoned from the galley, dragged Fritzen forward with the help of the other two sailors. Maq shook off the shock and amazement she was feeling and focused once again on winning the race.

* * * * *

The delay caused to the *Perechon* by picking up Fritzen enabled the *Katos* to achieve what it hadn't been able to do by means of its own power for a day and a half—take the lead. The ship had sailed well into the Eye of the Bull, putting almost a league between itself and the *Perechon*. These particular waters gave Melas little room to maneuver and regain the lead. Cliffs towered over the edge of the channel on the Mithas side so that waves pounding into their base were reflected straight back, where they often collided with oncoming crests, creating a thunderous crash and an almost vertical wall of water. On the Kothas side, the channel appeared calmer. However, Melas knew the surface hid treacherous currents and deadly reefs that sheltered sea hag coveys.

"We'll have to come up as close behind the *Katos* as we dare, then break for the lead as soon as we leave the channel!" Melas shouted, trying to be heard over the sound of the pounding water.

The *Perechon* pitched and bobbed as it followed the minotaur vessel through the Eye. The water churned and surged, and waves spilled up over the deck, sending sailors scrambling to find something to hold on to. Maquesta held on to the rigging and tried to climb higher on the rope ladder of the mainmast. She wanted to get a good view of how far ahead the *Katos* was. She gained about ten feet, then decided she had better stop. She wrapped her arms around the ropes and held fast while the *Perechon* continued to dance on the turbulent waters. Down below she saw one of the newer crewmembers latch on to the capstan and bend over and wretch from motion sickness. She grimaced. If her father saw the green sailor, she knew Melas would give him a stern talking to and force him to find work elsewhere.

A large wave crested over the bow of the ship, throwing a wall of water on the hapless sailor. Maq grinned, but then scrambled for her own purchase as the ship rocked and nearly dislodged her. She gripped the rope ladder even tighter, but her legs waved free below her, as if she were a flag blowing in the strong breeze. Glancing up, she saw the topsail strain against the masts, and she heard the tall timber creak, but she breathed a heavy sigh of relief when the ship passed through the Eye and the water began to calm.

The sick sailor regained his composure, and he busied himself checking the rigging. Smiling widely, Maq watched him for a moment, then climbed higher to get a better look at the *Katos*. Melas was maneuvering the *Perechon* close in behind the minotaur ship as they neared the end of the channel.

"Faster, faster," Maq urged as she climbed even

higher and inspected the sails. The cloth and the rigging was holding, though she made a mental note to talk her father into a new topsail when they had the prize money in their grasp. This one had been patched too many times.

Finally the *Katos* and *Perechon* emerged from the channel, and Maquesta descended the ropes rapidly and rushed to her father's side. "Pull!" he barked at her, thrusting her in front of the wheel. She gripped two of the wooden spokes that extended from the wheel and served as handholds and turned them rapidly to her right. The motion caused the system of pulleys attached to the rudder to move, and the *Perechon* pulled to the starboard side of the *Katos*. "Keep it up!" Melas yelled. His voice was raised to be heard above the crackling of the sails in the wind. "I'm going to adjust the rigging to see if we can get a little more speed out of her!"

Maquesta tingled all over with excitement. She'd been given the wheel at the most crucial part of the race. The *Perechon* had been entered in many such contests, but this was the first time a ship was presenting a serious challenge. She breathed faster and felt her heart hammering fiercely in her chest. Her course took the ship so close to the *Katos* that she imagined hearing the conversations of the minotaur sailors on deck. Risking a glance to the side, she saw the captain and his mates working the wheel. Another group of sailors were laboring over the rigging. She doubted they had her father's skill.

With her hand on the king's spoke, the largest handhold that pointed up when the rudder was straight, Maquesta turned the wheel hard to the left, taking her farther away from the *Katos* and closer to the treacherous shore. Maq doubted her father would have tried this maneuver, and likely would have stopped her had he been within arms' reach. She didn't want to risk the two ships bumping in the unpredictable water, and she wanted to attempt what Limrod had—but in a little deeper water. She knew the *Perechon* didn't sit quite as heavy in the water as the *Torado* had, and secretly she wanted to impress her father and prove something to the crew. A spray of seawater splashed in her face, refreshing and cooling her. Taking another sidelong glance, she noticed the *Perechon* had made some headway—it was pulling ahead of the *Katos*. Her maneuver had caused the *Perechon* to regain the lead!

Cheers erupted from the sailors on the *Perechon* deck. A loud cheer behind her signaled the approach of her father. Melas slapped her strongly on the back.

"Good job, Maquesta!" he beamed. "And it was a good thing I gave you the wheel—I certainly wouldn't have done that." More softly, he added, "And I'd better not catch you trying to do something like that ever again. I made a few adjustments, and that should help us pick up even more speed. It will tax the sails and the rigging a bit, but I want very badly to win this one."

She grinned up at him and stepped back, returning the wheel to his control and forgetting his gentle scolding. Nothing could dim her spirits now. She had succeeded at the *Torado*'s failed gambit—keeping the *Perechon* close to the Mithas coast. They had squeaked between the *Katos* and the shore, recapturing the lead with a vengeance.

* * * * *

The summer's evening sun still warm against her skin, Maq allowed herself to think about the celebration she knew would take place that night in Lacynos. Standing next to her father at the helm, Maq grinned up at Melas, who winked back. Maq had remained on the aft deck, within earshot of her father, while he continued to lengthen the lead they had on the *Katos*. As she had on countless occasions throughout her youth, Maq had performed tasks as ordered and listened as Melas explained his strategy to her: why the sails needed to be trimmed a certain way, what potential hazards or advantages particular waters held, how the king's spoke felt in his hand in certain conditions versus others. When she was younger, Averon would sometimes join them, and Maq and her father would spend hours discussing the finer points of navigation—with the boisterous first mate throwing in his opinion here and there. In more recent times, however, these had become exclusively father-daughter occasions. Everyone else, including Averon, was discouraged from interrupting unless the matter was extremely urgent. As Maq's knowledge and experience had grown, Melas had increasingly solicited her opinion, not Averon's. These times always caused a thrill of pride to course through Maq.

Now, once again, the *Katos* trailed the *Perechon* at a steady distance of about a league, unable to close the gap. With constant winds, Maquesta estimated they would sail into Horned Bay and claim their victory a good hour before darkness set in. She reminded herself to ask her father about purchasing a new topsail for the mainmast. While the minotaurs did not build their ships as well as other races did, she reflected, they were expert sailmakers—and certainly good sails were available in Lacynos.

Then an odd thought crossed her mind.

"Father, don't you think it's strange that we neither saw nor heard of the *Katos* before this race?"

"Krynn is not such a small place," replied Melas. "There are ports we have never visited in waters we have not sailed."

"Not so very many, and anyway, by its design the

Katos appears to be a Blood Sea ship. I would not have thought there were any ships unknown to us here," Maq said, staring thoughtfully at the *Katos*. "At least it looks like a Blood Sea ship except for one thing. Did you notice?"

"Yes. It's a bit out of the ordinary, but not unheard of, Maquesta."

They both referred to a striped awning extending from the base of the upper aft deck over the main deck of the Katos, with three sides so that it looked like a small, closed tent.

"I would hate to have to work around that on our main deck," Maq said. "I wonder . . . Wait a minute!" Maq, who had been regarding the *Katos* rather dreamily, snapped to attention.

"Did the winds change?" She hadn't noticed any difference. Checking the *Perechon*'s sails, Maq saw there had been no change. She looked back at the other ship. "Father, I don't know how she's doing it, but the *Katos* is gaining on us!"

"What!" Melas roared. "Maquesta, here!" He motioned her over to take the helm, then stood for an instant, hands on hips, staring back at the *Katos*. He pulled his spyglass out of his pocket, extended it, and raised it to his eye. A string of curses erupted from his lips. He shoved the glass back into his pocket, then vaulted down the steps to the main deck. "Averon, come help me here! Vartan, Hvel, to the foremast!"

Melas shouted one command after another, having the crew adjust first one sail, then the next, shouting directions to Maq at the helm. The sailors worked frantically. But still the *Katos* gained.

Maq grasped the helm, rendered nearly immobile. Her heart pounded wildly with joy—again she had been given the wheel at an important time. Her right hand gripped the king's spoke tightly. At the same time, a constricting band of nerves threatened to squeeze her heart to a dead stop. They were in jeopardy of being overtaken again!

Maq glanced back over her shoulder. Despite everyone's efforts, only an hour from Horned Bay, the *Katos* was steadily erasing the *Perechon*'s lead. How ignominious! Maq felt ashamed, ashamed at herself for having such self-centered emotions. But she burned with a combination of anger and shame at the thought that she was helming the *Perechon* as it might be sailing down to defeat.

The *Perechon*'s sails snapped loudly in the wind. Melas had ordered every scrap of sailcloth unfurled. He had directed their positioning to take utmost advantage of every puff of wind. The *Perechon* leapt and crashed through the waves with an energy rarely seen before. Sea spray dampened Maquesta's face and plastered her curls to the sides of her head. She was leaning every ounce of her body weight into the wooden spokes of the helm in an effort to hold the speeding ship to a steady course. Considering whether to tie a length of rope to the aft deck railing to aid her with her task, Maq cast her eyes around the deck to see what was available. When she looked up, she found her father standing next to her. His brows knit together in a frown, he was staring out to sea. One look at his face told Maq the news was not good.

But glancing backward, Maq nearly leapt with joy. The sea was empty! They must have completely outdistanced the *Katos*. But in the next instant, she realized the sea behind her was empty because the *Katos* sailed abreast of the *Perechon*. With a nod of his head at Maq, Melas took over the helm. Several moments passed, and both father and daughter shook their heads to clear out their ears. Yet each still heard it, though faintly at first: a high piping, for all the world sounding like a flute playing a rapid jig.

The *Katos* sailed quite near the *Perechon* now, still abreast but unable, it seemed, to finally pull ahead. The music grew louder, more insistent. Maq and Melas looked at each other with the same question in mind: where was the sound coming from? The slow realization that the source of the music was the *Katos* made Melas's brow furrow even more. Who in Krynn would be playing a flute in the final stretch of a race?

"If it's meant to improve spirits over there, I bet it's not working," Maq said excitedly. "I don't think they can outrun us! What do you think, Fa—"

She never completed the question. The jig stopped abruptly. Maquesta thought she noticed a bit of tension leave the *Katos*'s sails. Then across the waves the music resumed; this time the air carried a haunting tune, pitched in an even higher range than the jig. Inexplicably, contrary gusts of wind enveloped the *Perechon*, bringing with each blast gritty dust that stung the crew's eyes. The *Perechon*'s sails snapped and cracked, filling with wind blowing first one way, then another. The tall wooden masts creaked ominously as if they were in pain, strained almost to their limit.

"Take down the sails," Melas bellowed from the helm. "Take down the sails or we'll lose our masts!"

Holding her forearm in front of her face to try to shield her eyes from the blowing dust, Maquesta fought her way against the wind to the mizzenmast where Averon and several others were attempting to lower both sails.

"Someone's going to have to climb up to the boom," Averon shouted in her ear. "Part of the topsail rigging has snagged on something. Here, take my place holding this rope and I'll go."

Maq shook her head without saying anything and began climbing the rigging. She knew where the problem was, because she had fretted over the topsail before. She also knew Averon was saying something to her because his mouth was open—but the sound was carried away by the wind. Maq was one of the best climbers on board. She was certain she would be better at unsnagging the sail than at holding a rope, which demanded more strength than skill. And, as ever, she felt she had something to prove to the rest of the crew.

Buffeted by the wind, Maq inched her way up the rigging, by feel rather than sight. The dust was blinding and forced her to close her eyes. Then, when she had almost reached the boom, the wind squall died as suddenly as it had begun. Blinking her eyes to clear them, Maq observed that the sky was still cloudless, the sun shining, and the *Katos* now sailed far ahead, apparently unhindered by contrary winds. She worked the topsail until the fold was free, then she looked at the minotaurs' ship again.

On the deck of the *Katos*, she spied a lean figure, heavily cloaked and hooded. Not a minotaur, she judged, realizing that the outline of horns would have shown beneath the material. Before Maquesta could study the figure further, it stepped back beneath the striped awning.

Chapter 3
Betrayed

"Com'n."

The invitation was slurred. Maquesta had expected her father to sample the ale on board— liberally sample it. What surprised her was that he had retreated to his cabin alone after the *Perechon* had slipped, unheralded, into the Lacynos harbor—just in time to see a bedecked minotaur barge bearing away a group from the *Katos*, presumably to accept their prize for winning the race. He drank in solitude, accompanied only by a couple of large pitchers of the heady brew. She took one look at him and whirled around and left. She'd come back later when he was sober or sleeping it off.

With a book and an oil lamp in hand, Maq retreated to the upper aft deck. Her perch near the helm was predictably deserted now that the *Perechon* was moored in Horned Bay. However, though secluded on the opposite end of the ship from the galley and the sailors' quarters, Maq was able to hear much of the wake they held to mourn the *Perechon*'s loss and drown their sorrows.

Several hours later, most of the noise had subsided. A few of the sailors had stumbled up on deck and passed out, including Vartan, whom Maq could see sprawled on the main deck. Those remaining in the galley had settled down to some even more serious drinking. But Melas had still not emerged from his cabin, nor had Averon joined him, both of which Maq found odd. Normally the pair would be in the thick of it with the rest of the men. Maq rarely drank and never in the midst of the crew. She didn't want to risk losing control and opening herself up to ridicule.

Maq preferred reading as an escape, anyway. Her mother, a teacher from her elven village, had read to Maq often in both the tongue common to humans and in the lilting Elvish language—and Maq always associated the activity with her mother. She derived considerable comfort from it, even when her reading matter was an old sea map or mariner's journal. However, that night, brooding over the *Perechon*'s loss, Maq read very little before deciding to check on her father again.

When she pushed open the door to her father's cabin, Maq hesitated. The cabin was dark, lit only by the light of Krynn's moons, which entered through portholes on two sides of the cabin. Melas was slumped over his desk, its top strewn with pieces of paper, two empty pitchers by his feet.

Approaching him, Maq hoped her face didn't betray the sudden anguish she felt. Her father was crying. She hadn't seen his tears since that first year after her mother had disappeared. He had cried so much then, Melas once said, he had used up all his tears. But he was crying now.

"Father, what's wrong?" Maq knelt by Melas's feet, looking up at him. "It was only a race. There'll be other races to win. Other prizes to claim. The crew will wait for their pay. They've done it before. They won't leave you."

Melas turned his face away from her. "Ah, no, Maquesta. It was more than a race. It was the *Perechon* herself."

Melas's entire frame convulsed with a wrenching sob, then quieted. He swiped a burly forearm across his face, wiping away the last of the tears. He turned back to look directly at his daughter, seeming to have sobered up. "Now I've said it."

She looked at him and brushed her hand gently across the top of his head.

"Said what? What do you mean?" Maq regarded her father with a puzzled expression. "There's nothing wrong with the *Perechon*. She's as sound as ever. Nothing could have raced through that squall. All she needs is a new topsail." A twinge of guilt flashed over her at the recollection of her role at the helm, thinking perhaps she could have done something as the *Katos* passed them by a second time. Maq shook it off.

"Why, I was just reading in the *Manual for the Maritime-Minded* about a tremendous squall that . . ."

"No, Maquesta. The *Perechon* is still the best ship on the Blood Sea, and you did as well as anyone could have at the helm."

Even in his current state, Melas had known how she must be feeling, Maq thought with a rush of affection.

"It's just that the *Perechon* won't be our ship anymore," Melas continued, his voice sinking to a whisper. Once again, he averted his eyes from his daughter's.

Maq's stomach somersaulted. "What?"

"Averon and I were so sure; we were certain we would win the race, so we bet everything we had—we bet more than we had. You know how few coins we had between us. And it had been too long since the last time I paid the crew," Melas's words jostled up against one another, so quickly was he speaking.

"The minotaur betting master in Lacynos wouldn't take a signed pledge from us. In the event we lost, he wanted more than our names on a piece of paper. But we knew we wouldn't lose. *Couldn't* lose. And then, Maquesta, with the prize money plus our winnings . . ." A hint of the excitement that prospect created for him entered Melas's voice even now.

"With our winnings we wouldn't have had to worry about money for a long time," Melas finished. "Only the betting master wouldn't accept just our pledge. So we signed over the *Perechon*."

"I think it was not Averon's to sign over," Maq whispered, her voice strangled by emotion.

"Maquesta, you can't blame this on Averon. I did it. I wanted to do it. I just knew . . ." Here Melas shook his head, overwhelmed. "Averon feels terrible, just terrible."

"Where is he?" Maq roused herself from a grim line of reflection, heading toward the inevitable conclusion that she was to lose the only home she'd ever known. "Why isn't he here with you?"

"I sent him away. I didn't want to be with anyone. I needed—I *need* to sort some things out by myself," Melas said haltingly. His chin dropped down to his chest.

Maq circled her arms around Melas—though indeed they could not completely gird his immense bulk—and laid her head against his chest. Melas placed a hand on his daughter's wiry curls. Thus linked, father and daughter found some brief comfort.

She stayed with him until she was able to convince him to rest. "We'll think of something in the morning. Don't worry. Somehow things will work out . . . they always do." Then Maquesta gently closed the door to

Melas's cabin, turned, and came face to face with Averon. The first mate reached past her to open the door.

"Don't go in. I finally got him to get into his bunk. I think he's asleep." Maq fixed her eyes on Averon, who was doing his best to avoid her gaze, shifting his weight from foot to foot and shuffling backward as they spoke. Watching him, the gravity of what had happened crashed down on Maq.

"Averon, how could you have used the *Perechon* to guarantee those bets? How could you possibly have talked my father into it? He's your best friend. And now he's lost everything."

"Ah, girl, it seemed like the perfect plan," Averon responded lamely, continuing to edge away from her.

Anger left over from the undervest incident and frustration from the *Perechon*'s loss boiled up inside Maquesta. "This is how you repay Melas for being your friend, for always giving you a home and work to come back to after you've been gadding about for weeks—by roping him into one of your ill-considered schemes? And now soon none of us will have this ship to call home. We'll be stranded in this minotaur city!" She continued to sputter and advance on him.

Averon stopped his slow retreat, drew himself up, and thrust out his chin. Something she had said had touched a nerve. "I have done a great deal through the years for Melas and this ship, not that anyone has ever given me any credit. I won't stay here and be lectured!" Averon turned on his heels and stalked off.

Still seething, Maquesta stomped over to her cabin, located next to Melas's. Once inside, she paced back and forth, trying to calm down—without great success. Then she pulled out a book, lit a lantern, and sat down at her reading table. It was only a few minutes later that the tinkling of a bell suspended from the ceiling interrupted her. Maq glanced up at the bell, sighed, then stood. The small brass bell, which had continued to ring, dislodged itself from the spring that held it and fell, striking Maquesta in the head. Maq stooped, picked up the bell, and threw it, with all her strength, into the corner. "Lendle!" She spit out the gnome's name, following it with a string of muttered curses, as only a young woman raised around seaports could. She headed for the door, taking her foul mood with her.

* * * * *

Fritzen Dorgaard lay on his back on a cot Lendle had set up in the armory, which was occasionally used as a temporary infirmary since it was next to the galley where the gnome concocted his remedies. Maq leaned over the stricken sailor. Fritzen's green eyes were wide open, but unseeing.

Melas had said Fritzen was half merrow, or sea ogre, and Lendle insisted his sun-bronzed skin should have a hint of green to it. Instead, it seemed his skin had lost all color.

"Odd combination, sea ogre and human," Maquesta said, then pursed her lips into a straight line. "Well, I should talk."

She laid her hand against his forehead; it was cold and clammy. The skin around the gash on his face was puffy, pulling against the stitches Lendle just finished sewing.

"VerygraveverygraveIneedsomechatterwort," Lendle began, speaking at the typical gnomish pace, "orhecannotmakeitunlessIgetsomechatterwortsoon."

"Hold on, hold on. Your stupid summons bell fell down and hit me in the head. I've had some very bad news. It's late. I'm tired. In other words, I'm in no condition to keep up with your conversational speed records," Maq grumped.

Lendle pursed his lips in mild disapproval of his favorite crewmember. With a motion of his head, he indicated Fritzen.

"A simple *slow down, please* would have sufficed, Maquesta Kar-Thon. I also am tired and have no special liking for being lectured. I've spent the past three hours tending to our guest."

Maq flushed. Now she'd received two reprimands for lecturing, not that it was an unknown quality in ships' captains, which is what she expected to be someday, or had expected to be until the news earlier tonight.

"I'm sorry. How is Fritz? And what do you need me for? I'm not a healer."

"His condition is very grave. See this gash on his right forearm?"

Lendle grasped the half-ogre's wrist and rotated his arm outward so Maq could see the soft underside. A jagged slash about six inches long cut deeply into the flesh. The raw edges oozed a greenish slime. Maq grimaced.

"One of the hags may have had poison on its claws and sliced him before the hippocampi were able to rescue him," Lendle explained. "Or it could be something else. In any case, I need to rouse him to ask him about it before I can treat it. A sea hag wound requires special care. Unfortunately, he seems to be sinking more deeply into a state of shock. He's been through an awful lot, and he might not make it. Chatterwort might bring him round, but I have none. I want you to go into Lacynos to buy some. I still have several coppers and a handful of steel pieces. They should be more than enough. I've invested too much time in him to see him die now."

"Can it wait until morning? I'd like to get some sleep, and I don't relish the idea of walking the streets of Lacynos in the dark with everyone there having a long night of drinking under their belts."

"Yes, but leave as soon as it's light. And take someone with you, Maquesta. I'd go myself, but I think I should stay here with Fritzen Dorgaard."

Maq nodded, suddenly overwhelmed with weariness. She made her way back to her cabin, threw herself down on top of the bunk, and immediately fell asleep.

* * * * *

The next morning, Maquesta threaded her way through the streets of Lacynos, trying to stick to the drier ground and at the same time avoid the occasional drunken minotaur who staggered by. Even at this early hour, the air was heavy with heat and humidity, constant facets of the weather in this part of Krynn—and one of the reasons the roadways never completely dried out from rainfall to rainfall.

Hvel followed Maq's lead, maintaining a brisk trot in order to keep up with her long strides. Not much older than Maq, Hvel was a full head shorter, and portly. He nonetheless could move quickly and was a good man in a fight, knowing how to use his weight and size to the best advantage. Maq had that in mind when she asked him to accompany her, that and the fact that he was one of the few crewmembers stirring and sober when she was ready to leave. When alert, as he seemed now, he was also a man of few words—which suited Maq's current mood just fine. She had a personal errand she wanted to pursue after buying the chatterwort. Hvel was not the type to ask too many questions if she arranged to split up with him and rendezvous back at the wharf.

Nearly every block in Lacynos boasted a tavern or inn. And every one they had passed was open and occupied. They never closed in this port. Up ahead,

Maq spotted the shingle she was looking for, the Bay Watch. Lendle had given her directions and said the innkeeper, a human named Renson, also sold medicinal and magical herbs.

Once they stepped through the doorway, Maq and Hvel paused to allow their eyes to adjust to the gloomy interior. Only one candle burned in the half-dozen wall sconces. The dim dawn light, entering through the front door and two small rear windows, provided the candle little assistance. Maq scanned the common room for any sign of the innkeeper. At the back of the room, she observed a wooden ladder, which took the place of stairs in most minotaur buildings. This one led, presumably, to guest rooms. Unlike minotaur inns—that served only food and drink—the Bay Watch offered overnight lodging as well. However, from what Maq could see, most of the patrons had passed out at their tables, not bothering to spend a copper on a bed. Only one trio of well-armed human sailors—more than likely pirates, Maq thought—remained awake, still drinking.

Maquesta saw no evidence of the proprietor, but the sound of snoring drew her toward a rough wooden bar situated in the far corner of the common room. It offered a good vantage point on both the front door and the wooden ladder. As she and Hvel approached the bar, not only did the snoring grow louder, a spicy aroma cut through the stale barroom odor. Smoke wafted from small pots placed around the perimeter of the bar. Inhaling deeply, Maq leaned forward as she walked, only to smack her nose against a hard, flat surface while simultaneously stubbing her toe. She stumbled backward, cursing, saved from falling on her rump only by Hvel's steadying hand. Behind her, the pirates erupted into raucous guffaws.

"Wha-What happened?" Maq gingerly touched her throbbing nose to check if it was broken. No, just sore, she decided. Most definitely, she had run into something. Yet in front of her she saw nothing. From behind the bar, the snoring stuttered to a halt, replaced by a gravelly roar.

"Which of you thieving scoundrels was trying to pinch a free drink while I was catching me forty winks? I'll not put up with that! I charges me a fair price. I never cheats no one and no one had better cheat me!"

Brandishing an axe in one hand and a jagged-edged short sword in the other, the speaker—or roarer—of these dire warnings stood up behind the bar. A few stray hairs stuck straight up from his otherwise bald head. One eye glared at them from under a tufted eyebrow. Where the other eye should have been, a dark hole gaped.

"I assure you, we were not trying to steal anything," Maq spoke up clearly, ignoring the pirates' drunken laughter. "I am Maquesta Kar-Thon and this is Hvel Gamon, from the *Perechon*. We came to buy some chatterwort from you."

Mention of a commercial transaction immediately calmed down Renson, for that was who the man behind the bar introduced himself as. He peered closely at them with his good eye, obviously sizing them up. After half a minute, the innkeeper blew out whatever was lit inside the small pots and beckoned Maq and Hvel forward.

They both held back. Then Maquesta finally stretched her arms out toward the bar. Nothing. She moved forward slowly, repeating the motion with her arm, Hvel following her cautiously. Renson cackled.

"Don't worry, don't worry. Just a little illusion I create with some of my herbs—invisible smoke wall. Keeps those with grasping hands and big thirsts from helping themselves to the tap. The herbs have stopped smoldering, see? You'll be all right. I'll start them up again when we're finished. Can't trust everyone." Here Renson nodded his head toward the pirates, who had resumed their drinking. "Otherwise I'd never get any shut-eye."

Resting her forearms on the bar, Maq saw that a narrow cot covered with a dirty blanket was set up behind it. Renson had stowed his axe in an easy-to-reach cubbyhole and stuck his sword into his waistband, freeing his hands to tie a ragged gray patch over his empty eye socket. "Now what was it you said you wanted to buy?" he inquired once he had the patch in place, rubbing his hands together and taking on the air of an unctuous merchant.

"Chatterwort, about five drams' worth."

Renson's expression soured somewhat at the meagerness of Maq's intended purchase. "I'll have to check my storeroom. I should be able to help you." With that Renson lifted a trapdoor located in the cramped floor space behind the bar, and dropped out of sight.

Maq felt Hvel, standing next to her with his back to the bar and his eyes on the pirates, tense up. She turned to see one of the trio, a tall, muscular redhead, approaching them. He held his and his friends' empty ale mugs in one hand. Maq watched him. He moved gracefully, though he'd obviously been drinking for a while. Only a certain heaviness in his eyelids betrayed the amount of ale he must have consumed. She glanced down at Hvel, who nodded almost imperceptibly. They both knew that a drunken sailor, in a port as wild as Lacynos, needed careful handling.

The redhead set his mugs on the bar for refilling and looked at Maq appreciatively.

"Greetings and good morning. Fletch's the name. Me and my comrades sail with the *Bloodhawk*. Maybe you've heard of her?"

Maq nodded. A pirate ship with a reputation for speed and ruthlessness.

Fletch swayed slightly, grinning at her. "Why don't you dump your pudgy little friend here and join us? I promise we'll show you a good time." He winked at her and banged one of the mugs against the top of the bar. "What do you say?"

Maq looked over and saw the two seated pirates leering at her. She smiled sweetly at Fletch.

"I'm sure you'd try your best, but I don't really enjoy wrestling. Anyway, my little friend here is terribly ill. I'm buying medicine for him now, and I have to take him back to the ship before he collapses. I hope he's not contagious."

Hvel, who except for a pair of bloodshot eyes exuded sturdy good health, stood placidly beside Maquesta. Fletch stared at him suspiciously.

"Don't get too close," Maq warned, stepping between Fletch and her companion. "I would feel just awful if you caught it, too. So I'll decline your invitation. I'm really very sorry. Maybe we can do it another time." She continued smiling at the pirate.

Too drunk to know he was being insulted and lied to, Fletch took a step backward. "Barkeep! More ale!" he shouted in the general direction of the trapdoor. After a few minutes in absorbed contemplation of his empty mugs, the pirate seemed to forget his earlier conversational gambit. He moved on to another subject.

"You're from the *Perechon*, you say?"

Maq nodded again, still smiling.

"Someone on your ship must be happy, *very* happy—" He paused for emphasis. "And rich." He winked at Maquesta.

What was this fool talking about? Maq wondered. Not wanting to reveal too much curiosity, either to the drunken sailor or to Hvel, who like the rest of the crew had no inkling of Melas's failed betting strategy, she reacted guardedly.

"No one's happy. We lost," Maq stopped and took a breath, finding it difficult to say out loud. "We lost the race."

"Yes," Fletch wagged a finger in Maq's direction. "Too bad you weren't sailing with the *Bloodhawk*. We never lose once we set our caps for something. Why once, two years ago . . ."

Maq, eager to hear more about the harbor race, steered Fletch back to the subject at hand. "Yes, I heard about that. Remarkable. And it was someone from the *Bloodhawk*'s crew who was pleased about the outcome of yesterday's race?" she asked innocently.

"Not the *Bloodhawk*, the *Pere . . . Perek . . .*" Fletch gave up. "Your ship. I heard about it at the betting master's, over at the Breakers. Now that's a place where a fellow can at least get served a drink," he said loudly, looking around vaguely for Renson. Maq tugged at his sleeve. Fletch stared at her uncomprehendingly.

"The *Perechon*?" she prompted.

Fletch frowned, then perked up. "Right. Someone from the crew bet on the winning ship and came in to the Breakers to collect his winnings. Little guy. Bow-legged. Very happy. And rich."

He peered with renewed interest at Hvel, who had moved some distance down the bar after Maq's impromptu diagnosis of his condition, and consequently had not picked up much of the conversation. "Is everyone on the *Perechon* little?" Fletch asked.

Disconcerted by the pirate's description of the winner as someone closely resembling Averon, Maq was unable to make any response. With relief, she saw Renson's head pop up out of the cellar. Fletch's attention immediately shifted. "Barkeep!" he bellowed.

Maquesta joined Hvel at the far end of the bar, where they waited for Renson to serve the pirates before selling them the chatterwort.

"That sailor was quite a bit drunker than he looked," Hvel observed. "What was all that about one of us betting against the *Perechon*? Did I hear that right? And then he called me short?"

Maq managed to compose herself. "His mind was so fogged by drink, he didn't know what he was talking about. That story changed about ten times in the course of our five-minute conversation."

Hvel chuckled, returning his attention to a plate of sweet rolls on one of the shelves behind the bar. "Short. *Hmpf!*"

"Here's your chatterwort." Renson laid the herb wrapped in a twist of paper on the bar. "That will be twelve steels."

"Twelve!" Maq reacted indignantly, commencing the ritual of bargaining. Years of making ends meet on the *Perechon* had made Maquesta a very adept bargainer. In this instance, preoccupied by what she had just heard, Maq went through the process by rote and was not at her best. Nonetheless, she still achieved a significant reduction in Renson's asking price.

"And how much for one of those stale rolls back there?" Maq added. Hvel brightened. After a minute more of haggling, he had one of the sticky buns in his hands. Maq counted out the coins, and they turned to leave. But after a couple steps, she stopped.

"You go ahead, Hvel. I forgot to ask Renson something Lendle wanted me to find out about brewing the chatterwort. No use you standing through all the directions. I'll meet you back at the dock. This shouldn't take more than an hour."

Occupied with his sweet roll, Hvel nodded and continued out the door. As soon as he was out of earshot, Maq beckoned Fletch over.

"Can you give me directions to the betting master's at the Breakers?" She had intended all along to find the person or persons who held Melas's markers and try to negotiate an arrangement that would allow her father to keep the *Perechon*. Now, with what Fletch had told her, she had another reason to find the betting master. And find him soon.

Memorizing the crude instructions, she hurried out the door, her anger and curiosity mounting with each step. Several minutes later—and after making a few wrong turns—she was there.

"It's a miracle anyone can find this place to make a bet," Maq muttered under her breath. "There's not even a sign. And it looks abandoned."

She stood in front of a squat, narrow building sandwiched between two larger ones, having threaded through a maze of streets and alleys to get there. The paint around the windows was peeling. Weeds grew in profusion about the front of the place, and a lone window box held dead flowers. Still, the well-trampled roadway leading up to the betting master's threshold indicated the establishment's popularity. However, at this early hour Maq appeared to be the only customer.

Once she stepped inside, Maq saw that a bar cut diagonally across the far corner. Other than that, the long room less resembled a tavern than it did an empty storeroom. There were no tables and chairs for the patrons, only two chalkboards, one hanging from each side wall, obviously for posting the odds for given events, Maq suspected. Also, there was no betting master.

"Hello? Is anyone here?"

Maq cautiously paced the length of the packed dirt floor. After getting no answer, and trying several more "hellos," she headed for a door set into the back wall. She knocked, and in response the door was pulled open so rapidly and forcefully from the inside that she had to jump back to avoid getting knocked flat on her stomach.

Maq stepped over a raised threshold into a room, not

as long as the first, but just as narrow. It was lined by minotaurs armed with the spiked clubs they called tesstos. Facing her from behind a massive, slate-topped desk that was tall enough to allow him to stand—and with its surface inclined inward, preventing someone in Maquesta's position from seeing what it held—stood the one Maq assumed to be the betting master. In the uncertain light cast by two flaming torches set in wall sconces, his horns appeared to nearly touch the ceiling after first sweeping outward to cover half the breadth of the room.

He was a massive minotaur, regardless of the tricks the low lighting played. He was at least seven and a half feet tall, and his coat was a deep black, as dark as Nuitari. His head sat on broad shoulders, down from which extended long, muscular arms. Hands that were large and encrusted with rings fingered a knife lying on the counter. Maquesta found herself drawn to his eyes, which were bright blue, unusual for his people. They nearly matched the large sapphires that circled his neck on a thick, gold chain. The betting master wore a silky gray tunic that did nothing to conceal his well-defined chest. Everything about him was expensive, Maq decided.

He eyed her sternly, harumphed, and turned his attention to a piece of parchment. The contempt these creatures felt for her was palpable. Maq swallowed, squared her shoulders, and marched forward. The betting master himself ignored her, but Maq sensed the guards observing her every movement. When she had come to within about three feet of the desk, one of them stepped out, barring her way with his tessto. The betting master continued to attend to the parchments on his desk, not looking up at her. At this close range, Maq noticed that his fur was actually mottled with bits of dark brownish red here and there. Mottling only occurred on minotaurs well older than one hundred. Maq regarded him with intensified curiosity.

Minutes passed, and Maq begin to shift back and forth on her feet. The betting master gave no indication he was about to conclude the business at his desk and speak to her. Unfamiliar with the niceties of minotaur etiquette, but conscious of the need to return to the *Perechon* with the chatterwort for Fritzen, Maq decided to risk speaking up.

"Excuse me. I seek the betting master. Are you he?"

Finally, the minotaur looked up from his papers.

"Those without the sense to speak up when they have business with me are not worth my time. What do you want?" The betting master spoke the human common tongue with a fluency unusual for a minotaur. Yet years of reaping a profit as the fates parceled out wins and losses had left him even more arrogant than was typical for that bestial race, lending a harshness to his every utterance.

"I am Maquesta Kar-Thon, daughter of Melas Kar-Thon, captain of the *Perechon*. I—"

The betting master cut her off. "Then you have no business with me. I have paid the one from the *Perechon* who placed the winning bet, and I no longer hold your father's markers."

"But surely . . ."

He returned to his paperwork and snorted.

That fool from the *Bloodhawk* had told the truth! Even more than the name of the person who now held Melas's markers, Maquesta wanted to know the name of the *Perechon* crewmember who had bet against the ship. However, she doubted the betting master would simply tell her who the winner was.

"Who does hold my father's markers?" she asked, thinking quickly. "Averon sent me here to see if his winnings could be used to cover my father's bets."

"Oh?" The betting master allowed the question to hang in the air for a minute. "I would not have thought that was his inclination. But no matter. Not even the handsome purse I paid him would cover your father's foolish bets. Happily, that is no longer my concern. You need to take your case to Attat Es-Divaq. He bought your father's markers before the race. So I am now saved the trouble of having to dispose of your ship."

The betting master briefly looked down his snout at her, his disdain for humans obvious. He signaled one of the guards, then began gathering up his papers.

Maquesta barely registered the name of the minotaur who now held her father's markers. Her mind spun round and round the same name—Averon! Anger, hurt, betrayal, confusion threatened to overwhelm her. Maquesta had started to tremble so violently that she was afraid she would collapse in this room full of sneering strangers. A sharp prick in the small of her back refocused her attention. One of the guards had prodded her with his tessto in the direction of the door. Summoning every ounce of willpower, Maq turned, walked the length of the room, and stepped through the doorway. Once in the front room, Maq leaned her back against a wall, using the rough brick to support herself. No longer trembling, she was drained of all strength.

After a few moments, she began to think clearly. If this was how she felt at the news, she considered, it would devastate Melas. No, Maq realized, he would never believe it. He would refuse even to listen to such talk about his best friend. She needed a plan—not only for approaching this new minotaur lord, Attat, but for confronting Averon so he would openly admit what he had done. Only then would Melas believe it. Maybe then they could use the money Averon had won to cover some of Melas's bets and appease the minotaur lord.

Maquesta pulled away from the wall and hurried out of the betting master's, toward the harbor, her heart pounding in time with her quick footsteps.

Chapter 4
Caught

"Luckily for Fritzen Dorgaard, his wound was apparently not from a sea hag. He was dazed, but he managed to tell me that his arm caught on a piece of the reef when he was knocked overboard. I've made a poultice, and it's already started to heal." Lendle showed Fritzen's forearm to Maquesta, then went back to mashing a concoction of foul-smelling herbs with a mortar and pestle.

Maquesta looked at the wounded half-ogre and decided they had a lot in common—aside from having mixed parentage. Fritzen's ship had been dashed against rocks. Her hopes for the future had been dashed just as harshly, and soon her father's ship would belong to someone else. They were both pretty much homeless.

While still immobile and flat on his back, the half-ogre's eyes were closed, but the lids twitched slightly, and he did seem to be resting more comfortably. A little of his color had returned, which the gnome was quick to point out. Thankfully for anyone who ever became ill on the *Perechon,* Lendle's medicinal creations always worked better than his mechanical inventions.

"Did he say anything else after you gave him the chatterwort?" Maq asked the question idly, preoccupied with her scheme for bringing Melas, Averon, and the minotaur lord, Attat, together. Perhaps if she plotted well, the *Perechon* might not be lost to them after all.

"He is ashamed." Lendle stopped his mashing to regard Fritzen. "Ashamed and wounded where a poultice can't help him. He tried to tell his captain not to steer too close to the rocks, but his argument wasn't convincing. Not only did he lose the *Torado* to the sea hags, he wasn't able to save his captain. And in the end, he grabbed on to one of the hippocampi. He's cursing himself for abandoning the ship and the crew to save himself. I don't know if he will ever recover from that."

Yes, thought Maquesta, perhaps there are some wounds too deep to ever heal.

"Melas, Averon, I, and a few of the others will be going back into Lacynos later today. Is there anything else you need to take care of Fritzen?"

Lendle looked up at her sharply. "What business do you have in Lacynos? Your father does not seem of a mood to find the *Perechon* work so he can pay our wages. And more drinking of ale would not, I think, be to anyone's advantage."

"Don't worry, Lendle. We have a few things to straighten out, matters that might even lead to a payday in the near future."

Maq gave Lendle a tight-lipped smile that failed to reassure the gnome, then left the armory to arrange the shore visit with Melas. She strode quickly to his cabin, determined to make everything work out all right.

"Father?"

Maquesta pushed open the door to her father's quarters. Sunk in a black mood of despair, Melas had not left his cabin since the previous evening. She found him now seated once again at his desk, with Averon pulled up alongside him on a stool. Whatever the two had been discussing, they stopped when she entered the room.

Maq had not anticipated that the first mate would be with Melas. Unprepared, she feared the hurt and anger she felt showed plainly in her face as soon as she saw him. But Averon, sitting in profile to the door, did not look at her. He stared off, behind Melas's head, gazing through a porthole at the sea. She inwardly continued to fume at her father's best friend—a man she once considered a close friend, too.

"Father, I've found out who holds your markers. It's not the betting master. It's a minotaur lord named Attat Es-Divaq. Do you know him?" Perhaps, Maq thought, unknown to her, there was some bad blood between Melas and Attat.

Melas shook his head silently.

"I think you, Averon, and I should go to see him before he comes to collect his debt. We should offer to work off our obligations. It would mean being in the employ of a minotaur, but at least we would be able to keep the *Perechon*. And maybe there would be some extra steel involved to pay the crew."

It was only logical that Averon, as Melas's closest friend and first mate, should come along, and by making the suggestion in front of both of them Maq didn't see how he could avoid it. She felt certain that if she endeavored to bring Melas, Averon, and herself together in front of the minotaur lord who held her father's markers, she could provoke Averon into revealing his duplicity. But she expected Averon would try to avoid such a situation.

"Yes," Melas paused, reaching out to the idea tentatively. "Averon was just suggesting the same thing."

Why would Averon have made that suggestion? Could she somehow be wrong? That development troubled Maq. Yet she could glean nothing from Averon's current attitude. His attention remained fixed on the porthole. He wouldn't even look at her.

Melas, however, ever an optimist and a man who preferred doing anything to nothing, had begun to warm to the idea of visiting Attat.

"Yes, let's seize the bull by the horns, so to speak. We can make a good case for ourselves." Melas spoke to himself as much as to Maq and Averon.

"The *Perechon* is a prize—none better—but she's a much richer prize with the best crew on the Blood Sea. Yes!" Melas rapped the flat of his hand down on the desk, startling both Averon and Maquesta from their separate musings. The sparkle had returned to his eyes, and he was quickly shaking off the effects of all the drink he had consumed the previous night.

"We'll go after lunch," Melas continued. "Get a few of the men together to come along. The wisest course is not to be too outnumbered when we venture into a minotaur stronghold."

"I think you're right, Father."

He rose from the table, and in three strides had his arms around her in a friendly bear hug. "We'll make this work, Maq." He released her and slapped Averon playfully on the back, then he turned and went to the door. He opened it with a flourish and extended his hand, indicating Maq should leave first.

As she did, she heard her father speak to Averon. "Well, come on, isn't this what you have been asking me to do?" She did not hear the first mate reply, but Averon was close behind her.

While the crew seemed gratified to have their captain out among them once more, even Melas's presence could do little to enliven lunch that day. A number of sailors remained too disabled by the aftereffects of drink to drag themselves to the table. Those who did dined on a thin bean gruel, which was all that Lendle, preoccupied with Fritzen's care and with very meager supplies at hand, could whip up. A mood of uncertainty in the wake of the *Perechon*'s loss lingered over the entire crew.

Melas ate quickly, then rose from the table, giving orders with most of his old energy and authority.

"Averon, come with me. Maquesta, start lowering the longboat. We'll leave shortly."

Maq had put herself in charge of selecting the shore party, not wanting to chance Averon's doing it. Immediately after leaving Melas's cabin earlier, she had talked to Hvel again, and four others—Canin, Magpie, Micah and Gorz—telling each to be armed and prepared for trouble. Such advice was a given for any visit into Lacynos, so her words didn't surprise the sailors. Maq was glad Averon had gone off with Melas. She intended to repeat the advice again as soon as they gathered at the longboat. She wanted everyone to be on guard.

Standing herself, Maq signaled the others to rise. With irritation, she saw Vartan stand with Hvel. The two were best friends. When Maq approached Hvel, he had suggested Vartan come along. Maq had sternly vetoed the idea. The helmsman was an unproven commodity as far as she was concerned—just a pretty face. She shot Hvel a withering glance. He shrugged his shoulders, as if helpless. Maq decided not to make an issue out of it; she'd talk to Hvel about it later, after they'd returned to the ship. So now there would be an even half dozen coming along with her, Averon, and Melas.

The trip from the *Perechon* to the wharf passed quietly. The crewmembers still knew nothing of Melas's wagers and the risk of losing the *Perechon*. Maq had decided to keep that information from them until after the confrontation at Attat's unspooled. As far as they knew, they were accompanying Melas to an audience with a minotaur lord at which, most assumed, the captain would be soliciting an assignment for the *Perechon*. Averon's attitude still bothered Maq. She found it difficult to gauge. As the longboat drew closer to the wharf, both Melas and Averon exhibited growing agitation.

Once the longboat was secured at the wharf, Averon led the group off the pier, plunging ahead into the Lacynos streets.

"Shouldn't we get directions to Attat's?" Maq called from behind.

"Don't worry, I know the way," Averon called back, "just one of the many points on which I can be of service to you, Maquesta." Averon followed that remark with a joking aside to Melas which Maq could not hear. His bold assertion of the status conferred by close friendship offended Maq and steeled her determination to reveal him.

Attat's palace, it turned out, lay a good distance from the waterfront, a distance made greater by the fact that there was no direct way to get there through Lacynos's haphazard streets. The great majority of minotaur dwellings resembled the buildings Maq had been in earlier in the day—ramshackle, with ladders instead of stairs, never more than two stories high. A few of the very wealthiest nobles, however, had more elaborate homes. Maq had heard of the palace of Chot Es-Kalin, the self-proclaimed ruler of Lacynos, a veritable city within the city. Nonetheless, she was not prepared for Attat's palace.

Though still within the city walls, it sat surrounded by its own immense stone wall, which Maq judged to be at least twenty feet in height. Two massive minotaur guards clad in leather greaves and bronze chest pieces stood at the front gate, blocking their entrance. Each was armed with a bardiche, a long polearm with a curved, axelike blade on the end. It gleamed wickedly in the sun. Melas tried telling the guards what they wanted, but the minotaurs apparently did not speak the common human tongue. Vartan, it turned out, spoke some of the minotaur's language and was able to make their intentions clear. He smiled mischievously at Maq when it was obvious the minotaurs could comprehend what he was saying. The guards summoned a wretched-looking human slave, who went off and returned shortly with the message that Melas and the others could enter.

Melas led the way across a dusty courtyard, empty except for more armed guards, similarly dressed and equally as heavily armored as those at the gate. Maquesta wondered if there were likely other guards they could not see. Cautious, the group made its way to a pair of towering wooden doors inlaid with hammered silver, minotaurs' preferred precious metal. Maq was surprised at the doors' workmanship, which could have stood alongside the finest anywhere in Krynn. As she studied the panels, they swung open silently on well-oiled hinges—even before Melas could knock. The group entered a small anteway that gave onto a second entrance flanked by elaborately carved wooden columns. Two more guards, wearing breastplates made of steel, stood aside to allow them to pass into the palace's great hall.

Intended to impress as well as intimidate, the hall succeeded at both. Maq sensed the awe and trepidation in the other crewmembers, seasoned adventurers all, and felt it herself. Three times as long as it was wide, the hall extended nearly the length of the *Perechon*. Its upper reaches were hidden in shadows. Massive stone columns of polished granite marched down both sides of the room. Beyond them stood gloomy alcoves, some of which appeared to lead to other sections of the palace.

At the far end was a broad, richly carpeted dais on which the minotaur lord sat in an imposing, carved wooden armchair. He was surrounded by guards, several of whom snorted as Melas and his associates drew near. Spread-eagled between two smaller columns behind the chair hung the golden-scaled skin of some large, winged creature Maq didn't recognize. The scales twinkled softly and warmly in the light that entered the room through a wall of windows behind the dais. That light was augmented by wall torches that burned even now, in the middle of the day. The windows opened on to what looked to be a well-landscaped garden filled with plants, statues, and colorful birds.

In addition to Attat, his guards, and a few slaves, the great hall held a menagerie of fantastic creatures, each chained to one of the columns. A number of them Maq didn't recognize, but some she did. A griffon was chained directly across from a hippogriff—a cross between an eagle and a horse, which was the natural prey of griffons. Their proximity caused each constant agitation, an apparent source of amusement to Attat. An ice bear with startling white fur strained against its chain, occasionally emitting a growl of frustration. The distorted physique of a Gurik Cha'ahl goblin crouched near the base of one column, drooling and gibbering. The eyes of a mottled green, froglike creature bulged, and its tongue flicked out as they passed. "Bullywug," whispered Hvel at Maq's side. "Meat-eater."

Maq shivered. The osquip she and Lendle had seen a minotaur leading a few days ago was no doubt destined for here. It would have been chained to one of these columns, she suspected—had its escort not sliced off its head.

The lord kept his eyes on them from the instant they

entered the room, almost as if he were measuring them up as potential additions to his private zoo. Now that she stood before him, Maq's eyes opened wide, and she took in a great gulp of air. She realized that this was the very same minotaur she and Lendle had seen at the waterfront the day before the race, the one who had made short work of the osquip. They had passed by Lord Attat himself, never knowing he held the *Perechon* in his hands as tightly as he held the chain about the unfortunate beast's neck. In addition to the jeweled girdle he had worn the other day, Attat now sported silver wristbands and a collar studded with large gems—any one of which likely could have purchased a ship the size of the *Perechon*.

"How do you like my pets?" He addressed the humans in the common tongue, his voice deep, but not as guttural as Maq was used to hearing from minotaurs.

"I don't imagine they're too affectionate," Melas observed drily, stepping forward while the others hung back.

Maquesta watched her father and Attat closely. This lord obviously required his measure of recognition, but it was not in Melas's nature to pay tribute lightly. Maq hoped her father would keep himself in check.

"True, but I derive other pleasures from them. And the guests in my dungeon seem to enjoy them immensely," Attat replied with a silkily dangerous insinuation.

"I am Melas Kar-Thon and—"

"I know who you are, human," Attat interrupted. "The famous sea captain, master of the oh-so-swift *Perechon*." He made it sound close to an insult. "I have been expecting you."

Melas looked surprised.

"You made no attempt to hide your procession to my

humble abode," Attat explained. "And I am not without friends in this port who keep me informed of matters of interest to me." His eyes closed to slits, and he glanced briefly at Maquesta.

Toadies and spies, you mean.

For an instant, Maq feared she had lost her mind and spoken those words out loud, so strongly did she feel that they had been heard. But no. The lack of any reaction from those around her indicated she had kept her opinion of Attat's "friends" to herself.

"You saved me a trip, Melas Kar-Thon," Attat continued. "I had planned to visit the *Perechon* later today and claim what is mine."

Maq saw Vartan and Hvel, who were standing directly behind Melas, exchange surprised glances. She motioned them to be quiet. The minotaur's nostrils flared. He appeared to enjoy playing with them. Her hopes for a happy resolution to the question of remaining with the *Perechon* began to slip away.

"I hope to convince you otherwise. I have a business proposition for you," Melas responded.

"How interesting," Attat murmured. "So many propositions to consider, so little time."

Melas, intent on presenting his case, ignored that comment and continued.

"My idea is simple and benefits both of us. I and my crew stay on the *Perechon* and sail it where you direct until we've given you a value equal to the ship and bought it back."

"Are you suggesting you'd work without pay?" Attat asked, clearly intrigued.

"I would. And so would many of the others, I suspect. There are times we sail without pay as it is. For those who want pay, perhaps we could negotiate a reduced rate. We'd need something for repairs and maintenance of the ship, for food, and maybe some pocket coins for port visits," Melas said. "But it would be far less costly for you than running the ship and paying a crew full wages."

"Hmm." Attat paused, apparently interested. "Why should I pay any sum for a crew that's bound to be more loyal to you than to me?"

"Because, while the *Perechon*'s a prize, she's less of a prize without the best crew on the Blood Sea."

Melas stood with his hands clenched at his sides, waiting for Attat's decision. Maq noticed the tendons on either side of Melas's neck were stiff with tension. She needn't have concerned herself about Melas's remaining on good behavior. The future of his beloved *Perechon* would be decided at this meeting. And he knew it.

"It happens I do have an immediate mission in mind for the *Perechon*." Attat's remark refocused Maq's attention. "Tell me if it interests you.

"As you have seen, I collect exotic creatures." Attat waved his hand toward the chained monsters. "My collection is far more extensive than what you see here. I have built a zoo for them in my gardens." Here Attat nodded his head toward the windows behind the dais and proudly puffed out his considerable chest.

"Yet there is one creature that would perfectly round out my collection—a morkoth. Have you heard of them?"

Melas frowned in concentration, thought a minute, then shook his head. Hvel, who, it appeared, had a broad knowledge of Krynn's arcane zoology, jumped in.

"A wraith of the deep they're sometimes called. Wicked creatures, deadly, and very crafty. I understand they live in underwater tunnels, and they're difficult to find—unless you know where to look. Some say a morkoth looks human, but with fins and gills on the rest of its body, and a head like a squid with a lethal beak.

Others say they look more like a fish than a man, or are part octopus. I suspect there are actually few survivors to accurately describe one." Hvel stepped back, as if completing a recitation. It was obvious he was pleased with himself for knowing that bit of maritime trivia. He winked at Maquesta, and she grimaced in return.

"That's right, very good," said Attat, somewhat amused. "There are conflicting descriptions, and that is one reason why I am so curious about the creatures. I want to see what one truly looks like. I want to own one. I built a grotto in the garden for a morkoth. The creature will be the centerpiece of my zoo, an achievement of acquisition and subjugation that should finally demonstrate to everyone on Mithas my superiority to that ignorant brute Chot Es-Kalin, who dares call himself the king of Nethosak," Attat exclaimed, using the minotaur name for Lacynos.

"My scouts have acquired enough tales and rumors to pin down the approximate location of a morkoth in the waters called Endscape, off the northwest coast of Saifhum. It exists near a colony of kuo-toa. I am not interested in acquiring a kuo-toa. I already have a pair."

Everyone in the *Perechon* contingent knew of this race of fishmen who hated surface dwellers and were fearsome fighters. They did not want to tangle with kuo-toa.

"You pose a very difficult mission," said Melas. "However, I fail to see why you have a particular need of the *Perechon* to accomplish it."

"Well, I don't really need the *Perechon* for this mission, but a morkoth *is* what I desire," Attat said haughtily. "My ship, the *Katos*, is of course first-rate, but frankly not as fast as the *Perechon*. She never would have won the race except for that unlucky bit of weather you ran into."

Maq gasped. So Attat was the owner of the *Katos!*

That information, in the context of this meeting about his ownership of Melas's markers, made her deeply uneasy, though she wasn't sure quite why.

"Then, of course, using a crew of mercenary human sailors would ultimately be far less costly than having to recruit and train my superb crew of crack minotaurs. Besides, if anything untoward were to occur, I would hate to lose the minotaurs," Attat continued, his nostrils flaring, which Maq had come to recognize as the only outward sign Attat made when he was amused.

"To be honest," said Melas, "as you've described it, if the kuo-toa are nearby, they might be in alliance with the morkoth. If such is the case, and with the capture of a morkoth the goal, I think you would have to expect something untoward."

His statement made no obvious impression on Attat.

"Even were we to make it past the kuo-toa and capture the morkoth, how would we bring it back here? More to the point, how would we get to it in the first place, since none of us has gills for breathing underwater?" Melas asked.

"I have considered that problem. Guards!" Attat clapped his hands sharply. Two of the minotaur guards marched over to the wall of windows behind the dais. They pulled aside a curtain and swung open a set of double glass doors. As if they had been standing outside awaiting this signal, two other guards stepped inside, each roughly holding one arm of a tall sea elf. She had pale blue skin that glistened with a silver sheen. The knee-length white gown she wore was plastered against her slim body, indicating she had just come from a pool. Her long blue hair, slick and straight, fell to the back of her thighs and dripped water on the floor behind her. Eyes the color of emeralds looked furtively about the room, refusing to rest on Attat. Her webbed hands were bound before her. Her feet were shackled, so she was forced to shuffle as the minotaurs jerked her forward. The elf held up her head proudly, managing to convey both a fierce defiance and a profound humiliation at being thus chained and handled.

"Allow me to introduce Tailonna," Attat said mockingly. "One of the many guests staying in my humble home." The minotaur rose from his chair and waved a hand to his side, indicating the guards should bring his guest to him. Then he sat heavily and looked at the sea elf.

Tailonna, who had been dragged to stand just to Attat's right, stared straight ahead, refusing to acknowledge the minotaur or his introduction, and avoiding the gazes of Melas and his crew. Maq was impressed with the captive creature's dignity.

"Tailonna comes to us from coastal waters near the kuo-toa colony," Attat continued. "My scouts were lucky enough to . . . acquire . . . her during the same expedition as when they discovered news of the morkoth. Unfortunately, because of her ability to shapechange into an otter, and because she possesses a number of other magical capabilities, we have had to keep her in a special tank during her visit here and use these chains strengthened with a special lock spell when we do let her out. So I'm afraid she has found our hospitality somewhat lacking."

Tailonna maintained her stony facade throughout Attat's derisive speech.

"She should prove very helpful in any attempt to capture the morkoth," Attat added. "Among other things, she knows how to brew a potion of water breathing that allows humans and other surface creatures to breathe underwater."

Why should she help you? Maquesta startled herself with her own boldness. But when Attat didn't react, she realized she had only thought the words, not said them aloud, though once again her sense of having been heard was strong.

The question was a pertinent one, and Melas voiced it himself, couched more politely, a moment later.

Attat shrugged. "I've found Tailonna is more trouble than she's worth in terms of the amusement she provides me. If she helps capture the morkoth, once it is safely ensconced here, I have agreed to release her. Knowing how honorable the elvish people are, I believe I can trust her to help you." Again, Attat mocked his captive.

Melas looked askance at the sea elf prisoner. Nothing in his exchange with Attat had made him feel more uncomfortable. He held his fists clenched at his sides. Every aspect of his bearing conveyed tension, Maq observed with concern.

Again, Attat clapped his hands, this time saying nothing. Maq looked around the hall. Her search ended at an alcove just to the left of the minotaur lord's dais. A heavy red velvet curtain that covered the alcove's arched opening into the great hall was being pushed slowly to one side by someone or something standing behind it. A cloaked figure stepped forward from the alcove's dark recess, holding a tall staff that ended in a wicked-looking hook.

Maquesta stared at the figure, thinking she had seen it before. As she continued to gape, Attat motioned the figure to approach.

"Here is another useful addition for the *Perechon* crew during the morkoth expedition. Ilyatha, pull back your hood!" the minotaur commanded.

The figure had remained just inside the alcove's archway, declining to step into the main hall, which was well lit by the late afternoon sunshine streaming in through the windows behind the dais. A slender, clawed hand reached up and pushed back the hood. The creature's green eyes blinked rapidly, and it appeared to shrink away from the light.

Maq had no idea what she was looking at. It looked vaguely like a man, but short, smooth black fur covered its head and body, and under the voluminous cloak it was covered in an expensive-looking brocade tunic that looked more like a tabard because of its side slits. Its glance, as it surveyed Melas, Maq, and the others, suggested exceptional intelligence and commanded immediate respect. But the face, with its squashed-in appearance, pug nose, and sharp lower canine teeth protruding over its upper lip evoked the image of some sort of beast, perhaps an ape. Maq turned to Hvel and raised her eyebrows in an unspoken question. But even Hvel looked perplexed.

I am a shadowperson.

Even though she knew she hadn't voiced her question about the nature of this creature, Maquesta once again felt she had been heard—and this time, answered. Hvel had heard, also. His eyes grew round, and Maq realized why. Shadowpeople were the stuff of legends, not real! She stared at the creature.

I am, to my dismay in this instance, indeed flesh and blood. In your tongue, the closest rendering of my name is Ilyatha. Like Tailonna, I also am a prisoner of Attat's. The reasons for my compulsory attendance here are perhaps more subtle than hers, but no less real.

Ilyatha spoke with great sadness. Only Maq was looking straight at him, and she hadn't seen his lips move! Maquesta furrowed her brow and started to open her mouth, a question burning on her lips.

"Yes, Ilyatha is a telepath," Attat explained. "He not only communicates his thoughts without speaking; it is useless to try to hide yours from him. An annoying talent, at times, but one that should prove invaluable in your quest to outwit the kuo-toa and bring back the morkoth."

Melas regarded the shadowperson suspiciously.

"Can he sail?"

"Indeed, yes," said Attat, chuckling. "Ilyatha has a special proclivity for traveling by wind power. In fact, you saw a demonstration of it during the race. Ilyatha, show the honorable captain what I mean."

With apparent reluctance, the shadowperson drew a long, thin, delicately carved flute from inside his cloak. When he raised the instrument to his mouth, Maquesta, fascinated, saw that his arms were attached to the sides of his body by thin membranes, like the webbing of a bat's wing. He began to play a pure, high-pitched melody that soared and dipped and turned back on itself, tugging at Maq's memory. As the pace of the melody picked up, Maq noticed the curtains behind the dais begin to sway, the wall torches flicker. A light breeze tousled her hair, then a gust of wind caught Maq unawares, knocking her off balance and causing her to stumble into Vartan, who grabbed her by the arm and offered her a condescending smile. She could see he himself had planted his legs wide apart in order to maintain his footing against the wind that had inexplicably sprung up in the great hall.

Then Maquesta recalled when and where she had heard that music before—on the *Perechon*, during the race, when the *Katos* had finally overtaken them. Her fascination turned to fury at both Attat and Ilyatha. They had connived and used magic to make the *Perechon* lose! She looked over at her father and saw, by the storm gathering in his face, that he had realized the same thing.

The wind tore at a decorative metal shield suspended above Attat's chair, pulling it down and tumbling it off the carpeted dais onto the hall's stone floor with a loud clatter.

"That's enough!" a clearly vexed Attat bellowed. He snapped his fingers, and one of the guards rushed to pick up the shield.

Ilyatha took the flute from his lips. The wind died away instantly.

"You try my patience, Ilyatha, and that is not a good thing, as I shouldn't have to tell you." He glared at the shadowperson, who pulled his hood up over his head and stepped back into the dark alcove.

"What about *my* patience?" Melas demanded, his every word filled with unconcealed fury. "How can you expect me to take on this mission and sail the *Perechon* for your benefit with the aim of earning her back when you have so clearly demonstrated your untrustworthiness? You used magic to win the race! That is forbidden by the rules! I am going to complain to the Supreme Council!"

The minotaur threw back his head and laughed, the deep bass tones reverberating off the chamber walls. "Come now, Melas. Don't be foolish. I should simply deny it, as would every sailor on the *Katos*. Do you really think the highest minotaur ruling body would take the word of a human against that of one of its own nobles?" Attat asked, his nostrils flaring. "Oh, I suspect you'll go after the morkoth for me. I suspect you'll do it because it's your only chance, however tenuous, of getting back your precious *Perechon*."

For an instant, Melas stood erect with fury, staring at Attat. A pulse throbbed visibly at his temple. Then his shoulders slumped; his gaze dropped. The intricacy of Attat's plotting and arranging overwhelmed him. Was it possible the lord had this planned from the very beginning, intending to find a pawn for his creature hunt?

"Yes, I'll do it," he said, his voice pitched just above a whisper. "When do you expect us to leave? It will take a day or two to lay in supplies, and—"

"No!" The objection came from Averon, who had stood silently next to Attat throughout the meeting.

Averon directed his exclamation not at Melas, but at Attat.

"We had an agreement! I paid you! I am to be the captain of the *Perechon* on the mission to catch the morkoth!" Averon shouted, thrusting himself forward to the edge of the dais.

Melas looked in astonishment at his friend. "Paid him? Why? With what money? What do you mean, you would be the *Perechon*'s captain?"

"I wanted to help," Averon said, turning, wild eyes toward Melas. "Don't you see, I wanted to help you instead of you always helping me. I wanted to show I could captain the *Perechon* and help you get her back!" Averon pleaded, sounding more desperate each second. Melas stared at him in disbelief.

"Your friend here," Attat interjected sarcastically, "is the proud new owner of a tidy purse as a result of a bet he placed on the race, a large wager that the *Katos* would win."

The enormity of Averon's betrayal shattered Maq, even though she knew it was coming. He must have known the *Perechon* couldn't win, perhaps had even plotted with Attat to arrange the loss. Maq closed her eyes for an instant. She opened them in time to see Averon, uttering a strangled cry of protest, leap onto the dais, pull a dagger from his waistband, and lunge at Attat. In that same instant, Melas pulled his sword from its scabbard and leapt up after him.

Maq wasn't sure whether her father intended to hurt or help Averon. She simply couldn't tell. But it didn't matter. With a graceful series of movements, Attat rolled aside to avoid Averon's dagger, stood up from the chair, pulled a clabbard sword from his harness, turned and, holding the hilt of the sword with both hands, sliced off Averon's head.

Everything that followed took on a slow-motion,

dreamlike quality for Maq. Averon's headless body crumpled at Attat's feet, spurting blood, while his head rolled off the dais and landed with a sickening thud on the paving stones, the eyes open. His eyes blinked once, a muscle reflex, then became glassy and fixed.

On the dais, one of the minotaur guards next to Tailonna aimed his barbed shatang throwing spear at Melas, who stood with his sword drawn facing Attat. Just as the guard made a move to throw the shatang, the sea elf jostled against him, knocking the spear off its intended target at the center of Melas's chest. The shatang hit Melas in the shoulder with such force that it knocked him backward and pinned him to the dais.

"No!" Maquesta screamed, jumping forward to reach her father.

Guards moved in from both sides of the hall to contain Maquesta and the others. Instinctively, she swung her right leg out in a roundhouse kick that struck one of the guards in the groin, causing him to drop his shatang and double over in pain. She drove her elbow up into another guard's stomach, just below his rib cage.

The blow was well placed and caused the huge beast to pause, but only for an instant. He was upon Maq before she could draw her short sword. He struck her across the face, knocking her to the ground, where she lay, face against the cold stones, the guard's hoof in the small of her back, holding her down.

Vartan had managed to draw his weapon and wielded it expertly against one of the guards who looked clumsy with his. After a final parry, he stuck the guard through, but wasted too many seconds appreciating his own handiwork. With a roar, another guard leapt at Vartan from behind, bringing a studded tessto down on his shoulder, causing Vartan to drop his sword and fall to his knees, groaning in pain. Attat must have instructed his guards not to kill any of the sailors if there was trouble because Vartan's attacker, instead of finishing him off, kicked him, then sat on the human to immobilize him.

Micah was not so lucky, however. In the first moments of the melee, he had jumped on a guard's back, stabbing at the minotaur with a dagger. The creature smashed his antagonist against one of the stone columns, trying to dislodge Micah. The guard's aim was, perhaps intentionally, a little off. Micah's head flew back hard, becoming impaled on one of the daggerlike points of the metal torch holders. He hung there, the point protruding from his forehead.

Greatly outnumbered, Canin, Magpie, Gorz, and Hvel were swiftly and efficiently overpowered. A cacophony of roars, grunts, and howls filled the hall as the chained monsters vocalized either their bloodlust or fear. The guards looked for further instructions, but Attat only paced back and forth across the dais, occasionally kicking Melas savagely.

"Take them to the dungeon," he snarled, finally turning to address his lackeys. "Take them all below!"

Chapter 5
Attat's Dungeon

Maquesta drifted in and out of consciousness. The race played over and over in her mind, and she felt her body being tossed about as if she were constantly cresting one wave after another. Numerous times she stared at the crew of the *Torado* going down to the fangs and talons of the sea hags, and she watched Lendle tend to the only survivor, Fritzen Dorgaard. She also saw her father's grinning face, and she recalled many of the pleasurable moments they had shared on the deck of the *Perechon*. Then she saw his heartbroken expression when the *Katos* pulled ahead for the last time. She saw her mother's face, too; the details of that pale elven visage were distinct and beautiful and put Maquesta at ease. It had been fourteen years since the elf's disappearance, and with each passing month it became more difficult for Maquesta to remember just what her mother looked like. But it wasn't hard to remember in her dreams. She tossed and turned and her mind whirled, churning like the water around the Eye of the Bull.

Eventually the visions vanished, and she slowly pulled herself back to ugly reality. Sweating, her heart pounding, she finally opened her eyes. She must have been hit harder than she remembered. She recalled being dragged down narrow stone steps, slimy with mold and fungus. The steps ended in an evil-smelling pit of darkness. There must have been doors, because she heard a number of them creak open on rusty hinges, followed by the sound of bodies being thrown or pushed inside and the doors loudly slamming shut. Then it was her turn to be tossed inside, and a door closed behind her.

Maquesta rubbed her eyes and propped herself up on her elbows. She remembered the cell as being very small. Looking about the dim interior, she decided her memory was serving her well. Standing, with her curls brushing against the low ceiling, she grabbed her throbbing head with both hands. Maq tenderly felt about until she discovered a bump just above her left ear. They had been none too gentle in subduing her. She paced back and forth, only three good steps between the walls. Her stomach rumbled, and her throat and mouth were dry. Feeling her ribs and gauging her hunger, she guessed she had been in here several days. Frustrated, she selected a wall that felt less slimy than the others and leaned against it. Sliding down to the floor with her back against the cool stone, Maq could almost stretch her legs out and touch the opposite wall with her feet. She had to sit with her back angled away from the damp stones in order to avoid slipping into the open refruse trench that ran around the entire perimeter of the room. She sat slumped uncomfortably like that for she knew not how long. Hours, she suspected, as her head had started to hurt less and her stomach rumbled more.

The sound of groans eventually roused her from her state of despair. When Maq opened her eyes, she was feeling a little better, though she was weak from hunger. Her eyes, more perceptive than a human's, adjusted well to the lack of light. She easily could make out the cell's wooden door with its grated window. What illumination existed came through that opening. At the very top of the walls on either side of the cell, a long, shallow gap, also covered with an iron grate, presumably led to neighboring cells. Groans filtered in to her through one of these.

Listening closely, Maq thought she recognized the tones.

"Father?"

The moaning stopped.

"Father?" She leapt to her feet and made it to the door in two steps.

"Maquesta?" The voice that spoke her name quavered with ill health and fatigue. Nonetheless, Maq felt tremendous joy and relief. She had feared her father was dead.

"Thank the gods you're alive, Father! How is your shoulder? Did they tend to it at all?"

"No. They did nothing other than handle me roughly. I fear it is infected. I have no way to clean it. But don't worry, dear. Your mother has come to nurse me. She will take good care of me."

"Mother?" An icy hand gripped Maquesta's heart. Melas must be delirious, which meant his wound was indeed infected. She had to think of a way to get him out of here! Maq slumped back against the wall and cried.

* * * * *

The next time Maq woke it was to the sounds of guards conversing in the guttural minotaur tongue. She heard the repeated metallic clink of keys banging together on a large key ring. The guards sounded nervous. Moments later, several pairs of hooves came clicking down the stone stairs. Maq pressed her face against the opening in her cell door. In the eerie light cast by several large braziers of glowing coals, Maquesta saw Attat sweep into the central court of his dungeon, which Maq could now see was used for torture. She stepped back away from the door and let the shadows hide her.

She heard Attat stalk directly over to Melas's cell. He called for one of the guards on duty to open the door.

"You have ruined my plans!" Attat spoke loudly, but Maq wondered if her father were even consciousness. She heard a dull thud, followed by a wince of pain.

"Get up when I'm speaking to you!" Attat said something in the minotaur language to the guards. Maq heard a rustling in the cell, then a sharp exclamation from her father. The guards must have grabbed him by his arms and forced him to his feet, wrenching his wounded shoulder. She couldn't bear to listen.

"There, that's better," Attat continued. "Normally I would have had you all killed for daring to attack me. But with Averon dead, I wanted you to go after the morkoth. I thought a week in my dungeon would teach you to have greater respect for me. But I see now that you're of no use to me in your condition.

"There's nothing for it—I'll have to find a new captain and crew, and you all will have to die. You last, Melas Kar-Thon, so you can watch your sailors pay for your foolishness and so you can watch your woman pay for your affront to me."

"Lord Attat! Lord Attat! May I please have a word

with you?"

Maquesta summoned all her strength and presence of mind to call out to the minotaur noble. She had propped herself up against the wall for support, and maneuvered around to the door again, holding on to the bars with her fingers.

Attat, however, gave no sign of having heard her, or perhaps merely did not wish to respond. He began to walk toward the stairs.

"I can captain the *Perechon*! I can capture the morkoth for you!"

With a minotaur's infravision, his ability to see remarkably well in the gloominess of the dungeon, he turned and peered at each of the cells until his eyes lit on Maquesta's hands.

"And who might you be?"

"Maquesta Kar-Thon, daughter of Melas. I grew up on the *Perechon*. I've sailed my whole life. The crew knows me. I can do it. I even steered the ship through some tough conditions in the race."

"Daughter?" he purred. "I thought you were his doxy."

Attat's laughter echoed off the dungeon's walls. "I like a girl who has dreams, but not ones that I have to pay for," he said harshly. "I do thank you for one thing, however. Now that I know who you are, I can be sure to have you killed last, so you can watch your father die. Slowly."

Attat clapped his hands, and the guards came running. "I want them fed, though not much, and give them water. I want them reasonably healthy, clinging to life, thinking they have a chance. There's no satisfaction in it if they're praying for their deaths."

* * * * *

Over the next few days, Maquesta was forced to witness the horrific tortures of Magpie, Canin, and Gorz.

The guards brought both her and her father out of their cells to watch the macabre rituals. For Canin it was the rack. Then, weakened by hours of torment, he was thrown back into his cell with a bullywug, which finished him off and then ate him.

For Magpie, it was hot coals and branding irons, followed by a one-sided encounter with a griffon. When Maq closed her eyes and covered her ears, she could still see the blood and hear his screams.

Gorz hung from his wrists for hours while a case lined with sharp spikes slowly closed around him, piercing his skin. The guards sneered that they left him alive so they would have someone to torment tomorrow.

Maquesta cursed herself for selecting the men to accompany her, her father, and Averon to the minotaur lord's. If the men had stayed behind on the *Perechon*, they would be safe and free. Tears streamed down her face, and she wondered if the rest of the crew had already left the ship. At least they would not fall prey to Attat, she told herself.

Through the horror, Maq was still thankful she could be near her father, though his condition was rapidly worsening. When the guards were preoccupied with their amusement, Maq did what she could to clean Melas's wound. The infection seemed to be spreading down his arm. Most of the time, he rambled—about Mi-al, about sailing ships, about his youth, but never about Averon.

Only once did the fog seem to lift completely. He looked at Maq clearly. "I got you into this mess, Maquesta, and it's all because I trusted someone I shouldn't have. Never make that mistake—promise me. You can trust your family, but no one else. Promise me you'll never forget. Promise!"

He grasped her arm and held her gaze until she nodded. "Yes. I promise," she whispered.

"Money is something that will never betray you, either. Remember that, too!" She nodded again.

* * * * *

Maquesta studied the dungeon's layout and the guards' routines every chance she had in the hopes of divining some means of escape. The cells extended in a horseshoe pattern around three sides of the large central area where the torture implements were prominently displayed. The only prisoners were, or had been, the *Perechon* crewmembers—except for one minotaur, a muscular, imposing figure whom Maq had never heard speak. While clearly a prisoner, the minotaur had something of a special status in the dungeon. Maq had never seen him tortured, for one thing. With his legs shackled, he was sometimes allowed out of his cell by the guards and commanded to aid them by doing such things as handing them hot branding irons while they "worked." From the way the prisoner minotaur regarded such activities, however, that may have been a type of torture.

The narrow stairway leading up to the rest of Attat's palace was located on the fourth side of the torture chamber. The stairs afforded the only way in or out of the dungeon.

As a result, only two guards were routinely assigned to stand watch at a time, on rotating shifts. The two who worked at night seemed less responsible than the others, Maq had observed, occasionally bringing a flask of spicy spirits that they would imbibe late in the evening. It was during one of these episodes that Maq saw a dirk slip from one of the guard's harnesses. Without realizing what had fallen, the guard inadvertently kicked the dirk underneath one of the hot coal braziers, which sat on short legs, close to the ground.

The next day, Maquesta was let out of her cell to watch the final torment of Gorz, who was beaten until his flesh was bloody and then thrown in an iron-barred cage with an ice bear. While the guards watched the grisly scene with growing excitement, she edged away from them, squatted by the coal brazier, and reached about for the dirk. She burned her hand, but she managed to wrap her fingers about the weapon. Taking a quick look around before extracting it, Maq realized that the minotaur prisoner had seen her. His eyes met hers, and while his face remained impassive, she didn't believe he would sound a warning. Maq slipped the dirk into her back waistband and watched helplessly as the bear finished devouring Gorz.

Only Vartan, Hvel, herself, and Melas were left. She wasn't even certain Vartan was still alive, or what kind of condition he was in. He was never allowed out of his cell, so she hadn't seen him since they were all thrown into the dungeon. Still, Maquesta hadn't seen him tortured and killed, so that was some consolation. Hvel was alive. At night when the guards were drinking, he called to her. But he was not doing well. They were feeding him the same amount passed under the door to her, which was little, and the guards continued to berate him, teasing him about how he would be tortured and what creature he would soon fill the belly of.

Maquesta knew she had to act before she grew much weaker on the meager, gray gruel the guards fed them. She had to do something.

The next day when the guards dragged her and Melas out of their cells, she was ready. Maq watched until the guards unlocked Hvel's cell and started to drag him out. They barked some command in their language at the minotaur prisoner, who shuffled over to the cell. With all three of their backs turned to her, Maquesta braced her back against the wall near one of the hot coal braziers and used her feet to push it over, spilling the coals onto a pile of moldy straw. For an instant, she feared the straw was too damp to catch fire. Then the straw began to smoke and finally flames flickered up, dancing merrily in the still air.

"Fire!" She hoped the guards understood that word in the human tongue. Whether it was that or the smoke, they turned around in alarm.

One of them immediately ran over and began stomping on the straw. The flames licked about his hooves, and he howled as he continued his efforts, even thrashing at the straw with his club. Maq grinned—he was too stupid to realize the fire could not spread beyond the straw. It could not burn the stone floor or walls.

The smoke billowed about him, and he began to cough. Through the haze, she saw the other minotaur guard rush toward the steps. Hoping the smoke provided some cover, Maquesta slipped the dirk from her waistband and ran after the retreating guard. He covered the long distance quickly and placed his weapon against the wall while he fumbled about for his keys. She couldn't let him leave and sound a warning! Her feet pounded over the stones to close the distance, and she grabbed her side, which ached from the unaccustomed exertion.

The guard must have heard her coming, for he turned around and glared at her. She returned the menacing look and leapt forward even as he strode to meet her. Without hesitation, she shoved the dirk into the guard's chest where she expected his heart to be. He merely growled at her, raised his right arm, and slapped her away. She fell to her rump and was momentarily dazed. A shadow loomed over Maq, and she looked up to see the minotaur towering above her. With a grunt, he pulled the dirk out of his chest, looked at it, and growled even more loudly. He tossed the small blade to the ground and bent over to reach out for her. Maq deftly rolled to the side and pushed off from the stone in one fluid motion, landing on her feet. The minotaur's flailing hands closed on air, and he growled again.

Stooping to retrieve the dirk, she danced backward as he lunged at her. This time, however, his outstretched hand found her, his fingers closing about a mass of her curly hair. He pulled her to him roughly, and Maq felt as if he were going to yank her head off. Bringing her in to his chest, her face pressed up against his bleeding wound, he wrapped his arms around her and squeezed hard.

A jolt of pain raced up her spine, and Maq realized he meant to break her back! Clenching her eyes shut and futilely trying to block out the horrid sensation, she steeled herself and bit his wound. He howled in pain and eased his grip just enough so she could squeeze her hand out, the one that still firmly clutched the dirk. She jabbed at his side with the blade, repeatedly stabbing him until, with a groan, he let her go. This time he was the one to back up, shuffling to the wall where his own weapon, a large, curved sword rested.

No! Maq's mind screamed. She couldn't let him get that weapon. Then she wouldn't have a chance. "No!" she shouted aloud, as she used the last of her strength to melt the distance between them. She fitted both of her hands about the small pommel of the dirk, the blade pointed away from her. Closing to him, she jumped and shoved the blade upward, ramming it into his throat. The minotaur staggered backward, blood gushing from his wound. He thrashed about, and his hands clutched at his throat, trying to pull the dirk free. But Maquesta had used such force that the blade held, and the hapless guard fell heavily to his knees, then pitched over onto his stomach.

The clomping sound of hooves over stone behind her caused Maq to whirl. The second guard apparently had given up on the blaze and was running over to see what was happening. He was armed with a spiked club, which he swung at her as he approached. Maquesta squatted as the weapon whooshed in the stale air inches above her head.

Pushing off with her legs, she threw herself forward, her head and right shoulder hitting him squarely in the abdomen and knocking him back. The club clattered to the floor, and the guard swung his arms about, trying to keep his balance and stay on his hooves, as all the while he shouted what must be curses at her in minotaur.

Undaunted and determined to be free, Maquesta kicked hard, her foot striking him in the groin. Teetering, he bent forward in pain and surprise, then finally lost his balance and fell backward, his rump thumping hard on the stone floor. He groaned and toppled to his back, laying sprawled like a baby. Maq leapt over him and landed behind him, where his club had skittered. She bent to retrieve it, and her fingers closed about its thin handle just as he decided to struggle to his feet.

"No you don't!" she scolded. "You're not going anywhere."

The minotaur worked himself into a sitting position, his back an easy target for Maquesta. Dashing forward, she pulled the weapon past her shoulder, then swung it in an arc with all her might, aiming at the back of his head. Her aim was a little off, but she hit him between his shoulder blades, and he fell forward, his head striking the stone floor between his spread legs. Not sure if he would rise to fight again, she hit him a second time and grimaced when she heard the bones in his skull crack.

Finished with her ghastly work, she dropped the club and took in great gulps of the smoke-tinged air.

Coughing, she staggered to the first minotaur she had killed and rolled him over so the key ring on his belt showed. She pulled it loose and nearly gagged. She needed fresh air! The smoke from her fire had reached all the way over here. Clasping the key ring in her trembling fingers, she ran over to unlock Vartan's cell. He staggered out, disoriented and weak on his feet. Hvel, she saw, wasn't much better. Her heart sinking, Maq realized she would not be able to count on these two to help her get Melas up the stairs. They'd be lucky to make it themselves. She looked up at the captive minotaur, who had busied himself with trying to put out the flames.

"If you help me, we can all go free," she told him.

He simply nodded. "And if you help me stop this smoke, no one should be drawn here to investigate." Maq grinned and helped him extinguish the last of the flames. The smoke was thick where they stood, but it had not yet reached through the barred door that led to the rest of the palace.

Maquesta pointed to her father, who sat with his back against the stone wall. His head had fallen forward on his chest, and he coughed softly. She looked up at the minotaur. "Could you help me carry him?"

"Wait just a minute," the minotaur replied. "Let me try to break my shackles." His voice was deep and rumbled out of his chest. He placed the chain that held his feet together over the brazier that still stood. When the links glowed a fiery orange, he smashed them with a giant mallet the guards had used to drive wedges into the rack, in order to lock the gears in place. The chain broke apart as if it were made out of toothpicks.

"I am Bas-Ohn Koraf," the minotaur said somewhat formally.

"And I am Maquesta Kar-Thon," Maq grunted as she tried to get Melas's arm over her shoulder and lift him to his feet.

"Here, allow me."

The minotaur picked up her father easily, cradling him in brawny arms. Maq herded Hvel and Vartan up the stairs as the smoke started to dissipate around them.

* * * * *

Several minutes later, they slipped out through one of the glass doors leading to the garden, finally free of the dark confines of Attat's dungeon and his palace's twisting corridors.

"Let's head for that tall tree near the wall. We can climb it and jump over," Maq said urgently. She knew it wasn't much of a plan, but it was all she could think of, and she didn't want to wait around to come up with something better. The minotaur nodded.

Circling behind a half-moon of terraced rock garden, Maq had just turned to urge the minotaur to hurry when the look on his face caused her to turn back. Directly in front of her stood Attat and a cloaked Ilyatha, flanked by a troop of guards.

Maquesta's heart sank, and she fought back tears.

"I have to admit, I am impressed," Attat said, his voice betraying more menace than approval. "At the human, Koraf, not at you," he snarled at the minotaur carrying Melas.

"How did you track us so that you ended up in front of us?" Maq demanded.

"I had no need to track you, not with the help of Ilyatha here."

Maquesta could not see the shadowperson's face, but she glared in his direction. Ilyatha bowed his head. Maq couldn't decide whether the gesture was in acknowledgment or in shame.

"I may have spoken too hastily before," Attat continued, striding forward until he stood only a few feet away from Maquesta. "I think I will indeed allow you to captain the *Perechon*. I could do much worse, like with Koraf there."

"What about my father?" Maq's tone was brusque, almost demanding. She'd been pushed to her limits, and she no longer feared what the minotaur lord would do to her. "I want him to come with me. He can mend on the voyage and be of great help to me."

"No, no, no. I don't think he's quite up to a rigorous ocean voyage, do you?" Attat asked with mock solicitude. "I have other plans for him. He's my insurance—that you will come back. And your motivation—to successfully accomplish the mission."

"I want him to come with me," Maq said flatly. "I don't want him back in that dungeon of yours. I don't think he'd last another day there. And with my father dead, you have no insurance, and I have no motivation."

Attat smiled at her, his bull-like lips curling upward. He crossed his chest with his muscular arms, and his bracelets sparkled in the sunlight. "I'll concede you something, Maquesta. He won't be returned to the dungeon. While you are getting the *Perechon* ready for your voyage, I'll give him a room in the main part of the palace, have Tailonna tend to his wound. She will make certain he has something nourishing to eat. He'll be better by the time you leave. The only one going back to the dungeon is Koraf here."

Maquesta heard Koraf growl softly, and she decided to press Attat into a second concession.

"No. He comes with me." Maq stood with her arms crossed, mimicking Attat. "You've killed three sailors from my crew, four if you count Averon. I'm short-handed, and I've already seen that Bas-Ohn Koraf is an able worker. I'm sure I can teach him what he needs to know about sailing before we leave. You can do whatever you want with him once we return with your precious morkoth."

The minotaur lord threw back his head and chuckled, then leveled his gaze at Maquesta, his eyes seeming to smoulder. "Oh, you don't have to teach Koraf a thing about sailing. Shipbuilding is his trade."

Attat stroked his chin and looked at Ilyatha. The shadowperson faced him, and Maq suspected some kind of conversation was occurring between the two. She smiled weakly; apparently Attat was considering her demand to allow Koraf to go free.

At last the minotaur whirled to face her and took a step forward until he was now only inches away. She could smell the strong, musky odor of him, but she refused to move. Glaring down at her, he raised a lip in a sneer, then relaxed his expression.

"Go ahead, leave," Attat said abruptly. "Just you and the two others from the *Perechon*," he added, pointing at Vartan and Hvel. "I expect you back here in two days, ready to depart. I'll give you my decision then. In the meantime, Koraf stays here."

Maq looked into the eyes of the minotaur Bas-Ohn Koraf, but couldn't read what she saw there. He did nod slightly, as if giving her permission to leave.

After making sure Melas was settled comfortably, Maquesta grabbed Hvel and Vartan by their hands and hurried out the hammered silver doors, through the gate, and into the muddy streets of Lacynos.

Chapter 6
Leaving

"Lendle! Fritzen—you're well! But what are you two doing here? You both should be on the *Perechon*." Maquesta wanted to scold them and hug them at the same time. But she was too relieved to be free to do either.

She encountered the pair just as she, Hvel, and Vartan emerged from Attat's walled compound. Maq ran her left hand through her hair and came away with fingers full of dirt and spiderwebs. Her right hand held a leather bag Attat had grudgingly given her. Maq looked down at herself for the first time in more than two weeks, thinking about how she must appear. Her clothes were ragged and filthy. She was sure she smelled terrible. The bruise across her cheekbone from where a guard had hit her shone a sickly yellow through her dark skin. However, Vartan and Hvel looked little better.

Lendle eyed her up and down, his gnomish eyes lingering on her smudged face. "We've been keeping watch on the compound. I was trying to figure out a way to get inside. I had plans drawn up for a catapult large enough to send Fritzen over the walls. But I didn't have enough coins to buy the materials and equipment to assemble it." The gnome reached up and grabbed her hand and started pulling her away from the palace. "Of course, I still hadn't quite worked out how Fritzen would return, there being no catapult on the other side."

As they walked, Fritzen offered a crooked smile to Maq, Hvel, and Vartan. The stitches in his face had been removed, and only a slight red welt showed any indication that his face had been slashed. "The city's guards refused to help. They said what goes on inside Attat's walls is his concern, and no one else's. I had just suggested a direct approach: gather the crew and storm his front gate. I might have talked Lendle into it, too, but you happened to come out." He gave her a concerned look. "You've been gone sixteen days. We really thought we were going to have to go in to rescue the lot of you. And you do look like you're in need of rescuing."

Lendle stopped and whirled around, dropping Maq's hand and staring up at her. "W-Wait!" he stammered. "Waitwaitwaitamoment." He cast a quick glance back at the palace. "Where's Melas? Where's Averon? Whatabouttheothers?" Lendle began pouring out questions in his best gnomish fashion. "Where-aretheyMaquestaKarThon?"

Maquesta continued to stride away from Attat's home. "Slow down, Lendle. There aren't good answers for those questions. Let's wait to talk about it when we're back on the *Perechon*."

As the blocks passed on their trek to the wharf, Maquesta's pace slowed. Exhaustion finally swept over her in an overpowering wave, and she had to sit on a bench outside a tavern. She paused there only a moment to catch her breath, however, then she stood and forced herself to put one foot in front of the other to make it back to the docks. Vartan and Hvel walked just as slowly, asking from time to time to stop and rest. Lendle and Fritzen worried over the battered trio, but Maquesta was not in the mood for mothering.

* * * * *

Maquesta, Vartan, and Hvel did not protest when Fritzen said he would oar the longboat back to the *Perechon* by himself. His powerful arms brought them steadily closer to the ship, while the trio huddled together and tried not to doze off.

Once on board, Maquesta sat on a water barrel on the deck and motioned Lendle close. She handed the gnome the leather sack she had been carrying. Curiosity getting the best of him, he immediately grabbed it and stuck his face inside the opening. Inside were flour, beans, dried meat, spices, and other foodstuffs that made Lendle yip for joy. A smaller sack at the bottom contained three dozen steel pieces. "For provisions," she told the gnome. "I'm appointing you purser. You're family. I can trust you."

Lendle eyed her inquisitively. "Whoisthisfrom-MaquestaKarThon?" The questions tumbled from his rapidly-moving lips. "Whowouldgiveusfoodandcoins? Whereisyourfather? Didyoufindusework? Didhefindus-work? Whathappenedtoyouthatyoulooklikethis? Wheredidthisstuffcomefrom?"

"From a devil," Maquesta replied quietly. "We're working for a devil."

She stood and looked down at her gnome friend. "For the moment, I am the captain of the *Perechon*. I need you to buy some supplies. I'll trust your judgment. We'll be sailing on a procurement mission for a few weeks. Make sure you have plenty of food to keep the crew full. That will help keep them happy. Now, I'm going to my cabin to take a hot bath. A very *long*, hot bath. I'll talk to you when you return."

Maquesta shuffled away from Lendle, who still had a dozen more questions he wanted answers to. She washed herself, threw away the clothes she'd been wearing for the past two weeks, and then promptly collapsed into her bunk where she slept for half a day.

In truth, she could have slept much longer, but a knock on the door from Lendle awakened her. Without waiting for an invitation, the gnome bustled in carrying a mug of tannic tea. He thrust it beneath her nose as she sat, yawning, on the edge of her bunk. The tea's astringent aroma filled Maq's head, snapping her wide awake. She took a sip. "What is it?"

"Nevermindjustdrinkit," Lendle admonished. "Itwillhelpyouheal."

"I'm afraid it will take more than a strong cup of tea to do that," Maquesta said ruefully.

Lendle assumed an attentive, listening air that encouraged confession, and Maquesta poured out the story of Attat's palace, the fight, Averon's death, the dungeon's horrors, the mission she had agreed to lead in search of the morkoth, and the expected additions to the crew.

"We must be back at Attat's by sunset tomorrow to collect Father and the new crewmembers. Then we must be ready to sail the next morning," Maq said. "I had better get together the crew to explain what's happening and see if anyone wants to drop out. I hope they'll stay on. We've lost too many people already."

Lendle nodded in agreement while he rubbed some sweet-smelling salve into open sores on Maq's shoulders and arms, the result of the dungeon's constant dampness and considerable insect population.

"What about Fritzen Dorgaard?" Maq asked. "Is he fully recovered?"

"His body healed amazingly fast. But not his spirit, I fear," Lendle answered. "He ever wears a mask of good nature, though, to hide all the scars he has inside. I think he will be glad of something to do, and I suspect he'll stay on with the crew. He has nothing now that the *Torado* is gone. He's a skilled seaman and will be a great aid to you."

Maquesta stretched her arms out to her sides, then brought them in and felt her ribs again. She thought about getting something to eat, but realized there were more important things for her to attend to first. "I'll have to prepare the crew for the presence of the sea elf," Maq said, thinking out loud. "If she doesn't hold herself too aloof, they will come to appreciate her talents. She did what she could during the fight in Attat's palace. I believe she prevented Father from being killed.

"The shadowperson, though, I do not trust." Maq scowled at her recollection of Ilyatha. "He was the one who divined our escape attempt and betrayed us to Attat. In fact, he was the one who played the flute of wind dancing that caused us to lose the race in the first place. You must help me keep close watch on him, Lendle. And try to keep your mind focused on simple things when he is about. He can poke into a person's very thoughts."

"I do not think I would like that, Maquesta Kar-Thon," the gnome said, trying hard to speak slowly.

"And did I tell you that a minotaur sailor will be joining the crew?"

"A minotaur!" Lendle said, scowling. "What magical

abilities does *he* possess? He's the addition you'll have to pave the way for, after what we heard about how Attat and his lackeys treated you."

"Why? Have Hvel and Vartan been talking? Were they up and about before me?"

Lendle nodded vigorously. Maq frowned. She didn't want to be seen as requiring more rest and recuperation than her men.

Her men, she thought. Her ship.

"They were not as badly treated as you, I think," Lendle said, understanding her concern. "The stories they told about that place and its occupants, though, curled my toes," he added.

Maq grimaced. "Yes, but this minotaur, Bas-Ohn Koraf, was not one of Attat's beastly minions. He was his prisoner. And he helped us break out of the dungeon. He's an ugly cur, but far different from Attat, I think," Maq said.

"But Attat, him we must be careful of, even tomorrow when we are supposedly there to do his bidding. That one is smooth on the outside, but all jagged, poisonous, and evil on the inside. If it weren't for the fact that he holds Melas, I'd say we should just take off in the *Perechon*, forget the debt, see if he could catch us."

Maq pursed her lips. "Vartan and Hvel told you about Father?"

The gnome nodded sadly.

* * * * *

Maquesta stood on the upper aft deck, having just finished telling the *Perechon* crew, assembled below her on the main deck, about what lay ahead if they chose to stay with the ship under her command. Even before she had begun to speak, Maq sensed a new level of respect from the sailors. By then, Vartan and Hvel's story about how she had led the escape attempt from Attat's dungeon was known to everyone on board.

"Does anyone not want to ship out? I'll not hold it against you, nor will Melas. When it's time for him to sail again, I'm sure you can rejoin the crew. No hard feelings."

The men's silence gratified Maq.

Fritzen leapt up onto the steps leading from the main deck to where Maquesta stood. "Let's hear it for the new captain of the *Perechon*!" he shouted. "If we close our eyes, it's just like being captained by Melas Kar-Thon, himself. But once we open them, we know we're much luckier than that!"

The sailors erupted into cheers and whoops of laughter.

Maq blushed and grinned broadly. "Only that the first seaman who tries to sail with his eyes closed on this voyage is bullshark fodder," she called out to more laughter. "Now that we're all agreed that we'll make the voyage, let's get to work."

Fritzen, cutting a handsome figure, bowed jauntily to Maquesta as she passed him on the steps. His bronzed skin showed a hint of green, which Lendle told her displayed health in the half-ogre. His long blond hair was neatly braided and tied with a new leather thong, and he had shaved off the stringy mustache that used to dangle above his lip. Maq mimicked a bow in return and hurried to the galley. She was ravenous and decided now was the time to attend to filling her rumbling belly.

* * * * *

Fritzen was not with Maquesta when she set off for Attat's estate late the following afternoon. Minotaurs were far from his favorite creatures, he said. "I'd rather sail in to the rescue, than risk endangering you in the first place by losing my temper in front of their foul lot."

"You should try to overcome that blanket aversion you feel," Maq told him as she and Lendle climbed into the longboat. "Remember, one of them will be joining our crew, and we'll have enough on our hands without any fighting among ourselves."

"I think I can handle one minotaur," Fritzen said flatly. "He'll be in the minority here."

* * * * *

Eagerness and trepidation battled each other as Maquesta and Lendle cautiously entered Attat's compound. There were more sentries stationed in the courtyard this time, she noticed, and they were more heavily armed. She grinned slyly. Perhaps her having killed two of Attat's lackeys put the minotaur lord more on guard. She could not wait to see her father, but the thought of confronting Attat again caused the bottom of her stomach to fall away.

This time as she entered the great hall, Attat's "pets" were absent. On the dais at the far end stood two chairs, and on one of them, propped up with pillows and wrapped in a light blanket, his shoulder carefully bandaged, sat Melas. Maquesta ran up to him, tears of happiness sliding down her cheeks. He was dozing when she reached the chair, and she decided not to wake him. Looking him over carefully, she felt as if she were being watched. Glancing into the shadows, she noticed that Ilyatha stood to her left, obviously in attendance on Melas.

Maq quickly looked way from the shadowperson and tried to empty her mind of the hostility that sprang up the instant she saw him. She sensed, however, that her efforts were in vain.

Your father has been sleeping for some time now. He should wake at any moment.

Maq heard the words plainly, but saw that the shadowperson had not moved his lips. The proclamation was made inside her head. Maq continued to gaze down at Melas and refused to acknowledge Ilyatha's communication. But Lendle, whose shorter legs had just brought him to the dais, swiveled his head this way and that, trying to determine who had spoken.

Maq jerked her head in Ilyatha's direction. "He's a telepath, remember?"

Lendle, plainly curious, walked over to inspect the shadowperson more closely. Maq "heard" Ilyatha greet him. A second later, her father opened his eyes, and Maq became oblivious to anything transpiring between Lendle and Ilyatha. A broad smile creasing his ashen face, Melas leaned forward to embrace his daughter, wincing slightly. Though obviously still weak, he looked greatly improved. Father and daughter chatted about what was occurring on the *Perechon*, and for the first time in more than two weeks, Maquesta was happy.

"Where's Attat? Have we been announced?" she finally asked, anxious to gather up her father and the others and leave.

"He likes to keep callers, especially humans, waiting," Melas said. "But he's been very good to me these last couple days, Maquesta."

"Yes, well, I'm sure he had his reasons. And don't forget, he had a lot to make up for."

"The credit really should go to Ilyatha. He has cared for me day and night. And the poultices he made worked wonders on my shoulder. I think Lendle could learn a few things from him."

Indeed, if the gnome's animated gestures and grimaces were any indication, he seemed to be engaged in just such a conversation with the shadowperson at that moment.

A slave entered the hall, bearing a note to Maquesta. When she opened it, a bold, scrawling hand—Attat's she presumed—informed her that the minotaur lord had been delayed by his efforts to prepare something special for Melas. Maq should feel free to stay in the hall or visit the garden. Attat would be down shortly.

Maq snorted with impatience. By the time she looked up from reading the note, however, Melas had dozed off.

He does that quite often. Your father needs sleep in order to mend.

Maq again made no attempt to communicate with Ilyatha, unwilling to credit him even for helping her father. Maq motioned for Lendle to come over to stay with Melas. She intended to visit the garden to escape the sense that someone was eavesdropping on her emotions.

I would like to show you something, Maquesta Kar-Thon. Will you permit me?

The request caught Maq just as she was about to go through the glass doors into the garden. Ilyatha had followed the shrouded perimeter of the hall until he stood at its head, off to one side of the windows.

Maq sighed and nodded. The shadowperson was going to be on the *Perechon*, and she was going to have to get used to being around him, but she didn't have to like it.

Do you see those stone formations in the garden?

Maq nodded before she remembered she didn't have to show the shadowperson her response.

Visit them when you go into the garden, then come back, and I will tell you what you saw.

Tell me what I saw! Maq fumed at the creature's arrogance. She pushed through the doors in a huff, striding out into the welcoming, warm sunlight.

Attat's garden was truly lovely, filled not only with flowers and shrubs but occasional pieces of fine sculpture. Still riled up about Ilyatha, Maq held off doing what he had asked until she felt it was almost time to go back inside to await Attat.

At first, she didn't notice anything in particular about the stone formations. Then she realized that a number of them were actually hollow caves, and several of those caves had bars covering their openings. She was drawn to the largest one of these by whimpering and squeaks that sounded like an animal in pain. Because of how the cave was situated, it would have been in shadow for most of the day. But at this time of the afternoon, with the sun beginning its descent in the sky, strong beams of light illuminated the cave's interior.

Lying on its side on the floor of the cave, with its knees drawn up and its one arm and the attached membrane held out in a feeble attempt to block the sun's rays, was another creature like Ilyatha, only smaller, more delicate, and female. The creature seemed in terrible pain, and Maq found herself wanting to help it. The whimpering stopped as Maq reached the bars. The small shadowperson lifted her head and tilted it toward the front of the cave. Her eyes were open, but unseeing. She was blind, Maq realized with horror.

Father? the shadowperson asked tentatively. Then, probing Maquesta's thoughts and understanding that it was not her father but some stranger, the shadowperson laid her head back down. The whimpering began again.

Maquesta hurried back to the great hall. Ilyatha began communicating with her even before she entered.

That is my daughter, Sando. We live in an underground shadowperson community located on the other side of Mithas. Shadowpeople cannot stand sunlight. We venture to the surface world only at night when the hated rays of the sun are hidden. I am tormented by the memory of the night Sando convinced me she should come with me on an expedition to collect a piece of sculpture. I never should have said yes. It was in Attat's garden, the piece we wanted. It was to be a gift for a friend of mine, and I had brought gems to leave in exchange. Payment. I did not intend to steal it. But Attat's guards captured us. He allows me free run in his compound because he keeps Sando locked in that cave. For two hours each afternoon, sunlight streams into the cave. For Sando it is torture without the need for implements of torture. For me, it is torture also. The sunlight blinds Sando every afternoon. She recovers each night, but I am worried that the ultimate effect of this daily torment will be to leave her sightless, or perhaps maimed.

Attat has promised to remove Sando from the cave, and place her in an environment of constant darkness if I help you in your quest for the morkoth. I know that I affronted the balance of right and wrong by announcing your escape attempt to him the other day. I am sorry. But to have done otherwise would have been to risk my daughter's life.

Maquesta did not have to attempt to hide her thoughts from Ilyatha at the end of his explanation. Her thoughts reached out to him in sympathy and compassion.

* * * * *

"I wish you the best, Maquesta Kar-Thon." Attat's words rang hollow. But he continued to speak with false good cheer and feigned concern. Maq, Melas, Lendle, Ilyatha, Tailonna, and Bas-Ohn Koraf were gathered in front of the dais, facing the minotaur noble. Today he wore an embroidered tunic with black pearls sewn about the neck, armholes, and hem. His hands displayed more rings, and his throat was circled by a thick silver band set with purple stones. A cloak of rich satin hung from his shoulders. It was obvious to Maq that he was dressed regally to lord his position over her.

Attat lifted his hand, and a minotaur shaman, wrapped in a red robe embroidered with feathers and beads, stepped from behind the dais. He held a small pouch in one hand, sprinkling some dust from it onto Tailonna's shackles. The chains snapped open on their own. For the first time since Maq had met the sea elf, she saw a faint smile cross her blue lips.

"Now everyone is free to leave with you, Maquesta, even Koraf. There are times when simpleminded brute strength has its applications. With the addition of Koraf you will be well equipped to bring back the morkoth.

"I am, however, a worrier. I like having added insurance for a challenge such as this." The minotaur lord snapped his fingers, causing the bracelets on his wrists to jangle discordantly.

With that, two guards stepped forward, grabbed Melas, and threw him onto his back. A third pried open his mouth, and two more guards rushed toward Maquesta to keep her from interfering. The shaman stepped near Melas, this time holding a vial filled with a viscous black liquid. He poured its contents down Melas's throat. Maquesta, horrified, brushed past the guards and slid to her father's side. He gagged and then lay still, panting. Maq helped him to his feet. All the tentative good health and color that had started returning to his countenance had vanished, replaced by a sickly gray.

"What have you done!" Maq screamed at the shaman. She glared angrily at Attat. "We had a deal, and this was no part of it!"

The minotaur lord approached her slowly, then looked down his bull-like nose at her.

"Your father stays here. And just to make certain

you're properly motivated, we've given him a dose of slow-acting poison—a potion of choke weed," Attat hissed maliciously. He held up another vial, this one containing a golden liquid. "You have thirty days to bring back the morkoth. Within those thirty days, this antidote will save him. Longer than that, well . . ." The minotaur shrugged his shoulders. "If it takes you longer than thirty days, Melas will not survive."

* * * * *

In a somewhat more ramshackle compound not far from Attat's, a different sort of minotaur lord met with a pirate called Mandracore the Reaver.

Chot Es-Kalin, dressed in worn brown robes with a voluminous hood to mask his identity, went to the locked desk in the dingy office and picked up a piece of curling parchment. After turning the letter this way and that, he threw it at the pirate, a brutish half-ogre who sat in a rickety wooden chair.

"Why do they send me information this way? It's worthless!" Chot snarled. He waved his thick arm about for emphasis and spit in the direction of Attat's palace. Chot spoke minotaur, the only language in which he had any fluency. He stamped his hooves and glared at the pirate.

Mandracore scanned the paper quickly, then stood. "It says Attat is sending out another expedition for one of his prizes, off the coast of Saifhum." The pirate sneered. "He's just trying to add to his menagerie. Maybe he's after a bullshark or another sea elf. He's sending the *Perechon*, a ship he recently acquired after the race. It's of no concern to us."

"The ship's crew?" the minotaur persisted.

"Humans," Mandracore replied. "The same crew who used to man the ship, only now they're working for Attat."

The minotaur pulled the parchment from the pirate's hands and crumpled it angrily. "It is of concern to us. He's after something dangerous, else he would have sent a minotaur crew. Follow them, and if you can, destroy them!" Chot ordered. "It will be the perfect way to strike at Attat—to keep him from gaining something he clearly wants quite badly!"

Mandracore looked surprised. "We have other, more pressing business in those waters. I don't think our friends would be happy to see us stirring up trouble there . . . yet," Mandracore said silkily.

"Never mind what makes *them* happy. I'm not their lackey, though you are mine! And crushing Attat in everything he attempts makes me happy," the minotaur snapped. "Anyway, a talented half-ogre such as yourself should be able to keep everyone satisfied: our friends, yourself . . . and *me*. Now go!"

Chapter 7

Sailing The Blood Sea

Maquesta, still in shock that Attat would poison her father, said little on the way back to the *Perechon*. Lendle trotted at her side. Koraf dragged the cage Attat had given them to hold the morkoth, and Ilyatha and Tailonna trailed behind him. No one spoke, making the cortege seem like a funeral procession. At one point, Maq glanced behind her. If this mismatched group made up the core of her fighting team, she was in trouble, and her father's life was in a great deal of jeopardy.

It was dusk by the time they had rowed out to the *Perechon*.

"Where's Melas?" Fritzen asked as he helped the shore party climb aboard.

"Get the crew together on the main deck," Maq said curtly by way of reply.

Maquesta motioned for the others to come with her, leading them to the upper aft deck where they waited for the sailors to gather below. Most of them stared at Bas Ohn-Koraf, giving the minotaur a mixture of looks: surprise, puzzlement, fear, and apprehension.

"Melas won't be sailing with us," Maq announced when they were all together. "Lord Attat has poisoned him. My father slowly dies, and Attat will not save him unless we are successful in capturing the morkoth."

Angry mutterings broke out among the sailors, many of whom started pointing at Koraf and whispering "spy," "beast," and "lowlife." Their looks of puzzlement and fear gave way to hatred. The hostility was thick on the deck, and Maq did her best to try to dispel it, though she noticed even Fritzen looked with suspicion at the minotaur. "We have thirty days. If we present the creature to Lord Attat within those thirty days, Melas will be spared. I intend for us to be gone only twenty."

Then she proceeded to introduce the new crewmembers, ending with Bas-Ohn Koraf.

"For the duration of this voyage, Koraf will be my first mate." Jeers, hisses, and shouts of "No!" threatened to drown out Maquesta's words, but she gritted her teeth, waved her hands to silence the men, and continued. "He is worthy of the position, and you will accord him respect. Do not judge him because of his race. I have more reason to loath minotaurs than you. I will assign Ilyatha and Tailonna duties once I have a better understanding of their skills. Bear in mind that we must all work together as smoothly as possible, and we must sail as well as we ever have. There is no room on this voyage for petty hostilities. Anyone who can't follow these instructions should get off before tomorrow morning at dawn. That's when we'll be pulling anchor."

* * * * *

At first light, as the fishing fleet at the south end of the harbor was preparing to set out on their day's work, the *Perechon* glided past the galleys and merchant vessels, through the scummy brown water of Horned Bay harbor, out past the breakwater and into the open sea.

After a sleepless night in which she repeatedly questioned her decision to make Koraf her second, Maq took the helm. She had considered naming Fritzen, but Lendle had pointed out the half-ogre's continued depression, and counseled her against giving him too much responsibility too soon. Still, she had gone over her navigation route with Fritzen the night before. Her plan was to sail between the southernmost tip of Saifhum and the Outer Reach of the Maelstrom that churned the waters at the center of the Blood Sea, over the spot where the ancient city of Istar had stood before being struck down for its arrogance during the Cataclysm. The Maelstrom progressed in ever intensifying rings toward its center, the Heart of Darkness, as sailors called it. Any ship that broached the Outer Reach took the chance of being disabled by the constant storm that raged over the Maelstrom and sucked down to the bottom of the Blood Sea. The route Maquesta had mapped was riskier than it would have been to set a course around the northern tip of the island of Saifhum to reach the kuo-toa colony. But this route would save them considerable time. Bas-Ohn Koraf and Fritzen had reluctantly agreed.

Before the sun had completely emerged from beneath the horizon and begun its ascent into the sky,

Ilyatha briefly joined Maq on the upper aft deck. Though the light was still dim, he wore his hood pulled far forward, to shield his face. Away from Attat's palace and the massive minotaurs, the shadowperson seemed larger. He was several inches taller than Maquesta, and the cloak billowed about him in the breeze, making him seem wraithlike. And for the first time since making his acquaintance, Maq saw his lips move and audible words came out.

"I must remain below during daylight hours, but if you need me, just think my name. I will know immediately, and I will help as I am able." His voice was mellow and sonorous, pleasing to Maquesta's ears.

Maq smiled her thanks, comforted by his offer. Before she could speak to him further, he was gone.

Depending on the weather, Maq expected to approach the Outer Reach early the following day. She scanned the skies. A pearl-gray sea gull circled far above her head, following the *Perechon* out of the harbor.

* * * * *

After an uneventful day and an awkward dinner hour during which strange faces and grim memories squelched the usual camaraderie, Maquesta retired to her cabin. Fully clothed, she lay down on her bunk and immediately slipped into a deep sleep. However, the *Perechon*'s intensified motion, combined with pounding on her cabin door, awakened her during the night.

"Maquesta! You'd better get up!" Fritzen bellowed. "Koraf wants you on deck!" Even before she was fully awake, Maq realized by the way the *Perechon* pitched and rolled that a storm had hit. Rain pelted her portholes and the wind keened like something alive. Glancing out a porthole, Maq saw it was still dark. They couldn't have reached the edge of the Maelstrom yet.

She rubbed her eyes and gathered her wits for an instant before going to answer the door, annoyed at Fritzen's insistent summons. What was wrong with him, anyway? He and Koraf could handle the ship in a storm.

"Coming, Fritzen, com—" A high-pitched screaming and cackling cut through the shrieking of the wind. Alarmed, Maq yanked open her cabin door. She joined Fritzen on the main deck in time to see a macabre scene illuminated by a flash of lightening. The eerie light revealed a red mist seeping up over the deck on all sides. The red cloud carried with it the almost unbearable sound of screeching and wailing. As Maq watched, the mist covered the deck and began swirling up the masts. When it reached her feet, a clammy chill crept up her spine.

Then, before her eyes, the mist took on solid form—dozens of solid forms—small red figures with horns, clawed hands, long, sharp tails, and tiny, pointed teeth. "Blood Sea imps," Maq murmured, despairing. When the imps attacked, their aim was to disable a ship and murder the crew, dragging the bodies to the depths. She had heard the tales—but they didn't come from survivors. She hadn't ever heard of anyone surviving an encounter with the malicious little things.

The creatures raced about frantically and began pulling at the rigging. One floated up the mainmast and began clawing at the furled sail, rending it with his sharp nails. Two had climbed to the top of the mizzenmast and were jerking it back and forth in an effort to snap off the tip. Above the unnatural storm, the timber groaned in protest. A clatter of pots and pans sounded from the galley, where the imps must have been pulling down Lendle's hanging contraption.

Maquesta yelled in rage and darted back to her cabin to retrieve her sword. She heard the yells of her crew and the chattering of the imps behind her. Then she heard Koraf ordering the men to concentrate on one group of imps at a time. "Protect the sails first!" he hollered. As Maq raced from her cabin, short sword drawn, she saw that the men were complying with Koraf's command.

She watched in horror as Fritzen thrust a dagger in his teeth and started up the mizzenmast. Three imps grabbed hold of his legs and tugged him free, dragging him across the polished wood on his stomach. As she dashed toward them, the trio glared at her and attempted to carry him over the side of the deck. They nearly succeeded, as his legs were dangling over the side, but with a menacing growl, the half-ogre grabbed the railing and kicked out, sending one of the imps flying into the mist. He pulled himself forward until he was completely on the ship again, then he jumped to his feet and faced the remaining two. He balled his fist and brought it down hard on one of them. Maquesta saw the little creature's head cave in, but it just as quickly reformed to its original shape. Then she spotted its companion backing away from Fritzen and heading toward Vartan, an evil gleam its little eyes.

Individually, none of the imps could pose a serious threat to anyone. But in mass, like the wave of red that flowed outward from the galley, they presented a considerable challenge. Maq's legs pumped to carry her to the half-ogre's side. Coming at them were more than a dozen of the evil creatures—armed with butcher knives, iron pots, skewers, and all manner of other things Lendle used in his kitchen. Vaulting into a triple somersault, Fritzen scattered half of them easily. He swore loudly, however, as his blows and kicks passed through them without doing any damage. Maquesta was suddenly swarmed by the remainder, and she swung her sword in a wide arc. The blade passed through the torsos of the chattering creatures, but did not even serve to slow them down. Realizing she could do nothing to hurt them, but they could most certainly hurt her, Maq sheathed her short sword, crouched, then jumped straight up, grasping one of the sail's lines. Hand over hand, she hauled herself higher, and from her vantage point, she was greeted by the shocking scene below.

Members of the crew rushed on deck after being wakened by the storm and the noise. Their efforts to fend off the imps' assaults were likewise meeting with no success. Five of the creatures set upon Hvel and succeeded in dragging him to the armory hold and locking him inside. Another group tugged Vartan over to the wheel, where they tied him to it with excess line.

"The only way to attack a Blood Sea imp is with magic!" Maq shouted to Fritzen as he futilely continued his attempts to drive off the imps. "So the stories say!"

Casting about for a course of action, Maq thought of Ilyatha's offer. She concentrated, and a few moments later the shadowperson appeared on deck. Maquesta started to climb down, but he shook his head at her. *Stay where you are.* His words sounded inside her head as he took in the scene. *I fear I can do nothing to get rid of these scourges. Among my people I am a warrior.* Here Ilyatha held up the staff that ended in a sharp hook, a weapon he seemed never without. *Not a counselor. What charms I know have to do with healing, nothing else. And I see no other ships about, though I will try telepathically calling for aid.*

A paralyzing panic began taking hold of Maq. A small group of imps was now attempting to pound holes in the longboat. Fritzen ran at them, waving his arms and shouting, all to no effect. Near the bow Maq spotted Koraf. With a belaying pin in one hand and a sword in the other, he was swinging savagely at a pair of imps that were trying to break off the bowsprit. Two more imps crept up on Maq, climbing the line she was holding on to, and each attached itself to one of her legs. Their shrieks and cackles in such proximity made it difficult for her to concentrate. She began dragging herself higher on the line as they nibbled at her calves.

"But I can do something!" The voice was Tailonna's. The sea elf emerged from belowdecks, appearing cool and calm in the midst of the chaos. Tailonna quickly paced the length of the *Perechon*, appearing to do some sort of calculation. Reaching the bow, she turned to retrace her steps, drawing a half dozen delicate ornaments from her long hair—gossamer nets that held Tailonna's mass of locks braided with seashells in soft loops around her head and shoulders.

Turning first to the dozen imps wreaking havoc on the longboat, Tailonna took one of the nets, brought it to her lips and murmured several words into it, then tossed it toward the villainous creatures. In the air, the hairnet grew into a circular net of entrapment ten feet across. As the net settled onto the imps and tightened around them, they instantly stopped their shrieking and grew still, their eyes open but unseeing.

"A web net. She's hypnotizing them," Fritzen said admiringly as he continued to struggle with those creatures near him.

Tailonna repeated the spell each time she approached a group of ten or more imps. Sometimes other imps would rush over and attempt to free their comrades, but they were powerless to rend the net. Its shimmering strands held the imps as unshakably as a spiderweb holds its prey.

When Tailonna had used up all her nets, a couple dozen sea imps still remained. She met Ilyatha's gaze. After a minute, he communicated with the sailors still on deck.

She wants us to move upwind of her, and she wants my

flute of wind dancing, Ilyatha told Maquesta.

"Then give it to her!" Maq shouted as one of the little creatures bit solidly into the flesh above her kneecap. The storm winds buffeted the *Perechon* and caused Maquesta to swing on the line. "We don't need any more wind," she shouted. "We could lose a mast. But having any masts will be irrelevant if we're all dead!"

On the subject of Tailonna's intentions, however, Ilyatha remained silent. Handing her the flute, Ilyatha stayed beside her, apparently waiting for further instructions. The elf immediately began playing a variation on the jig Maq had first heard the day of the race. A dust devil sprang up at her feet.

Tailonna continued playing until it was fully formed, then nodded at Ilyatha. The shadowperson reached into the flowing cloak the sea elf wore, withdrawing a small pouch. He sprinkled a measure of what looked like yellow sand from the pouch into the center of the dust devil. Tailonna varied her melody, and the dust devil began to move up the mizzenmast to the two sea imps there. The tiny whirlwind spewed sand onto the pair. They dropped off to sleep, sliding down to the foot of the mast in the process.

Tailonna continued playing, directing the dust devil over the remaining Blood Sea imps, including the pair pestering Maquesta. Soon the deck was littered with tiny, snoring red forms. Unfortunately, the unpredictable force of the storm that continued to rage carried the sand into the eyes of several *Perechon* sailors. They also fell to the deck, fast asleep.

"We don't have unlimited time," Tailonna warned. "The sleepsand will wear off in about an hour; the webnet's hypnosis lasts a bit longer. We have to get away from this section of the Blood Sea!" Tailonna spoke in a breathy, musical voice that had something of the sea about it.

Maq slipped to the deck, rubbing at the small bites on her legs. "We can't risk raising a sail," she said. "The storm's force would break the mast. Then we'd be at the mercy of these things when they woke up again. We'll have to use the oars, but in these high seas I don't know how much progress we'll make. Wait a minute! Where's Lendle?" An image of the fire-driven contraption that the gnome had hooked up to the oars flashed through her mind. She wondered if she dared ask him to try it.

The gnome came running up to her from the direction of the galley, apparently summoned by Ilyatha. He was covered with a sticky mass of fruit and beans, and he pointed at the imps and shook his stubby finger. When Maq questioned him about his invention, Lendle grew very excited. He answered her, speaking with excruciating slowness.

"It is ready. I will have to go light the furnace."

"Well, go do it, Lendle," Maq commanded. "And hurry up. We have little time."

"Come and help me." The sea elf addressed Maquesta.

Maq whirled. Tailonna's request came perilously close to an order. Koraf and Maq exchanged looks. Without waiting for a reply, the sea elf began picking up the sleeping imps and tossing them overboard. Standing almost as tall as Koraf, Tailonna didn't need any help lifting the tiny monsters, just extra pairs of hands. Fritzen, Maq, and Ilyatha pitched in.

The mist continued to roll about the ship, its tendrils entwining around the rails and flowing up the lines of the mast. Maquesta cursed the crimson fog and peered into it to make sure no more imps were coming out. Satisfied, she ordered Vartan to gather up sheets. They were going to need to mend the sail on the mainmast as soon as they passed out of the storm. She looked over her shoulder to see Koraf inspecting the bowsprit.

Smiling, she decided she'd made the right choice in a first mate after all. Fritzen was collecting the knives and other implements the imps had raided from the kitchen. Satisfied that everything on deck was in good hands, she went to check on the gnome.

"Lendle, what's taking so long?" Maquesta stood at the top of the trapdoor leading to the cargo hold and called down. She could feel the heat from the furnace even where she stood.

"Inaminutewaitaminute," Lendle answered.

Maq had just started down the ladder when a percussive explosion rocked the *Perechon*. Sooty black smoke began billowing up from the cargo hold. She jumped back up to the main deck.

"Oh, Lendle," Maq moaned. She looked through the trapdoor—just in time to hear the sizzle as Lendle threw a bucket of water on something burning. More smoke poured out, making Maquesta wheeze. Peering through the cloud, Maq tried to see if the gnome was all right. Climbing out of the hold, he smashed into her.

"Justafewadjustmentsandwe'llbeflyingthroughthe water." He pulled a piece of paper and a stick of chalk from the pocket of his overalls and began jotting down calculations.

Maq left him and strode toward the poop deck.

"Koraf, gather enough sailors to man the oars and get them down there fast."

"What about Lendle's invention?" the first mate asked.

Maq shook her head ruefully. "You don't want to know. Just make sure the fire's out before you go down into the cargo hold.

"Fire?" Fritzen, who was heading toward the galley, blanched.

Maquesta didn't notice; she was watching Ilyatha, who was gazing intently into the skies above the ship.

Maq also looked up. The lightening and thunder had ended. The storm was breaking up, but not fast enough to permit their escape under sail power. Squinting up into the heavens she saw nothing but warm driving rain that stung her eyes. Then Maq thought she glimpsed the gray sea gull that had flown above them when they sailed out of Horned Bay the previous day. Within minutes, she perceived that something far larger hovered over the *Perechon*.

Fritzen set down the kitchenware, drew his sword, and held it by the hilt like a spear, prepared to aim it at the creature. Tailonna quickly walked over to him and pulled down his arm.

"Have you never seen a such a creature before?" Disdain showed in Tailonna's tones. "It is a ki-rin, and it can only be here to help us. Don't harm it in any way, or you will bring doom down upon us all," she ordered.

With difficulty, Fritzen restrained his anger at Tailonna's high-handed treatment. Developments with the ki-rin soon distracted him.

Amid gasps from the few crewmen left on deck, the ki-rin dropped down until it hung next to the *Perechon*, at deck level, opposite Ilyatha. Maq had never seen anything like it before. She judged the creature to be the length of two good-sized men put feet to feet. A single spiral horn that glistened like mother-of-pearl protruded from its forehead. A thick mane of burnished brass lay flat against its head and neck. It had a tail and hooves, of a similar color to the mane, but the creature did not really look much like a horse. Wings sprouted near its shoulders, small and feathered and tinged with gold. Even in the darkness, the ki-rin's coat showed a faint luminosity, revealing tiny golden scales that shimmered and twinkled like stars.

Without a word being audible, the creature and Ilyatha appeared to be holding a conversation. The shadow warrior gestured. The other occasionally nodded. After several minutes passed, Ilyatha bowed deeply and turned to face Maquesta and Koraf.

I apologize for our rudeness, he communicated, speaking directly to Maquesta. *This is Belwar, a ki-rin. Oh, I see you knew that already. I hope you don't object. I sent out a telepathic distress call while the imps were running amok. Belwar heard it. He has agreed to help us leave this place.*

The ki-rin circled the *Perechon* once at deck level. Ilyatha cocked his head to one side for a minute, then hurried forward. While the ki-rin waited off the bow, Ilyatha secured one end of line to the bowsprit, then threw the other end to Belwar, who caught it in his mouth. With powerful wings, the ki-rin began flying away, dragging the *Perechon* with him as if it were a toy boat being pulled by a child.

Tailonna began removing the webnets from the groups of hypnotized sea imps, whispering a few words to each group. Under her command, they lined up neatly and in precision filed overboard.

Maquesta threw her arms around Ilyatha and hugged him.

"This night ended far better than I could have hoped. I thought we were all going to die. Thank you. Perhaps this Belwar is a good omen."

"Let me out of here! Hey! I'm in the armory, let me out!"

Koraf was the first to hear the cries coming from the bow of the ship, as he and the rest of the crew cleaned up the debris left behind by the Blood Sea imp attack. He signaled for silence and cocked his head, listening, worried at first that an imp had remained on board and was playing some sort of trick. Then Vartan brushed past him, placing his ear against the armory door for a moment before yanking it open. A red-faced Hvel tumbled out.

"I thought I'd suffocate in there! I thought the imps

had taken over the ship! What happened? Why are we still alive?"

Vartan pointed to the ki-rin in the sky, its wings pulling strongly and surely, its coat shimmering a pale, clear gold in the dawning sun. Hvel forgot about being locked up and stared in awe at the magnificent creature. As they watched, the lead Belwar held in his mouth slackened. The ki-rin tilted its wings and began circling back on the *Perechon*. Hvel and Vartan scrambled out of the way as Belwar dropped the rope, following it down to perch gracefully on the edge of the upper deck.

Maquesta, who had been helping with the clean-up, strode forward to greet the creature and thank it. Since the sun was rising, Ilyatha had retired to his cabin belowdecks.

"Are you the captain?" the ki-rin asked as she approached him, his voice as melodious as the sweet singing of the thrush.

"I am captain of the *Perechon*, and I wish to thank you," replied Maquesta. "We would have been lost without your help, and other lives besides ours forfeit in consequence," she added, thinking of Melas and Ilyatha's daughter, Sando. "As captain, I accept the debt we owe as my responsibility and pledge to repay it in any way you wish." Maquesta stared into Belwar's glittering violet eyes, encountering great intelligence and compassion there.

"My pay is your smile," Belwar replied. "But tell me, what brings the *Perechon* to this part of the Blood Sea? You are approaching a dangerous passage between Wavend and Saifhum and the Outer Reach of the Maelstrom. What lies there could pale next to the Blood Sea imps."

Unwilling to reveal the full truth to a creature for the most part unknown to her, despite his brave actions, Maq decided to tell only part of the story.

"We have been hired by Lord Attat of Lacynos to pick up and bring back a special cargo. The sooner we return, the better our reward. I was attempting to save some time with this route."

The violet of Belwar's eyes deepened in anger to dark purple, and his regard hardened.

"Had I known you worked for Lord Attat, I wouldn't have helped you. I would have let the imps kill you and destroy this ship. He is my sworn enemy, and all the hate I hold in my heart is for him." Much of the music left Belwar's voice as he spoke these words. "I want nothing to do with any who traffic with him."

The ki-rin prepared to fly off. Just then, Tailonna glided forward, the shells braided into her long, blue hair clicking together rhythmically. When Belwar caught sight of her he paused and bowed respectfully. Standing next to Maq, Tailonna returned the acknowledgment.

"I fear our captain has told you too little of what we are doing here." Tailonna glanced sideways at Maq, with a look as close to a plea for understanding as one could get from an elf. Maq fumed inwardly at the Dimernesti's effrontery. "She does not understand the origin of your animosity."

Here Tailonna turned to address Maq directly. "When you were in Attat's palace, did you not notice the skin hanging behind the chair on the dais?

Maq thought a minute. That day now seemed so distant. She went back over her walk with her father down the length of that imposing hall. Then she nodded slowly. "Yes, I remember. I didn't recognize what creature the skin came from. It was golden, with scales and wings." Her voice died away. She turned back toward Belwar, who stood now with his head bowed, a great sadness evident in his demeanor.

"That was the skin of a ki-rin," Maq said.

Belwar nodded. He brought his head up, his eyes now flaming with anger. "Yes. It is the skin of my brother, Viyeha. We had been playing a game we sometimes trifled with in and around the peaks of tall mountain ranges. Tag, I think you call it. We were in the Worldscap Mountains, on Karthay. Viyeha misjudged the opening between two peaks and injured one of his wings. It was serious enough that we had to wait there a few days for it to heal before he could fly again. We used our magical abilities to create a comfortable lair and of course were able to conjure all the food and drink we needed.

"After two days I . . ." Here Belwar looked down. "I became impatient. I did not enjoy the inactivity. I began leaving for the greater part of each day, telling Viyeha I needed to patrol the island, but really just wanting to get away. On the fifth day when I returned from my flight, I found only the stripped carcass of my dead brother. And I found a great and irreparable sadness in my heart." Belwar's voice choked, and he paused to regain his composure.

"Attat had been leading an expedition into those mountains, trying to capture a new addition for his menagerie, when he stumbled upon our lair. Viyeha was asleep, or he would have anticipated the attack. As it was, the dozen minotaurs and half-dozen ogres Attat led were able to throw a net over my brother and slit his throat." Belwar spoke bitterly.

"An eaglet who nested above the lair witnessed everything and told me. It happened in the morning, soon after I had left. By the time I returned late in the day, Attat and his party must have vacated the island. I could not find them. But I have sworn vengeance. Some day when I find Attat outside his palace fortress, I shall exact it."

"We wish you all speed in doing so," Maq said fervently. "Tailonna was correct. I was not certain of your sympathies, so I did not tell you the whole story of why we are here. Attat holds leverage over us." She explained to Belwar about Melas; Ilyatha's daughter, Sando; Tailonna's capture; and Bas-Ohn Koraf's situation.

The ki-rin listened attentively. When Maquesta concluded the tale, he remained silent for a moment, then appeared to reach a decision. Belwar spread his wings, flapped them once, then spoke.

"I will remain nearby, keeping close watch on the *Perechon*, for the rest of your voyage. I have some responsibilities to attend to that may take me away from you on occasion, but never so far that Ilyatha can't summon me." Belwar paused, his expression serious.

"I will help you because you are deserving on your own merits. Your voyage may also present me with an opportunity to confront my enemy. But I fear there are other reasons to help. I have been troubled in recent years by signs of evil doings in the lands that lay to the west of the Blood Sea. I sense that the forces of good and evil are shifting out of balance, and we must all fight that in any way we can. And I think we can all agree which force Attat is aligned with."

Chapter 8
The Outer Reach

The next day's survey of the damage revealed the *Perechon* to be battered, but not ruinously so. Several of the sails were rent, and Vartan and Hvel were sitting on the deck, busy patching them with sheets and thin blankets. Vartan caught Maquesta's eye as she paced about, inspecting the damage in the bright sunlight.

"The sails won't hold, Captain," he told her. "Oh, they'll work for a day or two. Then I think Hvel and I will be back at this again. It's not that we can't mend the sails well. It's that these sails have been mended so many times that there will be more thread from our needles in them than cloth."

Hvel coughed to get her attention. "Maquesta, some of us have been talking, comparing how many coins we have between us. It isn't much. But . . ." He returned to sewing as he finished. "We've collected two dozen steel pieces. That, plus what you have left over from that evil Attat might get us at least one new sail."

She smiled and sat on the deck with them. "I appreciate that, Hvel, Vartan. We need new sails, that's for certain. I'll take you up on your offer, and the first time this ship makes some money, I'll pay everyone double who contributed for the sails."

She rose and resumed her inspection.

The imps had succeeded in battering a hole in the bottom of the longboat. Lendle assured Maq he could repair it, but she was skeptical when she saw him lay out a piece of parchment, grab his chalk, and start diagraming the repair—and a few enhancements.

The top of the mizzenmast, where the imps had been tugging to and fro, showed a hairline crack. Maq was seeing to this repair herself, reinforcing the wood and wrapping cord about it as added insurance. She scowled. If she had her way—and enough coins—she'd buy new masts *and* new sails.

Finished, she climbed up the mainmast and started scrutinizing it. She felt the wood and tested its strength. Her face clouded with concern. It was strong, but it was about as old as she was, and the ship had been through a lot lately. No cracks, but it was heavily weathered, and it would need to be reinforced. Looking down from her vantage point, she saw her crew working hard. No one was idle, and none of them seemed to be complaining. Even Tailonna was helping, though it was apparent the sea elf was not doing anything too strenuous.

A section of the deck railing had broken away and would have to be replaced with ropes temporarily. Fritzen saw to this, as his acrobatic talents let him dangle over the side of the ship and nimbly attach the ropes to the existing railing—while also inspecting the wood about the portholes, which some of the imps had chipped away.

Lendle's pot and pan holder in the galley was in tatters, a development that pleased Maq. The gnome indicated he would fix it, but first he had to finish his plans for the longboat and take care of replacing a connecting rod that had been destroyed by the explosion in his oar engine.

Koraf discovered that the most pressing need for repairs and replacements came not in the area of equipment, but supplies. The imps had methodically punctured all but one of the barrels of fresh water that the *Perechon* carried, and that crucial supply had drained away during the night. As much as she hated to take the time, Maq knew they would have to stop in the port city of Sea Reach on Saifhum to replace the water and purchase some more food with the dozen steel coins left from Attat. Perhaps they could buy a smaller sail with what the men collected. Koraf wanted the damaged crates, barrels, and bins to be junked. No use carrying around garbage, he said. However, he was quick to remove the iron rings about the barrels, thinking they might come in useful for something.

An hour later Maquesta found herself curiously eyeing the longboat, which was meticulously patched in the center. A lever-and-pulley mechanism had been installed near the front bench, and it connected to a rod that ran down the side of the boat. Following the rod, Maq saw that beneath the longboat was a bright green finlike projection on a swivel. She tested the lever, and miraculously it turned the fin this way and that. According to the diagram Lendle had left on the seat, the apparatus would make the boat easier to steer and would require less rowing. He saw her looking at his handiwork, grinned broadly, scratched his nose, and said he had other things to attend to.

With that, the gnome bounded away to his putterings, pleased that she had not criticized his invention. In the cargo hold and other indoor areas, he often had the company of Ilyatha, who had taken an interest in the mechanical workings of the ship, as well as a liking to Lendle. For the gnome's part, he confessed to Maquesta that in the shadow warrior, he had found the perfect companion—outside of another gnome that is. He, Lendle, could speak as fast as he wanted with Ilyatha. The shadowperson, with his telepathic abilities, always understood.

Maquesta, with her right hand firmly on the king's spoke, glanced to the horizon. The attack of the imps and the damage they had inflicted on the sails slowed the *Perechon*'s progress. And it hurt the crew's morale. Still, it was obvious they were a determined bunch, and she could think of no other people she would rather associate with. Shortly after midday the sea's rusty red waters began heaving into great swells, indicating their nearness to the Maelstrom's Outer Reach. The Blood Sea took its name from this color, the result of red sands stirred up when the city of Istar collapsed and kept in constant suspension by the resulting Maelstrom at the center of the sea. The *Perechon* began a sickening up-and-down motion caused by first climbing then slipping into the trough of the huge swells.

Maq leaned hard into the wheel, steering the *Perechon* always to the north, trying to keep to the far edge of the Outer Reach. She was so preoccupied she didn't hear Fritzen pad up behind her.

"You've a good crew," he said, startling her. "They've done about everything they can with the limited supplies. I've some contacts in Sea Reach. Maybe I can borrow enough coins to get you a new sail for the mainmast."

She turned toward him, a smile growing on her face.

"That would be wonderful, Fritzen."

"Fritz," he corrected her.

"All right, Fritz," she replied. "The men have collected two dozen steel. Perhaps with that—and with what your friends will loan you—we can purchase a few new sails. Better sails should improve our speed. And I wouldn't be worrying so much over them."

"Of course," he added, a touch of mischief to his deep voice, "if I get them to loan me the coins, I'll need some guarantee that I have a job here. My friends will insist that I pay them back. And I can't make any promises unless I know I've steady work."

"You'll have a job here as long as you want it," she replied, trying to sound businesslike, though she was giddy that he was asking to stay on long-term. "I should be the one to pay them back, though. Any money you earn is yours to keep." She paused and bit her bottom lip. "I should warn you, Fritz, sometimes a good bit of time goes by between paydays on the *Perechon*. We haven't had a lot of luck landing decent assignments."

"My friends will understand," he said softly. "Besides, after we get your father back, this ship's luck will change. Fortune could blow your way."

"Fritzen!" Koraf bellowed at him from the bow. The minotaur was motioning toward the bowsprit.

The half-ogre sighed. He was enjoying Maquesta's company, and he would have liked to stay with her a bit longer. "I told him I'd strengthen the bowsprit," Fritz said. "Your first mate is an able seaman, but I don't think he fancies tasks that might land him in the water."

"Minotaurs can swim," Maq replied laughing. "Very well in fact. But they are not the fastest of swimmers. Besides, you're the agile one. He's picking the right man for the job. That's the mark of a good first mate."

The half-ogre flashed her a wide grin, saluted, and dashed toward the bow.

For nearly two hours Maq fought the constant pull southward, toward the inner rings of the Maelstrom. An icy rain began to fall, and the sky erupted with thunder and lightening. Maq was about to call for help when she saw Koraf mounting the steps leading to the upper aft deck. He nodded to her by way of greeting, ever slightly formal. When he motioned that he would take over the helm, she gladly gave it up. As she had in Attat's dungeon, Maquesta felt she could trust this particular minotaur. Maq remained near the helm to ascertain that Koraf could indeed handle the wheel in this weather. She felt gratified at the level of skill he displayed.

After a few bad hours, the *Perechon* broke away from the pull of the Outer Reach, heading more directly northward, toward the port of Sea Reach. Just after they made the break, Maq spied a black sail on the horizon far behind them. Now and then during the course of that afternoon, she caught sight of it again. The sail could belong to only one ship, the *Butcher*, captained by the vile Mandracore the Reaver. Mandracore was the one true enemy Melas, and by extension Maquesta, had among those who sailed the Blood Sea regularly. He nursed an old grievance, something about how he and Melas had divided treasure they had scavenged from a sinking merchant vessel many years earlier.

The *Butcher*'s initial appearance troubled her. The fact that it seemed to be following the *Perechon* deepened that feeling. However, even though the *Perechon* was not sailing in top form, the *Butcher* never drew any closer that day. They sailed into the Sea Reach harbor as the sun set, and Maq put that particular worry aside.

* * * * *

Maquesta summoned several crewmembers after dinner that night. Hoping to keep their stay in Sea Reach to one day, or at the most two, Maquesta doled out various responsibilities. She and Lendle would go to the marketplace for foodstuffs and miscellaneous items, where she hoped their ingenuity at making money stretch would carry the day, since there were very few coins left in Attat's pouch to stretch. Fritzen would go to the shipyard to obtain a special compound designed to reinforce the mainmast, which, though not showing any cracks, had been subjected to a great deal of stress lately. After that, he promised to visit some friends and see if he could get enough coins to replace the largest sails. Hvel and Vartan would purchase the water. The assignments taken care of, Maq retired to her cabin for a nap. Sleep was a requirement, for she was to take over watch duty from Fritzen later that night.

* * * * *

Stars filled the sky and the air was still balmy when Maq relieved the half-ogre. He stayed on deck with her for several minutes, discussing the weather, the designs for the *Perechon*, and how the crew had fallen into an easy rhythm with a minotaur first mate. "Sailors are usually a skeptical lot," she told him. "But they are an accepting lot, also. There's a kinship about the sea that tends to erase racial boundaries. I knew they would eventually like Koraf."

Fritz's lips tugged upward into a smile. "And are you so accepting of other races, too, Maquesta?"

She hoped the handsome half-ogre did not see her blush. "I accept everyone until they've wronged me," she said simply. "You should get some sleep. Our day in port will come very quickly."

Maq settled in next to the helm, pondering her strategy for capturing the morkoth, trying not to worry too much about Melas, and working to keep her mind off

Fritzen Dorgaard. She didn't like the idea that he was occupying a lot of her thoughts. A captain has to keep her mind on the ship, she told herself.

She must have dozed for a few minutes, for she woke to someone gently shaking her shoulder.

"I do not sleep well most nights," said Koraf. "I would be happy to take this watch duty so you can get more rest."

"That's quite all right," Maq said defensively. Then, sensing the minotaur was not judging her, she added, "But I could use some company, and if you're not sleeping perhaps you'd oblige me on that."

Receiving no reply, and concerned that she had somehow offended him, Maq simply began talking. She talked about growing up on the *Perechon*, about the first time Melas allowed her to take the helm, about spotting the *Butcher* earlier in the day, about virtually anything that popped into her head. Gradually, she sensed Koraf relaxing.

"And what about you, Kof?" Maq asked, genuinely curious. "How did you learn to sail?"

Koraf remained silent. She wondered if he had fallen asleep. Finally, under the cover provided by the darkness, he began to talk.

Chapter 9

Bas-Ohn Koraf's Story

"For as long as I can remember, I have been fashioning boats from leaves, small pieces of wood and now, of course, solid lumber," Koraf told Maquesta. His resonant voice was soft, perhaps so no one else would overhear him.

"Because of that, when I was still very young, my family secured an apprenticeship for me with Efroth, the best shipbuilder in Nethosak. I do not come from a noble or well-connected family, so it was a very good apprenticeship, one of which I was very proud. Efroth had a thriving business, and four of us started with him at the same time—me, Diro, Thuu, and Phao. We studied and worked under him for many years, learning not only shipbuilding and design, but sailing as well. He taught us about the currents, weather patterns, how to spot an approaching storm by looking at the clouds and feeling the air upon our skin.

"I am not a braggart, and I have never considered myself arrogant, but I was his best student. The others recognized it and turned to me for help at times, all of them except for Diro. He was jealous, and he did nothing to hide his feelings. He began to try to shame me in front of Efroth by doing things that made my work look inferior, when my work clearly was not. Still, I knew I was good, and so did Efroth, so Diro's attempts to shame me did nothing except shame him.

"For a dozen years I learned and worked, worked and learned. That is not such a long time, Maquesta. You spent more than that many years at your father's side learning. It was a happy time in my life, and perhaps I was the happiest I have ever been when I was working with him. I owed him a great deal.

"Finally, it came time for us apprentices to set off on our own, and for Efroth to take in a new group. The next group would be his last, he claimed, for he was getting old and wanted time to himself. We each had to pass a final test in order to be certified as qualified shipbuilders. The test was to design and construct a sailing vessel, then sail it alone through a special course Efroth had set up off the coast. He would accompany each of us so he could observe and grade us.

"I put a lot of time into my small sailing ship, for I intended to sell it after the course and give the money to my family—my thanks to them for setting up the apprenticeship. Then I had plans to travel from port to port, building ships for cities and the nobility, grand designs the like of which the Blood Seas had never seen.

"I should have suspected, but I did not for I was foolishly naive then, that Diro would attempt to thwart me in this final competition. The night before the test, he entered the shipyard where our vessels were stored and weakened my ship's hull.

"The next morning, we gathered at the shipyard dock next to our vessels. One by one, Efroth sailed out with us, taking each of us through the course, judging the performance of the ship, how it was rigged, and measuring the skill of its captain. My turn was last. I'd like to think he took me last to ensure that none of the others felt inadequate.

"Diro had done well. He had honestly tried hard on his own merits, and I was pleased for him. But when my turn came I knew that I would do better.

"Everything began favorably. The winds were gusty, but I trimmed my sails correctly, and my ship was crafted to take the best advantage of the wind. Then, when we were about a mile offshore, I noticed water entering the ship. Before my eyes, the leak turned into a geyser and then, with a terrible noise, my ship split in two. I grabbed a piece of the wreckage and survived. Efroth was not so lucky. He was already old when we started with him as apprentices. And when the ship split, the mast fell and struck him on the head. He sank to the bottom and drowned before I could reach him.

"No one blamed me directly for his death. They just shook their heads at my unwarranted confidence in my skills. Even my parents seemed ashamed. I was in shock. I didn't know how I could have been so wrong about my abilities.

"That night I wandered around the waterfront, not knowing what I was doing. At one point, I entered an inn to ask for a drink of water. As I waited, I saw that a little ways down the bar stood Diro, Thuu, and Phao. I could tell by his loud talk that Diro, who had his back to me, was very drunk. Joining them was the last thing

I wanted to do, but I couldn't help overhearing what Diro was talking about. He was bragging about his cleverness and was showing the others a small pry bar he had used to weaken my ship's hull.

"Phao and Thuu, seeing me, tried to silence him, but could not. I succeeded in silencing him forever. Gripped by a white-hot fury, I walked over and strangled him. I made no attempt to escape. I was immediately arrested and sentenced to fight in the circus until I died."

Maquesta looked up into his tear-filled eyes. "But surely what Diro had done to you, and the fact that he caused Efroth's death, should have changed your sentence?" Maq asked.

"Our law absolutely forbids one minotaur killing another outside the circus—which are our organized combat games. Diro was already dead. He could not be sentenced."

"Then what were you doing at Attat's?" Maq probed.

"Sometimes, fighters in the circus are assigned 'keepers,' minotaurs responsible for maintaining us between bouts. In return, they receive a portion of every wager placed on our events. Attat is my keeper. I have been with the circus four years. I am undefeated, and as such, he draws good coin from my appearances."

"If Attat is your keeper, then why don't you just leave after helping us capture the morkoth? I'll tell Attat you escaped during the night, Kof. I'll drop you off in another port. You don't have to go back to him," Maq urged. "He's despicable."

Koraf sadly shook his head. "Two minotaurs are dead because of my actions—or my failure to take action. It is the law. And I honor the law. Also, allowing me to leave would be reason enough for Attat to throw you back into his dungeon. He is not someone to be trifled with."

Thinking of what Attat had done to her father, Maq could only agree. She nodded and gripped the king's spoke tighter.

Chapter 10

Sea Reach

The shore party set off, in good spirits, early the next day. Sea Reach was a far different place than their last port of call, Lacynos. Stone buildings with wide verandas, tile roofs, and bright, colorful awnings faced the waterfront, presenting a well kept and cheery face to visitors. Terraced farms climbed the rugged landscape on either side of the harbor.

However, Maq knew that—fortunately—the welcoming facade did not extend to all. The *Butcher* would not have dared sail into this harbor, nor would it have been comfortable for Bas-Ohn Koraf to accompany Maquesta and the others to town. Pirates and minotaurs were routinely driven off by galleys that patrolled the harbor and by armed guards who walked the waterfront.

Still, for the *Perechon* captain and crewmembers, Sea Reach was a very pleasant sight—or would have been if they hadn't been bailing out the water gushing in through the leak in the longboat. Maq scowled. Lendle's mending attempt did little but slow the amount of water bubbling in, and the lever on the side broke off the first time she tried to use it.

"ItisallrightitisreallyandtrulyallrightMaquestaKar Thon," the little gnome babbled rapidly. "Ihavea-plantofixitpermanentlyevenbetterthanbefore." He winked at her and looked at the leak. "I'll get right to work as soon as we finish all our errands!" he added, finally slowing down so she could understand him.

Maquesta simply grimaced.

After they had pulled the longboat up on a sandy section of beach and tried futilely to shake the water out of their boots, Fritzen asked for a change of plans. He drew her to the side and talked softly, watching Lendle to make sure he was occupied with inspecting the longboat.

"Maq, can you meet me at the shipyard after you finish at the market? I think we need to take the longboat over there for a quick patch-up before Lendle completes his permanent repairs—or we may not make it back to the *Perechon*. Hopefully I'll have some new sails with me, too."

Lendle, obviously overhearing, scowled at Fritzen, but then joined in Maq's laughing assent.

They all agreed to meet back at the wharf after lunch, understanding that they might have to postpone their return if the longboat still needed work.

* * * * *

Though Maq's family roots were set in Saifhum's soil, she had spent little time on the island. Every time she did visit, however, she vowed to return more often. Today in the sunny marketplace, watching Lendle bargain expertly with equally skilled shopkeepers, Maquesta was content to almost forget what lay ahead—and behind—her. Almost. Worries about her father never completely left her. Nor did she want to forget.

Wandering up and down the neatly swept streets, Maq and Lendle soon acquired their planned supply of fruits and vegetables, and the metal part Lendle needed for his gnomish engine.

"Do you want to come with me to the shipyard?"

"No, Maquesta Kar-Thon. I need to go elsewhere."

"Let me guess—you'll meet me at the Sea Reach Inn for lunch. If I get there before lunch, you'll be in the back room. Right?" Maquesta asked apprehensively.

Lendle beamed. The Sea Reach Inn was the largest such establishment in that port city. In addition to accommodations for overnight guests, it offered a large dining room with good, home-cooked meals served around the clock, and a back room where the card games never ended. The most popular games were Legion, Fates, and Bounty Hunter, the latter being a more complex version of a children's game, the Hunt. Lendle loved it. He had once played for three days and two nights in a row, Maq remembered. And he'd talked so much about the session that he forgot about his inventions for better than a week.

"Now, Lendle," Maq admonished, "don't forget why we're here and what we have left to do on this voyage. You can't have many steel pieces left; Vartan said you contributed to the sail fund. And I'd like you to hang on to your money in case we need to buy anything else."

"Maquesta Kar-Thon. You don't have to worry about me," Lendle said sternly, drawing himself up to his full three-and-one-half feet in height.

Maq knew Lendle never meant to get in trouble. It just

sometimes happened despite his best intentions. On the other hand, even as frugal as he was, she didn't think the gnome had enough coins left for a decent stake in a card game. After walking a few steps toward the shipyard, she turned to wave good-bye, but Lendle didn't see her. He had already pulled out his automatic wallet and was practically skipping down the street toward the inn.

* * * * *

"You let a gnome fix your longboat?" The elderly human shipbuilder laughed and laughed until it seemed he would never stop. Finally, he wiped the tears from his eyes, and with an obvious attempt to keep a straight face, said, "I'll see what I can do to fix the craft, though it won't be ready for a few hours. It will take at least that long to undo the gnome's work and repair it properly. I'll deliver it to the dock when it's finished." Stifling another laugh, he turned and walked away, shaking his head and talking to himself.

Maq and Fritz had rowed the longboat to the shipyard, getting their boots wet again in the process. Tired and hungry, Maq was in no mood to appreciate the shipbuilder's humor at their predicament, and she glared at the man's retreating back, biting her tongue to keep from saying something she'd undoubtedly regret.

"Relax, Maquesta," Fritz said, smiling broadly. "He means no harm. The boat will soon be fixed, and the new sails will be delivered to the ship this afternoon. I called in a few favors, promised to pay my friends a little interest, and—combined with the coins Vartan and Hvel collected—I was able to get enough money together to replace all your sails. We can use the best of your old sails for future repairs."

Maquesta jumped up and hugged him. "That's wonderful!" she cried. Then she instantly gained her composure and fell in step beside him, once more trying to assume a businesslike demeanor. "I meant what I said about paying back your friends as soon as I come into some coins."

"I'll take you up on it," he replied, "but only if you let me buy you something to eat." He jangled a small pouch at his side that had a few coins left in it.

"Let's go to the Sea Reach Inn," Maq suggested, all too conscious of Fritz's arm brushing against hers as they walked. "That's where Lendle's eating, and I have a feeling we should be checking up on him."

They walked slowly to the inn, enjoying the time together and feeling that perhaps things would work out after all. When they arrived, the inn's dining room was beginning to fill up with lunch customers, but Lendle was nowhere in sight. Once Maq and Fritzen made their way to the back room, however, he was immediately noticeable.

Lendle sat at a large round table, dealing cards to a group of players that consisted of two sailors, a merchant, a few locals, and a dwarf. By the large pile of chips in front of him, it was evident the gnome was winning—big. The game was Bounty Hunter, a forty-coin buy-in. As a child, Maq had often played the game with the Lendle, wagering fishhooks and seashells, and he had often folded so she could win. It looked as though, with his current run of luck, Lendle would have no need to fold this time.

"Maybe we can pay off your friends sooner than expected," Maquesta whispered to Fritz.

Maq signaled to the gnome, finally getting his attention. She circled her fingers in a wrapping up motion and mouthed the words, "Time to quit. Meet you in the dining room."

Lendle poked out his bottom lip, eyed his chips, then looked back at Maquesta and nodded happily. "Last hand for me!" he chirped to his companions, adding only after Fritz and Maq were out of hearing, "Well, maybe one or two after this one."

Once seated in the dining room, Maquesta inspected the slate menu, her eyes drifting down over delectables she hadn't tasted in months. "Beef. Chicken. Kipper." She sighed softly. "No eel stew. No bean soup. No hardtack. This is wonderful."

"Allow me," Fritz said, signaling a barmaid. "The lady would like a thick steak with potatoes and a glass of your best wine. The same for me, but bring me a mug of spiced ale."

The barmaid held up her palm for payment. "Hand over your coin first" she demanded. "At the Sea Reach, you pay before you eat."

Fritz pulled out his purse and counted out the coins, handing them over to the barmaid with a flourish.

"You're rich," Maq jested.

"Not after this meal," he replied, jiggling his coin purse that now only jangled softly. "But we've earned this." He looked into the coin pouch. "I think Lendle will have to buy his own lunch, though."

She giggled. "That's all right. From the looks of those chips, I'd say he can afford it."

The gnome had not yet joined Fritz and Maq by the time their steaming hot meal was brought to them. Maquesta didn't mind being alone with the half-ogre, but she was beginning to worry about Lendle. One bite of the steak, however, melted her curiosity, and she dug in as if she were starving.

Lendle had still not arrived by the time they were finished. Nor had he shown up by the time they had downed their second drinks. Maquesta shook her curls. "No more for me. I've got to keep my head clear. And it seems I may have to fetch our engineer."

Maq had just decided to go and retrieve Lendle, to

rib him about what a fine steak he'd missed, but suddenly a loud ruckus broke out in the back room, dashing her plans. In the midst of all the yelling, Maq made out the gnome's nasal, fast-talking voice.

"Youcantquit. Youhavetogivemeachancetowinitback andthenIcanpayyou."

"I have to do no such thing," a gruff voice replied. "You have to pay me *right now*."

"Yes! Pay him now, little man," another voice intruded.

"What's the matter, big-time gambler? Not good for your debts?" It was the gruff voice again.

"Imgoodformydebts. Letsplayonemorehandmaybe two. ThenIcanpayyouback. Honest."

When Maq reached the back room, with Fritz close on her heels, she saw that Lendle's pile of chips was completely depleted. The gnome had squared off with the prosperous-looking merchant, and had his small fists in front of him, as if he were going to duke it out with the much-bigger man. But when the other players sided with the merchant and the dwarf put his hand on a sharp-looking dagger, the gnome put down his fists and started babbling again.

At that, one of the gamblers dashed from the room, brushing past Maquesta and the half-ogre, who held up his three remaining steel pieces.

"I don't suppose this would even the score," he said.

Maq pursed her lips as she took in the scene, feeling dismay wash over her like a tidal wave. "I doubt it would even make a dent," she answered bleakly.

It seemed only moments had passed before the harbor guards arrived, led by the gambler who had run out of the inn. Fritz and Maq watched helplessly as the guards carted Lendle away, telling him he would have to work off his debt to make amends to the merchant.

It was either that or go to jail. For a long time.

Chapter 11
The Rescue

Maquesta grabbed a barmaid by the sleeve as she pushed by with an empty tray.

"Where do they take people arrested for not paying gambling debts?" Maq asked.

"Depends," the barmaid said, looking past Maq to the kitchen, as if anxious to pick up her order. "Best place to start is the chief constable's office, on the square." She tossed her hair over her left shoulder as she pulled away, vaguely giving Maq an idea of which direction to travel.

"I know where that is; let's go," Maq said to Fritzen, leading the way out of the inn and through the neatly kept streets of Sea Reach.

Because the island's steep hills crowded down

almost to the water's edge, Sea Reach had evolved as an elongated city, strung out along the bay without much of a city center. Toward the western end of the bay, though, where terraced farms had been cut into the hills, stood a small square with a large sundial in the middle. Stone buildings that housed the agencies conducting all the official business of Sea Reach—city clerk, deeds registrar, constabulary hall, mayor's office—ringed the square's well-tended greenery.

"Foolish ass-brained spawn of a misbegotten muck-dweller. It'd serve him right to rot in a cell here for a few weeks," Maq sputtered angrily as she stomped up the steep flight of steps leading to the constabulary hall's narrow entrance. "I can't dawdle too long in this town. We've got to be after the morkoth. I've a good mind to leave the muddle-headed ignoramus here and pick him up on the way back. Do him some good."

"Who taught you how to string insults together like that, a kender?" Fritzen asked wryly. "If you feel that way about the gnome, let's just leave him to his fate."

Maq shot her companion a withering glance. "How could you say such a thing? I'd sooner cut off my right hand. He's my friend. And I need him. But I'm furious that he got himself into this mess and that we have to take time to get him out of it. He knows the urgency of our mission."

At the top of the steps, Maq paused a minute to gather her breath, and her wits. Reflecting Saifhum's penchant for order, the constabulary hall dominated the other official buildings. Its massive, square-cut granite blocks reached up four stories, ending in a flat roof that was hidden by a parapet that, Maq was certain, itself hid a contingent of watchmen. If Lendle was being held here, they'd be hard pressed to extract him.

"Wait out here for me," Maq told Fritzen.

"But, Maq—" He began to protest, but she cut him off.

"I know what these islanders are like, and they'll think they know me because I look like them. On the other hand, you would just put them on their guard. And if they're suspicious, they might have someone start following us while we're in Sea Reach, which is a complication we don't need. I'll have better luck getting information alone," Maq explained. "I'll meet you on the square. If I'm not out by suppertime, then you can try to find out what happened."

"Yes, Captain," Fritz replied, making a mocking bow. "You ask, and I humbly obey."

Maq poked out her lips and put her hands on her hips. She opened her mouth to offer a retort, but thought better of it. Instead, she turned on her heels and went inside.

The Maquesta who entered the constabulary hall showed a far different mien than she had displayed on the steps. Suppliant rather than authoritative, Maq approached a tall counter that blocked access to the rest of the building. Behind it sat an officer busily scratching the nib of a feather pen across a long piece of expensive-looking parchment.

"Please sir, would you help me?" Maq asked plaintively.

"State your business," the guard said with an automatic brusqueness, still writing. When he looked up a moment later and saw an attractive young woman in obvious need of help, his manner visibly softened.

Maq smiled sweetly at him.

"My family and I live on the far side of the island, and I came into Sea Reach with one of our servants to visit the market. Only it seems he got himself in some sort of trouble at the Sea Reach Inn. Father will be so cross. Can you tell me how to find him and how to make amends for his offense?" Maq spoke softly, her hands held demurely in front of her. She still had the bags of provisions she and Lendle had purchased earlier, lending credibility to her story.

"Servant, eh?" asked the constable, looking her up and down.

For an instant Maq thought she had told the wrong sort of tale, that the constable wouldn't believe someone dressed as she was could come from a family with servants. But no, there were plenty of simple, hard-working folk on Saifhum, many of whom were wealthy enough to employ several servants.

"What's the servant's name? And is it a man or a woman?"

"Lendle, Lendle Chafka. He's a gnome."

"Gnome! Oh, that fellow. Couldn't miss him. He kicked Officer Rappa when they brought him in, hard, in the shins, yelling about how he had to go win back his stake," the constable said, tapping his pen on the desk. "We don't get many gnomes in Sea Reach—wouldn't ha' thought any lived on the island." A clear note of suspicion had crept into his voice.

"The *far* side of the island," Maq reminded him quickly, as she batted her long eyelashes. "He hasn't worked for us for long, and if this is how he's going to behave, he won't for much longer," she said, affecting indignation. "Is he here, then?"

"Nope. Can't work off a debt if you're in jail, that's Salomdhi's thinking. We would have locked the gnome up for awhile, but Salomdhi wanted him to come back to his place right away to start working," the officer said approvingly. "When there's money at stake, you'll not see Salomdhi taking a loss, that's for sure."

"Salomdhi?" Maq inquired.

"That's the fellow your servant lost money to in the card game. He's a merchant, the biggest in Sea Reach. Started out with one fruit stand and now he owns half the shops in the marketplace."

"Can you tell me where Mr. Salomdhi lives?" Maq asked. "Perhaps I can talk to him and arrange for my father to send him a payment. Lendle is our servant, after all. If he's going to work for nothing, he can do it for us."

"Sure. Take the street behind the hall and follow it until it ends. Salomdhi lives in a big white house with a red tile roof, the biggest house on the street. You can't miss it," the constable offered obligingly.

Maq had already thanked him and turned to leave when he called out to her.

"Young lady! Good luck in striking a bargain with him—Salomdhi's a tough customer." The officer chuckled, amused at the idea of the uneven match-up between Maquesta and the merchant.

Maq smiled to herself. He hasn't met a tough customer yet, she thought, but he will.

* * * * *

In the square, Fritzen was amusing himself by winging small pebbles at the backs of passersby then quickly turning the other way while they tried to figure out what had hit them.

"Don't you think one of the guards on top of the constabulary hall might spot you doing that? In this city, that could be enough to get you locked up," Maq said admonishingly.

"I live dangerously, and I like it that way." Fritzen grinned as he replied.

"Honestly! First Lendle, now you. I'm surrounded by a crew of juveniles—in behavior if not in age."

A sudden image of her father and Averon wrestling on the deck of the *Perechon* flashed through Maq's mind. She winced at the memory. With the thought of Melas, her sense of urgency doubled.

"Let's go. I know where Lendle is."

While she and Fritzen walked, Maquesta related what the constable had told her about Salomdhi and Lendle's sentence. Fritzen's eyes lit up at the news of the merchant's wealth.

"Sounds like there might be more to rescue at his house than just Lendle," he said mischievously.

"Fritz! We can't risk it. We have to concentrate on getting Lendle out of there and finding the morkoth," Maq said heatedly. "If you don't see that, maybe you shouldn't be on this voyage."

Suddenly serious, Fritzen reassured her. "I owe a great debt to both your father, for taking me in when the *Torado* sank, and to Lendle, who nursed me through a dark time." The half-ogre's face clouded as he mentioned those two events. "I am not one to either forget or neglect an obligation. You may rely on me, Maquesta."

Sea Reach was, in truth, not a very big place, and they arrived at the merchant's house quickly. Built near the foot of one of the rugged hills that encroached on the city, the house stretched up and down the street, but was not exceptionally deep. A white stone wall, half again as tall as Fritzen and topped by the same tiles that covered the house's roof, extended from either side of the dwelling until it reached the base of the hill.

Maq and Fritz decided to scout the walled garden before approaching the house's front door. Maquesta knew that though she had bluffed the constable into thinking the gnome was her family's servant, trying the same ploy on the merchant would be more difficult, especially if he had spotted her in the Sea Reach Inn. Fritzen knelt so Maq could climb on his shoulders, then stood up slowly.

"You're very light, you know?" he quipped. "I could carry you all day."

"Shhh!" she scolded. "Someone might hear you."

Peering over the top of the wall, Maq saw an extensive garden consisting of a number of vegetable and flower plots as well as a small cherry orchard. At first, Maquesta could not spot anyone. Then movement at the back of the garden, where it met the hill, caught her attention. She saw Lendle emerge from behind a door that blended into the rugged hillside so well she never would have noticed it if it hadn't opened.

He carried two hoes, a rake, and several other garden tools over to one of the vegetable gardens, where it looked to Maq as if he had already set up a pole on a cart with two wheels and a handle for pushing. Arms like spokes in a wheel extended out from the top of the pole. Despite the precariousness of her position, Maq chuckled. The gnome went about attaching the hoes and various other garden tools to his contraption. It looked as if Lendle were contriving some type of automatic weeding device, with the hoes positioned at just the right height to chop off the heads of the garden's vegetables. Salomdhi didn't know what he was in for.

"You know what I said about your being light?" Fritz whispered. "Forget it. You're getting heavier."

"Shhh!" she scolded again. "I'll just watch for a moment more."

Taking another look around the walled enclosure, Maq thought Lendle was alone, but she couldn't be sure. The place was too big. Even if he were alone, calling out to him would be risky. Sun glinted off the rows of windows that lined the back of Salomdhi's house. Because of the sun's reflection in the glass, she couldn't tell if someone were behind one of those windows, watching the garden.

Pondering what to do, Maq saw a rotund man with slicked-back hair and a prosperous air bustle out of the house. Maq ducked down slightly so her head wouldn't show above the top of the wall. She recognized the man from the card game. The merchant, no doubt Salomdhi, motioned the gnome to come to him, calling his name, "Lendle Chafka!" as if it were a disease. Luckily, the summons brought Lendle closer to Maq's vantage point, so she could listen in on the conversation.

"What's happening?" Fritzen whispered.

"Shhh. I'll tell you in a minute," Maq whispered back.

"No more *shhhhs*. What's going on?"

She poked her head up again. "I see Lendle. Shhh!"

"I have a business appointment," Salomdhi announced self-importantly. "Here, lift up your pantleg."

Maq didn't hear what response, if any, the gnome made, but she couldn't imagine he was very happy. She raised herself a little higher to get a better view. It looked as if Salomdhi were bending over and attaching something to Lendle's ankle. Maq ducked down again as the merchant stood up.

"There's no way out of this garden except through the house, and the servants will not allow you in," Salomdhi said. "You may as well not bother to think about escape. That charm locked around your ankle will allow me to track you, and I have the only key to unlock it. Of course, you're welcome to *try* to escape. That will give me your service for many more months. I've needed a gardener for quite some time."

As the merchant disappeared into the hillside cave, Lendle started to trail after him. Before the gnome got to the doorway, though, Salomdhi emerged carrying a burlap sack. The merchant looked around the garden, seeing little evidence of work having been done.

"Remember, I want all three vegetable gardens weeded by nightfall. You can start pruning the cherry trees tomorrow." With that, he left the garden as officiously as he had entered.

When Maq peeked over the wall again, Lendle, momentarily distracted from his plight by the introduction of this new toy, was fingering the ankle bracelet the merchant had put on him.

Maq jumped down to confer with Fritzen, who rubbed his shoulders and feigned a grimace. "The merchant's left," she said. "I don't think there's anyone in the house except servants. It would be easy to get him out, except . . ."

"Except what?" Fritzen demanded.

"Except that Salomdhi put some sort of charm on Lendle's ankle. Said it would let him track Lendle if he tried to escape."

Fritzen looked doubtful. "That merchant didn't look like the type to have magic charms lying around his house. Maybe it's a trick. Let's get inside first, talk to Lendle. Then we can worry about the trinket. Besides, maybe it's valuable and we'll want to take it along with us."

"All right," Maq agreed. She began climbing onto Fritzen's shoulders again.

This time he offered a weak protest. "I'm not a ladder."

"Just give me a minute," she sputtered. "I can lift myself over the wall by standing on you. But whose shoulders are you going to stand on?"

"No one's," Fritzen said as Maq stood on his shoulders. "Some of us need a helping hand," the half-ogre teased, "while others of us are self-sufficient."

At that remark, Maquesta kicked back at Fritzen, only half in jest, narrowly missing his nose. Looking up at the sky, Maq saw the sun had shifted a bit so there were shadows along the garden wall here that would provide her some cover in case anybody was watching from the house. With her arms braced on the top of the wall, she began to lift herself up and over.

Only when Maq had dropped lightly down to the ground on the other side was she noticed by Lendle.

Showing no surprise, he hurried up to her, a scowl playing under his big nose. "Wherehaveyoubeen?" he asked crossly. "DoyouhaveanyideahowlongIvebeen-waitingforyou?"

"Stop right there, Lendle. With all the trouble gambling has caused us recently, I'd think you would have known better than to get involved in a Bounty Hunter game, and then a brawl when you lost," Maq scolded. "We don't have time for this. My father. The morkoth. Remember?"

Lendle at least had the good grace to blush, a deep red suffusing his nutty brown skin, before plunging into his defense. "Ididntlose," he fumed. "Itwasatemporary setback."

Maq rolled her eyes.

"ThatbaboonSalomdhidoesntunderstandcard-playingetiquette," Lendle complained, warming to his subject. "Hedoesntunderstandhowtogardenorhow-tosetupaproperweedingsystem." Lendle grabbed Maq by the hand and began dragging her toward the back of the garden, toward the door she had seen him use.

"But, Maquesta Kar-Thon—" Lendle's speech started to slow, signifying growing excitement on his part. "You must come with me. That fool must understand *some*thing." Lendle said, continuing to tug at her hand.

"Hold on a minute, Lendle, I think Fritz is going to be joining us."

A thud against the outside of the garden wall signaled the half-ogre's imminent entrance. Fritzen had taken a running jump at the wall, leaping up as high as he could and using the small purchase his feet found on the vertical surface to push himself higher, so that his hands could grasp the top of the wall. In one smooth movement, he pulled himself up and over, doing a backward flip into the garden and landing easily on his feet.

"Show off," Maq said coolly. Fritzen grinned.

"What about the charm?" he asked.

"It looks as if you have enough charm," the gnome remarked, then resumed dragging Maq along with him.

"Lendle wants to show us something else first," Maq advised him.

Not having seen Lendle's earlier exit from within the hill, Fritzen looked duly impressed when the gnome opened the hidden door. They walked into a cool and spacious cave where Salomdhi stored garden implements, seed stocks, root vegetables, burlap sacks, and the like. It was virtually a gardener's paradise that attested to the merchant's wealth.

"This is what you're so excited about?" Maq asked in surprise. "Lendle, we have to get out of here. We don't have time for this."

"No. No. No, Maquesta Kar-Thon. You've got to see this." Lendle took them to the right rear corner of the cave. He picked up a gardening trowel and ran it along the rough-hewn rock of the walls until he came to an unobtrusive handle cut from the same rock. When Lendle jerked on the handle, Maq saw it was attached to a small, rectangular, metal plate that emerged from the rock as he pulled. Once the plate was pulled all the way out, what sounded like a weight shifting position echoed from within the wall, touching off a series of such shifts.

"Weights and counterweights," Lendle explained briefly. "Very ingenious."

An opening appeared in front of them as a stone door slid to the right. The main cavern received light from the open door to the outside, but the second cave was pitch-dark.

"Wait," Lendle admonished. He bent down, feeling on the floor just inside and to the left of the new doorway and came up holding a lantern. Fritzen struck a flint from a box he spied by a bag of turnips. When the half-ogre held up the lantern, Maq gasped.

A burlap bag filled with gold coins had split at the bottom seam, spilling some of its contents onto the vault's floors. That was the first thing Maq saw. Stacked behind it, extending down the left side of the cave and rising nearly to the roof, stood bag upon bag, also filled with coins, judging by their lumpy silhouettes. Assorted treasure was piled haphazardly around the bags: golden candlesticks inlaid with brilliant rubies, gold and silver bowls and platters, lacquered boxes and chests studded with jewels. Maq flipped back the lid of one. It was stuffed with a variety of gems, sapphires, diamonds, and emeralds.

The other side of the cave truly took her breath away. Metal shields, some inlaid with gold, leaned against the wall, coats of mail piled nearby. Leather weapon harnesses decorated with silver clasps and stiff leather breastplates occupied one corner. Nearby, bundles of swords, some with jeweled hilts, stood on their points, packaged together like sheaves of wheat. Tall spears lay on the cave floor next to a small mound of daggers.

Fritzen strode forward, selected a dagger with a ruby in the pommel, and stuck it in his belt. A pearl necklace found its way into his pouch, as did a small silver case the size of his hand. "We'll need some empty sacks," he stated.

"No!" Maq's tone was sharp. "This isn't ours to take. We're not thieves."

"Yeah? Well, I expect Lendle's merchant friend didn't come by this stuff honestly. And I'm sure he won't miss a bauble or two." The half-ogre stuffed gold coins into his pouch until no more would fit, then he strode across the small cave and pointed.

"Look at this." Fritz stood by a pile of helmets, fingering something. Maq and Lendle joined him. He was holding an elaborate, horned helm. The horns, long, slender, and curved, looked sharp enough to impale an enemy. Except for strategic openings for the eyes, the helmet would cover the wearer's entire head, front and back. It showed remarkable craftsmanship but was, at the same time, unspeakably hideous. He placed it on his head. "This is the helmet of a warlord, not a merchant," Fritzen said, adjusting it for a better fit, and running his fingers around the outside of it. "I've never seen anything like this."

"Nor should you have seen this one." A deep voice came from the doorway.

Startled, Fritzen and the others whipped around. Salomdhi stood in the entrance to the treasure vault. "Lendle!" he scolded. "What are you doing in here and who are these two with you?" The merchant stamped his foot. "I can see I'm not going to get my money's worth out of you! The constable warned me you might be more trouble than you're worth."

"No, I'd say the lot of them aren't worth much. But they might provide us some amusement," said a larger figure, coming up to stand behind Salomdhi. "And I so need to be amused right now, Maquesta Kar-Thon."

Maq started. The voice sounded familiar. Then the figure pushed Salomdhi aside and stepped into the cave.

"Mandracore!"

The pirate captain known as Mandracore the Reaver stood before her. A half-ogre like Fritzen, he did not stand quite as tall, but he was stockier, more muscular, and he had none of Fritzen's attractiveness. His coarse, broad features were dotted with warts. Maq had never seen his hair; he always wore a scarf tied tightly around his head. A gold earring in the shape of a grinning skull dangled from one ear.

"What are you doing on Saifhum?" Maq asked. She turned to Salomdhi and demanded, "What is he doing here with you? I've never heard of a Saifhum merchant dealing with pirates!"

Behind her Fritzen slid quietly to a bundle of swords. His back to them, he tugged one free and kept it hidden behind his legs.

Salomdhi looked acutely uncomfortable at Maq's accusations. "I—" he began.

Mandracore cut in. "My business carries me into quarters that are no concern of yours, Maquesta Kar-Thon. As to what we're doing in this particular cave—your little friend called us back."

Puzzled, Maq looked over at Lendle. Only then did she notice that the charm around his ankle pulsed insistently with a pale blue light.

"It's just good luck that this time my business dealings give me the opportunity to settle an old score," Mandracore added. "Too bad your father isn't here. I'd rather settle it with him, Maquesta. But you'll do." He snapped his fingers and two shadowy figures stepped up behind Salomdhi, completely blocking the doorway.

Being within the cave put Maq, Fritzen, and Lendle at a disadvantage for starting a fight—unless they could lure the pirates, or at least Mandracore, inside. She exchanged glances with her crewmates and saw they felt similarly stymied.

Salomdhi began backing out of the cave, keeping a wary eye on Mandracore. "What do you mean to do?" Then, apparently not reassured by the look on the pirate's face, he whined, "I want no part of this. I want you all off my property. This is not what your masters are paying me for, Mandracore. There'll be no murders here."

"Just what services are you providing these scum?" Maq asked.

"It's just an honest business transaction," the merchant said defensively. "I rent them this storage space, do some buying and selling on their behalf. I'm paid well. I don't ask any questions. What they're doing is none of my concern." Salomdhi puffed out his chest and stuck up his chin self-righteously. Seemingly fortified by his own rationalizations, he addressed Mandracore.

"You heard what I said—Get out, and take these . . . these . . . *spies* with you!"

With a raised eyebrow, Mandracore signaled his henchman, who each grabbed one of Salomdhi's arms and ushered the merchant into the treasure vault.

"No fat merchant talks to Mandracore the Reaver that way," the pirate snarled, shoving his face to within an inch of Salomdhi's. "Think your hands are clean, eh? Then I've got a little lesson for you. This should be very educational."

With Mandracore half turned away, focused on the squirming merchant, and the other two pirates occupied holding him, Maq saw her chance. She dropped to her knees and grabbed one of the daggers lying on the cave floor. Then she leapt onto Mandracore's back, circling her legs around his waist and her arm around his throat until she nearly cut off his breathing. She scraped the tip of her blade underneath his chin, warning him not to move.

In the meantime, as soon as Maquesta made her move, Fritzen ran a couple steps toward the pirates holding Salomdhi and jumped up, swinging both legs straight out in front of him in powerful kicks that caught the guards under their chins and sent them tumbling backward. They loosened their hold on the merchant, and fell awkwardly on a mound of spilled gold coins. The half-ogre drew the sword down to the larger one's chest and growled, the sound reverberating in the helmet and indicating that the pirate should stay put.

Freed from their grip, Salomdhi turned to run but was tackled around the ankles by Lendle, who then expertly flipped the merchant onto his stomach, twisting his arm behind him, inflicting enough pain to keep the man motionless but not, unfortunately, silent. Salomdhi, unused to physical distress, began screaming that his arm was about to break.

The other pirate knocked down by Fritzen had regained his feet and was circling the half-ogre with long, twin daggers drawn.

"Stay back," Fritz warned, "or I'll slit your friend's stomach as if he were a pig at the slaughterhouse, and his blood can wash all these pieces of gold."

Undaunted, the standing pirate laughed and circled closer. Fritz, frustrated, balled his fist and struck the downed man hard in the face, knocking him out and breaking a few of his teeth in the process.

Maq, still on Mandracore's back, didn't like the situation. Though the pirate facing Fritz was a human, and quite a bit smaller, he seemed agile and practiced, a potentially deadly foe.

"Tell him to drop the daggers!" Maquesta barked at Mandracore, pressing the flat of her borrowed dagger against his throat. The pirate clenched his jaw closed, refusing. "I'm not kidding!" Maq turned her dagger, pressing the point into the soft underside of his chin until a trickle of blood appeared. "Tell him!" she ordered.

"Yega!" Mandracore called in strangled tones. "Drop your daggers." Such was the fear-driven obedience that the Reaver commanded from his crew that the pirate obeyed his order immediately. Fritzen picked up the daggers, sticking them in the sash at his waist, and pointed to the ground.

"Lie down next to your friend!" Fritzen commanded. Again the words reverberated inside the helmet. Shaking his head, he pulled the thing free and dropped it on the ground. "How could anyone wear something like that?" he whispered to himself.

"Lendle, do something about that noise!" Maq sputtered as Salomdhi continued to wail. Lendle tore a strip from the bottom of Salomdhi's silken tunic, and to the merchant's obvious indignation stuffed it in his mouth, muffling the noise, though not completely stopping it. The merchant broke out into a cold sweat and squirmed harder.

"Slowly now, let's walk into the other part of the cave," Maq ordered as she tightened her grip on Mandracore's back. "Yega and the other one first, with Fritzen following, then Salomdhi and Lendle. We'll save the best for last, Mandracore." Maq assumed there would be rope in the first section of the cavern, rope they could use to tie up Salomdhi and the pirates. Then they would need to get back to the *Perechon* as quickly as possible. The charm on Lendle's ankle was still blinking. She didn't know if it was summoning anyone else to the merchant's compound, but she didn't want to take the chance.

Yega dragged the unconscious pirate to his knees and began pulling him like a sack of potatoes, angling him toward the outer cave. He threw Maq a look of icy contempt as he went. Just as the men were inside the entrance, Maquesta's eyes grew wide.

"Fritzen! Look out!" The warning came too late for the half-ogre. Mandracore had stationed a third pirate to keep watch in the garden while he and the others accompanied Salomdhi inside. That pirate, wielding a curved saber, now lunged at Fritzen from just outside the treasure vault's sliding door. Fritz ducked away at the last minute, but the blade still caught him solidly in the shoulder, causing him to wince in pain. The half-ogre brought his purloined blade up to parry, catching the next slash and easily deflecting it, but he was stunned from his injury.

This gave Yega an opening. The pirate darted away

from Fritzen, in toward his armed companion and pulled a dagger free from his belt. Now the two stood facing the half-ogre, and they moved in closer.

"Lendle! Go help him—I'll watch the merchant." Though Lendle was a skilled fighter, Maq was afraid if she went to Fritzen's side Mandracore would be able to overwhelm the gnome. Therefore, Mandracore was her responsibility, and hers alone.

Before the third pirate could strike at Fritzen again, Lendle leapt forward. The gnome dashed underneath the half-ogre's blade and swung out with a small gardening trowel, slashing the pirate's leg and causing him to howl. As the pirate bent over to inspect his wound, the gnome jumped as hard as his stubby legs allowed, thrusting the trowel at the pirate's chest. The point plunged through the man's colorful garb, finding his heart. He pitched forward, a glassy expression on his face. At the same time, the pirate with the dagger pressed forward, trying to slice at Fritzen's stomach. Still off balance, Fritzen was able to hold on to his borrowed blade, but the saber wound prevented him from using his right arm. Seizing the advantage, the remaining pirate jumped at the half-ogre. Fritzen rolled to the side, striking out with his good arm, bringing his sword up under the pirate's ribs until the tip of the blade passed out his back. The pirate fell, with a wounded Fritz practically on top of him. The last pirate, finally regaining consciousness, crawled toward his fallen comrade's saber. But Lendle hopped between the pirate and the weapon, holding him at bay with the small trowel.

"Dropitrightnow!" the gnome shouted.

The pirate looked at Lendle waving the bloody gardening tool, glanced at Mandracore, and pitched the dagger to the cave floor.

"Now, down on your belly," Lendle added, slowing his speech to make sure the pirate understood. When the pirate complied, the gnome sat on him and looked over at Fritzen. "You all right?"

The half-ogre groaned and pulled himself off the dead pirate. He looked at Lendle and grinned sheepishly. "So you can do more than cook," he jested. Then his eyes squinted in pain and he glanced at his shoulder.

Only the point of Maquesta's dagger and the certainty that she would use it kept Mandracore still. Salomdhi, on the other hand, slowly got to his feet and stood paralyzed by fear and horror, not even bothering to take the makeshift gag out of his mouth. His wide eyes took in the bodies and the blood.

"Lendle, tie up that pirate you're sitting on, and Salomdhi, too. Then help me with Mandracore," Maq directed. "Fritzen, how are you? Press down on that wound!" The half-ogre was sitting with his back propped against the wall, holding his bleeding shoulder.

"I'm doing what I can, Maquesta. I've lost some blood, but I'm better off than those two." He raised his arm in the direction of Mandracore's dead pirates. "I'll be able to make it back to the *Perechon*."

Maq slid down Mandracore and pulled his hands behind him, tying them with a piece of strong hemp. She jostled him to his knees, then shoved him forward. He turned his head to the side just in time so his nose didn't hit the stone floor.

"This gives me another score to settle with the Kar-Thons," he said bitterly. "I guess I'll be taking that account up with you from now on, now that Melas is out of the picture," Mandracore sneered.

"What do you know about my father?" Maq asked sharply. "What have you heard?"

"I have friends in Lacynos," the pirate replied. "I know Melas is living on a temporary stay, pending your return—and provided you're successful."

Maq frowned, troubled that the Reaver should know the purpose of the *Perechon*'s voyage. "Do your masters in Lacynos have anything to do with that treasure and weapons cache in there?" Maq asked, trying to puzzle out a connection.

"I didn't say masters, I said friends," the pirate answered harshly. "I have many interests, and in this instance my friends' interests and mine coincided in a way that is filling my purse," Mandracore added, enjoying Maq's discomfort.

"Well, my interests don't extend to solving riddles posed by vermin like you," Maq said, standing up. The pirates and Salomdhi were now all securely bound. Maq went to stand over the merchant, who was shaking and sweating and appeared to be going into shock.

"I've never seen anyone killed before," he whispered up at Maq.

She looked at him disdainfully. "I suspect your *honest* business dealings have set you on a path to witness many things you haven't seen before—and won't want to. Now, where's the key to Lendle's ankle charm?"

The merchant motioned his head toward his vest. In an inside pocket, Maq found the key. She removed the charm, a small disk of smooth gray stone embedded with white rings that continued to flash.

"Where did you get this?" she asked. Salomdhi nodded his head toward Mandracore, who smirked back at Maquesta. Knowing she would get no information from the pirate, Maq dropped the charm on the ground. "Maybe it will help someone find you."

"Let's go," she said, turning to Lendle.

Maq helped Fritzen up and supported him as they walked out of the cave.

"Till we meet again, Maquesta," Mandracore called out as she closed the hillside door.

As they walked through Salomdhi's house, Lendle

pulled a strip of linen off the dining room table and tied it around Fritzen's wound, trying to stanch the flow of blood. The trio could feel eyes watching them, but not one servant made an appearance or tried to stop them.

"You're a dangerous lady to be around," Fritz said jokingly to Maquesta as they reached the street.

"I thought you said you liked to live dangerously," she replied. Her tone was light, but her face showed concern. "We have to get back to the wharf and out to the *Perechon* as fast as we can. I have a feeling it won't be long before help arrives for those scum."

"I need to make one quick stop while we're at the wharf," Fritz said. "I've a pearl necklace in my pocket that will pay off the debt to my friends. Think of it as your comrade Mandracore buying your new sails."

Chapter 12
The Butcher

"A watcher charm—that is very old magic," Tailonna said thoughtfully.

Once the *Perechon* was sailing out of Sea Reach harbor—with new, crisp, white sails on the newly strengthened masts—Maquesta had asked the sea elf and Ilyatha to come to her cabin. She told them about what had transpired on the island, about Lendle's temporary servitude, the cache of treasure and weapons, Mandracore's appearance, and the charm.

"I am surprised that a simple merchant or even a pirate would know about such things as watcher charms, much less be able to put his hands on one," Tailonna continued.

"Well, Mandracore kept talking about the *friends* whose interests he was furthering. I wish I knew who they were," said Maq. She looked up from her thoughts to see that Lendle had slipped into the cabin. "How's Fritzen?" Maq asked the gnome.

Lendle had, once again, set up the armory as a temporary infirmary, with Fritzen as its sole patient. "He's stubborn, Maquesta Kar-Thon, and he keeps mumbling that being with you is very dangerous business. I am worried about him. He lost a great deal of blood, and he was still not fully recovered from the sea hag attack," Lendle replied, rubbing his chin in concern. "I am not certain what is necessary to treat him. I came to ask Tailonna and Ilyatha to consult with me on his care."

If the situation hadn't been so serious, Maquesta would have smiled at Lendle's phrasing. The gnome didn't like to admit to any gaps in his knowledge. And he wasn't one to ask for help.

"Tailonna, would you please take a look at Fritzen?" Maq asked reluctantly.

The Dimernesti nodded silently, and Maq suppressed a flash of irritation. Tailonna had already been of great help, and no doubt would be again before the voyage ended. But Maq found the sea elf maiden's remoteness annoying.

"We'll keep you posted on his condition," the gnome said. "Oh, one more thing, Maquesta Kar-Thon. Fritzen Dorgaard acquired pocketfuls of gold coins from the treasure cave. He had me divide them among the crew. Morale is much improved."

Maquesta grinned, pleased at Fritz's generosity. "Ilyatha, I'd like to have a word with you before you join them," she said unnecessarily. The shadow warrior had not made any move toward the door, having telepathically sensed Maq's desire before she stated it.

"Have you had any communication with Belwar since he left us the other day?" Maq asked once the other two had gone to the armory.

"No, I have not. Why do you ask?"

"See if you can contact him. If I know anything about Mandracore, he will try to follow us, and in Sea Reach he gave me cause to think he knew what our mission was," Maq said worriedly. "I know you, too, are anxious to return to Lacynos. Any interference from the Reaver could delay our return past the time . . . past the deadline Attat has set." Maquesta found she could not speak aloud words that referred to her father's possible death.

"How could the pirate know anything about what Attat has done?" Ilyatha asked, surprised.

"I don't know, but I intend to find out," Maq answered. "Mandracore referred to friends in Lacynos. The minotaur Koraf worked in the Horned Bay shipyards. I want to ask him what he has heard about the Reaver. I want your advice on how much I should tell him. Do you think I can trust Koraf? I made him my first mate because by doing so the crew would be forced to accept his presence. But could he be a spy Attat planted on the *Perechon*?" Maquesta realized she was asking the shadow warrior for his counsel as she once would have asked her father.

Ilyatha considered the question. "I sense a great anger in the minotaur, matched by an almost equal measure of gentleness," he replied finally. "His nature does not seem a duplicitous one. You have shown good judgment in your actions so far, Maquesta. Trust your own assessment. I believe you have his loyalty."

Maq smiled warmly at Ilyatha, grateful as much for his approval as for the advice.

* * * * *

Fritzen lay on a cot, pale and feverish, his eyes closed.

"Show me what medicinal supplies you have on

hand," Tailonna told Lendle, more a command than a request. But since the gnome himself had no sense of social niceties, he didn't take offense.

Lendle went to the corner where he had left his medicine case, a wooden box with a handle and a latch. However, instead of having a top that unlatched and flipped back, as most such cases would operate, this one opened on all four sides with spring catches. When Lendle pressed on one of the catches, intending to open the front panel only, all four sides fell away, leaving him holding the top and bottom of the case, which were connected at the corners by leather thongs. Three open shelves of herbs and potions were promptly revealed, and these immediately began spilling out onto the armory floor.

"This case I made makes it much easier to get at all my herbs," said Lendle as he hurriedly scooped up his supplies. "But this has never happened before. It always works correctly."

"Of course," said Tailonna, showing a rather rare flash of humor. She bent over to help him, murmuring the herbs' names as she replaced them in the case one by one.

"You have collected a very useful selection of medicines," Tailonna said. Lendle beamed at the compliment. "Let me examine Fritzen first, then we'll see if you have what he needs."

Tailonna leaned over the patient, and lightly touched the handsome half-ogre's chest. Fritzen's eyes fluttered open for an instant, held Tailonna's gaze, and then closed. She removed the bandage Lendle had applied and gently probed around the edges of Fritzen's wound. Despite her gentleness, the half-ogre cried out in pain.

Tailonna stood up. "The saber cut must have given the small amount of sea hag poison that was still in his blood the opportunity to grow stronger," she said, frowning.

"Will this happen every time Fritzen is injured?" asked Lendle.

"Just until his body has completely purged itself of the poison, but sea hag toxin is very potent. Many moons will cross the sky before that cleansing is complete. How did he receive the sea hag wound to begin with?" Tailonna inquired as she turned once again to the medicine case and began picking up various packets and vials. "I know of no survivors from sea hag encounters. My people stay away from waters where hags are reputed to dwell. We believe there is no need to present the vile creatures with victims."

Lendle told her briefly about the attack on the *Torado* during the race. "I thought Fritzen was injured on the coral when the hippocampi rescued him," he explained, "but that would not cause this infection. He was the only one of the *Torado*'s crew to make it to the *Perechon*."

"Ah, that explains the suffering I saw in his eyes just now, something that is more than bodily pain," Tailonna said. Lendle nodded. "This only survivor carries many wounds with him."

After considering the medicines before her for a moment more, Tailonna turned to the gnome. "There is something else that would help him, something I don't see here."

"Where can we get it?" Lendle asked. "I don't think Maquesta will permit a return to Sea Reach."

"It's not in Sea Reach, but a much greater distance away. Here, come with me," Tailonna said abruptly. "I may need some help getting off the ship."

Lendle followed Tailonna willingly, fascinated to see what she intended. The sea elf stepped through the armory door, out onto the main deck where she walked over to one of the side railings. Standing facing the sea, Tailonna took off the nets and seashells that held her lengthy hair. She handed these to the gnome, who eyed them with awe. He fingered the nets gingerly, remembering the magic they'd released during the imp attack.

Next, she closed her eyes and extended her arms out to her sides, holding her hands with the palms facing upward, thumb and middle finger touching. Tilting her head back, she chanted a few words that sounded vaguely musical. Standing behind her, Lendle watched as the outline of the sea elf maiden's body softened into a wispy haze of pale blue-green, then it seemed to dissolve into the surrounding air. After a minute, her entire body had taken on an amorphous quality, becoming almost translucent. Then it started shimmering and pulsing with energy, and the gnome felt goose bumps race up and down his arms. The very air seemed charged. Once the substance of Tailonna's body had separated into particles suspended in the sea air, that suspension collapsed in on itself, becoming a concentrated mass that spun gently just above the deck's surface and darkened to a deep blue, then turned earth brown. In another minute, that mass elongated and took on concrete form once more, as a sleek, silver-brown sea otter. The creature rose on its haunches and placed its front paws on the deck railing so that its muscular body was almost as tall as Lendle. The animal glanced out to sea and cocked its head inquisitively to the side. Then the otter glanced over its shoulder at the gnome, its eyes a shimmering blue-green that held Lendle spellbound. The otter chittered animatedly, nudged Lendle with its cold, wet nose, then looked out to sea again.

Lendle shook his head as if to clear it, then carefully set the hairnets and seashells on the polished deck. "OhyesIwillhelpyouTailonnatheotter," he gibbered. He lifted the otter's hindquarters, helping it slip over the side of the *Perechon*, into the waters below. Lendle watched with wide eyes as the animal rolled on its back and seemed to wave one of its forepaws at him. Then it turned on its stomach and swam off. Lendle gazed out over the gentle swells until the otter's small head was no longer visible. Then he looked around him on the main deck. Of the few sailors out tending to their duties, nobody else, it seemed, had seen Tailonna shapechange. Feeling privileged that the sea elf had shared something special with him, he bent over and scooped up her nets and shells. Then, jumping up and down with excitement, Lendle ran off to look for Maquesta.

* * * * *

Maq found the minotaur Koraf on the lower deck, checking and oiling the oarlocks. She stood by the foot of the stairs that led to the upper deck, waiting for him to notice her and considering exactly what she would say.

"Did you wish to speak with me?" Koraf asked, not looking up from his work.

"Yes, I need your help, Kof," Maq said. "Please, take a moment . . ."

The minotaur appreciated her honesty and, with the arrogance typical of his race, appreciated being asked for help. He put down his oil can and faced Maq.

She approached him and sat down on one of the rowing benches. She patted the bench next to her and, after a few moments of silence, the minotaur obliged, lowering his heavy frame onto the wood.

"Do you know a pirate named Mandracore?" she asked.

"Mandracore the Reaver? A half-ogre?"

Maq nodded.

"I know him all right." Koraf snorted. "He *wants* people to know him. He has a very high opinion of himself, that one does." The minotaur shook his bull-like head and ran his thumb around the outside of the oil can. "His ship, the *Butcher*, is often moored in Horned Bay. It's a good ship. Too good for the likes of him."

"Do you know what he does in Lacynos? Who he sees?" Maq asked eagerly.

Koraf snorted again and shrugged his shoulders. "I don't waste my time keeping track of braggart half-ogres. Why do you care?"

Maq related the essentials of her encounter with Mandracore on Sea Reach, including the fact that he bore a grudge against her father and seemed to have knowledge of their current voyage. Koraf thought a minute, absentmindedly fingering his waist sash. It was obvious he was uncomfortable talking about his experiences.

"Months ago, before I was imprisoned, I saw him down at the shipyard with Chot Es-Kalin. They were alone and had their heads together about something. I have no idea what," Koraf recalled. "But I thought it odd that Chot Es-Kalin, more wealthy and powerful even than Attat, would openly consort with someone like the Reaver. Some minotaurs believe that socializing with humans or other races lowers their station."

"But that was only once, months ago?" Maq pressed him.

"Yes, but I would have had no opportunity to see Chot since my imprisonment at Attat's. Chot and Attat are fierce rivals," Koraf pointed out. "Attat intends to surpass Chot in wealth and become the ruler of Lacynos. Attat might succeed if Chot is not careful. But Attat must be careful, too, of his tactics."

Maq nodded, remembering what Attat had said about the reason he wanted the morkoth for his menagerie. "The morkoth could help him," she said softly.

"On that count, Attat is deluded," Koraf volunteered.

"What do you mean?" asked Maq.

"Attat seeks to consolidate power by displaying his possessions. By capturing and dominating a collection of monsters, he thinks he is creating an impression, demonstrating his superiority," Koraf explained. "Chot seeks to consolidate power by using it. His method is more effective—at least for the time being."

"Then why does Chot care what Attat does? Why does the rivalry flow both ways?"

"Attat is like a thorn in Chot's side, an annoyance that by its constancy has taken on a greater significance," Koraf said. "He would like to humiliate Attat, and by humiliating him, destroy him. Where Chot could fail is if his attempts to humiliate Attat are unsuccessful. Then the humiliated one will be Chot, who could lose some of his influence."

Thinking about what he had said, Maq studied the minotaur before her. He displayed an acuity she didn't expect from members of his race. She was glad she had trusted him.

"I don't know how Mandracore figures into all of this, but I suspect he does, and that whether we want to or not, we're going to find out how," Maq said finally. "I expect him to come after us, and with Fritz down, we'll need everyone to stay extra alert."

Koraf grunted, turning back to his oil can and his self-appointed task.

* * * * *

By the next morning, the *Perechon* was approaching the east coast of Endscape and had started to turn north. It was making better time with new sails that didn't let the wind slip through all the patches and mends.

Tailonna still had not returned to the ship. From Lendle, Maq had heard a full account of the elf's shapechanging, and she wasn't pleased that Tailonna had left the ship without her permission. Perhaps she wouldn't be coming back. And without her, who could brew the potions that would let them breathe underwater? How could they capture the morkoth then?

Maquesta sought out the gnome and found him in the galley, brewing some tea. She had to duck her head when she entered, as Lendle had managed to string up his collection of pots, pans, and assorted utensils on a pulley system that looked even more complex than the previous design. Maquesta sighed and chose a route that would not take her near any knives and forks.

The gnome looked exhausted, having stayed up with Fritzen most of the night, catching a little sleep in a bedroll on the floor of the armory.

"How is he?" asked Maq, deciding not to scold him over Tailonna.

"The same," said Lendle in an unusually brief reply.

Maq, gripped by last-minute misgivings, hesitated before broaching the subject she had in mind to discuss with the gnome.

"Lendle, have you been able to make any progress in repairing your oar engine?"

The gnome's eyes lit up and his fatigue fell away. "Ilyatha and I managed to get most of the repairs done before we moored at Sea Reach. I still have a few adjustments to make before it's in working order, though. I'll see to it right away Maquesta Kar-Thon, if that is what you would like me to do."

Maq grimaced. Lendle and his adjustments. "When—and if—Tailonna returns, I would like her to take over Fritz's care, and for you to concentrate on getting the engine in working order," Maq said, fully aware that, as far as she knew, it had never yet been in working order. "We may need every trick we can muster to get back to Lacynos on time. The new sails are speeding us along, but still . . ." She paused and swallowed hard. "I want us to be ahead of schedule in case anything goes wrong. I don't want to jeopardize my father's life."

Lendle indignantly drew himself up. "My engine is no trick, Maquesta Kar-Thon. It is science, and it will help you get back to Lacynos with time to spare."

"Whatever it is, I think we'll need it," she said.

When Maquesta left the galley, Lendle was humming happily as he stirred his tea. She stopped briefly in the armory, where the half-ogre was resting. Standing by his side, she placed her hand on his forehead. His eyes were closed, his face pale and drawn. His skin was hot, indicating a high fever. She looked about for a wet rag, and finding one, placed it on his brow.

"I wish I could do something for you," she said quietly. "I feel as though this is all my fault."

"You could stay with me for a while," Fritz answered, still not opening his eyes.

Maquesta jumped; she'd thought he was asleep. Not bothering to reply, she pulled up a chair and sat next to him until his gentle snoring indicated he'd finally fallen into a healing slumber.

* * * * *

It was late afternoon when Hvel, on lookout duty, spotted the black sail on the horizon.

"Ship ahoy!"

The words brought Maq bolting from her cabin, where she had been devising a plan for capturing the morkoth. She ran up the steps to the upper aft deck where Koraf had the helm, and pulled out her spyglass. She didn't really need the instrument to see the *Butcher*'s black sail behind them, and to realize that it was gaining on them. Instead she focused on the men on deck to see how large his crew was. The pirates were all too numerous, and they were hard at work trimming the sails and working the rigging to get the best speed out of the ship.

Maquesta's lips drew into a thin, tight line. "He can't catch us. He just can't." Despite the *Perechon*'s improved speed, she was worried. The *Butcher* was a three-masted ship with more sails and the potential for faster movement if the wind was strong.

"Vartan!" she shouted. "Get up the mainmast and trim our sails a bit. Let's see if we can get a little more speed out of the *Perechon*."

"Yes, Captain!" he called back, then scampered up the rigging.

"Hvel, get belowdecks and summon Ilyatha. Tell him we need his flute of wind dancing!" Maquesta looked out over the rest of the crew. "Be alert. Mandracore's on our tail!"

Maquesta was concerned about using the magical instrument, as she didn't want to test the masts, and she disliked forcing the shadowperson on deck during bright sun. But she saw little alternative. Raising the spyglass to her eye again, she confirmed that the *Butcher*, with its many ebony sails, was gaining. Though easily visible through the tricks of perspective played by the open sea, the *Butcher* had in fact first appeared when it was far, far distant from the *Perechon*.

Ilyatha, clothed in a voluminous cloak, with his head hidden in the hood's shadows, padded on deck. *This must be important*, he communicated to Maquesta. *Being in this light pains me.*

Maq pointed at the *Butcher*, and Ilyatha read the rest of her thoughts. Nodding, the shadowperson took up a position near the bow and brought the flute to his lips. At first the tune was haunting, almost eerie. The notes floated out of the instrument and across the deck, billowing the sails. The ship pitched and rolled, but it picked up more speed. Then the tune changed, becoming brighter, faster, and in response the wind increased, blowing more briskly right around the ship and causing the masts to groan softly in protest.

Maquesta looked at the water. The waves within several yards of the *Perechon* were choppy and had growing swells. But the water farther out was calmer. There, the wind was not as strong, not touched by the enchanted notes from the flute of wind dancing. She felt something tickle at her mind and realized Ilyatha was speaking to her.

The Butcher *is too far away for me to slow the winds about its sails,* he communicated. *And I can use this flute but a few more minutes before it must build up its magic again.*

I understand, Maquesta concentrated, satisfied that Ilyatha had picked up her thoughts. She remembered that during the race the flute was not used long on the *Katos*—just at the most opportune time. And it seemed Ilyatha had used it well now, to pull the *Perechon* far enough ahead so that the *Butcher* looked like a black dot on the water. The magic temporarily exhausted, Ilyatha returned belowdecks, communicating to Maquesta that the flute could be used again when evening approached.

Through the long hours of the afternoon, the *Butcher* steadily closed the gap, its numerous sails taking advantage of an increasingly strong wind. At one point, Maq went to the armory. She called Lendle to the doorway and handed him a belaying pin, a dagger, and a short sword.

"If Mandracore and his crew board us, make sure Fritzen has a weapon in his hand. I don't want him to be defenseless," she told the gnome in a low voice. "Mandracore will have a grudge against you, and against Fritz as well. You each killed one of his men."

It was late afternoon, and Ilyatha told Maquesta the flute had not yet regained enough magical energies.

"Give it an hour or two more," he said. Maq knew they might not have that time to spare. Watching Mandracore's ship approach, Maq's blood started to boil. All thoughts of outrunning the *Butcher* left her. If Mandracore wanted a fight, she would give him a fight he would not likely forget.

"Everybody!" Maq had climbed up to stand near the helm. She addressed her crew.

"I think you all know the *Butcher* and her captain, Mandracore the Reaver." The sailors gathered below her muttered oaths by way of assent. "Well, it looks like he wants something from us. Are we going to give it to him?" Maquesta yelled.

"No!" several sailors shouted in unison, their fists toward the sky.

"If he wants his ship stuffed down his throat, then I think he'll get what he wants from us!" shouted Hvel from the back of the group. Everyone cheered.

"Prepare your weapons, then," Maq ordered. "If we can't outrun him, we'll give him a fight he won't forget."

* * * * *

Just for the pleasure of frustrating Mandracore, Maquesta tacked and otherwise maneuvered the *Perechon* to keep it out of the Reaver's reach for a while longer. Tired of being the mouse in that cat-and-mouse game, she knew to fight him—which was what she wanted—would risk the *Perechon*, her crew's lives, and her father. But Mandracore's ship kept gaining, and when the afternoon sun hung low in the sky Maquesta set a straight course and waited for the *Butcher* to pull alongside.

The first grappling hook thrown caught the *Perechon* amidships. Three other lines soon followed. As the *Butcher* and the *Perechon* floated side by side in a forced misalliance, Maq ordered Hvel and Rawl, who were standing by the main ballista, to start firing. Round missiles shot by the crossbowlike weapon began pummeling the *Butcher*'s sailors as they attempted to swing ladders across the gap between the two ships and board.

Noticing that the minotaur Koraf stood at the end of one of the ladders, waiting to engage the first pirate from the *Butcher* who attempted to set foot on the *Perechon*, Maq called out to him.

"Kof! Kof!" When she got his attention, Maquesta made a shoving motion with her arms. The minotaur nodded. Despite the fact that three of the *Butcher*'s crew had mounted the ladder and were attempting to cross over, the minotaur easily lifted his end, shoved it back toward the *Butcher*, then yanked it down so the ladder and its passengers tumbled into the sea. Maq mimed her approval.

Soon, however, in spite of other such tactics and the ballista, a dozen pirates from the *Butcher* had boarded the *Perechon* and were engaging Maq's crew in fierce combat. And more were coming. Ordering Vartan to remain at the helm, Maq jumped into the fray, drawing her short sword and shouting curses at Mandracore, who was nowhere to be seen. Swordplay had been an early game of hers. She'd played it often, wooden sticks standing in for weapons, with Lendle, Averon, and her father. Unlike many mariners, rather than a curved saber she preferred a straight-bladed sword. She wielded it now to disarm a pirate who had pinned Rawl against the steps leading to the upper aft deck. Rawl picked up his own sword and finished the job.

Maq scanned the deck, trying to spot Mandracore's bandanna, but she didn't see it anywhere. Just as she was turning to check on Vartan at the helm, she felt a stinging around her ankles and was whipped off her feet. Lying on her back, momentarily breathless, Maq looked up to see a hulking blue-skinned ogre from the

Butcher, holding a whip. He yanked on it, tightening its coils around her ankles. Convinced she was held securely, the beast straddled her, limiting her ability to roll away from an attack, and drew his sword. Maq grasped the hilt of her own weapon and tensed, preparing to evade the ogre's blow and strike back.

But before she could act, two massive arms covered with brown fur circled the ogre's upper arms and chest, applying a stunning pressure that caused the monster to drop its sword and whip. Maq quickly rolled away and began pulling the whip off her legs. Holding the ogre from behind, Koraf lifted the creature up even higher and slammed him to the deck. The wind knocked out of him, the beast staggered forward, but was too slow. Koraf growled and drew his dagger, grabbed the ogre by the hair, and slit his throat.

"Maquesta! Maquesta!"

Maq jumped out to see where the urgent summons was coming from. Koraf, wiping the blade of his dagger on his thigh, pointed to the bow with his other hand. Looking in that direction, Maq soon located Hvel, jumping up and down near the armory door, waving his arms wildly.

"Kof, come with me!" she commanded. The two of them fought their way forward, killing three of the *Butcher*'s sailors in the process.

When they reached Hvel at the door to the armory, Maq saw why she hadn't spotted the Reaver earlier. Lendle lay in a far corner of the room, unconscious, the color drained from his ruddy brown face. Blood ran from a nasty gash on his head and stained the gnome's white hair red. In front of him, Mandracore and three of his ogres stood around the head of Fritzen's cot, swords and daggers drawn. Fritzen smiled weakly at Maq as she and Koraf came to the door. The pirate captain held the belaying pin and the dagger Maq had given Lendle. He used the belaying pin now to viciously prod the half-ogre's injured shoulder. Fritzen clenched his teeth, refusing to cry out.

"I'm sorry, Maq," said Hvel, wringing his hands. "He said if I didn't call you, or if I tried to call anyone else, he'd slit Fritzen's throat."

"It's all right, Hvel," Maq said, patting the sailor's shoulder. "The Reaver likes to stack the odds so he never has to fight an honest battle."

A shadow of anger crossed the pirate's face, but he controlled it. "Tell your crew to stop fighting, Maquesta." Mandracore ordered.

"Why should I do that?" asked Maq innocently. "From the looks of things, we're winning."

"If you don't order them to throw down their weapons, I'll kill your sick friend here and slit the gnome's throat wide open. Then I'll come for you," the pirate snarled.

"I think you'll do that anyway," Maq said with a composure she didn't truly feel. Desperately, she cast about for a way out of this situation. With a glimmer of hope, Maq thought she saw Lendle, who lay on the floor behind Mandracore, open his eyes. Then she realized that even if the gnome regained consciousness, in his injured condition he could do little against Mandracore and the three others.

Because Mandracore knew Maquesta had spoken the truth, he made no response. The muscles in Maquesta's legs tightened, and she prepared to leap at Mandracore if any of them made a move to harm Fritz. Better to die fighting than sniveling for mercy at the hands of vile creatures such as these, she vowed. Only the thought that her death would inevitably result in her father's death caused Maq a pang of regret.

Lendle's eyes fluttered again and this time stayed open. Maq forced herself not to look directly at him, not wanting to give him away. Mandracore had just turned to one of his ogres when the noise of fighting on the deck outside the armory died away. The momentary silence ended with an explosive crack, like a clap of thunder—only there was no storm outside. Everyone in the armory stood frozen in their places.

"Captain Mandracore! Captain Mandracore!" First one, then a half dozen voices took up the call. The summons sounded faintly, yet persistently, in the armory. Cursing, Mandracore took another jab with the belaying pin at Fritzen's wound, then ordered one of the ogres to cover his back while he went to see what had happened.

"The rest of you," he barked to his ogre cronies, "stay here. You! Put your knife to the half-ogre's throat. You—watch the gnome! If any of 'em moves, kill the half-ogre first. He killed my first mate!"

Maquesta heard Kof growl softly beside her. She hoped the minotaur would restrain his temper until they were presented with a good opening—one that wouldn't risk Fritz's and Lendle's lives.

Out on the deck, only scattered pairs still fought. The rest of the pirates and sailors stood transfixed, staring at the *Butcher*, where chaos had erupted. Belwar hovered above the pirate ship in a halo of light that was caused by the rays of the setting sun reflecting warmly off his golden scales. Below him, the *Butcher*'s mainmast lay split in half, cracked by a metal ball the size of a boulder that had been dropped on top of it by the ki-rin. As the ball crashed through the main deck, fires had erupted, engulfing the ship in flames and smoke. Waves of heat from the flames swept over the *Perechon*. The smell of burning wood and canvas sails permeated the air. Pirates who had remained on the *Butcher* were jumping overboard or attempting to board the *Perechon*.

In the light cast by the flames, Maquesta, positioned

athwart the doorway to the armory, observed Ilyatha climb the forward steps from the lower deck, carrying his shadowstaff. The firelight glinted off additional weapons she hadn't seen before, attached to a girdle he now wore. Maq's eyes met his. Clearing her mind of extraneous thoughts, she concentrated on communicating essential information. *The half-ogre with the bandanna and earring is Mandracore.* Maq stared at the pirate captain and was relieved when she saw Ilyatha follow her gaze. *One of his ogre warriors is in the armory, poised over Fritzen's cot. Lendle is wounded but alert and is being guarded by another ogre.*

I will take care of Mandracore first, Ilyatha returned.

With new pirates coming over from the *Butcher*, the fighting on the *Perechon*'s main deck had resumed—this time more fiercely than before. Maq saw Hvel and Vartan each trying to loosen one of the grappling hooks to allow the *Perechon* to float free of the burning *Butcher*. But because they continually had to fend off attacking pirates, neither was making much progress.

Clearly furious at the fate of his ship, Mandracore had just pivoted on his heel to return to the armory to mete out a suitable punishment to Maquesta when Ilyatha attacked. Unobtrusive with his dark fur in the dusky light, the shadow warrior glided forward silently and with a swift motion drove his hooked staff deep into Mandracore's body. The pirate screamed, more in rage than in pain, and bent over in the middle, grasping at the staff, his expression incredulous. Just as swiftly as he had thrust the staff, Ilyatha twisted it, causing another flash of disbelief to cross Mandracore's face. The shadow warrior pulled the staff free, and Mandracore fell to his knees, then dropped face forward onto the deck. Ilyatha knelt and grabbed Mandracore's cloak, using it to wipe the blood off the staff.

The dim-witted ogre guard next to the pirate captain

had only just realized something was amiss as Mandracore began to crumple. With a blood-curdling yell, he lunged at Ilyatha, who was cleaning his staff. The shadow warrior dropped Mandracore's cloak and pivoted. He brought the clean staff up to block the new attacker, and the ogre's sword harmlessly bounced off the wood. Rising to his feet, Ilyatha made another strong thrust forward with the staff, driving the sharp end into the ogre's belly. The ogre stood only because Ilyatha held the staff, but when the shadow person tugged the weapon free, the ogre crumpled to join his captain. Again, Ilyatha cleaned off his weapon and looked about the deck for a foe. Seeing none within his immediate reach, Ilyatha ran toward the armory.

Maquesta saw a pirate rise up from behind a barrel of water and leap after Ilyatha. About to call a warning, she realized she didn't have to, as her thoughts were enough. Ilyatha pulled a cord with a sharp, hooked blade at one end and a weighted ring at the other from his girdle, spun around, and threw it expertly at the attacking pirate. The cord whipped around the unfortunate sailor's neck, driving the hook into his throat. The shadow warrior resumed his movement toward the armory, and Maq glanced inside. Not knowing what was happening outside the cabin, the remaining ogres had started to look nervous and a little confused. Out of the corner of her eye, Maquesta saw that Lendle was now fully alert, though he was feigning unconsciousness. When the ogre guarding him glanced away, Lendle snapped his eyes open and spotted his dagger, which lay on the floor between him and his guard—just out of reach. Whatever happened now had to happen quickly and silently, Maq knew, or there was a good chance the other ogre would simply bring the sword he was holding down across Fritzen's throat. The half-ogre was unaware of his peril, having lost consciousness again. Maquesta nervously chewed her bottom lip. She didn't want to lose Fritz. Not this way. Not *any* way.

Call out Mandracore's name, then step away from the door, Maq heard Ilyatha think. The minotaur, Koraf, standing next to her, must have heard a similar message, as she saw him blink and his brows furrow. Not yet completely comfortable with the shadow warrior's method of communication, Koraf started slightly, then glanced down at Maq, who nodded almost imperceptibly.

"Mandracore!" Maq called. She stepped outside with Koraf, leaving the doorway clear. In the same instant, Lendle slid forward along the floor and grabbed his dagger, folding his stubby fingers about the worn pommel. He prepared to leap up to protect Fritzen or to attack the ogre who was inadequately guarding him. The gnome's ogre guard offered invaluable assistance to their scheme by forgetting his orders. Seeing the doorway was clear, he plunged forward, apparently assuming Maq and the minotaur had joined in some new attack on Mandracore. The ogre standing over Fritzen barked a command that served to slow the running guard, who had just realized he shouldn't have left his post. Ilyatha appeared, seemingly out of nowhere, planting himself in front of the guard and using his shadowstaff, thrusting its wooden end at the ogre's chest, thumping him soundly and causing him to fall backward.

The ogre near Fritzen growled and raised his sword, preparing to bring it down on the half-ogre's throat. Lendle saw the attack coming and shot forward over the floor, stabbing the ogre in the back of the thigh and causing the brute to whirl and face him. The ogre laughed when he saw his tiny assailant. That was his undoing. The gnome moved in again, thrusting upward and sending his dagger deep into the pirate's belly.

Furious and in pain, the ogre reached down and grasped Lendle's shoulders, shaking the gnome so hard he dropped the dagger. Bringing the gnome up even with his eyes, the ogre growled menacingly and opened his mouth, angling Lendle so the gnome's short neck was even with the pirate's teeth.

"No!" Maq barked as she slipped back inside the armory.

Her shout momentarily drew the attention of the ogre, giving Lendle another opening. The gnome kicked forward with both legs, his feet smashing in the front teeth of the pirate. The ogre howled and dropped his small assailant, and Lendle landed crouched, but on his feet.

Maquesta drew her sword and charged, meeting and parrying the swing of the ogre's blade. She brought her weapon back and swung forward, but as she stepped into the swing, she slipped on the growing pool of ogre blood on the floor and ended up on her rump.

The ogre grinned, raised his sword above his head, and started to bring it down on Maquesta. She was quicker, though, and jabbed her short sword upward, piercing his abdomen and running him through. She rolled to the side, avoiding his falling form, and felt the floor shake when he landed.

Brushing off her hands, she rolled the pirate over and extracted her weapon. "Lendle, are you all right,?" she asked. The gnome still stood, a little wobbly from the drop. He nodded yes and picked up his dagger. Blood no longer flowed from his head wound, but his face was drained of color.

"OfcourseIamallright," Lendle protested, taking one step forward and collapsing to the floor in a dead faint next to Fritzen's cot.

"Kof. Stay here with Lendle and Fritzen!" Maq ordered. She knew it wouldn't be the minotaur's choice of assignments, but she hoped he would realize there were few others she would trust with the job of defending her friends. Koraf frowned, but positioned himself outside the armory door, weapons drawn.

Back on deck, an exhausted Hvel and Vartan had succeeded in loosening all the grappling hooks. Maquesta watched them toss the hooks and line back toward Mandracore's ship. The *Perechon* now floated free of the *Butcher*, which at this point was all but consumed by roaring flames, a brilliant orange torch adrift on the sea. Belwar wheeled and soared above the *Perechon*, using his horn and his hooves to help pick off those pirates who were still fighting. Not that many were. Demoralized by the sight of their burning ship and the spreading word of Mandracore's fall, most of the *Butcher*'s pirates who remained on board the *Perechon* stood together in stunned silence, their hands away from their swords and belaying pins. While they hadn't turned over their weapons, they made no attempt to use them. Their surrender was clear.

A number of pirates milled about in the water near their burning ship. Maq saw that someone had managed to lower the *Butcher*'s three longboats into the sea. Several sailors had already pulled themselves into the boats.

The *Butcher* had suffered heavy losses. With Mandracore injured, possibly dying, Maq didn't feel compelled to eradicate the crew at the cost of more injuries to her sailors.

"As captain of the *Perechon*, I declare victory!" Maq shouted. "Put down your arms. Anyone from the *Butcher* who wishes may join their comrades in the water. Those who don't will be thrown in our brig—to be turned over to the proper authorities when we reach port. This is a shipping lane, and you can take your chances at being picked up. Otherwise you're welcome to the hospitality of the next port's jail."

"And maybe the possibility of a noose!" Vartan howled.

The *Perechon* sailors cheered.

At that, every pirate who could manage to stay afloat went over the deck railing into the sea. Two ogres picked up the limp form of Mandracore, who was breathing shallowly, and they jumped into the water with their captain.

"Why'd you let them take Mandracore?" Hvel asked Maquesta. "You should have let us finish him off."

"I refuse to sink to his level, and if I put him in our brig, he'd die and stink the place up," she answered coldly. "And I don't want Lendle taking time to mend someone I want to see dead. Let the elements claim him. It's a more fitting end for him, anyway."

"And if the ogres get hungry . . ." Hvel laughed. "It will be something other than the sea claiming his remains."

Vartan organized a crew to throw the dead sailors from the *Butcher* into the water. Most were ogres, and required two or three men to pick up one body. No one objected to the grisly task; it was evident they wanted the bodies gone as quickly as possible. Vartan, looking over the *Perechon*'s crew, was pleased to tell his captain there were no fatalities—yet—though there were enough injuries to keep Lendle and Ilyatha busy for many days.

To everyone's amazement, once the *Perechon*'s decks were clear of pirates, the flames engulfing the *Butcher* vanished. Not even a whiff of smoke lingered in the air. Maq couldn't believe her eyes. The *Butcher* was still disabled with a broken mast, but it appeared not even to be singed. Belwar, hovering above the *Perechon*'s deck, erupted in deep, mellifluous laughter at the gaping faces below who looked up from the longboats.

"The fire was just an illusion created by Belwar," said Ilyatha, who had joined Maq.

"An illusion? How could that be?" she demanded. "I felt the heat. I smelled the smoke."

"A ki-rin's magic is very powerful," Ilyatha said simply.

Maq still stared at the *Butcher*. "But the mast, the broken mast is real?" she asked.

"Yes, the split mast is real, but the boulder that broke it was created by Belwar," Ilyatha advised her. "See, the boulder, too, has disappeared."

The hole in the *Butcher*'s deck created by the large metal boulder was still visible, but the boulder itself was not. "When the ki-rin creates something as hard as metal, it does not last long," the shadow warrior explained.

Maq sighed, turning to survey her ship. "Well, I wish he could create something soft and edible that would last," she said. "Lendle's in no condition to cook, we have a long night ahead of us, and I'm starving."

"Oh, but he can," said Ilyatha delightedly and called out to the ki-rin, repeating Maquesta's request.

Thus did an evening that began in rather desperate straits end pleasantly for the *Perechon*'s captain and crew, with a sumptuous supper of roast joint, bread pudding, and mushrooms for Ilyatha.

Maquesta, thinking about the meager provisions she had been so intent on bringing back from Sea Reach, looked at the banquet spread out before them and laughed aloud with joy. If only Father were here to see this, she thought.

If only.

Chapter 13
Awakenings

After snatching only a couple hours of sleep, Maquesta rose before dawn the next day to patrol her ship. She grimaced when she saw the six bodies covered by a tarp, the wounded sailors who had not pulled through during the night. They occupied a section of the main deck near the stern, and she planned to give a brief service for them shortly after full light. She sighed sadly. One of them was the young sailor who had gotten seasick during the race. She made a mental note to search his belongings and discover where his parents lived. They deserved a letter at least.

She bowed her head, thinking that each of the men had deserved better than to die at the hands of Mandracore's pirates. Then she cursed herself. These six men were dead because of her desire to help one man—her father. Had she traded their lives for his? And would Lendle and Fritzen trade their lives, too? What price was she willing to pay?

But to turn back now would mean the dead had sacrificed themselves for nothing, she thought. Maq mulled the possibilities over in her troubled mind as she walked toward the armory.

Aside from the personal loss Maquesta felt, losing the six sailors meant the *Perechon* would be dangerously undermanned for the rest of the voyage. Though not as undermanned as the *Butcher*, she thought with some satisfaction. Many others among the *Perechon*'s crew had suffered injuries in the fight, but those were relatively minor wounds—cuts and bruises mostly. Those sailors were resting in their hammocks, and Ilyatha, who had briefly tended to them, said they would be up and about in time for their duties later today.

The shadowperson also had tended to Lendle. The gnome's wound must have been grievous, for Ilyatha had hovered over him for hours last night. Still, the mysterious telepath declined to tell Maq just *how* serious—had in fact outright refused to tell Maq, despite her repeated questions. At one point in the evening, he went so far as to order Maquesta out of the makeshift infirmary.

Maquesta paused outside the armory door. She was going to get some answers this morning from Ilyatha. The telepath was going to tell her exactly how Lendle and Fritzen were faring. Taking a deep breath, she threw open the door and rushed in, a lecture already prepared that would get her some information.

"I was busy taking care of your friends last night," Ilyatha said, looking up and sensing her thoughts. "I didn't want to take the time to talk, to explain things, to make you worry about Lendle and Fritzen perhaps more than you should. You needed some sleep. Besides, I wanted time to pass, to see if they might improve on their own."

And . . . ? Maquesta thought, unable to put voice to her fears.

"And Lendle has shown some improvement, though not much. At least he is breathing regularly. He might be up and around in a day or two, but . . ." The shadowperson's voice trailed off, and he pointed at the gnome. "You must realize that injuries to the head are hard to predict. He could be unconscious for several days, a few weeks perhaps. Maybe longer. And he might not be himself for a while. The head is often more difficult to heal than the rest of the body."

Maquesta's eyes filled as she looked at the gnome, but she steadfastly fought back the tears. "He *will* be all right? Won't he? Tell me he will be all right."

Ilyatha's reply was soft. "My mind cannot touch his. I cannot sense his thoughts. That is what troubles me. I cannot tell you that he will be all right, simply because I do not know."

Maquesta bit her lip to keep from crying. Captains don't cry, she told herself. Captains aren't weak. "Lendle has to get well, or we will all starve," she said, trying to sound stoic about the gnome's condition. "Hvel and Vartan said they would try their hand at Lendle's eel stew—minus the potatoes. But they're lousy cooks." She stared at Ilyatha and tried to blank her mind. Maq was thinking that she was too young to captain the *Perechon*, that she couldn't handle life and death matters when they involved people she truly cared about, that she wished her father were here, that she wished Fritz and Lendle would be all right, that she wished she were stronger.

The shadowperson cast Maq a concerned but tired look. He did not respond to her troubled and private thoughts, but instead glided to a chair next to the gnome. He dropped to the thin cushion, stretched, and yawned.

When Maq asked about Fritz, Ilyatha just shook his head. "I am not familiar with sea hag venom, or many other aquatic toxins for that matter," he said sadly. "He is fighting for his life, but I fear he could be waging a losing battle. He worsened during the night. See how pale he is? The poison in his blood is strong."

"Can you sense his thoughts?" Maq asked out of curiosity.

The telepath nodded. "He dreams about his fallen comrades from the *Torado*—when he is not thinking about you."

Maquesta paced about the armory, looking at Lendle, her long-time friend, and at Fritzen Dorgaard, for whom she had strange and persistent feelings.

Propped up in the chair, the shadow warrior dozed along with his patients. Fritzen and Lendle lay on their backs, both of them breathing shallowly. Maq placed a hand on each forehead; they were hot. Her brow furrowed, and knowing that no one was awake to see her, she finally let the tears come.

Occupied with such bleak thoughts, Maq did not at first hear her name being called. When she did and left the armory to find the source of the voice, she could not see who was calling. The deck was empty.

"Maquesta," the voice continued. "Maquesta!"

Wiping the tears from her face, Maq finally glanced over the side railing. Swimming in the water below, her long hair floating away from her face like a fan, was Tailonna. The sea elf waved and told Maquesta to throw over the rope ladder used to board the longboat. Complying, Maq vacillated between relief at Tailonna's return and irritation at her lengthy absence.

The sea elf quickly climbed the ladder; once above the water the weight of the bulging sea-frond bags she carried strained at her shoulders. Maq made no move to help, but once over the railing, the elf handed her two large bags. Tailonna kept hold of the remaining two smaller ones.

"Carry those to the armory for me, Maquesta," the elf said as she shook herself, the seawater spraying all over—much of it on Maq. "I've brought ocean herbs to cure Fritzen." With that, Tailonna strode toward the armory door, not bothering to see if Maquesta was following.

Maq glanced at the retreating form of the elf and at the sea frond bags dripping water on her deck. Seething with anger over being ordered around, she opened her mouth to offer Tailonna a vicious retort, but thought better of it. The sea elf was going to help Fritzen. The retorts could come after the medicine was administered.

"Lendle!" Tailonna cried in surprise the moment she stepped inside the makeshift infirmary. "What happened to you?"

Ilyatha awoke at the sound of her voice and proceeded to explain to the sea elf all that had transpired while she was gone. Flustered and upset, the elf glided to an empty bench, knelt before it, and started unwrapping the bags, taking out various pieces of kelp, conch shells full of algae, stubby strands of sea grass, unusual-looking oysters, clumps of seaweed, bulbous roots, a six-legged starfish, and more. She placed each item carefully on the bench, making sure nothing touched anything else. "Maquesta, I need my other bags. Over here, and hurry. I must act quickly while my ingredients are still wet and fresh."

Maq dropped the bags at the sea elf's side, then went to stand next to Fritz, her gaze drifting between the half-ogre, Lendle, and Tailonna.

The sea elf opened the larger bags and pulled out fist-sized pieces of rock with tiny, colorful plants growing out of them. Next, she took one of the smaller, empty frond bags, placed her hand inside it to fashion a mitten, then reached inside the larger bags and brought out sea urchins, their sharp, spiny ridges lying limp in the air.

"I need a knife and a bowl," Tailonna continued. "And get me two cups. One each for Lendle and Fritzen. I think I have sufficient material to mix up enough potions to help both of them."

Ilyatha made no move to assist the sea elf, so Maq, huffing with resignation, whirled on her heels. "I'll get them out of the galley."

When she returned—her arms filled with several small bowls, four cups, three knives, a large steel spoon, and a wooden cutting board—Tailonna looked up, offered a slight smile, and indicated where Maq should set the materials.

"I didn't need that much," the sea elf said.

"That's all right," Maquesta replied. "I didn't want to make a second trip." Intrigued at what the sea elf was mixing, Maq pulled a chair next to Ilyatha and sat down to watch. She made no move to hide the animosity she felt toward the haughty Tailonna, and she briefly wondered if the shadowperson felt the same.

The elf used a frond to hold the spines of one of the urchins down, then she brought the knife through the little creature, cutting apart its brittle shell with a sickening cracking sound. Carefully holding the halves over a bowl, she waited until all the liquid—Maq suspected it was the equivalent of blood in a human—ran out. Tailonna did the same with two of the other urchins, then proceeded to mix the bulbous roots in with the liquid. She mumbled a few words Maquesta couldn't understand and waggled her fingers over the bowl. Apparently satisfied with her concoction, Tailonna rose, padded over to Lendle, and opened the gnome's mouth. Putting one hand behind his stubby neck, she tilted his head and poured the mixture down his throat. The gnome involuntarily swallowed most of it, but a good bit ran out of his mouth and down his chin.

"Clean him off, while I work on a poultice for Fritzen," Tailonna directed Maquesta.

Maq gritted her teeth and pushed off from her chair. Finding a small towel, she carefully wiped the thick, smelly liquid off the gnome's face, then strode to the elf. "What did you give him? And just what will it do?"

Tailonna was busy cutting up pieces of seaweed, soaking them in urchin blood. It was obvious she was going to use all the utensils Maq brought her. "A potion my father taught me to make," she said simply. "It has incredibly strong curative powers. There's a bit of magic about it." The sea elf reached past Maq and selected a couple of the odd-shaped oysters. Prying one open, she pulled out the meat and added it to her mixture, then stirred in some algae. "I'll need a cloth."

Fuming, Maq stomped to a cabinet. Finding no cloths or towels, and realizing the towel she had used on Lendle was the only one in the armory, she took off the sash from around her waist and passed it to the sea elf. "Will this do?"

"I suppose," the elf answered, taking it from her and soaking it in the pungent liquid. Rising, she glided to the half-ogre, sat at his side, and proceeded to wrap the sash around his arm and shoulder. "This will draw out the sea hag poison," she explained. "It should work rather quickly, especially since he has merrow blood in his veins. It is odd that though he is a half-ogre, he looks so human and is so handsome. Merrows are typically an ugly lot. Fritzen was fortunate he inherited none of the merrows' facial features, only their size and strength."

"Does this poultice have a touch of magic, too?" Maquesta asked curtly.

"Of course." The elf went back to her bench and

resumed her work.

"Now what are you doing?" Maquesta's tone was demanding, her impatience coming to the fore.

"I want to make an additional healing potion for Fritzen, and I intend to create a stimulant for Lendle. I suppose while I am at it, I should make as many healing potions as possible. You do seem to need them around here." The sea elf turned away from the bench, and her blue-green eyes caught Maq's gaze. "I do know what I am doing, Maquesta. My skills are considerable, and my potions will save them. But I could use some help . . . if you don't mind."

Ilyatha, whether sensing Maquesta's irritation or genuinely wanting to aid the sea elf, rose from his chair and moved to the bench. "Let me," he offered. "Maquesta has many other things to do on this ship, and many other pressing concerns."

"I have dead to bury," Maq said. Turning, she left the armory, fervently praying that Tailonna's skills and mixtures would be enough to help two people she cared deeply about.

* * * * *

Dawn came to the sea, the sun rising and coloring the water and tinting the sky a rosy pink. With it came sailors to the deck of the *Perechon*. Koraf took the wheel, and Vartan and Hvel busied themselves with trimming the sails. When enough of the men were gathered, Maquesta walked over to the bodies and pulled the tarp back from their faces. The crew gathered around.

She was nervous, but she tried not to show it. She'd watched her father give final words over sailors before, though never this many bodies at the same time. Now the task was hers.

Facing the rising sun, she ran her fingers absently through her curls, composed herself, then turned to face her crew. She slowly recited the names of the dead men. "These sailors gave their lives for yours, for the *Perechon*, and for the hope of returning Melas to us. They paid the highest price a sailor could, and we stand here honoring them for their acts of courage." Her voice was strong, and she noticed all eyes were on her. "May Habbakuk, god of the sea and of eternal life beyond the world, watch over them as their spirits embark on a new journey. Now we give our friends and comrades to the water. Let the sea embrace those who loved her dearly."

Koraf blew into a steel whistle, low then high, sharp tunes signaling the end of the brief service. Maquesta padded away from the rails, and the crew set about the business of sending their dead comrades overboard. She heard the splashes behind her as she walked toward her cabin, intent on putting the final touches on her plan to capture the morkoth, and flinched at the finality of the sound.

* * * * *

An hour later a persistent rapping at the door roused Maquesta from her notes. Before she could invite the person inside, the door opened wide, and Tailonna strode in. Her hair was once again artfully wrapped about her head with the small magical nets and decorative seashells in place.

"Where were you?" Maq sputtered. "We needed you."

"I was in the armory, you know that. I was tending to Fritzen and Lendle. I saved them."

"That's not what I mean," Maquesta continued, fuming. "Where did you disappear to for better than a day?

You didn't even ask my permission to leave."

"I don't need anyone's permission—" Tailonna began.

"No?" Maq pressed. "I'm the captain of the *Perechon*, a fact you seem to constantly overlook. Captains give the orders on their ships. It's that simple. And while you're on my ship, you're part of my crew. You follow my orders. Understand?"

Tailonna drew herself up to her full height and regarded Maq coolly. "I was obtaining the necessary herbs to help Fritzen. Fortunately, they are also helping Lendle."

"Where did you have to go for them?" Maq snapped. "Back to Lacynos? If you don't want to be a part of this, Tailonna, you're free to go. Though I would appreciate it if you first made us those potions that will let us breathe water." Maq rose. Hands on her hips, chin raised aggressively, she confronted the sea elf. "I don't think I've ever understood why you agreed to help in the first place. But if you stay with us, remember that you're under my command, and you don't leave again unless you've discussed it with me first!"

The sea elf's eyes darkened, and she returned Maquesta's icy stare. "I am going back to the armory. There, my talents are appreciated. When you can pull yourself away from your plans, feel free to visit us—but only briefly. My patients need rest and quiet." Like a dancer, the sea elf pivoted on the balls of her bare feet and glided out of the cabin.

It was clear to Maquesta that Tailonna didn't enjoy being reprimanded. "Well, I don't like being treated with disrespect," Maq muttered to herself. She glanced at her papers and decided to work on her plans only a little while longer and then go check on her friends. She wanted to see if Tailonna's magical healing could work the wonders the elf claimed.

* * * * *

Tailonna stormed into the armory, angry about being spoken to by Maquesta in such a rude manner.

"Well hello, fair lady," Fritzen offered as a greeting. The half-ogre was sitting up on his cot, his legs crossed under him and a blanket wrapped around his broad shoulders. "I understand from Ilyatha that I have you to thank for my improved state of health."

Tailonna's expression softened at seeing Fritzen. A hint of a blush crept to her face, and she sneaked a glance at the telepath. Ilyatha was hovering over Lendle, seemingly oblivious to her. Smiling, Tailonna glided toward the half-ogre and sat next to him. The sea elf was angry at Maquesta, and a little angry at herself as well, for being attracted to this surface dweller whom she considered a half-breed.

"You're strong," she stated. "I did not think my healing poultice would work so quickly."

"I'm not one to stay down long," he replied. "Bed rest is boring, and I've always believed one mends better by being up and moving around."

"Be careful not to overdo it," she admonished. "The sea hag toxin will be in your blood for quite some time, and any further injuries you suffer could give it a chance to take hold again." Tailonna brought her hand up to his forehead. "You're still a little warm, but there is not much fever left." She let her hand linger there, amused that she found herself captivated by the handsome half-ogre.

Tailonna, Lendle's waking up!

The sea elf heard the words inside her head. Ilyatha's urgings drew her away from Fritzen and over to the gnome's cot. Lendle's eyelids were quivering, and his head rolled slowly back and forth. At last, he opened his eyes and stared up at the shadowperson and sea elf.

"Myheadhurts," he gushed as he tried to push himself into a sitting position. "Someonestophittingmeintheheadwithahammer."

"Stay down." Tailonna's firm voice and even firmer hand on his shoulder kept the gnome in place. "You were seriously hurt. You need to rest."

"I've got to cook breakfast," he said, slowing his speech pattern.

"It is past breakfast," the sea elf scolded. "But if you're hungry, I can have something brought here for you."

Ilyatha backed away from the cot and started toward the armory door. "Maquesta will want to know they are both doing better. I will get her."

"Wait!" the sea elf called. "I really could do without her company for just a little while longer. Besides, she's busy working on her plan to go after the morkoth. She'll stop by later. Let her be for now, and let Fritzen and Lendle enjoy some quiet."

Ilyatha looked at the comely elf. *The captain needs to know,* he communicated. With that, he bundled his cape about him and pulled the hood over his head until his face was cloaked in shadows. Letting the sleeves fall below his fingertips, and taking a deep breath, he stepped out into the painful morning light.

"I should help Maq with her plans," Fritz announced.

"No!" Tailonna's tone was more of a scolding than a command. "Maquesta is doing fine alone."

The half-ogre looked quizzically at the sea elf. "You don't like her much, do you?"

"I think she oversteps her authority," Tailonna said simply. "She takes on too much responsibility, and she basks in being in charge."

"I think she's a good captain," he replied. "And I think you're too critical of her."

"It is my way. Sea elves are not like surface dwellers. We are disparate, set apart. We look at the world differently. Perhaps our lack of tolerance for others is because we expect so much. We have high standards." She returned to sit next to Fritzen, close enough so her shoulder brushed against his. "Your blood is tinged with the sea, too. You should understand how I feel."

He stared into her blue-green eyes. "I think all good sailors have a hint of saltwater in their blood and in their hearts. And I think you would do well to find it in your heart to afford Maquesta Kar-Thon some respect. I'd say you owe her an apology. She has more burdens on her back than perhaps you will ever know, and I think she is handling them admirably. Besides, I think she is uncommonly tolerant of you. I've served under many captains, and most of them would have thrown you off the ship for insubordination. They would not have put up with your attitude beyond the first day."

Before the sea elf could reply, the door swung open, the light framing a tired and relieved Maquesta. She grinned widely when she saw Fritzen sitting up, but her eyes narrowed when she saw how close Tailonna was sitting to him. Not bothering to say anything, she strode to the gnome's cot and sat on the edge.

"Maquesta Kar-Thon," Lendle said slowly, "I am glad to see you. And I am hungry. What is for lunch?"

"A passable eel stew. Get yourself well—quickly, my old friend. For I do not think my stomach can survive Vartan and Hvel's . . . masterpieces."

"Where's Ilyatha? He's been very good to me. I want to thank him for making me well."

Behind Maquesta, the sea elf opened her mouth to correct the gnome, to take credit for his recovery, but a stern look from Fritzen cut her off.

"Ilyatha's belowdecks," Maq replied. "He's sleeping in the darkness of the cargo hold. He stayed up with you all night. But he said he would come by to visit after sunset."

Maquesta turned to Fritzen and explained she had been planning the raid on the morkoth lair. "I think Belwar will help us, though he is nowhere to be seen today. Ilyatha thinks he is traveling on another plane. We'll discuss the plans tonight, after Ilyatha has rested. Perhaps Belwar will be back by then."

Rising, she nodded to Fritz and Tailonna, then left the armory.

* * * * *

"I'm sorry."

The words startled Maquesta. She was at the wheel, staring at the clouds on the horizon and hoping they did not signal a storm. Turning, she saw the sea elf standing behind her.

"I am not used to being around surface dwellers," Tailonna stated simply. "My way is not your way, and I apologize for not following your instructions. We have no captains under the waves. In my community our elders are wise, but they are few, and the hierarchy of authority is not so well defined. I did not mean to insult you. And I will try to remember to seek your counsel and permission before I act."

Maquesta's mouth fell open in surprise.

"I recognize that you are in charge of this ship," Tailonna continued, "and that you make all the decisions."

"But I frequently ask for advice," Maq said. "I need the knowledge and assistance of all of my crew. And I do appreciate what you've done for Lendle and Fritzen." She saw Tailonna's face brighten when she mentioned the half-ogre, and that bothered her. But she kept those thoughts to herself.

Tailonna reached her hands up into the air and wiggled her webbed fingers, enjoying the breeze. After a moment, the sea elf stepped in front of the wheel, looking between the spokes and into Maquesta's dark eyes.

"When I left the ship to search for herbs and other medicines, I swam to my home community. I learned a lot there, information that should help you—and concern you—in your endeavors to capture the morkoth."

Details about a kuo-toa colony adjacent to the morkoth lair tumbled from the sea elf's lips. "Though the colony is not allied with the creature, there exists an uneasy truce. The morkoth does not attack the kuo-toa, but neither do they prevent other creatures and animals from swimming into its lair. It is rumored the kuo-toa even make sacrifices to the morkoth. Their numbers are considerable, and to get to the morkoth, you and your group will probably have to go through the kuo-toa.

Maq groaned softly. "Nothing has been easy on this trip," she said, letting down her guard a little and feeling slightly more comfortable in the sea elf's presence. "It seems we're destined to ever be challenged."

"I will do what I can to help you," Tailonna offered. "I have no love for the kuo-toa, nor for their associates, who often capture sea elves and force them into slavery. My people tell me the colony works in concert with another nearby underwater community. It is a village filled with koalinth. They are similar to the hobgoblins that walk the land, but these are aquatic, and evil, perhaps worse than the morkoth and kuo-toa."

"I don't know if I have enough sailors to take on a colony of kuo-toa or the koalinth," Maquesta said thoughtfully. "Perhaps a better tact would be to find a way around them, directly to the morkoth." She noticed the sea elf's dejected expression and decided to offer a compromise. "With the morkoth secured and in Lord Attat's hands, my father will be returned to the ship. Perhaps we could recruit more sailors in Lacynos and come back. With a stronger force, and with your people aiding us, we would fare better in a battle against the creatures."

The sea elf nodded. "Fritzen is right: you are wise. And I have been . . . perhaps . . . difficult. To bridge our differences, let me offer you a boon."

Tailonna walked to the rear of the aft deck and retrieved a bucket. Attaching it to a coil of rope, she threw it over the side, let it fill with seawater, and then hauled it up. Carrying the bucket near to Maquesta and the wheel, the elf sat cross-legged on the deck and peered into the water. Taking one of the smaller seashells out of her hair, she gently blew on it, muttered some musical-sounding words, and dropped the shell into the bucket.

"I cast a spell that lets me divine moments in the past," Tailonna said. "Look into the bucket and concentrate. You will see familiar scenes and people familiar, but only the past can be known to you."

"My father?" Maq posed.

"If you concentrate, you can see moments—or years—into the past. It will be as if you were there, reliving whatever you choose to." Tailonna waved her hand over the bucket, and the water shimmered and formed glittering ripples.

Maquesta stared at the ripples and watched as they smoothed out, revealing Melas's face. Concentrating, the surface of the water rippled again, then smoothed to show the elder Kar-Thon lying in a bed, with a minotaur sage tending him. Out the window of the room, Maq saw herself, Tailonna, Koraf, and Ilyatha leaving the grounds of Attat's palace. The time must have been right after she agreed to Attat's foul mission and shortly after her father had been poisoned. Relieved that her father was receiving the care the minotaur lord had promised, Maq concentrated on a different time period.

Again ripples spread outward from the center of the bucket, and Maquesta saw herself as a young girl with long hair that was braided on the sides of her face. No more than seven or eight, she was scampering along the deck of the *Perechon*, running precariously close to the edge of the ship. It was a dangerous game she played when no one was looking, but this day it was especially dangerous because the sea was rough and water constantly sprayed up on the deck. Giggling, she ran faster, then she heard herself scream in surprise as one of her feet slipped and shot over the side of the boat. For an instant she felt herself falling, but then the sensation changed, and she was being lifted high into the air. Melas's strong arms rescued her, and he held her close, gently scolding her. The next time the *Perechon* sailed into a port, Melas had spent every coin he owned to have a railing built around the edge of the deck. It was the same railing that graced the ship today.

Again the scene changed; Maquesta was older, twelve she guessed by the way she was wearing her hair. It was short now, cut like many of the other sailors wore theirs, and her ears showed. But they were no longer pointed, so it didn't matter. Maq was visiting with her father at the wheel. Grinning broadly, he hefted a crate. Setting it behind the wheel with much flourish, he hoisted Maq onto it and put her right hand on the king's spoke.

"Steer the ship!" he commanded her in his rich, booming voice. "Take us toward the bay!"

It was her first solo behind the wheel. Melas nodded to her and strode toward the bow. He was trusting the ship to her, a mere child. He wasn't even watching her. What confidence he must have had. Maquesta felt her heart swell with pride as she relived that glorious moment. But it was so long ago, and the vision was fading now.

Concentrating harder, the ripples appeared to move faster, and the years melted away. This time Maquesta was little more than a baby, and she was being comforted in her mother's arms. Her mother, dressed in voluminous dark clothes to hide her elven nature, was singing a soft tune, trying to get Maq to fall asleep. It was an elvish song about forests, one that Maq had forgotten. But now the melody was playing over and over in her head as she looked up into her mother's eyes and stared at the beautiful, fair face. If elves hadn't been hunted, hadn't been forced to hide from humans in certain parts of the world, Maq's mother wouldn't have had to conceal her true nature.

Maquesta watched herself grow. She saw herself learning to walk, a difficult task for a child on the pitching deck of a ship, and she laughed as she tried to put everything remotely edible in her mouth, including her father's maps. Then she saw herself alone on the deck of the *Perechon* late one night. She couldn't have been older than four. Why would she be out here alone so late? No, Maquesta noticed, peering into the shadows by the capstan. She wasn't alone. Her mother was there. Her mother had carried her here, near the rope ladder that reached over the side of the ship.

"I cannot play this game any longer, sweet Maquesta," she heard her mother say. "I can no longer hide who I am, what I am. I cannot deny my heritage. I love your father, and I love you. But I also care for myself, and I must go to be with my own people—where I will have nothing to hide. You will not see me after this night, my child. But know always that you will ever be in my heart."

Maquesta watched her mother climb over the rope railing. There was a small boat, with two elves in it, waiting for her. One of the elves blew a glittery powder into the air, and Maq coughed as the cloud of it engulfed her. Then she saw the darkness swallow her mother, and she forgot everything that transpired that night. The next morning she saw her father crying, realizing his wife was gone. Melas thought she might have slipped overboard and drowned. Then he worried that someone had come for her during the night and stolen her from him. It was that morning Melas and Lendle cut the tips off Maq's ears, fearing that if someone discovered the little girl was a half-elf she would be spirited away, too.

Maquesta vowed to tell her father what really happened when he was back on the *Perechon*. He deserved the truth.

"Maquesta?" the sea elf broke Maq's concentration. The ripples faded. The magic was gone. "Are you all right?"

"Yes," Maq said. "Thank you for the vision. I saw my father. He was being cared for when we pulled out of the Lacynos harbor."

Tailonna took the bucket and threw the water over the side of the ship. "I could let you have another water vision tomorrow if you wish."

Maquesta declined. "I think I'll concentrate on the present."

The sea elf smiled. "I'll go back to watch over Fritzen and Lendle now. Fritzen is feeling much better, and I think he needs someone to talk to."

Maquesta was unaccustomed to Tailonna's new politeness, and disturbed that she would be spending more time with Fritz. She shook her head to get the jealous notion out of it. Fritzen is half sea-ogre and would be better off with someone closer tied to the water, she ruefully decided. Trying to focus on something else, she waved to Koraf.

The minotaur was near the capstan, talking with Hvel.

He nodded to her and moved quickly across the deck.

"I've been calling you 'Kof'," Maq said. "Perhaps I've been too familiar with you in doing so. I should have asked if you minded. It would have been more polite."

"Mine is an uncommonly difficult name for human tongues," he said, slightly amused. "And I do not object to the familiarity. It makes me feel . . . accepted."

Maquesta watched as the minotaur clomped back to Hvel. It seemed Kof had found a good friend among the crew. As the two chatted, Maq started humming a soft tune, an elvish one about forests.

* * * * *

Shortly after sunset Maquesta, Ilyatha, Tailonna, and Hvel gathered in the armory. Fritzen was sitting in a chair. Only a thin bandage on his shoulder hinted that he had been wounded. Maq was explaining her plan for trying to bypass the kuo-toa community to reach the nearby morkoth lair. Tailonna drew a map, showing where she thought the colony was, and a likely location for the lair.

"My people suspect the beast lives in this rocky ridge, where it could have constructed tunnels. We cannot be sure, though," she said. "I will make several vials of a potion that lets you breathe water. It will serve you in case it takes a while to find the beast's home."

Ilyatha looked at the sea elf's diagram. "I can use my telepathic abilities to reach out and attempt to locate the morkoth, while at the same time keeping us away from the kuo-toa."

Maquesta stood and nodded to each of her companions. "Then we are decided." They nodded in return. "I, Tailonna, Ilyatha, Kof, and Hvel shall go. Tailonna has volun-

teered to use her magical nets to capture the kuo-toa."
"MetoometooMaquestaKar-Thon," Lendle was sitting in his cot, excited at the prospect of breathing water and exploring a new realm.
"Not this time, my friend," Maq said sternly.
"What about me?" Fritzen stood and moved his shoulder. "I don't want to miss out on this. And I'm feeling fine."
"We'll see," Maq and Tailonna said practically in unison.

Chapter 14

The Morkoth

Fritzen was feeling much better—too good to remain cooped up in the armory-turned-infirmary with a mending gnome who babbled incessantly about various inventions, including how to construct a better mechanical wallet. Having heard enough, and wanting some fresh air and more pleasing company, Fritzen waited until Lendle was sitting up in his cot, busy diagraming improvements to his oar machine, then sneaked up top. He still favored his shoulder, but the view quickly took his mind off the dull ache. The sun was setting on the Blood Sea, and like an overturned bottle of paint the color spilled out over the choppy water, transforming it into an iridescent orange. Pink-tinged seabirds flitted above the waves, looking for something to eat. Finding a small fish, one released a haunting cry and climbed toward the cloud-filled sky with its wriggling prize.

Bas Ohn-Koraf stood near the prow, a spyglass pressed to his bull-like head and trained on the shoreline. Maquesta was at the wheel. She steered the *Perechon* toward the coast while she hummed a haunting tune.

Fritzen clung to the shadows for several minutes, watching her and trying to guess where she might take the ship. Adjacent to the point possibly, he mused. That was the place he'd select because it was close to open water, allowing them to get under way more quickly in the morning. The half-ogre's lips tugged upward slightly. He was finding himself increasingly comfortable in Maq's presence and was amused that he would seek her out. She seemed content behind the wheel, and the crew didn't hesitate to follower her orders. He certainly had no qualms about following this slip of a woman. But what would Maquesta Kar-Thon do, he wondered, if the mission was successful and her father was returned whole to the *Perechon*? Step down, of course, Fritzen decided. She'd return the ship to her father's care. But having a taste of being a captain, would she search for a ship of her own? If so, Fritzen suspected he would go with her.

Oblivious to the watcher, Maq ended the melody and deeply inhaled the salt air. She chewed on her bottom lip and cursed herself for not heading toward shore earlier. She did not want to be caught on the open water at night—the bout with the Blood Sea imps had been bad enough. As if mirroring her prayers, a gust of wind caught the sails, billowing them and speeding her course. The *Perechon* was near Endscape, she judged by a group of towering rock formations, a place her father used to tell her grand stories about. Her father. Maq shook her head and fought back a tear. Was he holding on? Was he thinking about her, too? She ran her slim fingers through her curly hair and looked at the point, considering anchoring the *Perechon* off it. No, she decided after a moment. Too close to open water. Instead she selected the cove, and the ship responded to her gentle turn of the wheel.

Fritzen quietly padded up behind her, intending to surprise her.

"Feeling better?" she asked, not bothering to turn around.

"How?"

"That healing poultice on your shoulder. It stinks. It smells like dead fish. In fact, it probably has dead fish in it."

Fritzen grinned sheepishly. "I see you're headed to the cove. Excellent choice. It's where I would've gone. Safer from the wind, harder to spot from the open sea."

She finally turned and caught his gaze. For an instant their eyes locked, and he edged closer, then she broke the moment and glanced at his shoulder.

"I'm fine, Maq. Really," Fritz responded to her unvoiced concern. "Tailonna makes wonderful magical healing potions. Lendle is feeling better, too. He was hard at work on a diagram when I left him, then he intended to visit the galley and instruct Hvel and Vartan in the art of seasoning soup. And speaking of food, dinner should be ready soon. Join me?"

"After we drop anchor," she said, returning her attention to the shore. "Then I want to check the sails and the rigging and lash everything down. Look at the clouds overhead. It's the stormy season on this part of the sea, and if those clouds are any indication, we could be facing a gale tonight. If so, the cove should keep some of the wind at bay."

Fritzen stayed with her until the *Perechon* pulled as close to shore as was safe given the draw of the ship, and he waited until Maq was certain the sails were lowered and in good condition. She fretted over this and that for another hour, then she, Kof, and Fritzen sat cross-legged on the deck and ate bowls of warm and filling oyster soup. As the clouds moved on, taking the hint of a storm with them, and the stars came out, the trio took turns pointing at the various constellations and telling old stories about sea monsters and about the gods coming to Krynn and meddling in the affairs of sailors. For the first time since leaving Attat's palace, the three began to relax and enjoy each other's company. But the mood was shattered as Maquesta yawned and rose from the deck.

"Time for us to get some rest," she announced. "Most of the crew turned in more than an hour ago. I told them we were going to get an early start." She wiped at a spot of soup that had spilled on her tunic. "Kof, stay up top for awhile. I don't like these waters—even near the safety of the land. Fritz, send up Berem and a lookout to keep him company. I'll relieve you later. We sail at dawn."

Fritz rose to go below, and Maq whirled and headed toward the steps. "Thanks for a pleasant evening, gentlemen," she added.

"Maq . . ." Kof's hushed voice halted her halfway to her cabin.

She turned and watched as the minotaur stiffened. His nose twitched, and a ridge of short, bristly hair stood up on the back of his neck. "There's something out there."

Maquesta started toward the capstan, where her sword rested. But she stopped short as she spied a clawed, webbed hand reach over the railing.

A scratching sound behind her sent her whirling around. Several more pairs of claws were on the other side of the ship—all attached to horrid bodies.

"Kuo-toa!" Kof yelled. "Dozens of them. Devils of the deep!"

"Fritz!" she barked. "Get below and sound the alarm. We're being boarded!" With that she dashed toward the capstan, flinging herself the last few yards and sliding on her stomach across the polished deck. She stopped herself as her fingers closed about the hilt of her sword, and she pulled herself to her knees and unsheathed the blade just in time to see a dark shape lumber toward her. The creature had a massive head like that of a sea bass, but its mouth was filled with jagged teeth that gleamed in the moonlight. It was covered with slime that glistened dully, and it stank of rotting seaweed. Maquesta swallowed hard and concentrated on not retching. The creature's torso was like a man's, though a little larger and covered with blue and green scales, and its arms and legs were nearly humanlike. But its feet were long flippers that trailed strands of kelp, and it had a fishtail that hung behind it and scraped across the deck. The kuo-toa wore crossed leather straps about its chest, with daggers evenly stuck into sheaths on them. Held by a thin cord to its back was a spear, which the thing reached for with its webbed claws as it slogged forward. Maq pulled her sword free of the scabbard and swung it in an upward arc that sliced the creature's belly open as it leaned toward her.

The creature screamed shrilly and looked down to see its entrails spill out. Maq jumped to her feet and swung again, this time higher. Her sword connected with the thing's chest, coaxing another horrid cry that trailed away. As Maquesta's victim pitched forward onto the deck, she leapt back and stared in mute horror as two more waddled forward to take its place. One had an ornate shield and was larger, more than seven feet tall. It wore an impressive necklace of coral and bones, signifying it was of some importance. The kuo-toa spouted a string of gargling gibberish, then thrust forward with its barbed spear. The smaller creature did likewise, jabbing at Maq's middle. She crouched to avoid being skewered and felt the creatures' slime drip onto her shoulders. Behind her, she heard Kof struggling with more of the creatures, his grunts mingling with their babbling gibberish and screams.

"Monsters!" she spat, as she released her sword and sprang to her feet. "You'll not take my ship!" She reached out and grabbed the smaller kuo-toa's spear and pulled hard. The surprised creature was momentarily thrown off balance and let go of its weapon to keep from falling. Avoiding another spear thrust from the larger creature, Maq twirled her borrowed weapon like a baton until the sharp metal head pointed toward her massive attacker. She took a step back, spread her feet for better balance, and waved the spear in front of her to keep the kuo-toa at bay and to give herself a moment to think.

The big kuo-toa's huge eyes rotated to take in the battle on the deck. Maq risked a glance over her shoulder and cringed as she saw Kof being borne to the timbers by a half-dozen of the kuo-toa. Thundering footsteps heralded the arrival of the *Perechon*'s crew, with Fritzen in the lead, but Maquesta knew her men might be no match for the malicious sea creatures.

A growl drew her attention back to the big kuo-toa. It, too, had its spear extended to keep her at a distance. To her horror, she saw the smaller creature pull daggers from its leather harness. She nimbly stepped to the side, avoiding the first missile, but the second nicked her arm and she nearly dropped the spear. Fire coursed through her limb. "Take care!" she cried to the crew. "I think they're using poison!" Out of the corner of her eye she saw the smaller kuo-toa catch a javelin in its chest and go down.

The large kuo-toa threw back its head and made a cackling-gurgling noise that sounded somewhat like laughter. Then it darted in, faster than Maq would have believed possible, and stabbed her thigh. The spear sank in deep, and Maquesta yelped in surprise and pain. She felt the warm blood flow down her leg as her attacker pulled the spear free, sending another jolt of pain through her. But she gritted her teeth, remained standing, and thrust forward with her spear at the same time. The large kuo-toa brought up its boiled leather shield, and Maq's spear tip lodged in it. The creature made a rumbling sound deep in its throat and tossed its shield—and Maq's spear—to the deck. Its eyes focused forward, and it took a step toward her. Behind her Maq heard the cries of her crewmen—shouts of pain and victory merging.

"See to the minotaur; he's down!" she heard one sailor cry.

"I can't get to him," called another. "We're surrounded!"

"Look out! There's more coming over the aft deck!"

"Ohmyohmyohmyohmyohmyohmy!"

"Where's the sea elf? Wait, she's coming on deck. Do something, Tailonna!"

"Start a fire! See if that'll keep them back!" yelled the helmsman.

"They've got weighted nets! I'm trapped!"

"Maquesta?" It was Fritzen's voice. "No! Maq!"

She felt the creature's webbed hands fold about her waist and lift her as easily as a child would carry a doll. Its claws dug in hard, and she slammed her eyes shut as the big kuo-toa gripped her in a bearhug. She felt the air rush out of her lungs, needles of pain poking her everywhere, and her world started spinning. Then she felt herself thrown backward, and she landed roughly on the deck, her head smacking hard against the wood.

Dazed, she slowly opened her eyes to see the half-ogre straddling her, pushing the big kuo-toa away. Fritzen danced forward, keeping the creature off balance, until the pair were clear of her. Then Fritzen leaped up and brought his leg straight out to strike the kuo-toa's chest, knocking it backward onto its rump. The half-ogre pressed the attack and jabbed his heel into the kuo-toa's face. But the sea creature quickly retaliated, grabbing Fritzen's ankle and yanking him down to the deck. As the pair grappled, Maquesta shook off her dizziness and sluggishly pulled herself up. The arm nicked by the dagger tingled all over.

She spotted Ilyatha hugging the shadows and creeping toward the forward mast. He motioned her to be silent, and she watched in fascination as he darted around behind a pair of kuo-toa occupying Lendle. He moved so silently not a board creaked, then he raised twin daggers and plunged them into the backs of the unsuspecting creatures. Lendle yipped his thanks and skidded to the side to avoid the falling bodies.

Beyond the gnome she saw a young sailor struggling with another creature. The man was stuck between the sea creature's shield and the railing, and he flailed about helplessly while the kuo-toa beat him. Maq grabbed the capstan for support. Her wounded leg and arm throbbed horribly, and she had to focus her thoughts to keep from blacking out. She looked about for a weapon, but there were none in easy reach. Dimly, she wondered where her sword was.

Still, she was determined to stay in the battle to its bloody conclusion, which she feared might come all too soon—signaling the end of the *Perechon*'s crew and her father's life. Pushing herself forward, she staggered toward the center of the deck, where she knew javelins and harpoons waited. Behind her she heard slapping sounds: kuo-toan feet moving over the polished wood.

At least one of the creatures was after her, she realized as she bit her bottom lip and tried to move faster.

"Get down, Maquesta!" The voice belonged to Tailonna. Maq fell forward onto the deck. She lifted her head just in time to see a gossamer webnet fly through the air. Getting to her hands and knees, she whirled to spot a trio of kuo-toa caught like insects in a spiderweb. Tailonna slid to Maq's side and helped her up. Then the sea elf pulled a second of the tiny nets from her hair. Flinging it toward another group of kuo toa, Tailonna gestured with her fingers and mouthed the words of a spell. The tiny net shimmered in the air and grew to the size of a fishing net. It landed on the sea elf's intended victims, trapping them. Another net Tailonna tossed toward the big creature struggling with Fritzen. Again a magical net found its mark, engulfing the massive kuo-toa. The half-ogre's legs were caught in the filmy tendrils, too, but he struggled to get himself free.

"Over there!" Maq pointed. Lendle, armed with a dagger and a wooden spoon, had become the center of attention again—this time with a quartet of kuo-toa circling him.

Tailonna nodded and released another web. This one struck the sea creatures about their heads and torsos, leaving Lendle space to dart free between their legs. "I told him to stay in the infirmary," the sea elf muttered. "Doesn't he ever listen?"

"HelpKofheisintroubledosomethingplease!" Lendle was pointing.

Maq and Tailonna glanced beyond the forward mast and saw a kuo-toa pushing the prone minotaur toward the rail. Unconscious, he would quickly drown. Again arcane words came to the sea elf's lips, but this time they produced lavender darts of light that flew from her fingers. They struck the kuo-toa in the shoulder and spun it around in time for it to receive another set of magic darts in the chest. Amid cheers from the *Perechon*'s sailors, the sea creature fell backward on top of Kof. The tide of battle had turned, thanks to the elf, and the sailors rushed forward to swarm the remaining kuo-toa.

"That must be their leader!" Fritzen called above the cacophony. He was pointing at the large kuo-toa in the net, the one that had wounded Maq. "I heard it snapping orders at the others, but I've got it." The half-ogre had retrieved Maq's sword and had the tip pointed through the webnet at the creature's throat.

Tailonna and Maquesta slowly moved toward the tall kuo-toa. "What will we do with it?" Maq posed. "We can't just let it go, but we're after a morkoth, not a sea-devil." She gritted her teeth and shook her injured arm; it was numb now, all but useless.

Fritzen rushed forward and grabbed Maquesta, hoisting her like a baby in his muscular arms and leaving Tailonna free to create more webnets. "I think you're the one in need of an awful-smelling healing poultice this time." His dark eyes showed concern, though his voice was light. "I'm taking you to the armory, where you'll be safe. Your crew can handle what's left of these things."

"Kof is going to be all right," Lendle called across the deck. He pushed the dead kuo-toa off the minotaur and grinned. Then he scowled when he saw Maq's bloody leg. "He's just stunned, in better shape than you are. I'll check on the others. Then I'll tend to you, Maquesta Kar-Thon."

"There're more kuo-toa in the water," Maquesta whispered to Fritzen. "I can see them. There must be at least two dozen. You're not taking me anywhere until I know for certain the *Perechon* is safe."

The half-ogre scanned the water and shook his head.

"I don't see anything."

"Trust me. They're are out there."

Tailonna moved to the bow, where she had six more kuo-toa trapped in her nets. Several yards behind her, Vartan and Hvel had convinced a dozen of the creatures to drop their weapons and surrender. The battle was finally over.

Tailonna motioned for Fritzen and Maq to join her. "I can understand what these things are saying. Well, a little of what they're saying. Their language is crude."

"I can understand everything they say." Ilyatha stepped forward and sheathed his daggers. "Though I'm not sure you want it translated. They are a malicious and insulting lot."

"I *do* want to know," Maq stated, nudging Fritzen to let her down.

Fritzen frowned, but he gently set her on the deck, supporting her to keep the weight off her wounded leg. All about them the *Perechon* crew pushed the dead kuo-toa overboard and were in the process of tying up those that were injured or had surrendered. Four *Perechon* crewmembers had died in the struggle and were laid out on the deck. Maquesta cringed. The price for her father's life had risen again, and now the *Perechon* would be operating with a skeleton crew.

Ilyatha began spouting the same gibberish Maq had heard the big kuo-toa speak. The shadowperson was bent over a pair tied back-to-back. A handful of sailors stood nearby trying to pick words out of the garbled noises.

"Their king ordered the raid," Ilyatha said, turning to face Maq and drawing her attention away from the dead sailors. "It seems you have royalty aboard—and practically an entire colony of kuo-toa." He pointed to the big creature Maq and Fritzen had fought. The tall kuo-toa was tied to the forward mast, where three sailors stood guard. "It was leading the colony to an underwater shrine. They were planning a special worship service to honor the Sea Mother, their evil goddess. They spotted the *Perechon* as we approached the point and decided to capture the crew for slaves and food—saving some of us for sacrifices to the Sea Mother, of course."

Maquesta stepped away from Fritzen. Ignoring the half-ogre's protests, she limped toward the king. "I didn't want to fight your kind," she said, suspecting that the creature couldn't understand and she was talking to herself, but continuing anyway. "We were going to bypass your territory. You shouldn't have attacked us." Maq fingered the coral necklace about the creature's neck and tugged the bauble free.

"I figured you were important. I just didn't realize how important. We're going to use you, *Your Majesty*. You're going to tell us where to find the morkoth. In fact, I think some of your loyal subjects should lead us to the beast—if they want to see their king live past dawn."

Fritzen's stern face broke into a broad grin. "You're brilliant, Maq."

He and Ilyatha rushed to the king, and once again Ilyatha voiced the weird kuo-toa tongue that sounded like growls, hisses, and gurgling water. The king's reply was loud, harsh, and punctuated by spitting. The other captured kuo-toa began to hiss and babble, too, and they struggled futilely against their bonds.

"He's telling them to escape," Ilyatha said. "He says they should free themselves in the name of the Sea Mother."

Fritzen growled and kicked the king harshly in the side. "Maybe he doesn't realize we're serious," he taunted. Standing on one leg he raised the other higher than his head—until his foot was even with the king's scowling visage. Quick like a cat, he brought the leg down, and the other swung up to miss the kuo-toa's head by less than an inch. "Maybe we should convince him we're serious."

Tailonna padded forward and began mumbling, weaving a pattern in the air with her hands. "We don't need any more bloodshed, though I cannot convey how pleased I am at the number of dead kuo-toa. Killing this beast will gain you nothing other than my satisfaction. But I can make it more cooperative. I can make it quite reasonable, in fact." A small blue orb appeared in the palm of her right hand. She blew on it, and it floated forward, enlarged, then surrounded the king's head. For an instant, the kuo-toa's face shimmered with the same blue light, then the color disappeared, as if the magic never existed. "Now try."

Ilyatha stared into the kuo-toa king's eyes and babbled in the creature's strange language.

"I can pick up a few words," Tailonna told Maq. "Ilyatha's telling it that its life will be spared—as will those of its captive warriors. But . . ."

"But it has to provide a guide to the morkoth's lair. Which it has just agreed to do," Ilyatha finished. "The pair by the bow are its sons. They'll take us to the morkoth, though the king warns that the beast is dangerous. Now we will not have to search for its cave. Hours will be saved. This cursed attack on us has turned into a blessing."

"ButyoucannotgoMaquestaKarThon." Lendle was at her side, pointing at her bleeding leg. He stuck out his stubby index finger and started wagging it at her as if she were a misbehaving child.

"And you should not be out on deck. You should be in the infirmary," she retorted.

"Aswillyoube," the gnome answered.

Maq thought to argue with him. The *Perechon* was

her ship and, as captain, she gave the orders. But wisdom prevailed, and she decided to back down. "I know, Lendle. I'm going to need some of your tender care and one of Tailonna's potions. But while you're seeing to me, I want Fritz, Kof, Ilyatha, and Tailonna to go after the morkoth. Tailonna's webnets and magic will be necessary to catch the beast."

Fritzen motioned to the minotaur, who was just regaining consciousness. "Right away, Maq?"

"No. In the morning. The sea's so dark at night it will look as though you're swimming in ink. You won't even be able to see a hand in front of your face." She shook her head and pointed toward the water. "Besides, those other kuo-toa are out there. And I want *His Majesty* to order them away."

"I see them, too," Tailonna offered. "Twenty or more I'd guess. I'll take care of it." With that, the sea elf started talking to the king.

"Kof!" Maq quipped as the minotaur walked to her side. "It's about time you got up and joined the fun. I want you to make sure all of our guests are secure in the cargo hold tonight. And throw his majesty in the brig. When that's done, have our dead wrapped in sailcloth. We'll bury them at sea tomorrow."

Then Maq was swept up in strong arms and found herself being carried toward the infirmary. Exhaustion claimed her as she was placed on a cot. The last words she heard before drifting off were Lendle and Tailonna's rapid instructions to Fritzen to start mixing herbs.

* * * * *

Morning found Fritzen hovering over Maquesta, wiping a cool cloth across her forehead as Lendle busied himself with another concoction. Her leg was wrapped in several layers of bandages and was propped up on a pillow, and she was regaining feeling in her arm.

"Your turn in the infirmary," Fritzen said. "There was venom on the kuo-toa's weapons, but Lendle and Tailonna mixed up something that is drawing out the poison. Tailonna is in the crew quarters, giving some to the others who were injured. She assures me her mixture is magical, and everyone—including you—will be back to normal in a few hours."

Maq smiled and tried to rise, but the half-ogre laid a firm hand on her shoulder. "You're the captain, and you can order me to let you up and I'll oblige. But I'd rather follow a healthy captain—one who's going to be around for quite some time. Rest, Maq. Kof will lead us after the morkoth, and by the time we get back, you'll be feeling much better."

Maquesta pursed her lips, but nodded. Though she wanted to be up on the deck to see them off, she knew that Fritzen was making sense. She hated feeling weak and not fully in control of the situation, and she was angry that all of her crew seemed to be taking turns in the infirmary. But she closed her eyes, tried to relax, and concentrated on listening to the gnome reciting ingredients to himself. A pungent odor filled the room, and Maq knew she was going to stink before this was all over.

"Take care of yourself," Fritzen whispered as he made a motion to rise. Then he stopped and stared at her. "Last night you saw more kuo-toa in the water. What gift do you have, Maquesta, to allow such sight?"

"No need to tell him," Lendle offered, obviously overhearing their conversation. The gnome went back to babbling ingredients and stirring.

"It's all right. I trust him," Maq replied, opening her eyes and staring at the ceiling. "I'm not wholly human," she began. "My mother was an elf. She left my father a long time ago. I don't know if she's even alive. She left when warbands of humans were hunting elves and their kin. I suspect she disappeared to keep attention away from the *Perechon*. My father, frightened for my safety, had Lendle cut off the tips of my ears when I was just a small child. He didn't want anyone to know I was a half-elf. He was afraid I would be lost to him, too. So I have the elven gift of sight. I can see things better than humans can, though not quite as well as most elves."

"So now you know Maquesta's secret," Lendle said sternly. "It is one shared by only those people in this room—and by her father leagues away. And it had better not go any farther." The gnome's beady eyes were trained on the half-ogre's. "Understand?"

* * * * *

On deck, Ilyatha, Tailonna, and Bas Ohn-Koraf were waiting, all armed with kuo-toan spears. The minotaur carried the end of a thick rope in his hand. Several crewmembers gathered around out of curiosity, and when Fritzen found his way between them, Ilyatha tossed him a large net and told him that it would hold the morkoth when they found and captured it. Tailonna reached into a pouch at her waist and pulled out six vials containing the magical elixir that would allow them to breathe water as if it were air. She gave two vials to each of them.

"One vial should last many hours, between eight and twelve, I suspect. It could have different durations for each of us," she added, looking at the minotaur and half-ogre. "But if we work quickly there should be no problem."

Kof nodded and tugged on the end of the rope he

was holding. At the other end were the king's sons; the long rope was tied about their necks as if they were dogs on a leash. "Let's just get it over with," the minotaur grumbled. "While I love the sea, I don't care much for swimming, and I care even less for the company of kuo-toa."

Fritzen nearly dropped his vials as a burst of yellow light brighter than a noon sun struck the deck. As the glow faded, Belwar appeared, his sharp hooves hovering inches above the wood. The ki-rin nodded a greeting, and the crew parted as he approached the quartet. "I will go with you," he announced. "I was away last night and returned in time to see only the end of the struggle. Though I was not able to help you then, I will lend my aid now. Morkoths are tricky and deadly."

"Then, to our success!" Fritzen toasted as he raised the vial to the sky, then brought it to his lips and downed its contents in one gulp." The others did the same, and as one they moved to the side of the deck and jumped into the water. The ki-rin dived over, too, with the resulting splash leaving the onlooking crewmen drenched.

Koraf gasped as he sank beneath the surface and thrashed around like a wounded fish, trying desperately to keep a grip on the rope attached to the kuo-toa. He held his breath and dropped like a stone, with Ilyatha, Fritzen, Tailonna, and the creatures following him. The ki-rin hovered just below the surface, watching.

Relax, Ilyatha's mind coaxed. *Breathe the water as if it were air. Breathe.*

The minotaur closed his eyes and inhaled a little. It was an odd sensation, water entering his nose and going down into his lungs. At first he feared that he was drowning, that the elixir was just some horrible joke concocted by Attat, who wanted to doom them all. Then he gasped in fear and took in great lungfuls of saltwater. It stung his throat, but only for a moment. The odd sensation passed, and he opened his eyes. He was breathing.

Reaching the sandy bottom, he tugged on the rope and stared into the eyes of the king's sons. He shrugged his shoulders and pointed in different directions. Then he tugged on the rope again. At last the kuo-toa understood what the minotaur was getting at, and the largest of the two pointed southwest.

It is being truthful, Ilyatha's voice said reassuringly inside Kof's head. *The morkoth's lair lies in that direction.*

Above, the ki-rin saw what was transpiring and began swimming to the southwest. Its great legs churned the water, and it was all the rest of the group could do to keep the mythical creature in sight. They passed over a coral bed, where sea fronds that looked like delicate fans waved back and forth in the current. A school of queen angelfish passed overhead, giving the unusual travelers a wide berth, and on the sandy floor crabs skittered out of their way. Kof began to appreciate his surroundings, and his bull neck constantly pivoted back and forth to take in everything. After nearly two hours of travel he spied a rocky ridge that cut across the sandy bottom like the spine of some sleeping giant. The kuo-toa pointed toward the ridge, and the minotaur looked at Ilyatha, who nodded his approval. The ki-rin dived to the floor, and the members of the group, wary and pensive, slowed their pace as they approached the rocks.

The ridge looked like what Tailonna had drawn the day before in the infirmary. If her diagram was true, what was left of the kuo-toa colony would be on the other side of the rise and slightly to the north.

As they neared the ridge, they spied a cave, which was little more than a narrow crevice. *The morkoth's home,* Ilyatha thought to each of them. *The kuo-toa are frightened of the beast and say it lives there. They beg not to be forced inside. Only one of them has been this close to the opening, when delivering a sacrifice several months ago."*

Kof looked at the crevice, then at the ki-rin, who would not be able to fit through it. The creature's horn glowed faintly, and he spoke through the water so everyone could hear him. "I will watch your captives, for I cannot follow you. Even my magic will not let my form fit inside. But I will aid you, nonetheless." He closed his eyes and fire danced along his golden horn, a magical blaze that ignored the presence of the saltwater. The flames leapt outward, striking the edges of the crevice and flowing deeper into the rock. "The fire is not real, at least not like a true blaze. It will not burn you. But it coats the walls of the labyrinth beyond. It will light your way, and it may serve to frighten the morkoth, who likes to dwell in darkness. I wish you well." The ki-rin took the rope binding the kuo-toa between its teeth and moved back from the crevice.

Bas-Ohn Koraf took a deep breath of the saltwater and stepped inside. Fritzen and Tailonna followed him. Ilyatha paused outside the crevice. The shadowperson feared bright light, and it took him several moments to realize the light from the fire would not harm or blind him. The flames raced up and down the walls like a roaring campfire, casting eerie light patterns all about. Kof had to step sideways here and there as the passageway thinned, and more than once the minotaur scraped his back against an outcropping. Deeper and deeper they went, until Kof believed they must surely come out on the other side of the ridge. Then the tunnel started winding downward, and it split in two.

The minotaur sniffed, but found his keen sense of smell was wasted beneath the waves. Flames flickered down both passages, but they provided no clue as to the correct course. Extending his spear in front of him,

Kof took a step into the left tunnel, then looked over his shoulder and motioned for Fritzen to take the right. The half-ogre nodded, and Tailonna followed him, leaving the shadowperson to follow Kof. The minotaur had not gone farther than a dozen yards when his hooves crushed something brittle. Bending, he discovered a pile of bones that had once belonged to a large fish, a barracuda perhaps, he mused. The firelight playing on their white surface made the shards glisten. Suppressing a shudder, Kof continued to pick his way deeper. He growled in his throat, releasing a stream of bubbles when he saw the passageway ahead divide again. He moved on toward the right, where he had to grip the walls to keep from falling. The floor sloped steeply, bending down in a sharp spiral. Glancing behind him, he spotted Ilyatha moving to the left tunnel. The minotaur waved his hairy arm and nearly lost his balance trying get the telepath's attention. Ilyatha looked at the minotaur quizzically.

I'll not split our numbers again, Kof concentrated, hoping Ilyatha would pick up his thoughts.

Very well, the shadowperson replied. *I will let the others know to stay together.*

In the other corridor, Fritzen and Tailonna discovered a similar sharp turn, one with a drop-off that sent them floating down nearly fifty feet. From there the tunnel continued, spiraling down even farther. The half-ogre gripped the sides of his head, dropping the net and spear. The pressure here was beginning to get painful, and he wondered how far they had traveled and how much longer the elixir would last. He reached into the pouch on his belt to make sure the other vial was still intact. Tailonna placed a soft hand on his shoulder and pressed by him. They were in the sea elf's element, and Fritzen, gathering his belongings, allowed her to take the lead.

Nearly an hour later, Tailonna and Fritzen stared across a chasm—on the other side of which were Kof and Ilyatha. The magical fire stopped at the edge of the pit, which descended like a funnel into unnatural darkness. The minotaur nudged the shadowperson and concentrated, his great brow furrowing as he tried to convey a message.

I agree with Kof, Ilyatha communicated across the chasm, his words sounding stern inside Fritzen's head. *I believe the morkoth lies below, and he is preventing the fire from spreading farther.* With that, the shadowperson stepped off the ledge, dropping into the pitch-blackness of the crevice.

Kof swallowed hard and joined him, quickly passing Ilyatha by as his great weight propelled him through the water faster. The darkness swallowed them completely by the time Fritzen and Tailonna joined them in the fall.

What seemed like hours later, the quartet emerged into a large cavern thickly coated with shadows. The pressure was significant here, indicating they had come a long way below the surface of the sea. They could see only a few feet in the darkness, and Ilyatha instructed them to stay together so they would not become lost. Alone, the shadowperson suspected they would be easy marks for the morkoth. Kof swung his spear back and forth in front of him, pressing forward until he reached a rocky wall.

Like cave explorers, the four circled the chamber until they discovered six openings, each so thin they would be a tight squeeze to travel through.

One for each of us and two to spare, Ilyatha thought. *We should select one and hurry; the elixir . . .*

Kof nodded, and despite Ilyatha's warning he decided each person should take a different passage, tenuously linked by the shadowperson's telepathic mind. He directed Ilyatha down the closest passage, Fritzen down the next. The minotaur passed by the following two passages, noticing the grades were too steep. Then he pointed Tailonna down one, and he took the other. Each walked into the darkness with a weapon in one hand, and the fingers of their other hand brushing along the wall to show them the way. And all of them lost their balance as the floor disappeared beneath their feet and they fell even farther, sliding down rocky passages that twisted and turned.

Again the four found themselves emerging into a shadowy cavern, the tunnels they followed all bringing them to the same place. Kof growled, emitting a long string of bubbles, then he directed the others to stay together while he circled the chamber, discovering the features of its walls with his hands. When he returned to them, his eyes burned with anger, and Ilyatha winced when he poked inside the minotaur's head to discover what he was thinking.

Kof says this is the same chamber we left several minutes ago. There are six openings—he claims the same ones we ventured down, Ilyatha said, sending the message to everyone. *I suspect we never left this chamber to begin with. I think it's an illusion and we're being manipulated. I don't know where we are, but . . .* Before the shadowperson could continue, the cavern's darkness receded, as if light were being slowly coaxed from a lantern, revealing rocky walls encrusted with gems. High above, the edge of the cavern was lit by the ki-rin's magical fire. The flames continued to dance merrily, pointing toward a black shape descending toward the cavern floor. The dark form stopped halfway to the bottom, floating above them.

The morkoth! Ilyatha communicated to everyone. *It has been toying with us.*

From the waist up the hideous creature looked like a

sea snake, though it had a spiky top fin that ran to the crest of its wide, fishlike head. Four spindly arms, like the legs of a lobster, stuck out of its scaly sides. They ended in thin pincers that opened and closed almost rhythmically, their clacking sound cutting through the water. The morkoth's eyes sat to the front of its face, as a human's would, but they were dark, round orbs with flecks of red in the centers. The creature had no ears, at least none that were visible, but it had a mouth that looked like a squid's beak. It opened the beak and snapped it repeatedly, the clicking noise somehow reverberating through the water and unnerving the quartet below. Then the morkoth extended a long pink tongue that looked like a segmented seaworm and wriggled it.

The lower half of the creature's body resembled an octopus, with writhing tentacles sporting suction cups. The morkoth was quite a bit larger than Kof, and all over it was as black as night, though it had faint, luminescent silvery patches of scales here and there. As it moved closer to them, descending slowly through the water, it continued to click its beak and wave its pincer-arms, and its tentacles undulated almost hypnotically, drawing tiny air-bubble patterns in the water. Ilyatha and Tailonna stood unmoving, staring at the creature. The spears in their hands fell to the cavern floor as their eyes followed the bubble patterns.

Snap out of it, Kof concentrated, praying that the shadowperson and sea elf would pick up his thoughts. *Think! It's mesmerizing you. Wake up!* But his thoughts went unanswered. Only he and Fritzen seemed unaffected by the morkoth's writhings. The minotaur growled and stepped in front of Ilyatha and Tailonna. Spear raised, he poked it at the morkoth, but the creature's tentacles remained just out of reach. It continued to writhe, and Kof felt himself grow light-headed.

Closing his eyes and blocking out the image of the patterns, he continued to jab upward.

Behind him, Fritzen reached the sea elf. Releasing his spear and tucking the net under his arm, he grabbed her by the shoulders and shook her roughly. To his side, the shadowperson sprang to life, and for a moment, the half-ogre's grim face showed relief. Ilyatha drew his twin daggers, then, just as it seemed he would leap at the morkoth, he turned to face Fritzen and rushed forward. The half-ogre let go of Tailonna and dropped to the floor of the cavern, gaping in surprise as Ilyatha swam forward with the daggers, slashing where he had stood just a moment before. The shadowperson pivoted and glared down at him with eyes that had red specks swirling in them.

The morkoth! Fritzen cursed to himself. First it had taken control of the sea elf, and now the danger had doubled. He rolled to his side, bowling over Tailonna in the process, then he crouched and pushed off the bottom with his strong leg muscles. The half-ogre shot up through the water, the shadowperson following him. They passed by the morkoth, which was continuing to twist about and create more bubble-patterns. Fritzen felt a wave of dizziness wash over him as he glanced at the bubbles, but he fought it off and concentrated on the advancing Ilyatha.

Ilyatha grinned evilly as he moved toward the half-ogre. Though Fritzen was a skilled acrobat, his talents were best used on land. The shadowperson easily outmaneuvered him underwater. Fritzen knew he would have to rely on his strength. Ilyatha pumped his legs, propelling himself toward Fritzen, and the half-ogre treaded water to stay in place and meet the charge. As Ilyatha moved in, Fritzen's arms drove forward, and his hands clamped tightly on the shadowperson's dark wrists, keeping the daggers from finding their target. Out of the corner of his eye, Fritzen saw Tailonna stir. She rose unsteadily to her feet and looked up at Fritzen and Ilyatha, then furtively glanced at the morkoth. The half-ogre thanked the gods there were no red flecks in her eyes.

The sea elf raised her hands and wiggled her fingers, mouthing words to an incantation. Grabbing one of the nets from her hair, she was careful to keep from looking directly at the morkoth's tentacles, and instead focused on a spot on its torso. As she finished the incantation, her magical webnet rushed through the water straight at the beast, but it stopped inches from the creature's grotesque body, hovering for the briefest moment. Then the enchanted piece of gossamer returned just as quickly to envelop Tailonna tightly in the net she had sought to use against the morkoth.

Fritzen cursed between his teeth. The sea elf had been their best hope. The shadowperson in his grasp wriggled madly, and the half-ogre tightened his grip until he saw a look of pain on Ilyatha's face. Kicking forward with his legs, Fritzen propelled the shadowperson roughly against the cavern wall. The half-ogre was trying to stun Ilyatha, but the dark warrior was determined and only struggled harder.

Below, the morkoth slowly descended toward Kof. The minotaur still prodded about blindly with his spear, fearing to open his eyes and be charmed by the vile creature's movements. Through her webnet Tailonna saw the morkoth shift to come down behind Kof.

"He's at your back!" she shouted. The sound of her sea elven voice carried faintly through the water, reaching Kof's sensitive ears. "He's stopped writhing. You can open your eyes."

Her warning came almost too late. One of the morkoth's tentacles snaked out toward the back of the minotaur's neck. But Kof whirled and opened his eyes in time to see it. He crouched and drove the spear forward, embedding its tip in the rubbery tentacle. Black blood spilled out into the water. Kof knew Attat wanted the creature undamaged, but with the sea elf's webnets ineffective against it, there was little choice but to battle it or be killed—or battle it *and* be killed. He tugged on the spear, but its barbed point had passed all the way through the tentacle and was lodged there. Grumbling, he released the haft and grabbed another tentacle and started to climb toward the creature's torso.

The morkoth emitted a shriek that cut through the water and brought tears to the minotaur's eyes. The pain in Koraf's head was excruciating, but he knew to release the beast would mean his doom. Clamping his teeth together, he renewed his efforts and struggled to climb higher. The creature's other tentacles wrapped themselves about the minotaur's legs, pinning him in place. In response, Koraf dug his nails into the tentacle he had hold of, causing more black blood to be released.

The creature started twisting now, trying to dislodge the persistent minotaur. Its pincer-arms clacked menacingly, and it doubled over so it could snap at Kof with its beak. The minotaur took advantage of the beast's maneuver and released his hold on the tentacle to grab the sides of its fishlike head. The beak dived in, driving at the minotaur's shoulder and sending jolts of pain through him.

Above, Fritzen continued to struggle with his mesmerized assailant, repeatedly striking Ilyatha against the cavern wall until at last the shadowperson lost consciousness. The half-ogre noticed Ilyatha was still breathing, and he gratefully eased the limp body to the cavern floor near where Tailonna still struggled with her webnet. Then he pushed off again, streaking toward the morkoth and Koraf.

The minotaur dug his fingers into the flesh of the morkoth's face, raking his nails through the skin and scales and causing the beast to scream. The creature's tentacles thrashed maddeningly and found a hold about Kof's thick waist. They squeezed tight, trying to force the water from the minotaur's lungs. Koraf felt himself blacking out, but he dug his nails into the morkoth's neck this time, trying to throttle the beast while he sucked in water.

Fritzen grabbed one of the tentacles that was holding the minotaur and tugged. Though he could not pull the tentacle free, he managed to relax its grip just enough so Kof could breathe. The minotaur spent his renewed strength by squeezing the morkoth's neck harder, trying to suffocate the thing. Fritzen squirmed his hand between the tentacle and Kof's waist, then he pushed harder and got his forearm between the tentacle and minotaur. After what seemed like forever, the morkoth weakened, and the tentacles released their hold. The minotaur, morkoth, and Fritzen drifted to the cavern floor in one heap. The morkoth lay motionless, and for a moment, and the half-ogre feared it was dead.

"No, it lives. Barely," Tailonna said. She was finally free of the webnet. "Kof nearly killed it, though, and it might still die if we don't get it to the ship and tend to its wounds. Though I'm not sure I can concoct a potion to heal it."

Fritzen shuddered, thinking about aiding such a malicious beast. *Perhaps Lendle can mend it,* he thought. *The gnome seems able to work wonders.*

Kof gently prodded his ribs and nodded his thanks to the half-ogre. The bite on his shoulder was deep, but small, and he pressed gently on it with his fingers. The minotaur grimaced, but shrugged off the ache. He'd suffered much worse wounds in the Lacynos arena. Satisfied he was all right, he moved to the shadowperson, who was groggily coming to. Kof bent and retrieved Ilyatha's daggers, then looked at the cavern walls. He turned to Ilyatha and furrowed his brow. He reached out and touched the shadowperson's thoughts.

Take the morkoth's body out of here and ask the ki-rin to carry it for you. I'm going to stay a few moments, collect some of these gems, the minotaur communicated. Ilyatha started to protest, but a stern look from Kof cut him off. *If the morkoth dies, or if Attat backs out of the bargain, Maquesta might need something of value to trade for her father and the* Perechon.

Ilyatha relayed Kof's plan. Tailonna passed her waist bag to him, then she helped Ilyatha to his feet and the two of them churned their legs to take them out of the cavern. Fritzen picked up the morkoth and wrapped it in the net. He laid a hand on the minotaur's shoulder and nodded. Then he pushed off, with his wounded prize in tow.

Alone, Koraf started about his work, prying emeralds, diamonds, rubies, and jacinths out of the walls of the morkoth's lair and stuffing handfuls of them into his pockets and Tailonna's bag. He selected the largest gems, the ones that best caught the light of the magical fire overhead. By the time he could carry no more and was certain he had a fortune, he began to get lightheaded. He suspected he had been gathering the treasure for a few hours. Fumbling about in the pouch at his waist, he retrieved his second potion and downed it.

Then he found his way out of the cave.

The ki-rin had taken the morkoth to the ship and returned for Bas-Ohn Koraf. The grateful minotaur, laden with his sparkling treasure, accepted Belwar's invitation and climbed upon his back. Within the hour they were approaching the deck of the *Perechon*.

Maquesta's fever was gone. She was on the port bow, talking animatedly to a still-soaked Fritzen and a blanket-wrapped Tailonna. A thin, white bandage was wrapped about Maq's leg, and she leaned against a spear for support, but it appeared the captain was much improved.

Ilyatha was nearby, babbling at the kuo-toa king, whose hands and feet were tied. The other kuo-toa had been herded up on deck, and they stood by the railing as the *Perechon* crew kept them at a distance with spears and harpoons. The ki-rin landed behind Maquesta, and she turned and grinned at Belwar and the minotaur.

"Belwar, thank you for returning my first mate. Lendle's watching the morkoth. The beast is in Attat's cage, which we've managed to lash to the aft of the ship—just enough of it underwater so the thing won't die. Lendle thinks he can pull the beast through; he's been sprinkling herbs in the water all around it. But we'll have to keep a close watch to make certain the morkoth doesn't use any of its nasty tricks. I think everything will work out," she gushed. "We'll be able to get my father back—and the *Perechon*."

The ki-rin nodded to her, but its eyes were sad. "I do hope everything works out for you, Maquesta. I must go now, but I will return if you need me."

The minotaur felt in his pockets for the gems, letting his fingers run around their smooth, faceted surfaces. Then he patted Tailonna's bulging bag at his side. "I have insurance, Captain," he told her, when he made sure the rest of the crew was occupied elsewhere. He produced a large emerald, holding it where she could see. "There are more. Enough to buy several ships, perhaps enough to buy every ship in Lacynos and pay for crews to man them."

The minotaur gave her Tailonna's bag and walked with Maquesta to her cabin, where he spilled the gems from his pockets across the top of her table. Maq's eyes sparkled. It was more wealth than she had seen in her entire lifetime, as much wealth as lined the Lacynos merchant's treasure cave.

"I hope we won't need all of these at Attat's," she said. "I can think of much better uses for them, including paying a crew that has been without full compensation for too long."

Maquesta secured the treasure under her bed, then she and Kof returned to the deck. Tailonna rushed toward the pair, requesting that the remaining kuo-toa be slain.

"We killed well more than half of the colony when they attacked the ship last night," Maquesta argued. "I think that is quite a significant loss, one that will take them years to recover from. To slay captive foes is butchery."

The sea elf nodded reluctantly. "Their numbers may no longer pose a threat to my people. If they do, we can deal with them now. The odds are in our favor."

With that, Maquesta motioned to Ilyatha, who cut the king's ropes and ordered the creature over the side. The crew prodded the other kuo-toa to jump into the water, as well.

"The king's sons are in the hold," Maq told Tailonna. "When we are far from here, they'll be released. The king has guaranteed us safe passage as long as they are all right. Now we sail for deep water. We'll bury our dead at sea, then be on our way to Attat's."

Chapter 15
The Return

"You don't have to stay with us any longer," Maquesta told Tailonna. "We can ease into the Endscape port for you. It's not far, and there's a deep harbor that we can move all the way into. It won't set us back more than hour, two at the most."

The women stood near the bow of the ship, looking out at the early morning sky and the rough water. The sails were full of wind and crackled with each gust, and the ship crested one wave after the next, rising and falling and spraying water over Maq and Tailonna. Despite the strong breeze, they were not making good time. Dragging the morkoth's cage slowed their progress considerably.

The sea elf turned to Maquesta, a grin forming on

her thin lips. "I know I could leave," she said softly. "With the morkoth captured, my obligation ends. But . . ." She paused and looked up at the cloudless sky. "I have to know how this all turns out, Maquesta. I've come this far, and I want to see this journey through. Besides, you can't afford to lose an hour or two."

"And after that?"

"This is a fine ship. I've learned you make an excellent captain, and you have an able crew. But if you keep traveling waters like these, you're going to need someone with a little magic." She winked at Maq. "Maybe I'll stay. For a while anyway."

"I think the crew would like that," Maq replied, still not sure if she would like the presence of the sea elf on board.

"I should catch some fish for the morkoth," Tailonna added. "My people said the beast eats only live animals, and I trust you want the morkoth returned healthy to Lord Attat. So with your permission . . ." The sea elf pointed over the railing.

Maquesta nodded, not accustomed to having Tailonna ask permission to do anything. Then Maq turned and walked toward the port side of the ship. Behind her, she heard a splash, signaling that the sea elf was overboard. Maquesta hoped Tailonna managed to catch plenty of fish. She and the crew could use some fresh food for dinner.

Maq passed by Kof, who was obviously enjoying his time at the wheel. She wondered what he was thinking. They were returning to Lacynos, where he would be the property of Lord Attat again. She would talk to him about this later, as she had been mulling over the idea of purchasing his services from Attat on a permanent basis. Waving to him, she sped her pace. The minotaur nodded a greeting in return.

Her leg had recovered, thanks to the sea elf's magical balm and Lendle's herbs, though it was still a little stiff.

She vowed to walk as much as possible today to help it limber up—the gnome's orders. For a moment she thought about going belowdecks and looking for Fritzen. She enjoyed his company, and she would like to hear again the story about the morkoth's capture and the twisting tunnels of its lair. But then she changed her mind. The half-ogre was with several of the other crewmembers, resting—hopefully sleeping. They would take over when night fell. With the cage slowing them more than she had anticipated, the *Perechon* had to continue moving, no matter the threats of traveling on the Blood Sea at night. There would be no more stops, and Ilyatha would use the flute of wind dancing each evening as long as its magic held out.

She spied Lendle leaning over the railing near the morkoth cage and decided to chat with him for a few moments. She wanted to thank the gnome for his help in mending her leg. She hadn't thanked him earlier—she was concerned about her ship, worried about the morkoth. In short, she thought to herself, she was taking the gnome for granted. That was a situation that would end now, she decided.

"YouaremostcertainlytheugliestcreatureIhaveseen," Lendle chattered at the morkoth. The gnome was leaning as far over the railing as his short stature allowed, ogling the beast and rapidly and loudly speaking to it. It was apparent Lendle wanted his voice to be heard above the sound of the wind and waves. Though the creature remained submerged, its head was just below the water, and it was looking back with interest at the gnome. Lendle watched its beak open and close and its red-flecked eyes narrow. The gnome tried to imitate the morkoth, then gave up and waggled his fingers in a childlike manner.

"Youbenicetome," Lendle sputtered. "Ikeptyoualive withmyherbs."

"Slow down, please." Maq reached his side and affectionately scratched the top of his head. "I can barely understand you, which means it's doubtful the morkoth has picked up on a word."

"Thinkso?"

"Yes, I think so."

"Hmm." Lendle rubbed the end of his ample nose and smiled. He made an effort to talk more slowly for Maq. "I wasn't really talking to him anyway. He's ugly, huh?"

"Yes."

"And he looks like a couple of creatures put together. Part octopus. Part barracuda. A little bit of squid thrown in. Maybe a sea snake or an eel, too. He'd make good bait for a really big fish. Too bad we have to get rid of him."

"Uh-huh."

"You know, Maquesta Kar-Thon, I could create a device resembling his tentacles, but straight. And I'd make them much wider and flatter, of course, like oars. Made out of steel or hard wood—that would be best. You wouldn't want them to wiggle the way his tentacles do. They'd need to be sturdy, and water-resistant, too. I'd spread them even, like the legs of a starfish, like spokes on a wheel, then I'd attach them to a barrel. See, just like the straight part of his body there. If I could affix it to a winch, something to make the tentacles turn, I bet I could hook the whole thing up to the back of the *Perechon*. I'd crank it up, wind it up like a child's toy, and it would help power us through the water. We'd go *much* faster."

Maquesta offered Lendle a weak smile. "It has potential," she laughed. "But how about you getting belowdecks and working on your oar engine? That device is already put together; it just needs to work properly. Because of the morkoth's cage we're not covering much distance. And we can't carry the creature any other way, because I suspect if we took him out of the water, he'd die."

"My oar engine!" The gnome beamed. "You most certainly could go faster, Maquesta Kar-Thon, if I got my engine to work!"

"Exactly."

"I'll get right to it."

"Wonderful idea."

"And I'll fix dinner at the same time." The gnome pushed away from the railing and headed toward the stairs. Then he stopped, scratched his head, and turned back to Maquesta. "What do I fix for the morkoth? Do you think it would eat my brown-bean soup? How about cornmeal muffins? Dried kipper?"

"Don't worry about the morkoth, Lendle. Tailonna is out catching some fish for it. She claims morkoths eat only living things. And I'd be careful not to get to close to its cage. Those tentacles are long, and I'd hate to tell the crew the cook has been eaten."

The gnome whirled on his tiny feet and resumed his course.

"Oh, Lendle?"

He stopped again and looked over his shoulder.

"Thanks for fixing my leg. And my arm. And for seeing to the rest of the injured crew. Without you, we'd all be in the infirmary."

The gnome smiled and waved his hand, dismissing her words. "It was nothing," he jabbered. "Besides, Tailonna and Ilyatha helped." Then he dashed belowdecks.

Maquesta stared through the water at the morkoth. It placidly hung floating inside the cage, glancing up at her occasionally. She reached over the side to touch the top of the cage and saw the red flecks in the morkoth's eyes grow more intense and brighter, and its tentacles began to undulate faster. When she withdrew her hand, the beast again seemed docile. Maq doubted the thing was subdued. She suspected it was just biding its time, waiting for someone to lean too close. She decided to instruct her crew to give it a wide berth. She couldn't afford to lose any more sailors—or the morkoth.

* * * * *

It fell to Tailonna to feed the morkoth every day. She would catch fish, then carry them to its cage and push them through the bars, careful not to bring her fingers too close to the creature's beak. It seemed to be growing stronger, and though the bars on the cage were solid, and the latch strong and out of the morkoth's reach, the beast's presence worried her.

"Do you think we'll have any trouble getting the morkoth to Lord Attat's?" the elf asked as Maquesta and Fritzen wandered over to watch a feeding session.

"No trouble at all," Maq replied. "I intend to make the minotaur lord come get it."

The three laughed for several long minutes, before Maquesta strolled toward the aft deck. Fritzen followed her.

"When we pull into Lacynos—" Fritzen started.

"If we make it on time," Maq interrupted. "The cage is slowing us, despite the magic of the flute. I'm troubled over it; the cage's drag was something I had not anticipated."

"We'll make it," he said. "And when we make it, what will you do, Maquesta?"

She looked at him quizzically.

"You've a taste of being a captain now. I can't see you doing anything else."

Maq had to admit she felt a satisfaction at the respect accorded her by the *Perechon*'s crew. No longer was there any hint of her being merely the ship's mascot or someone who had to be treated as special because she was the captain's daughter. She was the *Perechon*'s captain—at least for another week, and everyone on board recognized that. Once or twice it had occurred to her to wonder what it would be like with Melas taking over again as captain, and her following orders once more. But she quickly pushed such thoughts away as the ultimate disloyalty.

"My father is the captain of the *Perechon*. It's that simple."

"Kof brought back pockets full of gems. Enough to buy your own ship," Fritzen posed. "And a lot more."

Maq hung her head. "I know. I've been thinking about that. I want to offer some of the gems to Attat, an attempt to buy Kof. He deserves his freedom. Lord Attat is liable to not let him go—just for spite. But if Attat did go for it, there still would be enough gems left over to pay this crew a year's worth of wages and to buy a fully-rigged two-masted ship. I'd hate to leave my father. But, despite everything, I sort of like this. Being in charge."

Fritzen grinned. "It shows."

"I'd have to get a crew," she mused, dreaming.

"Well, for starters you'd have Kof, if Attat can be tempted. And you have me."

Maquesta looked up at him, and Fritzen drew her into his arms. He kissed her, and she lingered in his embrace, then she pulled away, confused, and worried that someone might have been watching. "I-I have to take the wheel," she stammered. "It's my shift."

"I'll relieve you in a few hours," he offered, grinning.

Maquesta nodded, backing away and realizing she must be blushing horribly. Turning and bouncing up the stairs, she allowed a wide smile to creep across her face.

* * * * *

As Lendle busied himself in the hold working on his oar engine, Ilyatha helped him, relishing the darkness of the ship's belly and delighting in the gnome's company. The shadowperson told the gnome that the work kept his mind off his daughter, Sando. Though from time to time Ilyatha stared off into the distance, as if in a trance. Lendle suspected he was trying to telepathically contact his daughter. Finally, the shadowperson's words confirmed it.

"We are still too far away for my mind to touch hers, to reassure her we are coming," Ilyatha said sorrowfully.

Lendle tried to be compassionate. "We're still many days out of Lacynos," he said. "She'll be all right. You'll see."

The shadowperson made some adjustments here and there to the gnome's odd-looking oar machine, then glanced at Lendle. "But what happens, my friend, if we are late? According to Kof, Lacynos is eight days away. Our thirty-day deadline is seven days away."

The gnome scowled and retrieved a crate of rods, cylinders, clamps, bolts, winches, and pulleys. "We'll make it," he said slowly and sadly. "Maquesta Kar-Thon will think of something. She will not allow us to be late."

* * * * *

Belwar continued to monitor the *Perechon*'s voyage. Every now and then the magnificent ki-rin would swoop out of the clouds and hover over the ship, sending the sailors friendly greetings and, on a few occasions, loaves of bread, wheels of cheese, sacks of oranges, or something else good to eat. Often the food was in the shape of mythical birds or long-finned fish, as the ki-rin created it from his imagination.

The great creature most often conversed with the sea

elf on these visits, though Maquesta sometimes was treated to his words of wisdom.

"I sense the evil growing," the ki-rin told her on one of these special occasions. It was nearing sunset, and he made it clear that during this visit his time would be spent only with Maquesta. "Snaring the morkoth stopped only a small speck of the wave of evil gaining strength in the Blood Sea."

Maquesta looked into Belwar's iridescent eyes. "You talked about this evil before, when we first met you. How can you sense this? And can you tell what the evil is?"

"It is in my nature to feel the good and bad pulses in this world. Too, I can sense good and evil in planes that exist side by side with your world of Krynn." The ki-rin shook his head sadly, his golden mane glittering and causing Maquesta to blink. "There is always evil in every world, but when the pulse of it gets stronger, when those with foul intentions become more powerful, it makes me uneasy. I am uneasy now, and that is why I know the evil is becoming more tangible."

The ki-rin hovered above the deck and looked to the sky. "I have business again on another plane, though I suspect it shall not keep me for more than a few days. I will return to you when my tasks are complete." With that, he climbed into the air, shimmered, and turned into a translucent, glittering cloud that dissipated in the wind.

* * * * *

As the *Perechon* approached the section of the Blood Sea known as Blood Cup, the site of many sunken ships, Maquesta stood near the capstan, her spyglass pressed to her eye. She was beginning to worry in earnest about making it back to Lacynos on time. The flute had been a boon, but they were four days out of the minotaur port city, and the deadline was three days away.

"There's something odd about the water."

Maquesta put the spyglass away as she saw Tailonna climb up over the railing. Maq had gotten used to the sea elf's frequent excursions into the water to catch fish for the morkoth—or just to swim.

"Odd, how?" Maq asked, padding over to join her.

"There are no fish. At least nothing small for me to catch for your beast." Tailonna shook herself, this time staying far enough away from Maquesta that she did not drench the captain. "I saw a couple of barracuda and one large bullshark. That was it. Though fish that size tend to keep the smaller fish away, I swam far enough that I should have seen at least a school of queen angels or some cuddlefish hanging near the bottom."

Maquesta looked toward the aft deck. Hvel was talking to Kof, who had the wheel. Maq rubbed her chin. "Maybe the presence of the morkoth is spooking them; the thing certainly has made me uneasy. That hasn't caused a problem with fish before now, but maybe because he is stronger . . ." She took a few steps toward the center of the deck and waved to Hvel. "Check on the morkoth!" Hvel nodded, and Maq resumed her conversation with the Tailonna.

Though Maquesta still considered the sea elf haughty and somewhat irritating, she was starting to warm to her. Maq had gained some respect for the comely Dimernesti. The sea elf had taught her about several drop-offs in the Blood Sea, things Maq was sure even her father didn't know about. Tailonna detailed where the coral cities of the mermen were and where other sea races frequented, and she explained that the mermen were often more than willing to trade with surface dwellers, though the mermen were shrewd bargainers.

"Far to the west is the Pit of Istar." Tailonna started to regale Maq with tales of another feature of the sea floor. "The water there is more than three hundred feet deep, and halfway down there is a whirlpool above an ancient rune-covered column."

Maq, listening to the story, glanced casually over her shoulder to watch Hvel. She squinted her eyes to see what he was doing. Working with the chain on the cage, she suspected, maybe pulling some seaweed free from it. Hvel worked and worried over the cage, then he started playing around with the mechanism that held it to the deck.

"No!" she shouted, finally realizing what he really was doing.

Maquesta broke away from the sea elf and darted toward the aft section of the ship, her sandaled feet slapping hard over the polished wood. A softer slapping sound indicated the barefoot sea elf was on her heels. "Stop it, Hvel! You'll release the cage!"

Hvel glanced up and smiled at his approaching captain. Nodding to her, he released the last clamp that held the morkoth's cage to the back of the ship.

"What have you done?" Maq screeched, as she slid alongside him.

Hvel looked at her blankly, and she spotted red flecks in his eyes. "The morkoth needed to be free," he said in a dull, monotone voice. "I couldn't open the cage, though. I tried real hard, too. So I let the cage loose. I thought maybe its impact on the sea floor might break it open. My friend the morkoth needed to be free. He told me so."

"All stop!" Maquesta bellowed at the top of her lungs.

Immediately the sailors on deck rushed to the rigging to lower the sails.

"Drop anchor!" Maq continued to shout orders. "Now!"

"Aye, Captain!" It was Vartan calling from the capstan,

where he was fervently working to lower the anchor.

A pounding across the deck brought Koraf and Fritzen to the aft section where the cage had been affixed. Hvel grinned at them and quickly explained how successful he was in freeing his new friend. He puffed out his chest in pride. Furious, Maquesta shook his shoulders. The red flecks faded, and a dazed Hvel stood looking out over the water.

"What happened to the cage?" he asked innocently. "Why are we stopped? Why are you all looking at me like that?"

Maq ignored him and whirled on the Dimernesti. "Tailonna, how long would it take you to mix up some more potions of water breathing?"

"Not long," the sea elf said. "But I likely have enough ingredients for only one." She rushed toward the armory, where the remainder of her herbs were being stored.

"Do it quickly!" Maq called after her. "I'm going after the cage." Then she wheeled on Koraf. "Get Hvel belowdecks. I want Lendle to look him over."

The minotaur half-carried the puzzled Hvel away, leaving Maq and Fritzen staring at the water.

"Let me go after the cage," the half-ogre offered. "I've faced the morkoth before—in his element. I know what to expect. Besides, I'm stronger than you, and that cage is heavy."

Maquesta firmly shook her head. "This task is mine. I have to do this." Her shoulders sagged. "And we were so close. How could this have happened?"

Fritz stood behind her and wrapped his arms about her waist. "We're not undone yet, but you'll have to give in to me this time. There is no way you can bring up that cage."

"Neither could you," she retorted, spinning and releasing herself from his arms. "Not even you are that strong. But I could use your help up top. Lendle has a collection of winches and pulleys down in the hold. I've seen them lying around next to his oar engine. If you could get them rigged up, anchored off the aft deck, I could hook a couple of cables to the cage and we could pull it up."

Fritzen stroked his chin in contemplation. "What if the cage has broken open, Maquesta? What if the morkoth is free?"

"Then we are undone," she said softly. "My father will die, and Ilyatha will never see his daughter again. But I'll not let another sailor die on this quest."

"Thebeastisfree?" Lendle hurried up behind them and poked his head through the aft rail. "Everyoneistalking aboutthemorkothescaping."

"Temporarily escaping," Tailonna said, as she approached, holding up a vial. "Enough for one potion, and not a large one at that. I suspect this won't last you more than a few hours."

Maq stepped away from Fritz and took the vial in her trembling hand. "It will have to be enough, then." She downed the mixture in one gulp, made sure her short sword and dagger were firmly hooked to her belt, then vaulted over the railing and plunged into the choppy water below.

Tailonna glanced at Fritzen and Lendle. "I'm going with her," she said. Then the sea elf was gone, too.

The gnome peered over the railing to watch their forms disappear as they swam deeper.

"Ihaveabadfeelingaboutthis," Lendle jabbered.

The half-ogre tapped him on the shoulder, nearly sending the startled gnome into the sea, too.

"Winches and pulleys?"

The gnome nodded and led Fritzen into the hold.

* * * * *

The water became colder the deeper Maquesta swam. Her tunic was plastered against her skin, making her movements awkward, and after several yards she tugged off her sandals and let them float away. She felt the water move in and out of her nose, deep into her lungs. It was an odd sensation, but the potion was working, and Maq was amazed that she was breathing water as if it were air.

Dark shapes loomed up below her. Rock formations, a small coral reef, the wreck of an old ship. She batted her eyes and pumped her legs harder, her efforts carrying her deeper still. Another wreck came into view, and another. She gritted her teeth. The morkoth had chosen the center of the Blood Cup to make its move. These waters were rumored to be filled with all manner of aquatic life, lured by the empty husks of once-proud caravels, schooners, warships, and carracks. Divers who sought out the Cup to harvest the riches of the hulks were rarely successful. Most succumbed to attacks from bullsharks.

Sharks were the least of Maquesta's worries now. In fact, Maq didn't see any fish at all. Wait! There was one bullshark, a massive one. It lazily swam over the largest wreck, probably searching for food. That explained the lack of smaller fish, Maq decided. Bullsharks would try to eat anything smaller than themselves.

Trying to keep a good distance from the large shark, Maquesta hovered several yards above the sea floor and peered through the gloom, trying to find the morkoth's cage. All she could see was the graveyard of unfortunate ships and rocky spirals reaching upward amid them. Judging where the cage might have gone down before the *Perechon* could stop, she started swimming forward, skirting the ships, suspecting the cage might lie beyond them. With each stroke she prayed the cage was intact. If the morkoth was free, it could be hiding in any one of these rotting vessels—or it could be swimming as far away and as fast as its tentacles would take its ugly body.

As her half-elven eyes became more accustomed to the darkness, Maquesta began to pick out details. Most of the ships had sat on the bottom for decades. The barnacles and algae that flourished on their sides were thick and covered up the names on their hulls. Broken masts pointed in all directions, as if the sea floor were a giant pin cushion. Rotting pieces of sails fluttered from some of the masts, looking like ghosts hovering in the water.

The *Golden Sailfish*, *Blood Sea Bounty*, *Felicia's Dream*, and *Red Roland* were some of the names she could discern on the more recent wrecks. Perhaps victims of the Blood Sea imps, she mused, as her course took her around the edge of the graveyard and to a sloping coral ridge just beyond. Fortunately the morkoth had not hypnotized Hvel at night, when the imps are about, she thought.

Something brushed up against Maquesta's legs, and she drew her dagger, twirled in the water, and stopped herself from stabbing forward with the blade. Tailonna hovered there. The sea elf pointed toward the coral ridge. Maquesta followed the Dimernesti's gaze and spotted the outline of the cage, just over the edge of an embankment. Squinting, Maq could tell the morkoth was still inside. But it was getting some help to get free.

No! Maquesta's mind screamed, as she kicked her legs furiously to take her closer to the coral ridge. A squid, apparently under the control of the morkoth, was hard at work on the bars, trying to pry them apart with its tentacles. The morkoth was assisting it, using its tentacles to do the same.

Maquesta's eyes grew wide as she watched the bars start to bend. The sea elf shot past her, propelling herself at the squid, and hitting the creature's bulbous body, pushing it away from the cage and impaling it on a jagged finger of coral. Maquesta swam faster, too, her lungs aching from the exertion. She held the dagger in her teeth and dived toward the cage. As she landed on the ridge by the cage, the sharp edges of the coral bit into her feet. Ignoring the pain, Maquesta drew her short sword, moved forward, and thrust the blade through the bars to keep the morkoth back. She examined the bars that were swelled outward. Not enough space to let the morkoth slip through, she decided, though more than enough space for a tentacle to slip out.

She glanced over her shoulder to see Tailonna finish off the dying squid. Another was moving slowly toward Maquesta and the cage, and the sea elf started shooing it away, like one might chase a naughty dog.

Maquesta looked at the morkoth, then let her gaze drift upward and to the south, where she vaguely made out the image of the *Perechon*'s hull. The bullshark was hovering under the ship now, probably curious.

You're coming back with us, she thought, as she gazed malevolently at the caged morkoth. There'll be no more of your tricks. You can try them on Lord Attat for all I care. But first, she added to herself, we've got to get you out of this cage so you can swim free. There's no reason you should be confined in this terrible cage.

Maquesta's eyes were flecked with red, mirroring the eyes of the morkoth. The creature hovered within the confines of its cage, its tentacles tracing patterns of bubbles in the dark water.

Maq watched the bubbles for several moments, then she pushed herself off the coral ridge and floated to the top of the cage. The solder on the bars was likely the weakest there, she decided, as she hooked her legs between the bars for support and started to work on the metal with her dagger. The tip of her weapon broke off, but the rest of the blade was still strong.

Faster, the morkoth urged her.

Faster, she answered inside her head.

Maquesta had just about succeeded in breaking one of the welds when she felt herself flying backward through the water, pushed by two strong arms. Tailonna thrust Maq away from the cage, propelling her down to the coral ridge, and slamming her into it, knocking the water from Maq's lungs.

You don't understand, Maq's eyes tried to tell Tailonna. My friend the morkoth must be free.

Tailonna grabbed Maquesta's head and brought her own face down to within inches of it. "Listen to me," Tailonna said. The tones sounded bubbly and distorted through the water. "The beast has hypnotized you, just as it did Hvel. As it did to Ilyatha in its tunnel-lair. Fight it!"

Maq blinked and tried to focus on the words, on the sparkling blue-green elvish eyes before her. Tailonna roughly shook her.

"The morkoth," Maq mouthed. "The morkoth lulled me!" Maquesta pushed off the ridge, away from the Dimernesti and toward the cage, fire in her eyes replacing the red specks. She brought the pommel of her dagger down on the top of the cage to get the beast's attention, then she narrowed her eyes and glared at it.

Maquesta stood on top of the cage and pointed her hand up, in the direction of the *Perechon*. Then she motioned to Tailonna, indicating she should go to the ship. The sea elf shook her head fervently, perhaps unsure if Maquesta was herself. But Maq pointed again, and then pointed at the cage.

Tailonna understood. She was to go to the ship and bring down a cable. The sea elf waited for several moments, until the bullshark moved on, then her powerful legs kicked off from the sea floor and started her toward the surface.

Maquesta watched the Dimernesti rise, feeling envious of her ability to swim so strongly and move so gracefully beneath the waves. Then a shadow fell across Maq's line of sight. She blinked and looked up, initially fearing another bullshark. Squinting her eyes, she saw the movement again. One of the rocky columns amid the sunken ships was quivering, as if it might fall down.

Then column began bending, contorting. At first Maquesta thought the image was a trick played by the currents. But as she continued to watch, she saw the other columns start to move, too. She glanced at the morkoth. It was still. Its tentacles were at rest, though its wide eyes glared back at her malevolently. Not an illusion created by the morkoth, she guessed. Tailonna was too far away now to see what was transpiring. Maquesta could see only the tiny reflection of the sea elf disappearing at the top of the sea, climbing up to the *Perechon*'s deck.

The wavering rocks bothering her, Maquesta pushed off from the cage, trying to get above the sea floor and get a better look at the living columns. As she rose, she saw that the rocky columns were attached to a larger rock, one that sat in the middle of the graveyard. Her stomach began to churn as she realized it wasn't stone she was watching, but a living creature, a leviathan rising from the sea floor. A pair of large eyes opened on the bulbous, rocky-looking body, and Maq's mouth gaped wide.

A giant octopus! Her mind raced. This was why the ships lay broken all around. They weren't the victims of the Blood Sea imps—they were the victims of this hideous monstrosity! And this was the reason there were so few fish. The bullshark was insignificant next to this thing. As the creature moved, barnacles and algae, the parasites that had clung to its tentacles, fell away, revealing smooth, green-black skin. The mantle of the octopus, its bag-shaped body, was larger than any of the ships that lay broken about it. Eyes wider across than a man is tall blinked at her from the base of its body. Eight tentacles, longer than huge sea snakes, writhed and whirled, stirring up sand. The undersides of the tentacles were much lighter in color and sported hundreds of small cups. As the tentacles wiggled above the sea floor, Maq glimpsed the creature's gaping mouth on the underside of its mantle. As she watched, the creature's color began changing, becoming lighter to nearly blend in with the sand and ruined ships.

The thing must have been sleeping for weeks, Maquesta realized, to have accumulated so much algae on its skin. What had awakened it? She glanced down at the morkoth and saw its eyes were practically glowing. A single tentacle flexed toward the giant, like a beckoning finger.

Maquesta shot up through the water, her legs pumping fiercely. She had to get to the *Perechon*, had to get the ship out of here. Retrieving the morkoth had just become too costly. She refused to jeopardize everyone on board.

A stream of bubbles trailing behind her, Maq saw the light growing brighter ahead, signaling that she was nearing the surface. *Ilyatha!* her mind called out. *Make them raise the anchor! Make them . . .* At the edge of her vision, Maq saw a mammoth tentacle wrap itself about the anchor chain. Like a child with a toy, the great beast began to pull, and she saw with anguish that the *Perechon* rocked in response.

Changing her tactics, Maquesta angled herself beneath the ship. Her side ached, but she pushed herself harder, faster. She was nearly under the ship now, near the chain. She groped about on her belt and discovered that her dagger was gone, forgotten somewhere on the sea floor. But her short sword was with her. Pulling it free, and swimming more awkwardly with it in her hand, she finally reached the chain.

Hear me, Ilyatha! she continued to concentrate on the shadowperson, hoping he would pick up her thoughts. *You've got to get the* Perechon *away from here.*

Wrapping her legs about the anchor chain, so that she was head down and pointed toward the octopus, Maquesta pulled herself closer to the tentacle and lashed out with the sword. She sliced halfway through the tip of the tentacle that held the chain, then drew back her weapon to jab at it again.

I'm here, Maquesta. The voice inside her head was Ilyatha's.

A giant octopus! Maq shouted back to the telepath. *It has the anchor. I'm cutting it free. Raise the anchor! Tell Kof to get the* Perechon *out of here!*

We'll throw a rope to you, Ilyatha communicated, an urgency to his telepathic voice.

Don't worry about me! Maquesta concentrated. *The ship. Save the ship.* She lashed out at the tentacle again, this time successfully cutting through the rubbery thing. Dark red blood, almost black, poured out into the water like a cloud. She felt the tension loosen about the chain. *Move the ship! That's an order. Tailonna can direct you around the Blood Cup!* Maq realized that with those thoughts her father's life had finally, irrevocably, slipped beyond her grasp. Without the morkoth, there would be no antidote for Melas. There would be no freedom for Ilyatha's daughter. But staying over the Blood Cup jeopardized the lives of everyone on the *Perechon*. She could not justify that.

Releasing herself from the chain the moment she felt it start to surge upward, Maquesta decided to buy the *Perechon* some time. Swimming at another tentacle, she thrust forward with her sword, stabbing at the rubbery mass. Myriad suctionlike cups wriggled at her, but she kept out of their way, hovering just at the end of the tentacles' reach. Withdrawing the sword, she plunged it in again and again. Then the world turned black around her as the water darkened like the midnight sky. She twisted her head all about, but it was pitch-black everywhere. Not even her sensitive vision permeated the darkness. Then her eyes began to sting, and she realized the octopus had released an inky substance, turning the water black.

Maq was disoriented, not knowing which way was up, which way to the ocean floor, where the octopus might be lurking. Kicking her legs, she began to move, guessing that she was rising toward the surface. She held her sword tightly, and waved it back and forth in front of her to keep any tentacles at bay. As a jab of pain shot through her leg, she realized a tentacle had found a way around her flailing weapon. Perhaps the leviathan could see through its dark cloud. The octopus tightened its grip, and Maq gritted her teeth, trying to block out the aching sensation. Twisting in the black water, she continued to flail about with her blade, hoping it would connect with something.

Again and again she dragged the sword through the water, until at last it met resistance. Jabbing there, she felt a rush of bubbles against her body. She must have hurt the leviathan. Stabbing again, she cringed as a tentacle found her sword arm. It gripped her tightly, but she kept her fingers wrapped about the blade's pommel, refusing to let go. With one tentacle also still holding her leg, the tentacles began to move away from each other—the octopus intended to tear her apart!

Maquesta fought back a wave of pain and groped out with her free hand. She felt the tentacle about her sword arm, and she fumbled frantically until she felt her captured hand and the pommel still held tightly within it. Grabbing the sword, she started sawing through the tentacle with it, trying to free her captured arm. The tentacle tugged more strongly, nearly wrenching her shoulder out of the socket, but she persisted. The tentacle tugged again, and Maq screamed, though no sound came out, only a stream of bubbles. She cut faster, and at last she was rewarded when the tentacle about her arm writhed away. Doubling over, she felt about her calf, at the tentacle still firmly holding her there. Again she started cutting. This tentacle released her quickly to avoid being severed, and she kicked her legs to propel herself away from the creature.

She felt herself rising, and she kicked harder. Maquesta knew that if this giant octopus was like its smaller cousins, it would be able to regenerate its rubbery limbs. But it would take several weeks, and she and the *Perechon* would be long gone. Her heart hammered wildly in her chest, the thundering sound filling her ears and increasing her terror. Her feet churned, and she felt out of breath, dizzy, but at last her head broke through the surface of the water and she started breathing air. She coughed, spewing out the saltwater that had been in her lungs. Blinking furiously as the light of the morning sun hit her full in the face, she turned about in the water, looking for the *Perechon*.

The anchor dangled from the ship, which was a little better than a hundred yards from her. As she watched, the sails reached the top of the masts and began to billow with air. Sheathing her sword, Maq started swimming toward the ship. No use trying to fight the giant octopus when she couldn't see it for all the inky water, she decided.

"There's Maq!" It was Fritzen's voice. "Wait for her!"

Don't wait for me! Maq's mind scolded, hoping Ilyatha was still reading her thoughts. *If I reach the ship on my own, all right. But get out of here before . . .* Her last thought trailed off as she saw a giant tentacle rise above the water and drape itself over the bow of the *Perechon*.

Panicking, Maquesta swam faster, taking great gulps of air into her lungs and watching as the sailors ran toward the rubbery mass that threatened to capsize the ship. As she closed the distance, the water began churning in front of her, bubbling like Lendle's soup caldron. An enormous, bulbous head broke the surface of the waves. The leviathan had risen, seeking to add another ship to its trophy collection on the sea floor.

"You'll not take the *Perechon!*" Maquesta seethed. "You can't have my ship."

The great beast seemed not to notice Maq, it was so intent on the ship. Waving another two tentacles in the air, it dropped them across the deck, one between the mizzenmast and the mainmast, and the other over the aft section. The giant octopus began to rock the ship wildly, and Maq saw Vartan and Hvel get pitched into the water.

On the deck of the ship, Koraf gave up trying to steer the *Perechon*. He drew his sword, grabbed a belaying pin, and rushed at the tentacle that lay between the masts. The rubbery tentacle had broken the railings on both sides of the deck and, like a snake, had begun to constrict about the center of the ship. The minotaur grimaced as he heard the wood groan in protest. Motioning wildly, he directed the bulk of the sailors to join him. Gathering on both sides of the thing, they began hacking on the leviathan's tentacle, cleaving into the thick tissue and trying to dislodge it.

Fritzen had grabbed hold of the tentacle on the aft section of the ship and was trying to pry it loose. His muscles bulged, and the veins stood out on the side of his neck. Wrapping his left arm about the tentacle where it tapered on the port side, he reached to his waist and his fingers closed about the hilt of his dagger. Drawing the weapon, he pulled it back behind his head, and then let it fall, stabbing deep into the beast's flesh. Dark red blood spurted out, making the deck slippery. It was all the half-ogre could do to keep his balance. Then the tentacle turned on him.

Releasing the deck, where it had splintered the wood, and leaving a gaping hole open to the galley, the tentacle rose up into the air. Like a snake, it came down and coiled about Fritzen. It picked him up from the deck and shook him as a baby would a rattle. The half-ogre concentrated to keep from dropping the dagger. As the thing flailed him about, he stabbed into the tentacle repeatedly.

A great cry erupted from the leviathan's wide mouth. Fritzen and the others were hurting it! In anger, the giant octopus hurled Fritzen at the mizzenmast. The half-ogre flew through the air until his back soundly struck the mast halfway up. The wind knocked out of him, he plummeted to the deck, near where Koraf and the others had just managed to sever the tentacle that had been wrapped about the ship's middle.

The half-ogre groaned and shook his head. For a moment it looked as though there were two minotaurs, two of everyone. He shook his head again, and his vision began to clear. Stumbling forward, he fell against the tentacle and began pushing the severed part into the water. The stump that remained started thrashing about maddeningly. Koraf ordered the sailors to back away, lest they be beaten by the thing. As they complied, the flailing stump hit the mizzenmast, cracking it. The tall beam teetered for a moment, then the top half of it snapped off and crashed to the deck, pinning two fleeing crewmen, and covering the rest with the collapsed sail.

Tailonna and Ilyatha struggled against the tentacle at

the bow of the ship. The sea elf hummed and concentrated, while the shadowperson struck at the rubbery mass with his barbed staff. Violet darts flew from Tailonna's fingertips, striking the tentacle and causing it to rear back in pain. As the tentacle pulled back, it struck Ilyatha, knocking him into the water.

Maquesta saw the shadowperson fall. Tangled in his voluminous cloak, he flung his arms about, but couldn't stay afloat. Maq swam toward him, noticing out of the corner of her eye that Hvel and Vartan had grabbed on to a section of the railing that was floating in the water. Panting, Maquesta finally reached the shadowperson and started pulling the sodden cape from him.

"I know the sun will hurt you," Maquesta gasped. "But you'll drown with all these clothes on." Letting the cloak and hood float away, she grabbed Ilyatha about the shoulders and swam with him toward Hvel and Vartan. Shouts from her crewmen on deck, and the cacophonous screeching of the octopus, filled her senses.

"Maq!" Vartan called. "We thought you were dead."

Maquesta pushed the shadowperson into Hvel's arms. "Hold him," she huffed. "I'm going after the octopus. If we can't beat this thing back, we'll all be dead."

She dived beneath the surface, breathing deeply of the water again, thankful that Tailonna's potion was still working. Maquesta angled herself away from the ship and under the octopus. From beneath its body, she saw its limbs waving wildly and noticed that two had been cut in half. Dark blood poured from the frayed edges. The creature's mouth was open, and its long, pointed tongue, covered with two rows of jagged teeth, wriggled back and forth.

As Maq swam toward its underside, short sword raised in front of her, one of the unharmed tentacles brought a struggling sailor to its mouth. She kicked her legs faster to close the distance, but the octopus stuffed the hapless sailor inside its beak, using its tongue to cut the man into bits before Maq could even discern his identity.

Maquesta closed her eyes for but a moment, not wanting to see the sailor's grisly end. Opening them slowly, she saw the octopus's beak open and close, chewing its meal. She thrust herself forward, slipping between a pair of tentacles and jabbing at the bulbous body from underneath. Again the octopus screamed, but this time the cry was louder than before. The leviathan pulled its tentacles away from the *Perechon* and started swirling them about its body in the water, looking for its attacker.

Struggling to keep herself away from the tentacles—and staying beneath the giant octopus where its eyes could not see—Maquesta drove the sword in again. Almost instantly she was surrounded by the inky blackness. Undaunted, she withdrew her blade and stabbed forward, certain that the great beast could not have moved far.

* * * * *

On deck, Fritzen and Koraf lowered a rope ladder to Vartan and Ilyatha. "Hurry, please!" Vartan called. "The thing got Hvel. Dragged him under. We'll be next!"

Tailonna jumped over the side and helped Ilyatha to the ladder. The shadowperson's eyes were closed, and he tried to draw his webbed arms about his face to fend off the sun's rays. Vartan leapt ahead of Ilyatha, climbing up several rope rungs then extending an arm down, indicating Tailonna should hand up the shadowperson.

After she was certain Ilyatha was all right, Tailonna dived beneath the water, searching for Maquesta, who she guessed must be somewhere in the cloud of blackness. She mumbled a few words, and a globe of glowing blue light appeared in the palm of her hand, cutting through the inky haze. She spied Maq beneath the giant octopus's body. Maquesta was quivering, and Tailonna noticed the leviathan's toothy tongue was wrapped around Maq's left leg.

The sea elf gasped, realizing the octopus must have released its nerve poison into the water, one of its last defenses. Maquesta must have hurt the creature badly, Tailonna mused as she swam toward the octopus's mouth, hoping she would be in time.

* * * * *

Maq felt her fingers growing numb and had to keep both hands about the hilt of her short sword so she wouldn't drop it. Shocks of hot and cold chased up and down her frame, and she felt a tingling in her leg where the tongue had grabbed her. She bit her bottom lip, hoping the pain might help her concentrate. Focusing, she stabbed forward with her sword, piercing the octopus's tongue.

The beast let go of her, and its tongue flapped wildly, her sword still embedded in it. Maquesta, weaponless, looked about and saw Tailonna swimming toward her. The sea elf had a dagger strapped in her belt, and Maquesta numbly swam toward her, motioning for the weapon.

Tailonna reached Maq in a few strokes and could tell by the glassy look in the captain's eyes that the nerve toxin was in her system. The sea elf shook her head and pointed away from the octopus, trying to get Maquesta to back off to safety. But Maq was determined. Reaching forward with unfeeling fingers, Maq saw her hand close about the dagger. She pulled the weapon from Tailonna's belt. Maq brought her other hand about the small hilt, too, not wanting to drop the blade. Tailonna's magical light source helped her see the giant octopus, which had now turned so it could watch the two tiny figures in the water beneath it.

The sea elf began mumbling again, calling forth violet darts from her fingertips that struck the octopus near its mouth. Its lidless eyes grew wide and dark, filled with anger, as it waved its tentacles to carry it closer to the small creatures causing it so much pain.

At the same time, a determined Maquesta swam awkwardly forward, luckily dodging a tentacle, and moving up against the creature's head. Its massive eyes regarded her balefully, and Maq stared back at the creature, pulled her lip up in a snarl, and plunged the dagger into the nearest eye.

In the next instant, the sea about the *Perechon* became a foaming, frothing expanse. Tentacles thrashed about, and the giant octopus screamed shrilly, causing those on board the ship to cover their ears. The ship pitched, sending many of the sailors to their knees.

"To the oars!" Kof bellowed. Only those sailors closest to him heard the order above the terrible noise coming from the leviathan.

Maquesta and Tailonna suddenly found themselves being propelled backward through the water. The giant octopus was shooting a jet of water through its body. The burst of speed sent the leviathan away from the *Perechon*, and the backlash sent Maq and the sea elf bumping soundly up against the hull of the ship.

"Grab the rope ladder!" Fritzen called out.

The feeling had started coming back into Maquesta's fingers. Mustering what was left of her strength, she pulled herself up the ladder and fell forward onto the deck. Tailonna scampered up behind her. As Maq raised her head, she took in the destruction.

The mizzenmast lay irreparably broken, in worse shape than the mast Belwar had destroyed on the

Butcher. The railing was nonexistent about most of the ship, and holes dotted the deck where the leviathan's tentacles had ripped up boards. All about Maq, the crew worked to pick up the mess.

Fritzen helped her to her feet. His eyes held hers, and this time she didn't look away.

"I thought I was going to lose you," he said.

"I lost my father," she replied simply. "The *Perechon* can't make Lord Attat's deadline now. The morkoth is at the bottom of the sea. And the only way we're getting anywhere is under oar power. It will take us weeks to get back to Lacynos."

Fritzen kissed her forehead. "We also lost Hvel," he said finally. "The octopus pulled him under. Beyond that, two sailors were injured when the mizzenmast fell, but their wounds are not serious. Ilyatha will be all right, too, if that's any consolation. He's in the armory, under a blanket. The sun burned his skin and temporarily blinded him."

Tears spilled from Maquesta's eyes. The price had become very high indeed.

* * * * *

For nearly an hour the only sounds on the deck were made by crewmen cleaning up pieces of the mast and folding the sail. Maquesta sat on the poop deck, looking out over the water. Vartan padded up behind her.

"At your request, we've organized teams for rowing. They'll be starting . . ." His voice trailed off.

A discordant collection of groans, wheezes, clicks, and whirrs issued from belowdecks. A loud, sputtering belch discharged, and a great gout of black smoke puffed up through every hole in the deck. Maquesta jumped to her feet and clamped her hands over her ears. The air became filled with a cacophonous clanking, grinding, squeaking, and banging sound. Smoke poured forth again, and then the *Perechon* jerked forward. Maq climbed down from the aft deck and dashed through the smoke. Standing at the side of the ship, she glanced over. The oars were moving. All in unison.

"Mymachineisworking!" cried Lendle.

The gnome rushed on deck, and all eyes turned toward him. A triumphant cheer went up from the *Perechon*'s crew, and Lendle's eyes filled with appreciative tears. His clothes were in tatters, and burn marks were evident all over his small form. The tips of his boots had burned away, and his toes, covered with soot, wiggled excitedly. There wasn't much left of his beard, and his once-white hair was now as dark as Maquesta's. His face was smudged all over, except for a small track, down each cheek, that his tears had washed clean.

"MaquestaKarThonmymachineisworking!"

She rushed to the gnome and picked him up, hugging him fiercely and covering herself with soot and dirt in the process.

His face broke into a broad grin, and he talked slower to accommodate her. "Now we can make it to Lacynos on time. With one sail and my oar machine, we'll make better time than ever before."

"But the morkoth!" Maquesta cried. "Tailonna! Do you think the octopus is still down there?"

The sea elf rushed to Maq's side and gave Lendle's head an affectionate pat. "I think that octopus is long gone from these waters. Let me take a cable over the side and see if the beast is still in the cage. If so, we'll hoist him up. If not, we'll go looking for him again."

Maq shook her head. "This quest has been too expensive already. I'll not jeopardize another life on Lord Attat's creature hunt."

The Dimernesti nodded, somehow understanding

what was going on in Maquesta's mind. She ran to the aft of the ship and dived over, hardly making a splash as her form cut through the water.

"Lendle, can you make the oars stop—without turning off your machine? Perhaps just raise them up out of the water so we don't go anywhere?" Maquesta looked into his bright eyes, hoping she wasn't about to make another mistake. "I'm afraid if you turn it off, you might not get it started again."

"Oh, it will work from now on, Maquesta Kar-Thon." Lendle was beaming with pride. "When you directed us to set up a winch and pulley on the aft deck to pull up the morkoth's cage, I had to take the big winch out of my oar engine. It seems I had a few too many parts in the engine, because when I closed it back up, and turned it on, it started right away. Of course, there is the matter of a little smoke."

"So you have a winch set up?"

"Oh, yes, Vartan and I did that while you were . . . busy underwater."

"And it looks like we're going to need that winch and pulley!" Fritzen was calling from the aft deck. "I'll need some help with the crank. Tailonna says the morkoth is still caged!"

* * * * *

Several long minutes later, Tailonna's head cleared the water. "I've hooked up the cable. And it looks as if the morkoth is decidedly unhappy about all of this."

As she climbed on deck, the sea elf explained that she'd had to chase away a veritable army of crabs that were hard at work trying to free the morkoth. The steel bars were tougher than their claws, and all the experience had done was make the little crustaceans grumpy, she added.

It took shifts of three men, taking turns working the

crank, to pull up the cage. As its top broke through the water, Maquesta ordered the men to look away. She dashed to the hold and retrieved one of the old sails that she had stored in the event her new ones needed repairs.

Tailonna drew the material about the cage, so the morkoth could not look out of the bars and hypnotize any of the men. She left only a small hole, just large enough to slip fish through to feed the beast. And the hole had a flap of material attached to it, so when the creature wasn't eating, it would not even be able to see a speck of sky.

"Reminds me of an orange parrot my mother had," Fritzen mused. "The little bird was so loud that she had to completely cover the cage every night. She used a white sheet, and when I was a child I would have nightmares about the ghost in the kitchen."

"I dare say the morkoth is more annoying than a bird," Maq quipped.

"I'm not sure you could convince my mother of that."

"At least you still have a mother."

"Somewhere," Fritzen answered.

The cage secured to the aft section of the ship, Maquesta nodded to Lendle to put his oar engine into its highest gear. All of the crew had assembled on the deck to watch the gnome's machine at work. They anxiously stared over the sides, looking at the oars that hovered just above the water. Finally, the oars began to move, their oarlocks creaking. Slowly at first, then gathering speed and power.

The crew broke into spontaneous applause, and Lendle's blush could be seen even through the soot on his face.

* * * * *

During most of the next day, Lendle tended the engine as if it were a newborn baby, emerging from the cargo hold only to take an occasional bite to eat, and forcing Vartan to stand in as chef. The *Perechon* was making better time than ever before—and was also making more noise than Maquesta would have believed possible. She made a mental note to ask Lendle—after they arrived in Lacynos—if he could make the oar machine work quietly. She didn't want to ask him now and risk him doing something to stop it from functioning.

Maquesta and Fritzen stood by the helm, listening to the odd collection of sounds and watching the sun drop toward the horizon. It was the evening of the second day that the oar engine had been in use, and the *Perechon*, within less than a dozen hours, would be approaching the entrance to Horned Bay—its prize captive in tow, and more than a half day short of Attat's deadline.

Chapter 16

Resolutions

Clanking, wheezing, and belching gouts of black smoke, the *Perechon* pulled into Lacynos's bay shortly after dawn the next day, beating Lord Attat's deadline. Sailors on the wharf looked up in amazement at the wounded ship that was sailing smoothly but loudly.

Maquesta directed Lendle to cut his oar engine, and the ship coasted into the fetid waters in time for the crew to see a minotaur crewman throw the entrails of some large animal over the side of a schooner. Maq turned up her nose in disgust and was thankful that within a few hours Melas and the *Perechon* would be out of Lacynos—forever as far as she was concerned. She doubted the minotaur lord would put up any argument to keep the *Perechon* when he spotted the ship's condition and lack of a mizzenmast. Fritzen asked about making repairs in the port, but Maq only scowled.

"As soon as we have my father and Ilyatha has his daughter, we're leaving. We can find another port a few days away. Maybe it won't have as good facilities, but I'm sure the hospitality will be better," Maquesta told him.

Bas-Ohn Koraf stood near the bow. Maquesta could tell the minotaur had sunk into a deep state of depression. Before sunset his freedom would be taken from him, though she was hopeful Attat would allow her to purchase him with some of the morkoth's gems. Then there would be the matter of her father getting used to a minotaur crewman. That might be difficult after everything Attat had done to him, but she had come to rely too much on Kof to simply dismiss the minotaur first mate.

Once the *Perechon* was safely anchored, Maq sent Vartan and Fritzen to shore in the longboat—with a message for Lord Attat. He was to come to the wharf, bringing Melas and Sando along with him. The message further detailed that Maq would meet him on the deck of the *Perechon*, at which time the morkoth would be turned over to his care, ending her obligation to the minotaur lord. An exchange of prisoners, she viewed it.

Maq had no idea how the minotaur lord intended to get the morkoth from the harbor to his palace, since she thought the creature would die when taken out of seawater, but that was not something Maq intended to worry about. She'd kept her part of the bargain, and she didn't care what Attat intended to do with the beast.

She waved as Fritzen and Vartan eased the longboat toward the docks, then began pacing, anxiously awaiting the return of her father. She had so much to tell him. Tell him! Of course! She raced belowdecks to where Ilyatha hid from the sun's bright rays.

"Ilyatha," Maquesta gushed, "have you been able to

contact your daughter? Is Sando all right?"

The shadowperson's face showed a hint of a smile. "My daughter is alive, though she is still in that hateful stone prison in the garden. The sun's rays are creeping toward her even now. But I have reassured her that she will not have long to wait. We will be together and free."

"And then the *Perechon* will carry you as close to your home as possible," Maq offered.

Maquesta was happy for Ilyatha, but needed to be reassured herself. "Can you touch my father's mind? Can you tell him that he will be back on the deck of the *Perechon* soon?"

The shadowperson shook his head slowly. "I can contact Sando from this distance only because she, too, is a telepath. And throughout our journey I was able to contact the ki-rin because he has a strong and magical mind—one far more developed than my own. My ability to reach those who are not so gifted is limited."

"But you knew we were escaping from Lord Attat's," Maq began. "You were able to . . ."

"His dungeon was at the edge of my range, as far as my mind could reach within his palace. He stationed me thus so I could monitor what transpired below."

Maquesta's shoulders sagged, but Ilyatha made her realize that the *Perechon* had made it back before Attat's deadline, an accomplishment of which she and Melas should be proud. There would not be much longer to wait.

Maq and the shadowperson continued to chat, about where Ilyatha and Sando would go, where the *Perechon* would be heading for the next several months, and whether Maquesta would try to buy her own ship. They pondered where the ki-rin could be, as they had expected him to accompany them into the harbor. But Ilyatha said his mind could not touch Belwar's—the ki-rin must be visiting another plane. When Maq realized quite some time had passed, she went up on deck. From the position of the sun, it was well into the afternoon—certainly past the time when she'd expected Vartan and Fritz to be back. Where were they? Had something gone wrong? Was Lord Attat biding his time, making her wait on purpose? Making her fret and worry? The crew knew she was nervous; Maquesta had done nothing to hide her feelings. They, too, milled about on the deck, waiting and watching their captain.

Tailonna paced about as well, though she kept her thoughts to herself. Finally, she looked up at Maq and waved.

"I do this as a gift to you, Maquesta." Tailonna grimaced, twitched her nose, and strode toward the bowsprit. Balancing on the railing, she glanced down at the water. Giving it a disgusted look, she held her breath, dived over the side, and started swimming quickly toward the dock.

Maq rushed to the bow to watch her, noting the sea elf darted around floating barrels, patches of insect-laden scum, and the bloated remains of animals. She dived beneath other bits of refuse littering the harbor; nowhere within fifty yards of the shore was the water clean. When Tailonna climbed out on the dock, Maq scowled. The elf's once-beautiful blue skin was a dirty brown, and clumps of filthy moss hung from her hair and clothes. She futilely tried to shake herself off, and stared irately at the sailors on the dock, who were laughing, slapping their legs, and pointing at her.

To Maquesta, it looked as if Tailonna offered them some kind of retort, as one of the sailors jumped up and started running at the elf. Tailonna simply stepped aside, letting him fly off the dock and into the putrid water. As his comrades doubled over in laughter, the sea elf slipped into the longboat and rowed it back to the *Perechon*.

Tailonna waited in the boat and motioned Maquesta

to drop the ladder. "I'm going into Lacynos to get cleaned up and buy some new clothes. Of course, you'll have to pay for them." The sea elf grinned. "While I'm doing that, you can visit Lord Attat."

Wait for me, Maquesta, Ilyatha communicated. *I will brave the sun to see my daughter.*

No! Maq thought harshly. *I'll not let Attat find a reason to sway you to his side, to reveal what I might be thinking or planning on doing. You will stay here. I'll bring Sando to you.*

Maquesta clambered down the ladder, with Lendle close on her heels. Before the trio could push off, Koraf leaned over the side and started down the rope ladder, too. "I am coming," he said flatly. "I will not let you go to Lord Attat's alone. I know the palace, and I know my master. I do not relish returning there. But I have no choice."

Fingering the pouch at her side, Maquesta thought to herself that perhaps it would be better to have Kof along. She had plenty of gems with her that could hopefully buy his freedom. As the minotaur guided the boat back toward the dock, Maq thanked the sea elf and pressed one of the gems into her palm.

"That should cover some beautiful new clothes," Maquesta said. "And it should serve to get rid of the harbor stench."

"The bath definitely comes first," the sea elf said, wriggling her nose. "The harbor water is poisonous. Nothing prospers there but slime and insects and small, venomous serpents. The minotaurs should be slain for harming the water so."

* * * * *

Several minutes later Maquesta and Koraf strode along the wharf, with Lendle doing his best to keep up with them. The trio passed by one long dock after the next on their way to the main street that would take them to Lord Attat's imposing manor.

"MaquestaKarThonpleaseslowdown!" the gnome scolded. Lendle was nearly out of breath, taking four steps to each one of Maq's and Koraf's long strides. The gnome puffed and bounced along, his arms flapping out to his sides, as if, like a bird's wings, they might speed his course.

"I'm in a hurry, Lendle," she snapped back. "I'm worried." Her expression indicated her concern, but the gnome acted oblivious.

"Pleasewalkslower," he huffed. Then his eyes grew wide, spotting something Maquesta and her minotaur first mate did not see. "StopMaquestaKar-Thon!"

Perturbed, Maq halted in her tracks, and Lendle, who had not stopped walking, bumped into the back of her legs and nearly knocked her over. "Look!" he shouted, pointing out into the harbor. "Look what I see, Maquesta!" When it appeared Maq was too busy to be distracted, the gnome shook her hand and pointed again.

Finally, Maquesta turned to see what had caught the gnome's attention, and her heart sank. Anchored several ships over from the *Perechon*, in the shadow of a great caravel, was the *Butcher*. She couldn't have seen the ship from the deck of the *Perechon*. Which meant, she hoped, that the *Butcher*'s crew—what was left of it, anyway—couldn't see her ship either. The *Butcher* looked nearly as bad as the *Perechon*. She saw a crew working to repair the mainmast, the one Belwar had ruined. Another group looked as if they were fixing the hole on the deck. A longboat was still tied up near the center of the ship. Perhaps no one was ashore.

"We've got to hurry," she told the gnome. "We've got to collect my father, Fritzen, Vartan, and Sando. And we've got to get out of here. I don't want any trouble."

"Oh, I'd say you've already found trouble, *Captain* Kar-Thon."

Maquesta and Koraf whirled to see a gruesome sight. Striding toward them was a bedraggled-looking Mandracore. He was flanked by a pair of merrow, aquatic ogres. Looking as if they could be twins, the ogres each had a tangled mass of hair that resembled dried seaweed. A blue-green tinge to their skin, they had scales covering their shoulders, necks, and parts of their arms. They each wore a leather breastplate that did little to hide their bulging muscles.

Mandracore, too, wore armor, black leather studded with bits of steel. His face was recently scarred, the most prominent wound being a long, pink welt that ran from just above his right eye down through his cheek. Looking closely, Maq noticed his right eye did not move, and the pupil was glassy. He wore a heavy gold chain about his neck. A large charm in the shape of a closed fist dangled from it. She suspected it was a piece of jewelry taken from the merchant's treasure cave.

As the pirate chieftain approached, his billowing red cape carefully covered his right arm, and he walked with a discernible limp. She was concerned he hid a weapon, so she brushed in front of Lendle and put her hand on the hilt of her short sword. Koraf growled deeply, the sound rumbling in his thick throat.

"You'd fight me here?" Mandracore pronounced, as he waved his left arm in an arc. Maq followed his gesture and noted shop owners looking out their windows and passersby pausing to watch. "Why, look, there's a city guard! A rare sight in Lacynos, to be sure. Maybe he'd look the other way, eh, Maquesta? Maybe he wouldn't see you run me through. Or maybe he'd see you draw your blade against this humble and respected visitor and throw you in jail—for a long time. Perhaps you'd end up in Lord Attat's dungeon. I hear he buys prisoners and puts them to work in the arena. I wonder how long you'd last there? Of course, you could ask your first mate. I hear he's a star among the lord's pit fighters."

"I left you for dead," Maquesta hissed.

"Ah, and you were very nearly correct, my dear," Mandracore replied silkily. "Bullsharks." He threw back his cape, revealing a stump where his right arm used to be. "If it hadn't been for my trusted ogre friends, the sharks would have eaten all of me. As it was, the beasts had to settle for a few of my sailors—and my sword arm. I was barely able to reach the *Butcher*, no thanks to you. During the entire voyage back here I burned with a rage I had never felt before. What you did to me was far more severe than what your father did years ago." The pirate snarled, the ale on his breath strong and pungent.

"We've been repairing the *Butcher* for days, and with each sunrise I prayed I would see you again. Today, those prayers were answered when I saw your ship thunder into the harbor. If the *Perechon* were in any better shape than my own ship, I'd take it and leave you what's left of mine."

Mandracore took another step toward Maquesta, and she made a move to draw her blade. A small hand on her wrist stopped her. Lendle's eyes narrowed, and he shook his head, nodding toward the Lacynos guard.

Mandracore's not worth it, the gnome mouthed.

"You owe me *Captain* Kar-Thon," Mandracore sneered. "You've cost me my sword arm, some of my best sailors, and a considerable amount of coin. If I had stopped your efforts to retrieve whatever beast you were catching for Lord Attat, I would have gathered quite a tidy sum. So, my dear Maquesta, you will make good your debt. Do you understand? Maybe I will collect while you are in port, while what few authorities there are look the other way. Or maybe I will collect while you are on the open sea. But I guarantee you this, *Captain* Kar-Thon, as sure as the sun rises on the Blood

Sea I will collect everything you owe me."

The ogres brushed by Maquesta, Koraf, and Lendle, the sweaty stench of their bodies filling the air and nearly making Maq gag. Turning to watch Mandracore's small procession, a shiver raced up Maquesta's spine.

"I should have made sure he was dead," she whispered. "Never leave your enemies with a breath in their lungs." Mandracore the Reaver had important friends in this port city. She knew she couldn't raise a hand against him here, though she suspected he could do what he liked to her and the *Perechon* with impunity.

"We have to leave Lacynos soon," she whispered to Lendle and Kof. "Mandracore's enemies have a way of disappearing, and it looks as if I just made the top of his list. He's probably at least a day away from having his mainmast repaired. I mean to be long gone before he can raise a single sail."

The gnome nodded and scurried after her, once more trying to keep up with her long, swift strides. Koraf took one last look at the harbor and at Mandracore's crippled pirate ship. Then he hurried to catch up.

As the trio neared Lord Attat's manor, Maquesta noticed the streets were quiet. No one was about in the few blocks surrounding the palace. Doors were closed; windows were shuttered. It was almost as if the neighbors were expecting misfortune. Gritting her teeth, she ignored the nervous feeling in her stomach, and strode to the main gate. A pair of burly minotaurs barred her way.

"I'm here to see Lord Attat," she barked. "He's expecting me."

The minotaurs glowered at her, and she returned their stare. "Let me inside now!" she fumed, her hand finding its way to the pommel of her sword. Still, they did not move. Furious, she barked a few words at them in their own language, words she had learned from Koraf.

Finally, the guards nodded to her, understanding her

intent. They stepped aside, allowing her, Koraf, and the gnome to pass. Lendle nudged her hand as they entered the courtyard, pointing out the minotaurs watching them. Maquesta had never seen so many minotaurs milling about in one place. There were more today than after she and the others had broken out of Attat's dungeon. Each was armed, and they seemed to regard her with obvious interest. That Attat felt the need of this many guards to deal with her gave her a large dose of satisfaction.

She strode purposefully toward the main building where the doors opened for her, and she continued on her course—through the marble-floored hallways where innumerable treasures of art were hung, past the sitting room with its valuable stringed instruments, and into the minotaur lord's immense chamber.

Attat was sitting on his throne beneath the ki-rin skin on the wall, a cage resting in his lap. He was poking a thin-bladed knife at whatever was inside. The room was too long for Maquesta to make out all the details, though she could tell the hapless creature was gray, perhaps a squirrel or a large rat. The two imposing guards on either side of the minotaur lord stepped closer to their master. As she moved farther in, they gripped their massive spears. Once again, chained to the pillars were Attat's creatures—the great white bear, which growled angrily as she passed by; the griffon and hippogriff, still menacing each other, though the chains about their necks kept them from touching; and a few beasts she hadn't seen before. Among them was a thick reddish-brown snake with golden spots that had wrapped itself about its pillar. Maq guessed if it were uncoiled it would be at least twenty feet long. There was also a man with a hawk's head and with dark yellow claws for feet.

"A kenku," Lendle whispered, "A most unusual

creature who dislikes elves and humans."

"And minotaurs now, I'll wager," Maquesta whispered back.

As she, Koraf, and the gnome padded forward, more of the columns came into view. One had chained to it a yellow-skinned ape with large, pink eyes. It must be nearly nine feet tall, she judged as she returned its gaze. The ape jumped back, revealing two more of Lord Attat's captives. Maquesta shuddered. Fritzen and Vartan were chained to the farthest pillar. From the looks of them, they'd been beaten. The half-ogre lifted his head when Maq approached and offered her a weak smile.

"Greetings, Maquesta Kar-Thon," Attat boomed. "We've been expecting you."

"What have you done to Fritz and Vartan?" she sputtered. She closed the distance to the dais, the guards moving forward at the same time to make sure she didn't threaten Attat. Closer, Maq could now see what was in the cage on his lap. It was a miniature elephant that had gashes on its sides from where the minotaur lord had been poking it.

Roughly setting the cage on the floor, Attat stood. Not so regally dressed today, the minotaur nonetheless was wearing an expensive robe that nearly matched the deep purple cloak that bunched about his shoulders.

"What did I do to them? Why, I punished them, of course. They didn't bring you, they didn't bring Bas-Ohn Koraf, and they didn't bring my morkoth." Attat regarded her coolly, showing a measure of contempt. "The deal was for you to bring the morkoth to me. At least you have returned Koraf. There is a match in a few days' time in which I intend to enter him."

"The morkoth is in the harbor, in the cage you gave us," Maquesta fumed. "I have no way of getting him here. I have no wagon, and I have no large vat of water in which to move him."

"That can be arranged," Attat replied, thoughtfully stroking the beard on his chin.

"Nothing will be arranged until I have my father and he has been given the antidote. And I want Fritz and Vartan freed now." Maq's voice was strong, insistent. "I'll need Sando, too. Her father waits for her on the *Perechon*."

"Ah, your precious *Perechon*. My spies in the harbor tell me your ship is in disrepair."

"My father, Lord Attat? I've kept my part of your grisly pact."

The minotaur gestured, and one of the guards strode off the dais, clomping to a curtained alcove. The guard drew back the heavy fabric and motioned to Maq.

"You know the way to my dungeon, don't you, Captain Kar-Thon?" Attat's eyes narrowed to thin slits. "Your father is down there. Bring him up, won't you, Maquesta? The antidote awaits." The minotaur lord reached into the folds of his robe and pulled out the vial containing the golden-colored liquid. "While you are down there, instruct the guards to cage Koraf for me. By the time you and your father have returned, your men will have been released." The minotaur lord motioned toward one of his guards, who jingled the keys on his belt.

Maquesta glanced at the alcove, then faced Attat. "I would like to acquire the minotaur Bas-Ohn Koraf," she stated in a businesslike tone. "He's an able sailor, and I could use him in my crew."

"Oh, I consider Bas-Ohn Koraf priceless. He's my greatest fighter, undefeated, and he's not for sale. At *any* price." Attat glared at Koraf and pointed to the alcove. "Return to your home, slave, and with all due haste. Maquesta's father hasn't long to live."

Maq looked at Koraf, but the minotaur's gaze

revealed no emotion. He stoically nodded to her and strode to the alcove, his hooves clicking harshly on the marble floor. Maquesta, swallowing hard, followed him. The pair made their way down the long, twisting stone steps that led to the dank belly of Attat's palace.

"I won't have you caged again." Maq's tone was soft, not wanting any errant guards to overhear her. "There has to be another way."

"In this city I am Lord Attat's property," Koraf replied. "You don't have a choice. And you won't get your father well any other way."

When they reached the bottom of the steps several moments later, Maquesta saw the familiar hallway lined with cages. A pair of guards strode up to her, nodding, each taking one of Koraf's arms.

"We're glad to have you home," one of them taunted as he directed Koraf toward his old cell.

Maq watched as her first mate was led away. Rage burned inside her, and her mind churned with possibilities. "No!" she screamed before they made it halfway down the dank corridor. Drawing her short sword, she rushed forward. The guards whirled, but not in time. Her blade sank halfway up to the hilt in the side of one. Groaning, the guard crumpled and twitched on the floor. Maquesta pulled her sword free and bent her legs, ready to deal with the other guard.

The second guard released Koraf and drew his own weapon, a curved-blade sword nearly twice the size of Maq's weapon. Growling menacingly, he hauled it back over his shoulder to swing, and Maquesta darted in, slicing at his abdomen and leaping away before his descending sword could touch her. The guard looked at his stomach incredulously and saw a line of red forming where she had cut through his leather armor. Bellowing in rage, he lowered his head and charged forward, intending to gore her. Again Maquesta darted away, narrowly missing his horns and the swing of his sword.

She danced around to where Koraf stood and held the sword in front of her, waving the tip and taunting the guard.

"Don't do this," Koraf warned her. "Attat will kill both of us if the guards die."

"I'm already committed," she panted. "Why don't you help me?"

Leaping backward toward the dungeon's torture chamber, Maquesta crouched to meet the guard's next rush. As he closed in, she drove her blade upward, thrusting hard through his armor and piercing the flesh underneath. She gritted her teeth and tugged the blade free, then she dropped to the ground and rolled. The guard was seriously wounded, but he continued to stalk her. From the corner of her eye she saw the first guard start to rise. "Kof!" she barked. "Don't let him get away!"

She watched Koraf slide forward, bringing his hoof down on the back of the prone minotaur's skull. A crunch signaled that he wouldn't be going anywhere.

Momentarily distracted, Maquesta was not ready for her attacker's next move. He charged in, with his sword pulled back over his shoulder. He swung in wide, as if she were a fly to be swatted, and though she tried to dodge, the blade glanced off her shoulder. Maq backed up against the wall and looked at her arm. It was not a deep cut, but blood flowed freely from it, covering the sleeve of her tunic. She snarled and looked up at the guard. He took a step forward and raised his weapon again. There was nowhere for Maquesta to dodge now, and his reach was much longer than hers. She crouched, waiting for his next move, then she gaped in surprise as he crumpled to his knees and fell forward, his head thudding soundly on the hard stone. The other guard's weapon was lodged firmly in the middle of his back.

"Kof?"

"I couldn't let you die," he said, "though now the blood of more minotaurs is on my hands."

Maquesta knelt and tore free a piece of the guard's cloak. She wrapped it tightly about her upper arm, trying to stanch the bleeding. "Help me find my father," she urged.

"And then what?" Koraf posed. "We've killed the guards. Lord Attat will know and will have us both tortured to death."

"Don't be so cheerful," she said as she cleaned off her sword and sheathed it. She smoothed her tunic, and twisted her sash to cover up a spot of blood. "Attat thought I would meekly obey him and have you caged. He hadn't counted on the fact that his mission already has been too costly. There'll be no more sacrifices made for the minotaur lord."

Maquesta rushed from cell door to cell door until at last she found the small chamber in which her father lay. "The keys! Quickly." Looking through the barred door, she held her hand behind her back and wriggled her fingers. Koraf took one of the dead guard's key rings and placed it in her hand.

Fumbling with several keys before she found the one that worked, Maq softly called out to her father, but got no response. Throwing open the door, she rushed inside and knelt by him.

"Father?"

Melas's skin was the gray of slate, and his face was gaunt and skeletal. His chest barely rose and fell, and with each breath he took, he made a faint wheezing sound. Maq picked up his hand and noticed how bony it was, and how cold and clammy he felt. Tears spilled from her eyes, and she sobbed so hard she barely heard Kof enter the cell behind her.

"Father?" she repeated.

His eyes fluttered open, and he stared at her quizzically.

"It's me . . . Maquesta," she said softly. "I've come back for you."

His cracked lips turned upward in a grin. "Maq?" he whispered hoarsely.

She nodded and leaned forward and kissed his cheek. "I'm going to get you out of here."

Rising, she breathed deeply a few times, then reached her arms under his knees and shoulders. Bending slightly, she picked him up and turned to face Kof. Maq adjusted her father's position until his head lay against her wounded shoulder, hiding the blood. "See? Attat won't know anything happened down here," she said smugly, as she padded toward the door, her steps slower under Melas's weight. "Follow me up the stairs—after you've freed any other prisoners he might have down here, and then stay behind the curtain. I'm going to get us all out of here."

The minotaur looked at her with a puzzled expression on his bull-like brow. "At least let me carry him up the steps," he offered.

Maquesta shook her head. "There's not much left of him, Kof. He's not that heavy. Besides, I'll be winded by the time I make it back to Attat's audience chamber. If you carry him, I'll not have reason to look so tired. I don't want Attat to suspect anything."

The minotaur nodded and retrieved the key ring. Maquesta heard the cell doors opening as she started her long climb.

Pushing the curtain aside, she saw that Fritz and Vartan were still chained to the column. Lendle stood near them, chattering. She glowered at Attat and stepped into the chamber. The minotaur lord held out the vial.

"Your antidote," he said, running his thick fingers

along the smooth glass. He tilted the vial so the torchlight caught the liquid and made it sparkle.

Maquesta took another step forward, and watched in horror as he raised the vial above his head and brought it crashing to the floor, the golden liquid trickling into the cracks between the marble tiles.

"Fool!" Attat blustered. "I had no intention of allowing your father to live. Or you! You were only tools to retrieve my morkoth. Guards!" The minotaur lord clapped his hands, and the two guards at his side vaulted down the dais steps and rushed toward her.

"No!" she screamed. Setting her father on the floor, she somersaulted over him, narrowly avoided the spears thrust at her. Leaping to her feet and spinning, she saw the guards whirl and come at her again. Gripped with rage, and realizing she had only once chance, she dashed at them, hearing the encouraging shouts of Fritz and Vartan in the background. As she darted in, she grabbed one of the guard's spears and yanked with all her energy. The weapon came free, though she fell backward onto the floor in the process.

Without getting up, she spun the spear around, as she had seen Ilyatha do with his staff, impaling the very guard she'd borrowed the weapon from. He pitched forward on the spear, his weight pushing him down farther on the shaft, and she dropped the weapon and rolled to the side to avoid his falling body and the other oncoming guard.

Lendle rushed in, his small sword drawn. He waved it at the remaining guard and darted in to slash at his legs. The minotaur stepped back toward the dais.

"Guards!" Attat cried again.

Maquesta knew he was calling for those who stood beyond the chamber, and she knew she would have to act quickly. Rushing up the dais steps, she slipped by the guard and bowled into Attat, sending him reeling backward and knocking over his massive wooden chair in the process. It splintered and loudly cracked. The clattering noise continued, though it took her a moment to realize it was no longer the broken chair making the racket.

Bas-Ohn Koraf had arrived, wielding one of the fallen guard's curved swords. He roared into the room and headed straight toward the minotaur charging at Maquesta. The guard halted for the briefest of moments, enough to give Koraf the time he needed.

Koraf changed his grip on the sword and angled the weapon over his shoulder. In the next instant, he hurled it through the air like a javelin, the flashing blade dancing in the light of the torches. The weapon flew true and caught the surprised minotaur in the center of his thick throat. The guard was dead before he hit the floor, and Koraf rushed forward, picking up the dropped spear and tossing it to Maquesta.

She caught it just as Attat began to struggle to his feet and the chamber door burst open and a half-dozen minotaur guards poured in. Thinking quickly, she jabbed the spear against Attat's side.

"Tell them to keep back!" she spat. "Tell them!"

The minotaur lord glowered at her, and his guards pressed forward, hesitating slightly. One growled loudly and took a step toward the dais.

"I'll kill you! I swear I will!" Maquesta shouted. "You signed my father's death warrant, and you said you would kill me, too. What do I have to lose *Lord* Attat? Now, tell them to drop the weapons or I'll run you through!"

The minotaur lord nodded slowly, his eyes smoldering with hate. "Your weapons," he began. "Drop them and back away. Do it!"

The guards obeyed, and Koraf and Lendle dashed forward, picking up an assortment of spears, scimitars, axes, and knives, depositing them near Fritz and Vartan. Koraf strode over to the two dead guards and turned them over. Finding a key on one of their belts, he headed toward the captive crewmen.

"You must have more of the antidote somewhere," Maquesta fumed. "Where is it?"

Attat laughed, his deep tones reverberating off the chamber walls as he struggled into a sitting position. "There is no more antidote, Maquesta," he hissed. "And even if there were more, your father is too far gone for it to do any good. He failed quickly and would have needed the antidote days ago to survive."

Maquesta knew his words were true, and she choked back a sob. "You and I are leaving this place," she stated through clenched teeth. "We're going to the *Perechon*. You're my prisoner now."

The minotaur lord laughed again. "You think to kidnap me? I am powerful in this city. To kidnap me would invite your own destruction."

She prodded him until he awkwardly rose to his hooved feet, then she edged him down the dais steps and nodded to Fritz and Vartan, who were finally free of their chains. The half-ogre looked over the collection of weapons and selected one of the curved swords and thrust it in his belt. Vartan chose an axe and waved it at the guards, who held out their hands to their sides in response.

Next, Fritzen dashed up the dais steps and yanked down a cord that tied back one of the heavy drapes. The half-ogre grabbed Attat's arms, pulled them behind the minotaur's broad back, and wrapped the cord several times about his hairy wrists.

Glancing up, and satisfied the minotaurs were keeping a safe distance, Fritzen padded toward Melas, knelt, and picked him up. The half-ogre cringed at the sight of the emaciated man, and his heart went out to

Maquesta, who he knew was suffering horribly. Fritz nodded to her.

"Kof, see if any of those keys will release Sando from the garden!" Maq said. "She's in a small cave, near a statue of a centaur."

Koraf retreated from the chamber, and Maquesta and the minotaur lord walked between the pillars toward the far doors. Fritzen and Vartan followed close behind. Lendle hurried to catch up; he carried the cage with the tiny elephant in his left hand. By the time they reached the last pillars, Koraf had returned, the small shadow-person cradled in his arms.

"She's blind," Koraf said simply. "Carrying her will be easier."

Maquesta nodded toward the door and jabbed the heavy spear at Attat's side. At that instant, one of the minotaur guards rushed forward. Vartan heard his hooves pounding over the marble and whirled. Though the guard was weaponless, he had his head down and was charging like a maddened bull.

Vartan drew back his axe and rushed forward, slicing the guard's thick arm and causing him to spin. The minotaur skidded backward across the polished floor—into the reach of the chained griffon. The animal reared up on its haunches, spread its eaglelike wings wide, and grasped the shoulders of the guard with its razor-sharp talons. The griffon drove its beak into the guard's neck, and the minotaur screamed horribly. The scene was enough to keep the other guards from trying to free their lord.

Maquesta jabbed Attat again, this time letting the spear head sink into his side and draw a little blood.

"Open the doors!" Attat barked. As they passed under the frame, he added. "You will not get out of my palace alive, Captain Kar-Thon. I have many guards in the courtyard. They will not let you get away with this."

Prodding him again, Maquesta led her small entourage through the manor's museumlike corridors and out into the walled yard beyond. Koraf quickly bundled up Sando, trying to keep the bright light from hurting her any more than it already had.

"LookMaquestaKarThon!" Lendle happily gushed.

A pleasing sight greeted their eyes, and Maquesta's face broke into a wide grin. Scattered about the sculptured trees and bushes were magical nets—and trapped inside them were Attat's guards. In the center of the courtyard, merrily splashing in a fountain, was the sea elf, her now-clean clothes hanging from a stone minotaur that spewed water from its mouth.

"I was wondering when you'd be coming out," Tailonna said as she ducked into the water, letting only her face show. "I hope the lord doesn't mind my using his fountain. The inn I stopped at didn't cater to sea elves. And I really needed a bath." She winked at Maquesta, then her tone turned serious. "My nets will be good for about another twenty or thirty minutes, so haste back to the *Perechon* would be a good idea."

Maquesta nodded and poked Attat to keep him moving. "Won't you be joining us?" Maq called over her shoulder to the sea elf."

"I will as soon as all of you get out of here so I can get dressed."

* * * * *

Behind Maquesta's procession trailed a dozen tatter-clothed humans, prisoners from Attat's dungeon. They shuffled along, idly chatting among themselves. Koraf told Maq he didn't know what crimes they were guilty of, but all of that could be sorted out later. What the prisoners had in common was a fervent desire to leave Lacynos, and all of them were willing to work on the

Perechon in exchange for passage. A couple of them seemed to be able warriors, as the minotaur had seen them fight in the ring and survive.

Minotaur and human passersby, shopkeepers, street corner vendors, and sailors stared at the odd parade. Maquesta's group passed by two minotaur guards who made a move toward the *Perechon*'s captain—until she jabbed Attat and he instructed the guards to leave them alone. The minotaur lord was being too agreeable, Maq thought as she prodded him again, encouraging him to walk faster.

Halfway to the harbor, Maquesta told Fritz and Lendle to take the lead. The streets were getting busier, and she wanted someone in front of her so the minotaur lord could not bolt. Vartan stepped to her right, and Koraf, who was carrying Sando, stepped to her left. Attat was boxed in.

Still cradling her father, the half-ogre led the procession down the main street and to the dock where the *Perechon*'s longboat was tied. Maquesta instructed the former prisoners to wait on the shore. It would take more than one trip in the longboat to get everyone on board the *Perechon*. Lendle, cradling his elephant, waited with the men, as Fritzen led the rest of the group out onto the dock. They were approaching their longboat, which was tied near another moored longboat filled with four minotaurs, when Lord Attat threw back his head. "Help me!" he bellowed to the minotaurs. "They mean to kidnap me!"

Maquesta cursed as the quartet of minotaur sailors drew their cutlasses and clambered up onto the dock. Their hooves pounded over the planks as they advanced. Vartan rushed past Fritzen, and drew his small sword. The half-ogre stepped back and started retreating with Melas.

"Take him to shore!" Maq called to Fritz.

Attat's muscles bulged, and he strained against the cord that held his hands. Maquesta jabbed the spear firmly into his side.

"Tell them to stop, Lord Attat," she spat, "or I'll slay you here and throw your body into Horned Bay."

Attat growled, and with a burst of strength severed the cords. His leg shot out behind him, his sharp hoof driving into Maquesta's calf. Maq staggered and nearly dropped her massive spear. But she gritted her teeth, balanced the weapon, and thrust it at him again.

The minotaur lord pivoted, the jagged spear tip piercing only his purple robe. Grinning, he lunged forward, trying to bat the spear out of her hands, succeeding instead by throwing her off balance. Maquesta fell to her knees, still holding on to the spear. Her eyes grew wide as she watched Attat bound past her, straining to reach Fritzen, who was carrying her father to the shore.

"Fritz! Look out!" she called.

The half-ogre spun about, then nimbly stepped to the side, avoiding the charging Attat.

It was then Maquesta realized the minotaur lord had not meant to attack Fritzen, but to get past him. His hooves drummed over the planks, then with one leap he was on the shore. Using the spear for support, Maq pulled herself to her feet and started after him. But a clash of swords behind her stopped her progress. She turned to see Vartan struggling against the minotaur sailors. Koraf placed Sando gently on the street and drew his curved blade.

Because the dock was not very wide, only two of the sailors could reach Vartan. The other two stood behind their fellows, growling encouragement. Wielding the borrowed axe, Vartan swung it through the air and sent its sharp edge into the chest of one assailant. The wounded minotaur roared and fell back. Vartan pressed forward and followed him down the dock, allowing two of the minotaurs to move up and the other one to step behind him. He was surrounded.

Maquesta rushed forward, close behind Koraf. Vartan screamed as one of the minotaurs drove his blade deep into the human's thigh. Another minotaur brought his cutlass high above his head, meaning to bring it down on the sailor. But Koraf was faster. Pushing the wounded Vartan out of the way, Maquesta's first mate raised his own sword and parried the cutlass.

Maq thrust forward with her massive spear, sending the tip deep into the belly of another sailor. The minotaur crumpled, and Maquesta pulled hard to free her weapon. At the same time Koraf swung his blade, striking his assailant's hand and sending the cutlass to join the garbage in the harbor.

"Surrender!" Koraf barked to them in the minotaur tongue.

The sailors quickly complied, dragging their wounded comrades with them into their longboat.

"WegothimMaquestaKarThon!" Lendle called. His small feet slapped over the deck. "Wegothim!"

Maq turned to see Lord Attat's former prisoners surrounding the minotaur. They were treating him none too kindly and jostling him back onto the dock. Behind them strode Tailonna. She motioned to Maquesta and gestured at the longboat.

"My nets will be wearing off!" she called.

Maq nodded. She padded toward where Sando stood, alone and confused. Picking up the frightened child, she felt Sando's mind touch hers.

It's going to be all right, Maquesta thought. *We're taking you to your father. He's on the* Perechon.

He told me you'd protect me, Sando concentrated in reply. *He's waiting for us.*

Maquesta looked past the sailors, to Fritzen on the shore. He gently picked up Melas, and started down the dock toward Maq.

Lendle jumped into the longboat, then reached over and grabbed the elephant cage and set it beside him. Maq carefully passed the shadowperson to the gnome. Because the sun was starting to set, Sando was getting stronger. She sat on the gnome's right side and waited for the others to join them. Maquesta, Attat, Vartan, and Fritz, holding Melas, filled the seats for the longboat's first trip to the *Perechon*.

Once on deck, the crew surrounded the minotaur lord, and Ilyatha rushed forward to grab his daughter and hold her close. Fritz gently laid Melas on the deck, and Maquesta sat beside him. His dark eyes fluttered open, and he coughed and winced in pain.

"Remember the lesson of my life, Maquesta," Melas whispered. "Trust no one." His mouth opened again, and she leaned closer so she could hear. "Take good care of the *Perechon*, Captain Kar-Thon."

Melas took his last breath, and Maq sobbed openly.

Fritz placed a gentle hand on her shoulder. "We'll bury him at sea," he said softly.

She nodded and let him help her to her feet. A sailor brushed by her with a tarp. Behind her, the longboat returned from its second trip to the dock. As Tailonna, Koraf, and a group of former prisoners started up the rope ladder, the *Perechon* was engulfed in a flash of bright light.

With a scream of anger, Belwar appeared in the sky above the ship's mainmast. He dived toward the deck, and the sailors surrounding Attat fled in panic, leaving their prisoner an easy target. The ki-rin's horn, aimed at the quivering minotaur lord, crackled with lightning.

"You slew my brother!" Belwar shouted. "Now I shall do the same to you!"

The ki-rin's horn sank into Attat's shoulder, and the minotaur's body was instantly covered in a pale gold, crackling light. Belwar shook the minotaur free, and let his quaking form fall to the deck, then the ki-rin placed his front hooves on Attat's chest and peered into his dark eyes. The minotaur lord was whimpering, begging for his life. Belwar ignored his feeble protests.

"You are part of the evil that is spreading across the Blood Sea. Ending your pitiable life will serve justice *and* revenge."

Belwar shook his mane and glanced about at the crewmembers. "You!" he called to Koraf and Fritzen. "Pull up the morkoth's cage."

Maquesta watched as Kof, aided by the half-ogre, complied, winching up the steel cage and breaking the weld on the top. As Koraf slowly opened the top of the cage, Belwar opened his mouth and grabbed the minotaur lord's tunic. Dragging the protesting lord across the deck, the ki-rin tossed Attat into the cage.

"Let Lord Attat have his precious trophy," the ki-rin stated. He nodded to Koraf, and the minotaur lowered the cage's lid.

The ki-rin touched his horn to the mechanism holding the cage to the *Perechon*, and the metal clasp severed. The cage dropped to the floor of the harbor, and the water instantly churned red about the ship, signaling the end of the Lacynos minotaur lord.

Satisfied, Belwar rose slowly above the deck and floated toward Maquesta. "I am sorry for the death of your father," the ki-rin offered. "There was nothing even I could have done to save him. But know that his spirit is in a kinder place, and that he sails on a beautiful, endless sea." The ki-rin's horn shimmered, and the creature soared higher. "I will watch the morkoth and make sure it kills no innocent souls in Lacynos. And from time to time I will watch you, Maquesta Kar-Thon."

Another flash lit the growing night sky, then the ki-rin was gone.

Maquesta looked about the deck. Ilyatha still hugged Sando, his webbed arms wrapped about the diminutive shadowperson. Maq intended to drop the pair off on the other side of Mithas. From there they could get home easily enough.

Tailonna was escorting the last of Attat's former prisoners over the railing. Maquesta wondered how many of them would stay on. She needed more sailors, and she had gems with which to pay the crew their wages. Some of the gems would also pay for new masts, and would buy the gnome plenty of equipment and parts.

Vartan was directing a crew to raise the sails on the mainmast. Another group of sailors was lighting lanterns and hanging them about the aft deck and near the bow.

From somewhere belowdecks she heard a groaning and sputtering racket. Lendle had his oar machine working. She felt the ship surge and looked over the side to see the oars already in motion. A gout of smoke erupted from the cargo hold, and the *Perechon* was under way.

Fritzen, stepping up behind Maquesta, hugged her fiercely. "You're going to be all right," he told her.

She nodded and glanced at the tarp covering her father's body. "I know. But it will take a while."

"Any orders, Captain?" Koraf called. The minotaur had made his way to the aft deck and was behind the wheel.

"Take us out of the harbor, Kof," she said, her voice brightening slightly. "I want to go as far away from Lacynos as the wind and waves will take us."

Dragons of Summer Flame

An Excerpt

by Margaret Weis
and Tracy Hickman

Chapter One

Be Warned . . .

It was hot that morning, damnably hot.
Far too hot for late spring on Ansalon. Almost as hot as midsummer. The two knights, seated in the boat's stern, were sweaty and miserable in their heavy steel armor; they looked with envy at the nearly naked men plying the boat's oars. When the boat neared shore, the knights were first out, jumping into the shallow water, laving the water onto their reddening faces and sunburned necks. But the water was not particularly refreshing.

"Like wading in hot soup," one of the knights grumbled, splashing ashore. Even as he spoke, he scrutinized the shoreline carefully, eyeing bush and tree and dune for signs of life.

"More like blood," said his comrade. "Think of it

as wading in the blood of our enemies, the enemies of our Queen. Do you see anything?"

"No," the other replied. He waved his hand, then, without looking back, heard the sound of men leaping into the water, their harsh laughter and conversation in their uncouth, guttural language.

One of the knights turned around. "Bring that boat to shore," he said, unnecessarily, for the men had already picked up the heavy boat and were running with it through the shallow water. Grinning, they dumped the boat on the sand beach and looked to the knight for further orders.

He mopped his forehead, marveled at their strength, and—not for the first time—thanked Queen Takhisis that these barbarians were on their side. The brutes, they were known as. Not the true name of their race. The name, their name for themselves, was unpronounceable, and so the knights who led the barbarians had begun calling them by the shortened version: brute.

The name suited the barbarians well. They came from the east, from a continent that few people on Ansalon knew existed. Every one of the men stood well over six feet; some were as tall as seven. Their bodies were as bulky and muscular as humans, but their movements were as swift and graceful as elves. Their ears were pointed like those of the elves, but their faces were heavily bearded like humans or dwarves. They were as strong as dwarves and loved battle as well as dwarves did. They fought fiercely, were loyal to those who commanded them, and, outside of a few grotesque customs such as cutting off various parts of the body of a dead enemy to keep as trophies, the brutes were ideal foot soldiers.

"Let the captain know we've arrived safely and that we've encountered no resistance," said the knight to his comrade. "We'll leave a couple of men here with the boat and move inland."

The other knight nodded. Taking a red silk pennant from his belt, he unfurled it, held it above his head, and waved it slowly three times. An answering flutter of red came from the enormous black, dragon-prowed ship anchored some distance away. This was a scouting mission, not an invasion. Orders had been quite clear on that point.

The knights sent out their patrols, dispatching some to range up and down the beach, sending others farther inland. This done, the two knights moved thankfully to the meager shadow cast by a squat and misshapen tree. Two of the brutes stood guard. The knights remained wary and watchful, even as they rested. Seating themselves, they drank sparingly of the fresh water they'd brought with them. One of them grimaced.

"The damn stuff's hot."

"You left the waterskin sitting in the sun. Of course it's hot."

"Where the devil was I supposed to put it? There was no shade on that cursed boat. I don't think there's any shade left in the whole blasted world. I don't like this place at all. I get a queer feeling about this island, like it's magiced or something."

"I know what you mean," agreed his comrade somberly. He kept glancing about, back into the trees, up and down the beach. All that could be seen were the brutes, and they were certainly not bothered by any ominous feelings. But then they were barbarians. "We were warned not to come here, you know."

"What?" The other knight looked astonished. "I didn't know. Who told you that?"

"Brightblade. He had it from Lord Ariakan himself."

"Brightblade should know. He's on Ariakan's staff. The lord's his sponsor." The knight appeared nervous and asked softly, "Such information's not secret, is it?"

The other knight appeared amused. "You don't know Steele Brightblade very well if you think he would break any oath or pass along any information he was told to keep to himself. He'd sooner let his tongue be ripped out by red-hot tongs. No, Lord Ariakan discussed this openly with all the regimental commanders before deciding to proceed."

The knight shrugged. Picking up a handful of small rocks, he began tossing them idly into the water. "The Gray Robes started it all. Some sort of augury revealed the location of this island and that it was inhabited by large numbers of people."

"So who warned us not to come?"

"The Gray Robes. The same augury that told them of this island also warned them not to come near it. They tried to persuade Ariakan to leave well enough alone. Said that this place could mean disaster."

The other knight frowned, then glanced around with growing unease. "Then why were we sent?"

"The upcoming invasion of Ansalon. Lord Ariakan felt this move was necessary to protect his flanks. The Gray Robes couldn't say exactly what sort of threat this island represented. Nor could they say specifically that the disaster would be caused by our landing on the island. As Lord Ariakan pointed out, perhaps disaster would come even if we didn't do anything. And so he decided to follow the old dwarven dictum, 'It is better to go looking for the dragon than have the dragon come looking for you.' "

"Good thinking," his companion agreed. "If there is an army of elves on this island, it's better that we deal with them now. Not that it seems likely."

He gestured at the wide stretches of sand beach, at the dunes covered with some sort of grayish-green grass, and, farther inland, a forest of the ugly, misshapen trees. "Elves wouldn't live in a place like this."

"Neither would dwarves. Minotaurs would have attacked us by now. Kender would have walked off with the boat *and* our armor. Gnomes would have met us with some sort of fiend-driven fish-catching machine. Humans like us are the only race foolish enough to live in such a wretched place," the knight concluded cheerfully. He picked up another handful of rocks.

"It could be a rogue band of draconians or hobgoblins. Ogres even. Escaped twenty-some years ago, after the War of the Lance. Fled north, across the sea, to avoid capture by the Solamnic Knights."

"Yes, but they'd be on our side," his companion answered. "And our wizards wouldn't have their robes in a knot over it. . . . Ah, here come our scouts, back to report. Now we'll find out."

The knights rose to their feet. The brutes who had been sent into the island's interior hurried forward to meet their leaders. The barbarians were grinning hugely. Their nearly naked bodies glistened with sweat. The blue paint with which they covered themselves, and which was supposed to possess some sort of magical properties said to cause arrows to bounce right off them, ran down their muscular bodies in rivulets. Long scalp locks, decorated with colorful feathers, bounced on their backs as they loped easily over the sand dunes.

The two knights exchanged glances, relaxed.

"What did you find?" the knight asked the leader, a gigantic red-haired fellow who towered over both knights and could have probably picked up each of them and held them over his head. He regarded both knights with unbounded reverence and respect.

"Men," answered the brute. They were quick to learn and had adapted easily to Common, spoken by most of the various races of Krynn. Unfortunately, to the brutes, all people not of their race were known as "men."

The brute lowered his hand near the ground to indicate small men, which might mean dwarves but was more probably children. He moved it to waist height, which most likely indicated women. This the brute confirmed by cupping two hands over his own breast and wiggling his hips. His own men laughed and nudged each other.

"Men, women, and children," said the knight. "Many men? Lots of men? Big buildings? Walls? Cities?"

The brutes apparently thought this was hilarious, for they all burst into raucous laughter.

"What did you find?" said the knight sharply, scowling. "Stop the nonsense."

The brutes sobered rapidly.

"Many men," said the leader, "but no walls. Houses." He made a face, shrugged, shook his head, and added something in his own language."

"What does that mean?" asked the knight of his comrade.

"Something to do with dogs," said the other, who had led brutes before and had started picking up some of their language. "I think he means that these men live in houses only dogs would live in."

Several of the brutes now began walking about stoop-shouldered, swinging their arms around their knees and grunting. Then they all straightened up, looked at each other, and laughed again.

"What in the name of our Dark Majesty are they doing now?" the knight demanded.

"Beats me," said his comrade. "I think we should go have a look for ourselves." He drew his sword partway out of its black leather scabbard. "Danger?" he asked the brute. "We need steel?"

The brute laughed again. Taking his own short sword—the brutes fought with two, long and short, as well as bow and arrows—he thrust it into the tree and turned his back on it.

The knight, reassured, returned his sword to its scabbard. The two followed their guides deeper into the forest.

They did not go far before they came to the village. They entered a cleared area among the trees.

Despite the antics of the brutes, the knights were completely unprepared for what they saw.

"By Hiddukel," one said in a low voice to the other. " 'Men' is too strong a term. *Are* these men? Or are they beasts?"

"They're men," said the other, staring around slowly, amazed. "But such men as we're told walked Krynn during the Age of Twilight. Look! Their tools are made of wood. They carry wooden spears, and crude ones at that."

"Wooden-tipped, not stone," said the other. "Mud

huts for houses. Clay cooking pots. Not a piece of steel or iron in sight. What a pitiable lot! I can't see how they could be much danger, unless it's from filth. By the smell, they haven't bathed since the Age of Twilight either."

"Ugly bunch. More like apes than men. Don't laugh. Look stern and threatening."

Several of the male humans—if human they were; it was difficult to tell beneath the animal hides they wore—crept up to the knights. The "man-beasts" walked bent over, their arms swinging at their sides, knuckles almost dragging on the ground. Their heads were covered with long, shaggy hair; unkempt beards almost completely hid their faces. They bobbed and shuffled and gazed at the knights in openmouthed awe. One of the man-beasts actually drew near enough to reach out a grimy hand to touch the black, shining armor.

A brute moved to interpose his own massive body in front of the knight.

The knight waved the brute off and drew his sword. The steel flashed in the sunlight. Turning to one of the trees, which, with their twisted limbs and gnarled trunks, resembled the people who lived beneath them, the knight raised his sword and sliced off a limb with one swift stroke.

The man-beast dropped to his knees and groveled in the dirt, making piteous blubbering sounds.

"I think I'm going to vomit," said the knight to his comrade. "Gully dwarves wouldn't associate with this lot."

"You're right there." The knight looked around. "Between us, you and I could wipe out the entire tribe."

"We'd never be able to clean the stench off our swords," said the other.

"What should we do? Kill them?"

"Small honor in it. These wretches obviously aren't any threat to us. Our orders were to find out who or what was inhabiting the island, then return. For all we know, these people may be the favorites of some god, who might be angered if we harmed them. Perhaps that is what the Gray Robes meant by disaster."

"I don't know," said the other knight dubiously. "I can't imagine any god treating his favorites like this."

"Morgion, perhaps," said the other, with a wry grin.

The knight grunted. "Well, we've certainly done no harm just by looking. The Gray Robes can't fault us for that. Send out the brutes to scout the rest of the island. According to the reports from the dragons, it's not very big. Let's go back to the shore. I need some fresh air."

The two knights sat in the shade of the tree, talking of the upcoming invasion of Ansalon, discussing the vast armada of black dragon-prowed ships, manned by minotaurs, that was speeding its way across the Courrain Ocean, bearing thousands and thousands more barbarian warriors. All was nearly ready for the invasion, which would take place on Summer's Eve.

The knights of Takhisis did not know precisely where they were attacking; such information was kept secret. But they had no doubt of victory. This time the Dark Queen would succeed. This time her armies would be victorious. This time she knew the secret to victory.

The brutes returned within a few hours and made their report. The isle was not large. The brutes found no other people. The tribe of man-beasts had all slunk off fearfully and were hiding, cowering, in their mud huts until the strange beings left.

The knights returned to their shore boat. The brutes pushed it off the sand, leaped in, and grabbed the oars. The boat skimmed across the surface of the water, heading for the black ship that flew the multi-colored flag of the five-headed dragon.

They left behind an empty, deserted beach. Or so it appeared.

But their leaving was noted, as their coming had been.